To Lara Oct/20

A small "Thank you"
for keeping me
supplied with Library
books.   *Sarah*

Changing Places

By

D1809118

Sarah M Jefferson

Sarah M Jefferson

Changing Places

by

Sarah M Jefferson

©2015

(2nd edition)

Published by Ex-L-Ence Publishing a division of Winghigh Limited, England.

Also by Sarah M Jefferson: 'The Ranee's Tears' and 'The Major Meets his Match'

ISBN: 978-1-909133-75-4

Contents

Prequel

'Please believe me, Mr. Greening, I mean it when I say I have no plans to marry again.' It was Martha Grey's third refusal of him in as many minutes. She sighed in exasperation; why did the wretched man persist in bothering her now, just when she was so busy closing up the house. But her words were again unheeded, for Mr. Greening was far away, imagining as pretty a picture of their wedded bliss together as any man could wish for.

She tried again, 'Mr. Greening...'

He held up a plump hand, 'Now my dear Mrs, Grey... er... Martha, if I may be so bold, hear me out. You will be very comfortable at Greening House, I assure you, I built it, as you know, but two years since, after making my considerable fortune as an army contractor. The recent hostilities against the tyrant Bonaparte were a boon to me, a veritable boon. I was able to take some very nice profits...' He hastily recollected what a widow of a Lieutenant of the Royal Navy owed to the recent war and gave himself time by clearing his throat. 'Er... um... yes... as I was saying, Greening House is very comfortable, all of the latest improvements, and you need not be afraid of not being the mistress in my house for, once we are married, I shall dismiss the housekeeper... she is not as thrifty as she might be... as you will wish to look after the house yourself. Oh, yes, you would be able to call the house your own.

Martha stamped her foot, 'Mr, Greening, listen to me. Please.'

He was disconcerted, 'Eh! My dear Mrs, Grey, did you speak?'

'Yes, I did. Please pay attention to me. I must decline your offer for I do not wish to marry again.'

'Not wish to marry again? Nonsense, every woman wants to be married and I am proposing a very eligible connection, it is not as if you would bring much to the marriage. I was able to ascertain that the late Miss Gilbert's Will treated you shabbily. Besides,' quite sure the added inducement would clinch the matter, 'my dear children are looking forward to having you as their Mamma. I would put you in sole charge of them, I would not interfere with their upbringing.'

'No! Mr. Greening.'

'Yes, in sole charge, that is what every woman wants... a family. You no longer have a roof over your head and I am offering you one.'

'I have a perfectly good roof, as you call it.'

'No, you have not. I happen to know, remember, how badly Miss Gilbert treated you.'

'Mr. Greening you know nothing of the matter. I am leaving Seacliffe in a few days.'

Ignoring her words, he seized her cool hand between his hot damp ones. 'I know what it is,' he exclaimed coyly, 'You want me to propose to you in form and you are refusing me until I go down on my knees.' He dropped her hand and, to her horrified embarrassment, began to bend a knee. It then occurred to him the bare boards might be dirty, so he straightened up, pulled out a large blue and white spotted handkerchief from his tail-coat pocket; opened it; spread it carefully on the floor; and, knelt on it.

Looking down into his face, Martha could see that most of his female acquaintances would regard him as a good looking man, an excellent catch for any woman, especially a widow of ten year's standing with, as far as they knew, the merest pittance to live on. Fortunately, Martha was not destitute. She did not like Mr. Greening and liked him even less after this interview. She could not help remembering the poor, wispy creature who had faithfully brought forth a daughter punctually every year for five years. The last one, stillborn, proved too much for her and she quickly followed it to the grave, leaving an inconsolable widower for no longer than three months and a hopeful bridegroom thereafter.

He had been reviewing his female acquaintances with the object of replacing his late wife with someone more robust when, some months ago, his eyes lit upon Martha. A competent nurse, she was looking after the demanding Miss Gilbert with care and kindness; an excellent housekeeper, she had run number 24 Charlotte Terrace with skill; a handsome woman with a charming figure – healthy and strong – just the person to give him the son he craved; and last, but by no means least, the widow of the only son of a baronet.

Grabbing her hand in an uncomfortably tight grip, he gazed up at her soulfully. 'Will you marry me?'

Pulling her hand away, Martha's voice rang out clearly, 'Mr. Greening, I most respectfully decline your flattering offer of marriage.' And with a delicate emphasis which was lost on him, she added 'It is an honour for which I have done nothing to deserve… Oh, please get up, do!'

Ignoring her protestations, he drew breath to renew his offer. Desperate, and knowing nothing less than a direct attack would prick his armour of self-esteem, she interrupted him briskly.

'I shall have to ask you to leave. The house is being closed today and I still have a lot to do.'

As soon as the words left her lips, there was a tremendous crash in the hall. Grasping for any excuse to end this embarrassing episode, she ran to the door.

'Jessica, are you all right? You did not fall down the stairs?'

'No, my dear, I was just popping on my bonnet to take these books back to the Circulating Library. I had them under my arm you know, whilst I was standing on tip-toe to see myself in the looking-glass you keep so inconveniently high on the wall, when I dropped them. Is my bonnet straight?' She swung round catching sight of a red-faced Mr. Greening, who had risen hastily from his knees and was mopping his forehead with the blue spotted handkerchief. 'Oh! I did not know you had Mr. Greening with you – how do you do?' He bowed stiffly, looking rather sheepish.

'No, no, Jessica, Mr. Greening is just leaving.'

Before he knew what was happening, his beaver hat, gloves and caped great-coat were given to him, his hand shaken warmly and he was outside the front door. Bewildered he paused on the top step, hat in hand, trying to decide where he had made a mistake. He knew he had made a mess of his proposal and he was reluctantly coming to the surprising conclusion that the lady would never have him. Her undoubted charms would never be his, a great pity – although she was looking tired and a bit peaky of late and there were dark circles under her lovely eyes – such beautiful hair, and those lips... no, come to think of it, he had never noticed it before but those soft lips could become quite stern and as for her chin, it was definitely stubborn.

He descended the steps, perhaps Mrs. Grey would not be an accommodating wife after all. Not like Miss Long, ah, yes, all was not lost, if he had read the signs aright, he would have a wife soon. Miss Long may not have Martha Grey's looks but she did possess money. He must call on Miss Long as soon as possible, in fact if he hurried he would be in time to take tea with her this very afternoon.

Closing the front door with a shove, Martha looked at her friend, 'Jessica, you cannot go out in this wind, we can return the books tomorrow.'

Removing her bonnet Jessica said 'Oh, no I only dropped the books as a pretext, my dear, I thought you were in difficulties, your voice had risen considerably.'

Martha giggled, 'Bless you, yes, it was most uncomfortable, he would keep on proposing and would not take no for an answer. I did not want to hurt his feelings and I was too soft to begin with, I had to become quite brusque in the end. As inducements, if you please, he laid at my feet that pretentious house, sans housekeeper, of course, and his four little darlings who, he assured me are longing to call me "Mamma", as if those poor little white mice ever uttered a word unless spoken to, or ever dared express an opinion.'

'Really!' Jessica was fascinated 'what an extraordinary way to propose. Some men are so foolish.' Jessica peered discreetly out of the window. Keeping her eye firmly fixed on the view she asked slyly, 'You do not feel you could accept him? He really is very rich and you should marry again.'

'Certainly not to him, for all his eligibility, I do not think him kind. He was monumentally selfish to his wife and his children always look crushed. His housekeeper told Mrs. Bunnett that, except where his own comfort is concerned, he cheese pares... Jessica, what are you doing at the window?'

'Watching him. He seems to be talking to himself. Ah-ha, I knew it, he's not going home, he's going to see Miss Long instead.'

Martha ran to the window, 'How can you possibly tell?'

'Easily. He's walking towards the Parade instead of towards Prince Street. My dear, you have lost him, if you will not have him, she certainly will.'

'Well, I hope she'll be happy, she has been wanting a husband for years and I think she will be kind to the children. I just hope she can manage him.'

'I have no doubt of that, Martha, she has money of her own and three brothers to look after her rights. Oh, Martha, are you sure you do not want him?'

'Absolutely, why?'

'I had hoped you would marry and settle down here. I shall miss you so. Promise me if you do not like being at home again, you will come back.' She regarded her friend with great sadness.

Martha laughed, 'I am not going to the ends of the earth, we shall write and when I am settled you and Henry must come for a long visit.'

Jessica would not be comforted, 'It'll never be the same. Is there no one here you could possibly marry and settle down with – what about -?'

'We have been over this time and again, Jess. Going home has been the reason for my last ten years in bondage, or exile if you will. When I first came here I promised myself that after I had reached my goal I would return home. The old man is dead, he cannot hurt me anymore. In fact, if he were still alive that would not stop me now. Besides, there are some business matters I have to attend to.' She looked around the room, 'This used to be a pretty room and I was fairly content in this house. But Marcia's death has made it a natural time for me to leave. Today we have rolled up carpets, covered the furniture, put away ornaments, and mentally I've done the same with my life here. Now is the correct time for me to move on.'

Jessica sighed, 'You are right, I know you're right, I only wish it were not so.' She followed Martha from the room, remarking, 'By the way, Mrs. Bunnett has made us some tea. I told her to serve it in the kitchen, it is the only habitable place in the house.'

'I am dying for a cup, refusing Mr. Greening is thirsty work,' Martha replied gaily.

Young Johnny Jackson was running an errand. Mr. Tufnell had given him a penny to deliver a letter that had just arrived at the Receiving Office. Johnny could not see the urgency, the lady to whom it was addressed had lately died, but if Ol' Man Tufnell had paid him a penny, he supposed some strange grown-up reason must make immediate delivery necessary. Anyway he did not mind, at ten years of age he found it exciting to lean against the wind as he walked up Cliffe Road.

At the corner of Charlotte Terrace he paused for breath and looked without much hope across the Bay. No ships to be seen today. Time was, he remembered wistfully, when he was just a little boy before Ol' Boney was beat, he could depend upon seeing at least one man-o'-war, East Indiaman or other merchant vessel, beating their way up or down the Channel. And one glorious never to be forgotten day, he had actually watched a daring French privateer capture a cutter right at the entrance to Seacliffe Bay, just out of range of the guns angrily banging away on the Head. The cutter had been boarded and the prize crew had brazenly sailed it away to France. Now all had changed, Boney was in exile and only merchant vessels or dull ol' coasters and fishing smacks passed by now-a-days.

As he arrived at the back gate of No. 24, he found Tig hunched in the shelter of the wall. The tiger-striped cat greeted him with a miaow and a flick of his tail. Johnny opened the back door and was joined by Tig, his fur ruffled and fluffed by the wind. They shot through it together and Johnny had to lean hard to close it.

'Who's there,' called his Auntie Bunn, 'Shut the door, drat it.' She entered the passage, 'Oh, 'tis you Johnny, have you come to help me?'

'No, I mean yes, I mean – I've brought a letter for Miss Gilbert.'

'But she's dead.'

'I know, but Mr. Tufnell said I was to –'

'Well, give it here lad, I'll speak to Mrs. Grey about it. Why, Tig you naughty puss, wherever have you been ? I've been looking for you all over. It's too late to feed you now, you must go into your travelling box right away.' After picking up and kissing the unappreciative cat, she bundled him into a large wicker basket.

'You stay here, Johnny. No gingerbread men today, we're all at sixes and sevens. I'll make you some tomorrow.'

His Auntie Bunn was a notable cook and as she was coming to live with his family, he was content to perch on the kitchen table and think about all the tasty meals she would make.

Mrs. Bunnett bustled along the passage to the front rooms where she found Mrs. Grey and Mrs. Thistlethwaite had just completed a last minute tour of the house.

'Everything is in order, Mrs. Bunnett, and we are ready for that tea.'

'Thought you would be ma'am, it is on the kitchen table.'

'I expect you want to be off,' said Martha, 'no sign of Tig, I suppose?'

'I was just going to tell you, he came in with young Johnny, I have not fed him, I popped him straight into his box, he was that cross… I shall miss him, we had such lovely talks, Tig and I.' They entered the kitchen, 'Off the table Johnny, we are going to have a cup of tea, you can have milk if you like.'

'Tig's crying, Auntie, can't I let him out?'

'No, I'm afraid not,' said Martha, 'he's been missing for three days and if he escaped again we might never catch him. I think he was bewildered by the upset in his house. I'll feed him when we get to Mrs. Thistlethwaite's – Highness and Voltaire are already there. They will all probably be even more upset by the time they reach their final destination.'

Johnny was interested, 'Where are they going ma'am?'

'To a place in Gloucestershire,' his Auntie replied.

'Glossersher?' he looked blank, 'Where's that?'

'A county to the north-west,' said Martha, kindly adding, 'Near Wales.'

'Oh, Wales!' He grinned, 'A long way away.' He looked puzzled, 'Why are you sending them there. I would love to have –'

'That's enough of your whys, Mrs. Grey wants her tea in peace.'

'No, please let me explain it to Johnny. It is a surprising thing to him that the animals should travel all that way when perfectly good homes could be found for them here.' Martha sipped her tea gratefully. 'You see Johnny, when someone dies, as Miss Gilbert did, she leaves her wishes for the disposal of her belongings in a Will, which is a document drawn up by an attorney, in this case Mr. Thistlethwaite. Well, in her Will Miss Gilbert left some jewellery and Tig, Highness and Voltaire to her niece, a Miss Frances Gilbert, and she lives in Gloucestershire. So Mr. Thistlethwaite is obligated to send them to her, but Miss Gilbert put him in an awkward position, she insisted that no one in her family be apprized of her death. There had a dreadful quarrel many years ago, so Mr. Thistlethwaite could not write to them and ask if they wanted the animals. They live on an estate and must have cats, and dogs like Highness and who knows perhaps even a parrot, like Voltaire, of their own. I am to explain to the family what has happened. Which is fortunate for me, because I'm going to my home in Herefordshire, and before you ask where that is, young John, it is the next door county to Gloucestershire. All very neat you see, Mr. Thistlethwaite will hire a coach for me and my baggage and I shall travel in style with my menagerie.'

'The least he could do' murmured Jessica, 'after Marcia left you so little. When I think how you looked after her, with all her complaints and...'

'Please, Jessica, you do not understand. All the clothes she left me are magnificent. I shall not need half of them where I'm going. She had excellent taste, as you'll be the first to agree, and we were so alike in colouring and figure that I shall be too fashionable for Stretton Wakefield, that is,' she giggled 'until they begin to go out of fashion and by that time I'll be known as the eccentric Mrs. Grey who has not changed her style since Waterloo year.'

'Never,' exclaimed Mrs. Bunnett, 'you're much too clever with your needle to let that happen. When I think –' suddenly recollecting Johnny, who was gamely trying to follow the conversation, she turned to him and said, 'run home, Johnny, and ask your Dad to come with the wheelbarrow, or the donkey, to help me with my bags, there's a good boy.' As the door closed behind her nephew, she continued, 'when I think how you had to scrimp and scrape to keep looking the way you did, an' how Miss Gilbert, God rest her soul, was that critical of everything...'

'So true, Mrs. Bunnett,' agreed Jessica, 'but although you are only saying what I've been saying all along, you will not find Mrs. Grey in agreement with us.'

'Please both of you, I know you mean well, but I was scrimping and scraping for a purpose. I spent as little as possible on myself because I was saving up to go home to Stretton Wakefield. My salary was generous. And I have my widow's pension, and Miss Gilbert expected a certain standard from me.'

'Be that as it may,' said Mrs. Bunnett, 'you nursed her right to the end and she ran you ragged with her "run down and get this" and "run down and get that" and her not liking the nurses and wanting you near her at night. Why you are that thin you've been taking in your dresses by the handful and your wedding ring has quite slid off your finger'.

Involuntarily Martha's hand went to the gold band on the chain round her neck, 'True,' she smiled, 'but now I can get into Miss Gilbert's clothes with little or no alteration, she was always slimmer than I! Mrs. Bunn, just think of those glorious furs and how warm I'll be.' She shivered, 'I could do with one now.'

'I still think she could have left you some money, they way she did us servants, and more than the year's salary we all got. Plenty enough is going to them orphans, and why only her second best jewellery to her niece? Paltry, I calls it.'

Marcia Gilbert would have been the last person to appreciate any defence of her motives, but Martha felt honour bound to give some explanation of her late employer's actions.

'Please do not think that way, I've been amply rewarded. Ten years ago Miss Gilbert gave me a home when I needed one. She was not always the cross old maid she became, if you remember, we had some very happy and amusing times before she became ill. She was always physicking herself, I know, but that only became serious when Mr. Farrell married. Until then her hypochondria never stopped her from doing anything really interesting and she always took me with her.'

'I remember when Mr. Farrell was courting her,' said Jessica, 'it was just after I married Henry and met you both. She was so gay and happy then. Only five years ago and now she is in her grave and he is now the father of two more children.'

'Yes, I think it was the thought of step-children, six of them, and perhaps some of her own made her hesitate. Then when a handsome and younger woman came to Seacliffe, Mr. Farrell transferred his interest. It was such a dreadful blow to her, she never recovered. The hypochondria worsened and when the real illness began no one believed she was really ill – it was horrible. Poor thing, she did not want to die, right to the end she put up a tremendous struggle.' Tears filled Martha's eyes, and she shivered again. While soft-hearted Jessica patted her hand, the practical Mrs. Bunnett said, 'Another cup, ma'am, before I damp down the fire?'

'No thank you, we must be ready for Mr. Thistlethwaite, and Johnny will be back soon. I want to thank you, dear Mrs. Bunn for all the help you have given me. You've my address and I shall write to you as soon as I am settled in Stretton Wakefield. I hope the new owners of the house will take you on. If not, Mr. Thistlethwaite will help you find a position, will he not Jessica?'

Putting on her cloak as she spoke, she turned and gave Mrs. Bunnett a hearty kiss and put into her hands a bulky parcel. 'This is for you, you saw me making it, but I have not worn it.'

'Oh, ma'am... it isn't? She gasped, her eyes lighting. The wrappings were eagerly torn off. 'It is... the cloak you lined with your old fur wrap. Thank you, ma'am.' She was crying. 'I'll think of you every time I wear it.'

'Then it's not to be kept for best, it's to be worn whenever it is cold, like today. Put it on and let us see you.' The proud new owner pirouetted. Not even her cousin Mary, who had married well and gave herself airs, had anything like this. Just wait until church next Sunday, she would wear it even if there were a heat wave.

Her renewed thanks were interrupted by Johnny, who came in with his father. Farewells were made once more; Mrs, Bunnett made sure she had all her boxes; Tig was peered at between the withies of his basket; the house keys counted and tears began to flow. Whereupon, her male relations bundled her out of the back door. Johnny came running back.

'Auntie Bunn says she forgot to give you the letter I brought, she left it on the mantelpiece. It's for Miss Gilbert and auntie thinks Mr. Thistlethwaite should have it.' Martha pressed sixpence into his grubby paw and his eyes nearly fell out of his head. What a day... seven whole pence. He blushingly thanked her all the while thinking of where to spend his riches.

In spite of her cloak, Martha shivered in the icy blast as she waved the little party goodbye. She was glad she was returning to the more sheltered county of her birth and get away from the incessant wind. As she pushed the back door to she heard Tig yowl and Jessica trying to soothe him.

Martha went to the mantelpiece and picked up the letter, glancing at it casually her eyebrows rose. Interesting, it came from Gloucestershire.

The ring of the front door bell drew her attention and she went to answer it. Henry Thistlethwaite was on the top step.

'Are you and Jessica ready? Or, shall I walk the horses?'

'No, we're quite ready thank you Henry, come in quickly, this wind is terrible. We've found Tig and have just seen Mrs. Bunnett off, complete with the keys. Tig is in his basket and is in the kitchen. This bandbox is all I have, your man came for my trunks this morning.'

Tig and the bandbox were quickly stowed in the carriage, Henry handed in the ladies and climbed in after them. As the equipage clattered down Charlotte Terrace, Martha looked back at the house where she had spent so many years. This was the moment she had been waiting for, saving for, and now, instead of elation, all she felt was apprehension. For years her determination to return to her home had kept her going, but now fear of what lay ahead numbed her and left her feeling flat.

'Mrs. Bunnett seems content to remain on as caretaker, does she not? Remarked Jessica.

'Indeed, she hopes the new owner will keep her on,' replied Henry.

'The other servants have found their new places satisfactory, Martha?'

'According to Mrs. Bunnett,' she replied. In the effort to maintain her part in the mundane conversation, Martha was able to deflect her disturbing thoughts.

It was not until they were settled by the fire with the tea tray after dinner that Martha remembered the letter. Giving it to her host with a brief explanation, she and Jessica discussed their tiring day while he read it through – twice.

'Hm,' he handed it to Martha, 'you had better read it,' Seeing his wife's face, he added with a grin 'aloud.'

Martha began, '*Cobbleigh, January 15th, 1816.*'

'Why!' exclaimed Jessica, 'It has taken its time getting her.'

'Ssh... listen,' said her spouse.

'"My dear aunt Marcia,

You must forgive me for writing in this manner, but I have the sad duty to inform you that my dear father, your brother Gerald, died suddenly ten days ago. He had been in excellent health until he caught a chill hunting on Boxing Day... he would not look after himself and continued to go out in all weathers. He got so much worse that his lungs became congested and the doctor said his heart gave out with the strain of his trying to breathe. My father's affairs were left in very bad order and my trustees inform me that I will have to sell Cobbleigh. This I cannot bear. They want me to go to Bath and live with my Grandmamma, but I cannot and will not do this without trying to save Cobbleigh; there have been Gilberts here for hundreds of years, although you and I are the last. I have pleaded with my trustees to stay until the last possible moment but they are embarrassed by the fact I do not have a suitable chaperone, for my grandmother is old and delicate and could not make the journey. This why I am taking the liberty of writing to you. Please, aunt Marcia, if you have ever loved Cobbleigh, please, please come and help me in my efforts to save it.

I beg you.

Your despairing niece,

Frances Gilbert."'

The silence following the reading of the letter was broken by Jessica disgustedly remarking 'Such a pity Marcia Gilbert left all that money to build a wing onto the orphanage. Her niece could have done with it, all she gets is the second best jewellery and the animals... really it is too bad.'

'The second best jewellery was her mother's, the more ostentatious pieces belonged to Miss Marshall who had them from her father, the Nabob,' said Martha.

'Well, if family feeling made her leave her second best to her niece, why could she not have left her the rest, and the money.'

'Probably because all the money came from the Marshalls. Although I do wish those unfortunate orphans could have been left something more useful than a new wing to house the staff. A dowry for each girl on leaving, perhaps, either for marriage or to enter a respectable trade. Heaven knows being an orphan is bad enough, but with no money behind them they have rarely more than two alternatives... service or the streets.'

'Martha, really'. Chided Jessica.

'But it is true, and either choice must be hard for them because that orphanage does not give them enough education to set them apart from their peers. Marcia would be better remembered if she had given the orphanage the "Gilbert-Marshall Dowries" rather than the "Gilbert-Marshall Wing and Garden".'

'Who is to say she did not do both?' said Henry with a twinkle in this eye.

'Henry, you didn't?' his wife's eyes were round.

'Did, my dear.'

'Wonderful,' she said proudly.

Faced with this domestic interchange, Martha waited patiently. She had met their ability to communicate cryptically before and never ceased to be amused by it and wondered if she and Tom would ever have become so perfectly attuned to one another, if he had not been killed so prematurely. She had to admit she did not see how her marriage would ever have mellowed into the comfortable security that enfolded the Thistlethwaites. She had only met that perfect mutual trust in one other couple – her friends the Blakes.

'You are far away. Dreaming of Mr. Greening?' Teased Jessica.

'No, I was wondering if it is permitted for a mere mortal to ask what you two are talking about/' Laughed Martha.

The Thistlethwaites exchanged amused glances and Henry said, 'I prevailed upon Marcia Gilbert to give the trustees, amongst whom I am now one, wide latitude on the expenditures and, as long as everything is labelled "Gilbert-Marshall", that is what we have.'

'Did she take much persuading.'

'Of course she did, for she enjoyed making me run back and forth and work for my fees. She changed her mind nearly every week. I think her games with me prolonged her life a little, She had quite an amazing grasp of business affairs, I suppose Miss Marshall taught her that for I believe the old lady was formidable in more ways than one. Miss Marshall decided never to marry and in the face of convention adopted her niece as her daughter, Of course, she was so rich that all was forgiven, especially when she told her cronies, in strictest confidence, that Marcia and Gerald fought so much and were so jealous of each other that they could not be brought up in the same household. How much of that is true, and how much pure fabrication on her part so that Marcia could never be returned to the family, I do not know. Do you, Martha?'

'All I know of the story is that Gerald, who was eight or nine years older than Marcia, blamed her for his mother's death. The poor woman died giving birth to

Marcia. It seems to me the whole family acted very stupidly and cruelly to a young child, no wonder she never wanted to have anything to do with them. In fact I think the better of her for leaving a small remembrance to her niece.'

'Let us turn again to that poor girl's letter, I must do something about it promptly,' said Henry.

'It will not be a pleasant task,' said Martha 'to break the news of her aunt's death when she is counting upon her aid very much.'

Jessica's kind heart was touched, 'Poor child, I am sorry for her. She should have someone by her side that she can depend on.'

'I think I have it,' said Henry, 'Martha, my dear, I am afraid I'm going to impose upon you, but the Gilbert estate will recompense you handsomely.'

'Oh, no,' protested Jessica, 'Henry, you cannot ask Martha..'

'Will have to.'

Martha was amused, this time she knew what was coming. 'You want me to break the news to Miss Frances Gilbert, do you not?'

'Yes, I am afraid so, I will write a letter of course, but I think it kinder if the blow to her hopes came from you in the first instance.' Martha nodded her head in agreement.

'But that is not all, Martha, I shall have to ask you to leave as soon as possible, instead of staying a week or two with us. I am sorry, my dear, I know you and Jessica had all sorts of plans and I know you need a rest after all that nursing and the trials of closing the house, but I really do not feel Miss Frances can be kept in suspense any longer,'

The ladies were very disappointed and Jessica was quite cross with her husband.

Suddenly Jessica became more cheerful, 'Perhaps she'll ask you to become her chaperone, you were saying that you would eventually look for another position.'

'What's this?' exclaimed Henry, 'I thought Martha was returning to her home. You have not changed your mind?'

'No, not really, but I cannot help wondering what it will be like in Stretton Wakefield now. The closer I get to leaving Seacliffe the more trepidation I feel. It is very odd, after all these years of being absolutely determined to return, I now find I'm reluctant.'

'But why are you so reluctant, your father-in-law is dead and there's no one left to make your life miserable. Unless of course the new baronet…?'

'Charles? Oh, no. Charles would never be unkind to me. Sir John was just as hateful to him and his mother, as he was to us. I think it is because I am ten years older and, even if my memories are of golden days and perpetual summer. I know it could not have been so. I owe it to myself to return after having striven for so long to clear the debts my father left. If I am not happy there I can now live quietly and pleasantly where ever I choose.'

'Is that what you have been doing all this time?' marvelled Jessica, 'you never told us. I knew you were saving your money for something.'

'My father left a grossly encumbered estate just like Mr. Gerald Gilbert. Poor dear Papa was a good farmer, but he was not very successful in the speculations he attempted. By the time he died, little was left unmortgaged of what used to be a fair-sized holding that we Wakefields had held for centuries. I was very fortunate in my attorney, a young man who had taken over from my father's man on his retirement, and he threw himself into the task of helping me. It was he who discovered, hiding behind nominees, that it was my father-in-law who had foreclosed on the mortgages my father had unwisely taken out. Sir John never liked me and he hated my father with a passion, a passion made all the more violent because it was one-sided. Fortunately Mr. Todd, my attorney, was able to compound with the creditors (Sir John still hid behind the nominees) and we sold practically everything. Mr Todd, an excellent and wise young man, stopped me from stripping myself of all my worldly goods and we managed to retain the Manor House, Home Farm and several cottages. Then he took out new mortgages on them, needless to say not with anyone remotely connected with Sir John Grey, and he found good tenants for the Manor and Home Farm, putting the rents to paying off the mortgages.'

'How shameful,' exclaimed Jessica, 'your own father-in-law. Why did he hate your father so?'

'Jealousy, pure and simple,' replied Martha, 'Father married the girl they both loved – my mother, and when Sir John married in due course, Lady Grey could not help but know she was second best because Sir John never made any bones about it, so she did not like us either...'

'What a horrible man' muttered Jessica.

'...Actually, it started before that, when they were very young if not exactly when they were in short coats, They were at school together. They were both studious and athletic but father nearly always came first. Then at Stretton, although the Greys had settled in the neighbourhood at the time of the Civil War, on what had been sequestered Wakefield land, I might add, and by cleverly changing sides obtained a baronetcy at the Restoration, the Wakefields were always the first family in the neighbourhood. Sir John tried to best father at every opportunity and the buying up and foreclosure of the mortgages was one of his better ploys, It killed my father.'

'With this rivalry,' asked Henry, 'How came you to marry his son?'

'It was not rivalry in the true sense,' replied Martha, 'because father never paid much attention to it, in fact he laughed at Sir John's attempts, which of course infuriated Sir John and amused our friends and acquaintances vastly. I married Tom because we were in love and we married in haste because Tom was joining his ship. I was under age but Tom was twenty-one, so only my father's consent was necessary. I think he believed the marriage would ease Sir John's jealousy, but I am much afraid that our marriage prompted Sir John to foreclose.

'I was living in Plymouth, where Tom's ship was refitting and had been married six months when I found I was increasing. Just as I was becoming used to the idea of motherhood, I was called back to Stretton to nurse my father. I arrived three days before he died. Almost the last words he spoke to me were "Forgive me, I should never have given my consent, but your marriage should protect you now". At the time I thought he was sorry I'd married Tom, he'd never really cared for him, However, when I found out about the mortgages I knew then what he'd really meant,' She sighed heavily, 'Poor father.'

'And later you lost your husband and suffered a miscarriage, said Jessica sadly. 'That is when you came to Seacliffe?'

'Yes, my kind friends the Blakes looked after me until I was well. I could not live off them forever, even though they wanted me to stay with them. He was a Commander then and was most helpful in arranging my affairs as Tom's widow. He is now Captain Sir Alexander Blake and they are stationed in the West Indies.

'I knew I had to earn a living because I'd made a vow never to return to Stretton Wakefield until all the debts were settled and I felt I could return with honour. Helena Blake understood and it was she who heard of the position with Marcia Gilbert. I was warned that Marcia had run through at least six companions in the previous three years, but I was attracted to the position by the very handsome salary and the realisation that I needed a challenge to make me forget all that had gone before – "Take me out of myself" as my nurse used to say. So now you understand why I return to Stretton Wakefield.'

'Remarkable story,' murmured Henry.

'We never knew the half of it,' said Jessica, 'you kept everything so quiet. No one would have suspected all the troubles you've experienced.'

'Yes,' agreed Martha demurely, 'everyone thought I was straight out of the egg, when I arrived in Seacliffe.'

They laughed and Henry said, 'I'll see about hiring a coach tomorrow Could you be ready to leave the day after?'

As Martha nodded in agreement to his suggestion, Jessica said, 'And I think it is high time we all went to bed. Martha, my dear, you must be dropping with fatigue. Henry will give Highness her run.'

'Thank you, both of you,' replied Martha as she picked up her candle, 'I must admit I am very tired. I'll see you both in the morning – Goodnight.'

A large old fashioned travelling coach, roomy enough to accommodate Martha, her baggage and her three charges, rolled to the door three days later. The delay had been caused by Henry being particular in his choice. It took him some time for him to find a reputable coachman who could be relied upon to take every care of his passengers.

After describing his find to Martha, Henry remarked 'It make take you longer on the road. But with a coachman owning his own horses I am sure you will arrive in very good order. For February, the roads will not be too bad either, all this frost means no mud and when you reach the Post Roads, the new Macadam surface will make your journey smoother.'

Having to say farewell to two such good and dear friends was very hard. Jessica had cried a little, then recovered to press upon Martha a beautiful cashmere shawl to help counteract the inevitable draughts, a hamper of tempting delicacies in case she should feel hungry between inns and a hot brick wrapped in flannel for her feet. With tears in her eyes Martha thanked them both warmly, kissed Jessica rather blindly and allowed Henry to hand her into the conveyance.

It took them a few minutes to settle the interior of the coach. Highness, an over-excited black-faced fawn coloured pug, was leaping from one seat to the other yapping merrily, while a very disgruntled Tig was howling in his wicker basket. The parrot, the only creature who should have been vocal, was silent. Voltaire was the most taciturn of birds, Martha did not think she had ever heard him utter more than a morose and unintelligible grumble in all the years she had known him.

With Henry's help she subdued Highness and made her lie down on the seat opposite. There was nothing to be done for Tig except wedge his basket securely in the corner and hope he would eventually fall asleep. Voltaire's cage was set on the floor and a blanket draped over it to exclude any draught, then Martha took the near-side corner seat facing the way of going, put her feet gratefully on the hot brick while Henry carefully tucked her travelling rug over her knees. He checked that a demijohn of water for the animals was at hand, put Marcia's initialled jewel box beside Martha and moved the dressing case, also Marcia's but now part of Martha's inheritance, to a more secure position and said cheerfully, 'There, I really think you are ready to leave, have a safe journey and write to us as soon as you can.' He took her hand and dropped a fat purse into it. 'Take this, it should cover all your expenses.' Before Martha could thank him, he climbed down from the coach, shut the door firmly and briskly told the coachman to move off.

Blinking back tears, Martha waved to her friends until the coach turned the corner and she could no longer see them.

By the time they reached Chichester that evening, the novelty of being looked upon as a lady of consequence by obsequious landlords had quite worn off. To begin with she had been childish enough to enjoy such attention as she had not received in many years, since she had travelled with her father. Jim, the coachman's helper, was careful to see that she had every comfort, and it amused her that he behaved towards her as if he were a family retainer of long standing. But, by the end of the day she had a headache, for Tig had howled unremittingly and an over-excited Highness had been sick, providentially on some straw Jim had wisely laid on the floor of the coach.

The next day the miles from Chichester were accomplished without incident, Tig still complained hoarsely. Highness, at least seemed to have become a hardened traveller, spending the day looking out of first one window and then another. But Martha had not fared so well, her headache was still with her and it was with relief she looked upon their destination, the tall columns flanking the modern portals of the White Hart at Salisbury.

After a restless night, the headache still lingered, but Martha thought it her duty to press on instead of spending the day at the comfortable inn. As the coach ponderously rolled on from Salisbury she heartily regretted her decision, the day had become very much colder. Martha hugged Highness to her for, in spite of her fur coat, shawl and travelling rug, she was soon stiff with cold. Upon their arrival in Bath, where they would spend the night, nothing could disguise the fact that the vague uneasiness and various aches and shivers suppressed during the last few days of frenzied activity were resolving themselves into one of her worst types of sore throat and head cold. She retired to bed early with a hot posset brewed for her by the sympathetic landlord's wife and the next morning she did feel better. She hoped she was on the mend for Jim informed her that, barring accidents, they could expect to arrive at Cobbleigh that very afternoon. Mindful she was entering a house of mourning, she regretfully put aside her fashionable topaz brown travelling dress, sable hat and muff in exchange for an equally smart black wool dress, softened by white lawn ruffles at her throat and wrists and completed her toilette with a black pelisse, large muff and toque of black fox fur, which set off her rich red-brown hair and fair complexion admirably. Only faint purple shadows under her eyes gave any hint that she was still feeling far from well.

She took her place in the coach, thankful it was the last stage in her journey. She was not looking forward to the task awaiting her at Cobbleigh, but at least it would be over and done with by evening. She gazed unseeingly at the passing fields and tried to think of the most tactful way of breaking the sad news she bore. She was withdrawn from her pondering by the coach drawing to a halt. Jim appeared at the window.

'The near wheeler has cast a shoe, ma'am, we passed a Smithy a mile back an' if you are agreeable we'd like to turn around. We could cold shoe him, Ma'am, but 'is 'ooves have thin walls an' we'd prefer not, an' we cannot go with 'is shoe of neither.'

'Very well,' replied Martha, 'I quite understand the problem, we had a horse like that – but are we not closer to Nailsworth?'

'No, ma'am, Nailsworth is a good five miles further on. We can still reach Cobbleigh today,' he added reassuringly.

However the delay proved longer than anticipated, The smith had gone to a nearby farm and had to be fetched by his apprentice.

The small inn where Martha waited was not very comfortable. The landlady had insisted upon placing Martha in the rarely used front room – obviously kept for best. A fire was lit but, because the chimney was cold, it smoked and gave off very little heat. Martha managed to open a window after a struggle, hoping the smoke would escape, but this led to a piercing draught so she closed it quickly.

Eventually they were on their way again. Not really warmed by a few mouthfuls of watery soup she had managed to swallow at the inn, Martha was feeling quite ill. Her head was aching worse than ever and Tig had recommenced his complaints, even though she was holding him on her lap.

By the time the hired coach passed through Stroud to enter the valley of the Cobb, Martha was no longer looking out of the window. She lay back against the squabs with her eyes closed. For warmth and comfort, she cradled an unhappy cat on her lap, while the pug, exhausted from barking at every dog the coach passed, snuggled her stout body into Martha's side. Voltaire, hidden under the rug wrapped around his cage on the floor of the vehicle, occasionally rattled his wings, or cracked a seed. In pain, and longing for the journey's end, Martha wracked her tired brain, seeking the kindest way to break the bad news she brought with her.

The coach lurched sharply. Martha's eyes flew open. The equipage was turning to enter between a pair of elaborately wrought iron gates, one of which sagged off its hinges. They had arrived at last. The carriage bounced and juddered from one pothole to another and she and Tig were nearly thrown onto the floor. Martha clutched the indignant cat with one hand and with the other held tightly to the hanging strap. Highness woke up. Snuffling with excitement, she jumped stiff-legged on the seat, peering out of the window, her short nose leaving smears where she pressed it to the glass.

After what seemed an age, the coach drew up before the steps of a large square house of honey coloured stone. The front door, sadly in need of a coat of paint, was flung open and a young girl, dressed in rusty black, ran out, followed more soberly by her butler.

Jim, opened the coach door and let down the step. Before he could hand Martha down, Highness jumped out barking. Tig, seeing freedom at last, launched himself from her lap, using his claws to gain extra purchase. He sailed past Jim's head and flew up the steps into the house. Martha stood up shakily. Having difficulty in seeing where the cat went, she swayed in the coach doorway, calling out, 'Please butter his paws.' Hazily she realised it was a ridiculous thing to say. Blackness closed in around her... dots of light flashed behind her eyes... she fainted.

1 - Misapprehension

Afraid of the light, Martha cautiously raised her eyelids, the firelight, filtered through her lashes, did not hurt, so she opened her eyes wider. Disoriented, she stared up at the unfamiliar tester overhead. Where was she? Her bedroom at Wakefield Manor was not furnished in pink damask, nor did her bed sport a tester. Her bed was a four-poster, curtained in blue brocade with a pattern of herons woven into the cloth. This one had leaves. Where were her herons? She frowned... she was tired... Meg would know... yes... ask Meg... so tired... she drifted off.

She was conscious of warmth... voices... she heard voices. Someone was there... whispers... gentle hands moving her... smoothing her pillow... cool cloth on her face... 'Meg?' she murmured, 'Hush,' said a voice, 'sleep.'

Later, the same voice said 'See if you can drink this.' Obediently, she managed to swallow the broth gently spooned into her mouth, before she drowsily sank back...

The next time she awoke it was night. Firelight danced on the pink tester that puzzled her so.

She knew where she was. Not in her bed at her beloved Wakefield Manor yet, but she was on her way home, home to Stretton Wakefield where Meg, her old nurse, awaited her. She sighed contentedly and snuggled down into the bedclothes, she was comfortable and warm. Her bed freshly made, sheets scented with herbs. She had been ill. Remembering feverish dreams, she put a shaky hand to her brow, her fever was gone. She was much better, but what was wrong with her hand? Outlined in the fire's glow, it was so thin almost transparent... something missing. What?... a ring... her wedding ring... weak tears welled in her eyes... where was it? Feebly... distressingly weak, she felt the sheets and pillows around her. It was not until her hand brushed her neck she found the chain. Ah! Now she remembered, recently she had lost so much weight, the ring was forever sliding from her finger. Rather than lose it, she had threaded it onto the chain around her neck. It was all becoming clear to her now... Seacliffe... companion to Marcia Gilbert... Marcia's illness... long days... long nights nursing her... an exacting patient... and Marcia never wanting her out of her sight... the pain Marcia suffered... the strain of attending her protracted deathbed... the horror of it all came flooding back...

Clutching the ring as a talisman, Martha fell deeply asleep…

A sound roused Martha. She stirred and opened her eyes. The girl, who had run down the steps upon her arrival, was leaning over her.

'Miss Gilbert?' said Martha, struggling to sit up.

'Please call me Fanny, aunt Marcia.'

Martha blinked, and shaking her head to clear it, protested, 'But I'm not...'

'You are not truly awake yet, I know,' Fanny bent over her smiling. 'There's some broth prepared, would you like it?'

'Yes, please, I am famished. Have I been asleep for long?'

While she vigorously and inexpertly rearranged Martha's pillows, Fanny said she had been abed for five days.

'Good gracious,' exclaimed Martha, 'I am so sorry to cause all this fuss.'

'Not at all,' Fanny smiled, 'The doctor said you had a chill, were too thin and dreadfully overtired. He prescribed rest until you felt like getting up. Do you remember his examining you?'

'I do have some recollection... I feel so much better, I am sure all I needed was a good sleep.' Martha gave a cat-like yawn. 'It is true I have been very tired recently, and the journey from Seacliffe was not the easiest. Oh! Did someone see to the coach?'

'Daly, our butler, used the money in your purse to pay the coachman, do you not remember?'

'I only remember fainting in that silly fashion, I have never done such a thing before.' She replied with a rueful smile. 'And the animals, how are they? Has Tig settled down?'

Fanny laughed, 'When you fainted you were telling us to butter his paws, so we did, but he is such a grumpy cat I'm afraid it was not a success. The dear little dog...'

'Highness,' murmured Martha.

'Highness,' amended Fanny, 'she has made conquests of us all, even father's gun dogs. And as for the parrot... well... he talks so loudly... never stops... we have banished him to the box room with a cloth over his cage.'

Martha was astonished, 'What an odd thing. Voltaire has never uttered intelligently before, I always thought him a useless bird, quite unworthy of his namesake.'

'For shame, aunt Marcia, your own pet too!'

'Yours now, my dear... er, Fanny. Er... Fanny, I must tell you...'

Fanny laughingly flung her arms around Martha's neck, effectively smothering whatever she was going to say, 'What a lovely present... oh, thank you, thank you... I love him, he says such droll things... "belay that... heave ho... splice the mainbrace...".'

Immediately diverted, Martha said, 'Excessively nautical, let us hope he does not swear. Sailors' oaths can be quite ripe. 'Tis extraordinary, I wonder if the coach journey made him think he was at sea... one would suppose he was a sailor's mascot.'

'You do not know?'

'No, for he was Miss Marshall's pet originally.'

'Miss Marshall? Oh! Your relative who adopted you when you were ten,' said Fanny carelessly, more interested in her new pet. 'But how old would he be?'

Martha smothered a yawn, 'Probably about forty years.'

'That old. I never knew parrots lived so long,' she laughed, 'Oh, aunt Marcia, when I saw you arrive with all your trunks and your pets, I was never so happy in all my life. I thought to myself, she has answered my every prayer, now everything will come right, she will help me and I will not be alone any more.

'Is it very bad?'

Fanny nodded, 'As I wrote to you in my letter, p-papa d-died so s-suddenly, Taken Ill, and d-dead in a w-week,' she suppressed a sob, 'and m-my t-trustees do not understand. All they do is shake their heads and purse their lips, say no hope for it, with all papa's debts... we have to sell up.' Then she said in joyful hope, 'but now you are here. You will help me, I know you will.'

Martha was appalled at the mistaken faith Fanny put in her. Appalled, but also it was in her very nature that she immediately longed to help her. Desiring to know more, she said 'But Fanny, why are you so sure a mere aunt can accomplish what your trustees cannot?'

'It is not that, Aunt Marcia, 'tis just that you can talk to them for me and make them heed you. They treat me as if I was still in the nursery. They cannot understand – or will not – I mean it when I say I do not wish to leave Cobbleigh. They think I am being missish and melodramatic when I tell them I would die away from this dear place. But you understand me. Please say that you do... that you do not think me silly and childish not to face facts.'

'No, my dear, I do not think it for one moment.' With all her heart Martha wished she was the person Fanny mistook her for. 'But, my dear Fanny, I regret I cannot help you for I am not...' The disclaimer was lost, Fanny, who had only heard the first sentence, danced about the room with the exuberance of a six-year-old, chanting, 'I knew it, I knew it, you have come to help me, all will be well.'

In the face of such enthusiasm, Martha hesitated to disillusion her and an opportunity to right matters slipped by.

When Fanny finally subsided into a chair by her bed, Martha asked, 'Do you think you could bring Tig to me? You see he is a town cat and he loathed travelling. He had never been so affronted in his spoilt life – shut up in a wicker basket, tossed about in the coach for days. Perhaps if he were permitted to lie on my bed he will settle down.'

'I'll fetch him immediately... oh, this is dear Mrs. Daly, our housekeeper. See she has your broth.'

Mrs. Daly, tall, bony-faced and soberly clad in black bombazine, strode across the floor. The keys of her calling rattled on the silver chatelaine attached to a chain encircling a waist whose slender proportions emphasized her generous bosom. Like the prow of a ship her bust jutted before her, its bounteous curves restrained by whalebone stays. A crisply starched, frilly white cap perched on her iron grey curls, its wide lappets tied in a frivolous bow under her angular chin.

She presented a steaming bowl to Martha, 'Now Miss Gilbert, drink this up and you will feel better directly.'

'Thank you, but, I am not...'.

'Not hungry, Miss Marcia? I never heard of such nonsense, you have not supped since yesterday and doctor says we are to fatten you up.'

Martha recognized the voice, so gentle and kind, as belonging to the one who had tended her during her fever. Its quiet authority now reduced her to a cosseted child in her nursery again, and Martha meekly took the bowl and spooned up the broth. It was so delicious she finished it.

In the meantime, Mrs. Daly drew back the curtains revealing a charming room. Whilst the housekeeper busied herself with stoking up the fire, Martha studied her surroundings. Furnished in faded pink damask and old-fashioned walnut furniture, a lovely Persian carpet on the floor, all was well-polished and immaculately kept, but the apartment did need refurbishing.

'You cannot know, Miss Marcia, how eagerly Daly and I have been awaiting your response to Miss Fanny's letter. Poor Miss Fanny has had too much to bear, and she needs her own kin to look after her. She has had to withstand much for one so young.'

'Of course, her father's death must have upset her terribly.'

'Yes, Miss, but more than that, she has had to put up with... and her so young and her not knowing how to take it.'

'What do you mean by more?'

Mrs. Daly, a hand to her bosom, cast her eyes upward, 'Why, the "goings-on" in this house. Her being treated as if she were a nobody. It fair made me cry at the way she become so quiet. Her eyes getting bigger and bigger in her little face. That's why we were so pleased when you arrived, instead of just writing her a letter, as we feared you might. It's fair done us all a treat, bless you, miss, to see the way Miss Fanny has perked up. I said to Daly, I said, mark my words, Miss Marcia has come to help us and help us she will an' even if she cannot save Cobbleigh, at least she will do right by Miss Fanny, which the poor lamb deserves after all she has been through.'

Martha gazed into the distance while digesting this speech. It opened up various possibilities, and she would dearly love to know more. Almost involuntarily, she came to a decision. 'Mrs. Daly, apart from finding herself penniless, what else has happened to upset Miss... er... m-my n-niece?'

'Corbys,' the housekeeper replied with disgust.

'Corbies?' Martha wrinkled her brow, thinking vaguely of large, black Scottish birds, 'What can they possibly have to do with her?'

'Everything. They were dear friends of the Master's.' The scorn put into the word "dear" was worthy of a Sarah Siddons.

'Oh! I see. Mrs. Daly, please sit down and start at the beginning.'

'Well, Miss, I would like to but I hear Miss Fanny in the passage.'

'Perhaps you could return later?'

'Certainly, Miss Marcia, 'twill be a pleasure.'

Fanny entered, with difficulty, she carried the unhappy Tig. Thoroughly displeased, the cat's marmalade striped body drooped a deadweight in her arms. 'Oof!' she said, as she put him on the bed beside Martha, who remarked, 'To look at him now you would not believe he was the terror of the neighbourhood. There, there Tig, come and settle down,' Tig, his normally shining coat dull in his misery, mewed a pathetic recognition, Murmuring to him she gently smoothed his disordered fur. This soothing treatment calmed him. He relaxed, and slowly settled down, curling himself in a circle against Martha's side. He then bethought himself of urgent business, and licking a paw he washed the horrors of the last few days from his face. Martha and Fanny grinned at each other in delight.

'Some people,' Martha announced, 'may think "Tig" is short for "Tiger", but those in the know realise he is called after an important river, the Tigris. For all he looks so poor now, he is a very important cat.' Fanny, stifling a giggle, hastily agreed, Then catching the twinkle in Martha's eye, she allowed her delighted laughter ring out.

It was the first time in, she did not know how long, Mrs. Daly had heard that laugh. As she left the room, her cap frills nodded happily. She would tell Daly that even if Miss Marcia could not save Cobbleigh, she would at least prove to be of lasting benefit to Miss Fanny.

Fanny, suddenly recollecting she should not tire this fascinating lady, said, 'I'll leave you now so that you may rest. I'll return at dinner time'.

'Yes, you run along I must not keep you as I do believe I could sleep some more. I'll see you later.'

The door closed behind Fanny and Martha was left to think about the rash act she was contemplating. Impetuously she had, as usual, allowed her curiosity get the better of her. She had not insisted upon correcting the natural mistake the people of the house had made upon her unorthodox arrival. She liked Fanny, who had apparently received shocking treatment in her own home. Martha allowed all her sympathy for the girl, caught in a predicament so like Martha's own, to govern her in the formulation of an outrageous plan.

If she was to tell them who she really was, it must be now... it was almost too late already. At a pinch, she could still get away with admitting to her true identity, with the excuse she was still befuddled by her fever.

Before she committed herself to taking such an irrevocable step, and, putting to one side the stimulation of even thinking of such a masquerade, she must ask herself a serious question. Could she take Marcia's place successfully? Why not? Cobbleigh had no seen Marcia since she left for Seacliffe at ten years of age, thirty years ago. And who but a constant companion, such as herself, knew every detail of Marcia's history? As to looks, Marcia herself aided her in that, for she had left all her beautiful clothes to her in her Will. And, in the days before Marcia's illness, strangers often mistook them for sisters, much to Marcia's disgust. True Martha's hair was a deeper chestnut than Marcia's brown but, in the unlikely event she was questioned, these differences could be put down to the quality of the light.

Martha tingled with excitement at her daring. After long years of serving in bondage as a companion, her independent character continuously subordinated to the

8

whims of another, she was now free to take command of her life.

'What shall I do, Tig?' Tig, of course, ignored her question. 'I would like to know what really is the trouble here, and if I tell them I am Martha Grey, I know I'll never truly find out, nor would I have the right to help that charming girl. 'Tis too bad your late mistress and her brother hated each other so, and she left her all to the Seacliffe Orphanage. The orphans need it, of course, but there is no doubt Marcia's considerable wealth could have saved Fanny and Cobbleigh,' Martha sighed, 'Instead, all I've brought her is the second-best jewellery and you three animals. If only...'

Tig, stretching luxuriously, butted his head against her hand when it ceased its delicious stroking, but Martha was once again sunk in sleep.

Carrying a lighted candelabrum, Fanny entered and lit the candles in the sconces. As she drew the window curtains against the night, she said, 'I have asked for our dinner to be served up here by your bed.'

'Nonsense,' cried Martha, yawning widely and stretching her arms above her head, 'I'm going to get up. I'm tired of lying down.' Fanny looked dubious, so Martha added, 'I am much, much better, truly, all I needed was a good long sleep. I shall be up tomorrow. I do not mean to be more of a nuisance than I can help.'

They were still discussing the matter when Mrs. Daly entered. It was she who settled on the compromise of a table set up by the fire. Noticing it had burned low, she muttered, 'Those dratted housemaids, lolly-gagging about,' and set about repairing it.

After a discreet knock, the stately butler made his appearance, followed by two footmen carrying a Pembroke table. Daly superintended its placement by the hearth, and made sure the two places were laid with all the ceremony due to a Lord Mayor's banquet. Then the underfootman entered reverently carrying a bottle of wine. Martha watched all this in awestruck silence.

In five minutes, an appetizing and extravagant meal awaited her and Fanny. Mrs, Daly dismissed her husband and his minions from the room and personally served the repast. Martha, a shawl around her shoulders, was ensconced in a comfortable wing chair with her feet on a footstool. Fanny sat opposite her vying with Mrs. Daly in pressing her to try all the various dishes making up the bountiful meal. When they at last realized Martha was satisfied with some grilled sole, a slice of roast chicken and a syllabub, they desisted. Sipping the excellent wine, Martha watched while Fanny ate with a hearty appetite. A pretty girl, with character in her face, she would soon blossom into an unusual beauty. Without thinking, Martha remarked, 'Is it not time you put your hair up, Fanny? A loose knot at the back would suit you, I think.'

Fanny pulled a face and tugged at a fair ringlet, 'I was not allowed...' her face clouded, then quickly she said, 'Perhaps Annie could do it, after all I am nearly eighteen.' Smiling, Mrs. Daly nodded her approval.

Pursuing her own thoughts, Fanny looked up and said suddenly, 'I am so glad you are here to stay and help me.'

Martha flushed slightly and steeled herself, it was now or never. She opened her mouth to tell the truth when something inside her made her say briskly, 'You asked for my help, and I shall stay as long as I may be of service.' There, it was done. She had set herself on a devious course and she prayed she would do no harm, even do a little good. 'Now, tomorrow I shall get up and you may start by showing me around after breakfast.' To the chorus of remonstrances from her audience, she relented and amended, 'All right, I will not rise until after breakfast, but I shall wish to visit the estate as soon as may be.'

'I know,' cried Fanny, 'I will take you in the gig tomorrow afternoon. If it is fine and you are well wrapped up.'

'Excellent,' approved Martha, 'And Mrs. Daly perhaps you would show me around the house in the morning? I would like to see it... er... see any changes.'

'Of course, Miss Marcia, Now, I'll ring to have this cleared away and, Miss, shall I bring you some tea later?'

'Yes, please, I do like a good cup of tea.'

When only Fanny remained in the room, Martha said, 'Fanny, kindly tell me, please, why are you wearing that ugly dress. 'Tis too short for you and has obviously been altered. I'm afraid black is not very becoming to you either.'

Fanny's stricken face made Martha realize she had been less than tactful.

'This is all we could do in the way of mourning. 'Tis the only one that took the black dye properly.'

'Could you not have bought something more becoming, my dear?'

'I have no money, and Mrs. Daly and Annie did what they could.'

'Surely your trustees...?'

'I did not like to ask them after they told me there's no money. We have to clear Papa's debts.'

'You poor dear, you are not destitute, of that I am sure.' Conscious of having made the decision to embroil herself in Fanny's affairs, she was in danger of becoming reckless Martha temporized by saying, 'We will go into that later. For now, something must be done about that dreadful dress... can you sew?'

'No, my maid Annie is the seamstress.'

'Where are my trunks?'

'Annie has unpacked them.'

'What, all of them?' Hastily Martha mentally reviewed her possessions and, she was relieved to remember, there were no items that had more than her initials on them, and Martha Grey's initials were, of course, the same as those of her late employer – Marcia Gilbert.

Fanny her eyes shining said, 'She unpacked all of them... you have such lovely things.'

'Well, fetch Annie and we shall see what we can do for you.'

She smiled at the girl's turbulent exit. Really Fanny would be quite lovely once she was dressed properly. Her golden hair, pale skin and blue eyes made her look washed out in unadorned black, and little could be done about that. But at least properly fitted clothing would be a vast improvement.

By the end of the evening, Fanny was beside herself with excitement. Annie and her aunt discovered they were kindred souls. While the talk of fashion was quite out of Fanny's ken, she was now the proud possessor of a length of pearl grey cloth – to be made into a walking dress; a white dress for the evening, trimmed with violet ribbons, and a black dress to wear in the morning, whose plainness was offset by a square neckline filled with pleated white lawn which became Fanny very well. Because Martha was taller than Fanny, Annie said she would take the dresses up immediately, and settled by the fire with her sewing basket. Martha suggested Fanny bring all her clothes for inspection to see if anything met with her approval. To Fanny's pleasure, the only items to reach Martha's exacting standards were her personal favourites... her riding habits, a grey cloak lined with red, and a dark blue pelisse.

'You can wear those,' said Martha, 'even if you are in mourning. You are in the country and everyone knows of you and your circumstances. As soon as may be, we will buy some more clothes, The rest should be thrown out or given away.'

'I do love you, aunt Martha, thank you so much. I am so glad you are here.' Fanny kissed her warmly on the cheek and Martha had the grace to feel ashamed.

'Now, Miss Fanny,' said Annie, gathering up her sewing, 'you must leave Miss Marcia be, she must go back to bed now and have an early night.'

Quickly obedient to the suggestion of her maid, Fanny kissed Martha once more, bade her sleep well and quietly followed Annie from the room.

Martha retired to bed, not to sleep but to ponder over the events of the evening before Mrs. Daly returned. She was not unsatisfied with her evening's work. If ever anyone needed taking in hand, Fanny did. She could laugh and joke as naturally as any spirited seventeen-year-old, but when no longer animated, while Martha watched, her face became sad and forlorn, lending her a maturity far beyond her years.

2 - Martha Accepts the Part

'Well, Molly, me old love, are ye making me a cup of tea then?'

Molly Daly looked fondly at her husband sitting unbuttoned beside the fire in their sitting room. Relaxed, feet in carpet slippers, coat off, stock loosened, he puffed his churchwarden pipe contentedly. She never ceased to marvel that, at the first sound of a bell, he could be ready for any service within the space of thirty seconds.

She picked up the chased silver teapot from the side board, 'Would you like some, Harry? I'm taking a tray to Miss Marcia, she wants to talk to me about Miss Fanny.'

Removing the pipestem from his mouth, he pointed it at her, 'I should be careful there,' he warned.

'Oh! Why? I thought you...'

'We don't know anything about her an' it may not be such a good idea to trust her too far. I remember what a nasty, spiteful child she was.'

'Harry Daly! 'Twas was you who suggested Miss Fanny write to her, an' you who gave Miss Fanny the hope...'

'I only did it because we had to do something, fast. She was that desperate, an' Miss Augusta was no help. A broken reed. You'd think Miss Fanny's grandmother could have bestirred herself, an' come in person 'stead of sending her daughter. Fat lot of good Miss Augusta was, telling Miss Fanny nothing but that when she came to live with them in Bath she could share her duties in entertaining her Grandmamma. Enough to send Miss Fanny into hysterics.'

'Miss Augusta was ever the foolish sister, not like my Miss Charlotte. Not but it must be a dismal life Miss Augusta leads. Nothing to do. Under Mrs. Powys's thumb, for 'tis she who holds the purse strings – tight. Boring too – Mrs. Powys forever believing herself delicate. Only does what she wants to do. An' Miss Augusta lets her, ever resentful, but she hasn't the nerve to say "boo" to her mother. No, my Miss Charlotte was always the more spirited of the two sisters.'

'Spirits... talking of spirits, that Miss Augusta is overfond of the sherry, she ran through dunnamany bottles.'

'Aye,' she agreed, pouring hot water into the teapot to warm it, 'but thank goodness her drop too much enabled me to put her to bed before they read Mr. Gilbert's Will. With all that there todo with them Corby's, she'd have gone straight to her mother, tattled the whole tale, an' Miss Fanny would have been sent for post-haste. 'Twas bad enough as it was, when the trustees told Miss Fanny she would have to live in Bath with Mrs. Powys and her aunt Augusta. Of course, if old Mrs. Birch had been in England at the time, matters would have been managed differently and we would not have to have bothered Miss Marcia.'

'Aye, Mrs. Birch is the gamest old besom there ever was. Even if the old lady is not a real relation of Miss Fanny, she would never have said she was too ill to attend the funeral and, what's more, she would never have allowed Miss Augusta to be sent in her stead. Mrs. Birch can be depended upon to know Miss Augusta would celebrate slipping her mother's leash by getting tipsy amongst the funeral meats.'

Pouring the water from the now warmed pot, she scolded him with laughter in her eyes, 'Harry! Not but I know just what you mean.' And unlocking the tea caddy she carefully measured the tea leaves into the pot. 'What then am I to do about Miss Marcia? She is going to ask me questions an' I will have to answer 'em.' She poured boiling water over the tea leaves. 'In fact, I want to, I trust her. She seems a very capable lady and kind, she gave Miss Fanny some of her lovely clothes.'

'That is as may be, but you'd better be careful. There was no love lost between her and the Master, and I mind she was ever a sly one.'

15

While waiting for the tea to draw, the housekeeper stood, hand to bosom, thinking over her husband's words. 'Well, I'll do as you say, I will be careful.' Absentmindedly she straightened her cap, 'But I'm going to trust her, I think.'

She poured out his tea as he said, 'Go slowly then, an' think before you speak. Won't do no harm to go slowly.' She left him sipping the hot drink with relish.

But she was in a very confused frame of mind when she carried the tray upstairs. Her husband's instructions upset her. Intuitively, she had trusted Miss Marcia and now he had made her doubt her own instincts, in consequence she was tense with worry when she opened the bedroom door.

'I saw Miss Fanny off to bed, an' I brought the tea right away,' she said abruptly, setting the tray on the bedside table.

'I hope you brought a cup for yourself, so we can talk in comfort.'

'I did not take the liberty, Miss,' was the prim reply.

Oh! Lord, dismayed Martha sank back on her pillows. Mrs. Daly had had a change of heart. She wondered what had brought it on, she quite thought the housekeeper approved of her. Now she hoped Mrs. Daly would not prove too difficult to handle. While these thoughts whirled through the back of her mind, she said, 'Do go and get a cup, that is, if you like the stuff.'

Looking rather grim, Mrs. Daly left the room, and Martha was left trying to account for the remarkable change in attitude in so short a time.

When she returned, Mrs. Daly made a ceremony of pouring tea into both cups, enquiring meticulously into Martha's preference as to the matter of milk and sugar, then in silence she handed Martha's cup over. She took her own cup, and remained standing beside the bed, where her tension was betrayed by the creaking of her stays.

'Please bring that chair beside the bed and make yourself comfortable.' Mrs. Daly obeyed in silence, the fold of her lips making her look as if red hot pokers judiciously applied would not bring her to utter a syllable.

Martha regarded her with trepidation and then decided there was no point in waiting for her to speak.

'How long have you been at Cobbleigh? I should not remember you, should I?' It was drawing a bow at a venture, but she felt she could safely claim that thirty years away from a place tended to make one forgetful.

Relieved at being asked a question to which she could answer freely, Mrs. Daly replied, 'Oh, no, Miss Marcia, I came as maid to Miss Charlotte Powys, Miss Fanny's mother, when she married Mr. Gilbert. Then I married Daly when he was promoted to butler... you might remember him as the footman, perhaps,' Martha murmured she was only ten when she left Cobbleigh, and asked her if she had any children.

'Just the one, William, he's the underfootman,'

'A fine looking young man,' approved Martha.

'Yes,' said his mother proudly, 'he takes after his father. He was the one that carried you upstairs when you fainted.'

The conversation languished while Mrs. Daly stared into her cup. That has ended that subject, thought Martha, and she cast about for something new to break the stony silence.

'Can you tell me why Miss Fanny was wearing a dress that was too short and in such an unbecoming style? She told me there was no money, that I cannot believe.'

The housekeeper looked reluctant and then said, 'It was Mrs. Corby.'

'You have mentioned the name Corby before, who is she?' Silence. Martha probed again, 'Was Mrs. Corby her governess?'

'No.'

'Her chaperone?'

'No.'

'Well what? And where is she now?'

'I really could not say, Miss Marcia,' she folded her lips uncompromisingly. For a moment Martha studied her over the rim of her cup, then she put the cup in its saucer with a sharp click.

'Mrs. Daly,' she said earnestly, 'while I admire your discretion, it will neither help Miss Fanny nor Cobbleigh if I am kept in the dark. I want to help, but I cannot do so unless I am apprized of all that has gone on here. Miss Fanny and I need your help, everybody's help, because I feel that something must be radically wrong if an estate such as Cobbleigh can come to such a pretty pass that the trustees' only solution is to sell up. And you know what would probably happen if the place is sold; the new owners might not take on any of the servants or the farm workers; changes would be made which might not benefit anybody, and apart from these considerations, it could quite conceivably break Miss Fanny's heart. Now, Mrs. Daly, please, please, be frank with me, I do not want to have to ask Miss Fanny questions she might find distressing.'

Molly Daly was heartily ashamed of herself, but only said, 'Yes, Miss.'

Sighing, Martha tried again, 'So Mrs. Corby was not Miss Fanny's governess. Did Miss Fanny ever have a governess? How was she educated?'

'She had a very good governess up to last year, then Miss Bramble was dismissed by the Master.'

'Why?'

'I really could not say, Miss.'

'What did Mrs. Corby do here?'

'I really could not say, Miss.'

Martha was annoyed, 'Really, Mrs. Daly, I respect your reticence and you're not wanting to gossip about your late employer, but I must know what has gone on, for Miss Fanny's sake.' Leaning forward she said, 'Believe me,

Mrs. Daly, nothing you say to me will go further than this room.'

Slightly unnerved by the fixed look Mrs. Daly bent upon her, Martha waited hoping she had at last broken through her reserve. She knew she had when she saw a beautiful smile transform the austere features into those of a handsome woman. The lines had been placed there by worry, Martha realised, there was no doubt a fearful strain had been placed upon the household.

'Forgive me, Miss Marcia, but I'd heard such things about you, I was not sure really you could be as interested in setting things to rights as you appeared. I was that worried and, after discussing it with Daly, I thought I would test you a little, please forgive me.'

'Miss Fanny is a lucky girl to have such friends about her,' commented Martha. Then quite forgetting her role, she asked, 'But pray, what things had you heard about me?'

'The Master used to rant and rave about you and your, excuse me Miss, your sneaky, underhand ways. That you were very rich and...'

Back in her part, Martha smiled and supplemented, 'and selfish, and mean, and lazy. I know what he used to say of me. I had letters from kind relatives who made sure I knew, 'til they died off, My brother always hated me. You see, he believed I killed his mother.' Seeing Mrs. Daly's horrified face, she continued, 'Oh, you did not know that? Well, our mother died of childbed fever just after I was born, as I am sure you probably know. But as Gerald was only seven or eight at the time, naturally he blamed me. Anyway, enough of that, please go on and tell me about the situation here, that is...' she added with a smile, 'if you trust me?'

'Oh, Miss,' Mrs. Daly, abashed at Martha's gentle teasing, smiled shyly and said, 'I will tell you all from the beginning.' She put down her cup and edged her chair closer to the bed.

'Everything was well until my Miss Charlotte died, poor thing, She was never robust and caught a disease of the lungs, and coughed herself into an early grave. The Master, he loved her so, he was never the same after her death. Of course, Miss Charlotte for all her frail body, was the stronger character of the two and it was she who kept them going when they lost the two little boys they had before Miss Fanny, the measles it was, and both of them went, 'twas so sad. So we was very happy when Miss Fanny was born, but no more came after that. Anyway, as I was saying, at Miss Charlotte's death the Master changed. He lost all interest in everything, his horses, his dogs, his friends, hunting, everything. In the beginning the estate did not suffer for Mr. Buchan was alive.'

'Mr. Buchan?' asked Martha.

'Mr. Buchan was the bailiff, as nice a gentleman as you could meet, an' a very good bailiff. They do say that they is very well connected in Scotland, and the family came south because of troubles during the '45 rebellion. Alas, Mr. Buchan died three years ago and that is when matters went awry. When Mr. Buchan died the Master did not replace him. Work continued, we kept going as best we could, but 'tis a crying shame that as fine a place as this should have come to such a pass. Anyway, one day the Master went to Cheltenham, he was only supposed to be away two nights, but he stayed a se'nnight. When he returned he brought Mr. Corby with him.'

'Aha,' cried Martha, 'at last we come to the mysterious Corbys.' Ms. Daly grimaced ruefully, 'We were all delighted because we thought at last the Master had thrown off his melancholy. Very cheerful they were. But after Mr. Corby left Cobbleigh the Master went back into his shell. About a month later, Mr. Corby returned, this time with his wife, at least we are led to believe she was his wife.' The tone was vicious.

Startled and intrigued, Martha prompted, 'Go on, do.'

'They stayed a fortnight and when they left, the Master went with them. And so it continued, he would be here for a week or two, then away for a time. The Corbys treated the house as if it were their own. What's more, the Corby's brought their friends and the Master saw less and less of his own friends, who dropped off for they did not care for the Corby circle. Well, Miss Bramble and I knew what to call those people, an' we kept Miss Fanny out of sight as much as possible. Until about a year ago, Miss Bramble could not contain herself any longer an' she remonstrated strongly with the Master about the incessant gambling, the wandering up and down the corridors at night, and so on. But the Master lost his temper and dismissed her forthwith, not without a character though, he was not that far gone, an' she now has a good post in a nobleman's household.' Mrs. Daly's remarkable bosom heaved as she paused for breath, 'Oh, Miss,' she cried, 'It was unhappy days – an' Miss Fanny never said a word, just looked more pinched and sad, so Daly and I were sure she knew exactly why she had lost her dear Bramble.' She rose and went over to the fireplace and held up the teapot, 'More tea, Miss Marcia?'

'Please... and pray continue.'

After filling both cups, Mrs. Daly replaced the pot on the trivet and returned to her chair.

'Anyway,' she resumed, 'the Master told Miss Bramble, and she told me, that he would brook no interference in household matters. When Miss Bramble left, in tears, she begged us to look after Miss Fanny as well as we could. Which we have done.' Her stays creaked audibly as she sighed gustily, 'The Master, well, the Master did not seem to realize what them Corbys were up to. They, of course, encouraged him in every extravagance. Gambling, though Mr. Corby rarely won from him.'

'Good policy,' murmured Martha.

'Yes, well, the Master lost enough to the others, Daly used to tell me,' she threw up her hands in horror, '...and the drinking. A crying shame, all your father's fine cellar is in a fair way to being finished, Daly was beside himself at the waste of letting that crew swill it down their gullets.'

'There was nothing wrong with that bottle we had tonight,' observed Martha.

'Yes, well, Daly managed to hold some of the very best back, and after they got fairly will along with their wine, he would substitute inferior stuff he brought in specially, put into the empty bottles with the good labels.'

Martha laughed out loud, 'Resourceful fellow, your husband, and no one caught him?'

'Well, the Master did sometimes look at his glass a little peculiarly. Daly said he was the only one with any pretensions to a palate, but he was afraid the Master was fast losing it.

'As I was saying, the Corbys encouraged the Master to spend money recklessly. The Master even allowed Mrs. Corby to re-decorate "her" bedroom and footed the bills without a murmur. Miss Fanny and I think it in the most awful bad taste. I'll show it to you tomorrow – an' me crying out for new curtains for the library. Because he no longer sat in that room, the Master said he could not afford them. Then he hired a maid for Mrs. Corby.' Mrs. Daly sniffed, 'a dresser she calls herself, stuff an' nonsense, I call it.

'An' he bought a curricle an' pair for Mr. Corby, an' he paid for the lot.' Her face pink with indignation, she shook her head at the recollection, 'an' poor Miss Fanny,' she continued, 'Mrs. Corby was that jealous of the way she was growing into such a pretty girl. And Mr. Corby made it worse by drawing her attention to it. Anyhow, that woman persuaded the Master into allowing her to supervise Miss Fanny's clothes. It was a crying shame, she went out of her way to make Miss Fanny look young and coltish. Putting her into clothes as unsuitable as possible. I cannot prove it, of course, but 'tis my belief she padded the bills, an' still the Master paid. He did remark that Miss

Fanny did not look as well as she used to, but that... that woman insinuated Miss Fanny was going through an awkward stage. Awkward! Miss Fanny was never awkward, she has Miss Charlotte's grace.

'What a poisonous female!' Exclaimed Martha.

'Yes, it's no wonder Miss Fanny escaped to the stables as often as she could. Which was a mercy, it took her away from the "goings on". I had a bad enough time keeping Mr. Corby away from the maids as it was, an' I caught him ogling Miss Fanny in a nasty, sly, way I did not care for. It put me on my guard, thank goodness... he tried to corner her once, I was nearby an' I saw him off with a flea in his ear... Never tried it again, I made sure o' that.'

'Odious man!' Exclaimed Martha, 'And her father did nothing?'

Mrs. Daly's corset creaked alarmingly as she leaned over, 'Yes, well, Miss Marcia,' she said confidentially, 'towards the end, 'tis my belief the Master realized how foolish he'd been, an' when he caught his chill he did not seem to want to recover. He would not stay indoors and rest, went out in all weathers, and so died. Then there was a commotion, Mrs. Corby wailing and crying as if she was his widow, an' poor Miss Fanny absolutely stunned. Mr. Corby tried to quieten his wife an' I actually heard him say to her, "Be quiet you little fool, you are mentioned in his Will, he told us so". I was never more shocked in my life. Then came the reading of the Will after the funeral. Mrs. Corby sobbed into her handkerchief the whole time,' She shuddered, 'It was dreadful, Miss Marcia, though I'll say this for the Master, he had the last laugh. He'd mentioned Mrs. Corby in his Will right enough, but it was as guardian to Miss Fanny, no money, nothing.' She smiled with relish, 'You've never heard such a fuss. Mrs. Corby was so indignant, she nearly burst a blood vessel, Mr. Corby hanging onto her arm to keep her in her seat. Miss Fanny as white as a sheet, saying nothing, but you could see she felt as if a knife had gone through her. Mr. Ackland and the Reverend looking thoroughly disgusted. Then Mr. Ackland, bless his heart, suggested I take Miss Fanny out of the room. Daly told me later how it was. You see we was mentioned in the Will, left us a tidy sum we were, not that we've got it yet, as Daly said, how could we take the money when Miss Fanny was in such a way.' Mrs. Daly stirred in her chair.

'What happened then?' Urged Martha, engrossed in these revelations.

'Mr. Ackland questioned Mrs. Corby closely and it came out that she had no intention of acting as guardian and chaperone to a gawky schoolroom miss, I use her own words Miss Marcia, a gawky schoolroom miss who, she said, was so close to her in age as to make it quite ridiculous. Close to Miss Fanny in age, indeed, thirty if she was a day and beginning to show it. Especially, as she then made plain to Mr. Ackland, there was no money. In fact she had the gall to say that anyone could see that Cobbleigh was on its last legs. All this time Mr. Corby was trying to hush her and explain away her statements by saying she was overwrought. However, Mr. Ackland seized his opportunity. Would she sign a document in which she relinquished the duty of guardian to Miss Fanny, and she eagerly agreed. Mr. Corby did not want her to, but he realized it was no use when his wife would not support him, she was too jealous of Miss Fanny. Mr. Ackland did not waste a minute, he drew up a paper and they signed.'

'Oh! That was well done,' said Martha.

There was a glint in Mrs. Daly's eye as she picked up the thread of her tale, 'Then he and the Vicar became very stern, and told the Corbys to pack up and leave immediately. Daly was told to supervise the packing of Mr. Corby's effects and I was to do the same for his wife. You can be sure we were extremely vigilant. 'Tis my belief Mr. Corby had taken a few things before the Master died, for Daly had no trouble. She was a different matter, I had to stop her taking a fur wrap of Miss Charlotte's and one or two knickknacks from "her" bedroom including the silk sheets and pillow cases. It was with the greatest of pleasure we escorted them to the coach; Mr. Ackland would not let them take the curricle bought for Mr. Corby. The coach took them to Gloucester and they caught the Bristol Mail and that's the last we've seen of 'em. They took Mr. Corby's valet, but left behind the dresser. Hah! Dresser indeed, a more stuck-up useless doxy I never saw.'

She stopped her narrative, shaking her head sadly. Absentmindedly, she picked up Martha's cup and placed it on the tray. 'We were overjoyed to think the Corby's were gone for good, we never thought we would have further trouble until the next time the trustees visited us, then the blow fell. Mr. Ackland had received notices of the Master's debts and was so shocked by the amount involved, he knew Miss Fanny would have very little left to live on, for the estate has swallowed money recently. He and the Vicar put their heads together and decided all must be sold up and Miss Fanny should go and live with her grandmother in Bath. Miss Fanny could not believe them. She tried desperately to get them to change their minds. 'Twas Daly who thought of you and Miss Fanny fastened upon you as her saviour and even persuaded the trustees to wait until she had written to you and had your reply. Thank God, Miss, you came in person, and so quickly too. Only you can convince them trustees that something can be done about the state of things at Cobbleigh, then perhaps they will not be so swift to sell.'

'Matters are very bad?' Asked Martha.

Mrs. Daly threw up her hands, 'Parlous! I ran the house as economically as maybe, but there was such extravagance and wastage, a crying shame it was. And there is no one to direct what must be done over all. Miss Fanny does her best, but she only knows how to run a stable.'

'You put a lot of faith in me,' said Martha. A surge of energy ran through her. What a challenge. Her fingers twitched as if longing for action. However, some native caution made her say, 'I cannot promise miracles mind, but I believe between us, we will have a good try.' She smiled and said warmly, 'I am so glad you trusted me. You have painted an appalling picture. Thank God Mr. Ackland got rid of those... those leeches, he sounds a good sort of man.'

'He is,' conceded Mrs. Daly, 'but I cannot help feeling he and the Vicar find Cobbleigh a burden.'

'We must see what we can do to lighten the load,' remarked Martha, 'you have given me much to think on. It must be late, so go to bed, we will start taking action tomorrow,' They smiled at each other, and it was as allies they parted for the night.

3 - Charles and the Hidden Cupboard

Charles, Captain Lord Biscay, K.C.B., of his Britannic Majesty's Navy, was in his library at Stretton Court. From habit he stood with his elegantly booted feet planted sturdily apart on the polished floor. It was as if he had forgotten he was not at sea and expected the wooden boards to heave under him at any moment. The bent head and square chin resting on the immaculate cravat, accentuated the slight stoop acquired from years of cracking his head on low beams. My Lord was scowling dreadfully at the letter he held in his hand.

It was from the batch of papers loosely bunched at his feet. They lay where they had tumbled out of the cupboard in the wall. Earlier, his seaman's eye irritated by a picture hanging out of true, prompted him to straighten it. But, in spite of all his efforts, it persisted in dipping to the left. This made him look behind the picture, where to his astonishment, he found it masked a hidden cupboard, its door flush with the wall. The picture, a portrait of some of his late uncle's dogs, was now on the floor leaning against a chair-leg. The cupboard was locked, of course. In vain he tried every likely key from the ring handed over by Jennings, his land agent, on his arrival at the Court.

'Barlow!' he roared in a voice used to being heard above high winds and seas.

'Yes, my lord?' Barlow appeared so promptly he must have been hovering outside the door. Charles smiled at the stalwart figure, thinking his rough and ready presence must upset his uncle's finicky butler no end. Well, the people at the Court will have to get used to two naval men and their seafaring ways, they were here to stay.

'I cannot open this cupboard, none of the keys fit, See what you can do.'

'Aye, sir.'

Barlow was a man of many parts. After observing his steady competence in several tight situations, Charles had taken him as his servant straight from the lower decks. He had never enquired too deeply into the man's previous life, or how he was press ganged into the Navy, but he was continually amazed at the wide range of skills at Barlow's command. Now he watched the stubby fingers delicately manipulating the thin bladed knife Barlow was never without, together with another slender instrument, hooked at its end. There was a click, and the door swung open bringing with it a cascade of papers and dust.

Both men looked at the untidy pile at their feet. Charles sighed, 'Thank you, man. Now I'll have to go through them all. I do not think my uncle, or my grandfather before him ever threw away a single scrap of paper. Probably infallible receipts for the curing of crib-biting in horses, potions for mange and the like, but they must be looked at.'

'Shall I pick 'em up for you, my lord?'

'No, no, I'll sort 'em. Thank you.'

'Aye, my lord.'

Charles was still amused at his new title. Honours had flowed on him so thick and fast recently. First he was plain Captain Charles Grey. At present without a command and on halfpay, this state was no longer of consequence to him. He had inherited vast wealth and the baronetcy from his uncle, Sir John Grey. Before that, he had been made Knight Commander of the Bath for his services to the nation. And later, irony of ironies, he was ennobled owing to an incident which Charles, after hardships and exciting years at sea, classed as trivial.

A little of this was running through his mind, while he re-read the prickly little letter which made him scowl. He had come so far from the penniless boy whose widowed mother was dependent upon the uncertain generosity of his late uncle. Charles never ceased to be thankful he had risen to the rank of Captain, and was also lucky in the matter of prize money, and thus personally ensured his mother's comfort in her later years. That she had died before his succession to his uncle's estate, was a great sadness to him. How dearly she would have liked to preside over the Court.

Instead, just as he was starting to enjoy his riches, it looked as if his newly inherited wealth was not rightly his. Well, he would not be penniless again to be sure, but he would lose the Stretton estate. A hard fact to contemplate. He had always loved the Court, its lands, and the village... He raised his head, that reminded him, he must look at the estate map again. On his first cursory glance, it had appeared to him his lands covered a far wider area than he remembered from the days when he was a boy. Uncle John had truly prospered.

And, here he was, the paint of his newly augmented coat of arms barely dry, standing in his library fearing that most of his worldly goods were forfeit, at least, according to the letter in his hand. But, he reflected, standing here staring into space was not going to solve his problems. He must investigate further. He stirred the pile of paper with his foot, and turned up several more letters. He picked them up and turned them over. Curious, he thought, their seals are broken and with different addresses. Hm, how very odd. He read them all carefully. After the last one he grunted. Well one matter was cleared up, however, the girl – no she would be a woman grown by now – was owed some compensation from the Greys.

Who could answer some ticklish questions? Jennings as his agent, obviously, and there must be others who remembered events of ten years ago.

He put the papers away carefully and went in search of his agent. He found him in the estate office. 'Ah! Jennings,' he said, 'You have lived in Stretton Wakefield for a good many years, have you not?'

'Fifty years, man and boy, my lord.'

'So you must know everything that has happened to the Greys during that time?'

'Yes, my lord. Indeed, I remember your father as a young man, and a fine young man he was...'

'Yes, yes, but 'tis of more recent times I am thinking of... about ten or eleven years ago when Master Tom married Miss Martha Wakefield.'

'Yes, my lord.'

'Well, Jennings?'

The agent hesitated.

'Come, man, you cannot tell me anything I do not know, or suspect, already. I understand 'twas an unhappy business. I have a particular reason for asking.'

'Very good, my lord.' He ran a hand over his face, then scratched the back of his head. 'It was a shame it was, the way Sir John carried on. Miss Martha was a nice young lady, and she could control Master Tom when he was carried away in one of his starts, but I heard that Sir John favoured Master Tom marrying a Miss Vernon, one o' they Vernons over Bredenbury way. A matter of some land I believe. Anyway 'twas Sir John and Mrs. Vernon who wanted the match. An' 'twas all over the village as how they threw Miss Vernon in Master Tom's path at every opportunity. You knew Master Tom, my lord, he was ever one to go his own way, an' he up and married Miss Martha, sudden-like. He was of age, o' course, but Miss Martha couldna' be more'n eighteen, but her pa, Mr. Wakefield, he gave his consent. Anyway, after the wedding, that Mrs. Vernon, well, she could not bear to be thwarted. She was in a rare taking, went round the neighbourhood saying Miss Martha an' her father trapped Master Tom, an' they do say that was why...' he stopped.

'Go on, man. I'm particularly interested in what happened to Mrs. Tom.'

'It was like this, sir. Sir John now, he was furious at being flouted. He refused to receive either of 'em after the news of the marriage was broke to him. Threw them out of the house. Made Lady Grey very unhappy. Torn she was. Sir John ordered her not to receive Mrs. Tom – said Master Tom could visit her only if he came alone. Master Tom would not come to the Court without Mrs. Tom, an' that Mrs. Vernon went on creating mischief between 'em all. Then the Peace of Amiens collapsed and Mr. and Mrs. Tom went back to Plymouth.

'And after?'

'All quietened down, though Sir John raged against Mr. Wakefield something cruel for agreeing to the match. An' Mr. Wakefield had his seizure and Mrs. Tom came back to nurse him. He died and Mrs. Tom had a hard time saving anything from the estate for Mr. Wakefield was near to bankruptcy... made unwise speculations, 'tis said... all had to go... that fine estate...' Jennings shook his head sadly, 'An' what shocked the neighbourhood was that Sir John had, over the years, bought up all Mr. Wakefield's notes and mortgages without anyone being the wiser. A lot of money he made too.'

'Good God! So that's why the Stretton estate is much larger than I remember... What a terrible blow for Mrs. Tom. But surely she inherited something, didn't she?'

'She did, my lord. But only because Mr. Todd, her attorney – a downy bird – advised her.'

'Where is she now?'

'I don't know, my lord, an' that's a fact. No one knows except maybe Meg Swan, an' Mr. Todd of course.'

'Meg Swan? Is that the Meg that was Mrs. Tom's nurse?'

'Yes, my lord. She's living at Vine Cottage. It still belongs to Mrs. Tom. Vine and Rose Cottages, the Manor an' the Home Farm are all she saved. The Manor and Home Farm are rented, so is Rose Cottage.'

'That's all that is left of the Wakefield estate?'

'Yes, my lord. Sir John bought up and foreclosed on the mortgages of the rest. Y'see, my lord, Sir John hid behind nominees an' Mr. Wakefield had no notion 'twas him. As you know, sir, there was never any love lost between them two gentlemen.' Jennings leaned forward, 'You're too young to remember this, my lord, but Sir John and Mr. Wakefield loved the same woman, an' Mr. Wakefield married her. Never forgave the Wakefields, did Sir John.'

Charles grunted his disgust. Action suiting his frame of mind, he stood up saying, 'Thank you, Jennings. Order a horse for me, please, I'm going to see Mrs. Swan.'

Meg Swan stared up at the man towering over her. She knew who he was, of course, she recognized in him the boy she once knew, even though he was changed, and grown so grand. Politely, she waited for him to make the first acknowledgement.

'You are Mrs. Swan?'

'Yes, sir.'

'Meg, don't you recognize me?'

'Oh yes, my lord, but I did not want to be forward.'

'We are old friends are we not, so you could not be forward,' he smiled charmingly at the beaming Meg, 'Aren't you going to ask me in ?'

'Of course, my lord, come this way if you please.'

She led him into her cosy parlour, a formidably neat room and fiercely polished.

'Please sit down, master Charles, may I offer you a glass of my homemade wine?'

'Do you still make your cowslip wine? 'Tis long since I've tasted it and I remember how good it was.'

Flattered, she said, 'This instant, my lord,' and disappeared into her kitchen like a rabbit into its burrow.

Alone, Charles studied the room, full of mementos of the young Martha Wakefield. He admired a miniature of her, taken when she was about ten. She stared out at him with solemn hazel eyes, her thin face surrounded by a cloud of chestnut hair. His wandering gaze fell on some books, he opened one and recognizing the immature signature, closed it. There were two watercolours of

Wakefield Manor, indifferently executed, by Martha he suspected. He returned to the miniature, a sweet but strong face, and the painter had not truly succeeded with the eyes.

He was standing looking out of the window, his hands clasped behind his back, when Meg returned with a laden tray.

'Do you know why I am here?'

'I suspect 'tis 'cause of Miss Martha, but further than that I cannot guess.' She said pouring out the wine.

'Yes, 'tis about Martha.' He sat down with a glass in his hand. 'I want to find her immediately. A great wrong has been done her.'

'A great wrong!' Meg cried out angrily, 'She was tormented and harried. Malicious people treated her so badly she left, or was driven, from her beloved Stretton Wakefield, where her family have been for many generations longer than yours, and she has never returned.' Meg's eyes were so full of tears she used a corner of her apron to wipe them away.

'But you know where she is?'

'I promised her I'd never tell.'

'I am sure you did. But if I swear I wish to find her for her own good?'

'How do I know you are any different from the rest of the Greys. The Grey family has brought nothing but sorrow to her,' she cried out in distress.

'Eh! But don't you trust me, Meg? You always liked me better than cousin Tom.'

'That's not saying much.'

'Do you mean to tell me you did not like Tom?'

'Oh, I liked him well enough... for someone else but never for my Miss Martha. Sadly unsteady, he was. He should've married that Miss Vernon as wanted to have him, and left my lamb alone.'

'That's the second time today I've heard the name of Vernon. Tell me more.'

'Mrs. Vernon wanted Master Tom for her daughter, an' Sir John and Lady Grey were more than agreeable. When Miss Martha married Master Tom, Mrs. Vernon kicked up no end of a fuss. Made up spiteful lies about how's Master Tom was forced to marry my lamb. Said Miss Martha entrapped him. Which was not true, sir, I swear, An' Miss Martha was only in her fourth month after eight or nine months of marriage. An' I was the first to know. She was here at the time, nursing her Papa. But Mrs. Vernon went on stirring up trouble, working on Sir John's resentment, well, you know what he was like. Anyways, she got her comeuppance, Mrs. Vernon did, that Miss Vernon ran off with a penniless dancing master, or some such, and is ever so unhappy with at least eight children... so far.' She said with justifiable malice.

Charles could not help laughing at this last. Then he said seriously, 'Now, Meg, this is what I want to do. If you will trust me, I want to find Martha and see if she is alright. She's not remarried?'

'No. She's been far too busy. She's scrimped and scraped to save every penny of her wages, she's that determined to keep together what's left of the Wakefield estate.'

'Her wages!' He said in consternation, 'She's employed? Where? How? As what? Not as a governess, I hope?'

'Oh, no sir, as a companion to a rich lady.'

'Little Martha as a companion, How did this come about?'

'There's nothing wrong with being a companion,' said Meg stiffly. 'Besides, how else was she to make enough money?'

'Didn't Tom leave her anything?'

'Oh, yes,' she said scornfully, 'a mere pittance.'

'Meg,' he said earnestly, 'you must trust me. I want to help Martha, bring her back here and make the neighbourhood realise how badly she was treated. As

Tom's widow she has the right to a generous allowance. After all it would have been an entirely different matter if Tom had lived. I would not be here today for one thing. Even Sir John would have become reconciled to them eventually. He did not like me either for that matter. I feel sure he wanted to cut me out of his Will. Couldn't of course, because of the entail on the property. As it is, I am surprised he didn't will the Wakefield property away from me. Quarrelled with all our other relatives too, I've no doubt.'

Meg sipped her wine while she thought hard. 'Master Charles,' she said at last, 'I do believe you, but before I tell you anything about my lamb's whereabouts, I must consult with Mr. Todd, Miss Martha's attorney. I'll send him to you. I want what's best for my lamb, but I will not tell you where she is unless Mr. Todd says I may.'

'Good, then I shall expect Mr. Todd as soon as maybe.'

'Some more of my wine, my lord? Ever so excited I was when I heard you was made a lord.' She poured him a generous glass, 'Who'd a thought it. Master Tom dead, my lamb a widow, gone from here, an' you who was not welcomed by Sir John, now in his place. I mind the time...' and they fell into reminiscing of days gone by when they were young. When Charles and Tom, and the even younger Martha trailing behind them, got into all sorts of mischief.

'You know, sir,' said Meg, 'you were always there to help my lamb. Master Tom did not care for her, in those days. It changed after you left, of course, he came to depend upon her and she worshipped him. But she should never have married him, he brought her nothing but heartache and trouble.'

'Tom has been dead these ten years, and you and I Meg, will see what we can do for Martha, or rather what she will allow us to do for her. She always had a valiant soul and a remarkably independent mind.'

'Lord knows, she's had to have,' said Meg with a sigh.

When Charles took his leave of her, Meg watched him ride off down the street, a speculative look in her eye. He seemed mightily keen to find Miss Martha, and she wondered why. As a new thought crept into her mind, a smile stole over her face. Then she pulled herself up short, saying to herself, 'Now, now Meg Swan, early days yet, early days.'

The next day Charles studied with new eyes the boundaries of his enlarged estate. Armed with his recently acquired knowledge, he could clearly see a good half again of his property was made up of Wakefield lands. Jennings had shown him the various deeds and mortgages and, however Charles might deplore his late uncle's ethics, every transaction was completed well within the law.

Some days later the butler announced Mr. Todd and, at Charles's behest, showed him into the Estate Office.

Mr. Todd was one of those people whose name truly fit his personality and countenance. His hair was the beautiful red of a healthy dog fox. He had questing brown eyes, a long narrow nose, and a reddish pair of eyebrows that quirked up when he spoke. Fortunately for him, he had an excellent reputation for probity which gave the lie to his air of foxy cunning. Mr. Todd, who loved a joke, often alluded to his vulpine characteristics, which trait endeared him to many. Whenever he met a promising prospect, he mentally twitched his whiskers and swished his brush. On this first meeting with Captain the Lord Biscay, his metaphorical brush and whiskers were working hard.

'How do you do, my lord, Meg Swan told me you wished to see me.'

'Sit down Mr. Todd, please. Now, did she explain why?'

'Yes, she asked my opinion of your wishing to find my client, Mrs. Thomas Grey. Mrs. Swan has vouched for you, said we should furnish you with Mrs. Grey's present address. Now, I am not so easy to please. I would like to know more before I commit a breach of confidence.'

Charles poured them both a glass of Madeira, then sat back and told Mr. Todd of his recent findings, and his reasons for tracing Martha.

Mr. Todd listened quietly, his head on one side. Without comment, he studied the map when invited, read the letters when they were handed to him and preserved a judicial silence until Charles had finished. He sat thinking for a minute then came to a decision.

'My lord, do you propose to look for her yourself, and immediately?'

'Yes, as head of the family, I feel 'tis the most pressing of my obligations. Of course, I am sure you will tell me if she is in actual want. But I need to satisfy myself that all is well with her.'

'She is well. Up until six weeks ago, that is, when Meg last heard from her. Her employer, a Miss Gilbert, was very ill and Mrs. Grey nursed her until her death. After closing the house, Mrs. Grey expected to be with us almost immediately, but she has not yet arrived. And we have had no further word.' He handed Charles a slip of paper, 'She's at this address.'

'Seacliffe I see, and that's on the Sussex coast, not far from Brighton, I collect. Well, I am going to London soon. I'll make a point of visiting Seacliffe from there as soon as may be. And I'll let you know what I find there.' He rose, 'You will stay to luncheon?'

'Thank you, my lord, I shall be delighted.' As they moved into the dining room, Mr. Todd said, 'I own I am a little worried about Mrs. Grey, and am with you in thinking she should come back to Stretton Wakefield. All her father's debts are repaid – thanks to her diligence and in compounding with the creditors. We applied the rent from the remaining properties to the balance owing, and all is settled. I feel if she does not return now, she never will and it would be a shame. Now is the time for her to return before she takes another position.'

Two days later Charles set out in his uncle's, or rather his own, post-chaise and four, a luxury he had never before experienced in his adventurous thirty-seven years. As the chaise swept through the village, he saw Meg running down her garden path waving her white apron. Smiling at her vigorous "God speed", he energetically waved his acknowledgement of her farewell through the carriage widow as he swept by.

4 - Fanny's Worries

Fully recovered and feeling full of purpose, Martha ate an excellent breakfast. It was difficult for her to remain quietly in bed however. She had put off listening to her conscience long enough and knew she had to seriously weigh the pros and cons of becoming a thorough-going imposter. She was so sure she could help Fanny that she longed to take charge of Cobbleigh and set things in order. Her conscience told her she no right to meddle in Fanny's concerns, but Martha was made of stern stuff. Fully aware of her capabilities, she yearned to exercise skills suppressed during years subordinated to the whims of an exacting employer. She also knew that if she did not take a hand in the game, by all accounts there would be nobody else who would even try to rescue Fanny from her predicament.

These thoughts had rattled around in the back of her mind ever since she had made her impulsive decision the day before. Martha knew what it was to be left in debt and, although not precisely penniless, had learnt to watch every penny. It seemed to her that an estate such as Cobbleigh could surely support one girl and her household. It would be a great pity for Fanny to be forced to leave Cobbleigh, without a push being made to save it. Surely debts could be compounded. 'I know what it is, my girl,' she said to herself, 'you're of a managing disposition, and your curiosity is getting the better of you again.'

Should she reveal who she was? If she did that, she would have no authority, and if she understood anything of the situation, authority was what was needed. Meg was awaiting her. She would write to her and say she was delayed. Could she become Marcia? Of course she could. Having lived with Marcia for ten years, she knew more about her late employer than anyone else at Cobbleigh.

And yet, a small voice at the back of her mind persisted in asking, how would the masquerade end? Impatiently, she brushed the thought aside, confident that when the time came she would think of something.

Would she hurt Fanny by her pretence? She vowed she would be a much better aunt to her than Marcia Gilbert would ever have been.

Having won her battle to her entire satisfaction; Martha was getting out of bed when another thought occurred to her; what would her friends, the Thistlethwaites, think? Henry, as Marcia's attorney, would understand, but would he condone such an action? She ran over her arguments again and, thankfully, came to the happy conclusion that he would definitely approve of her helping Fanny although he would deplore her methods. Jessica, while agreeing with her husband, would approve Martha's impulse to help. She nodded her head, that settled it then, she would take the chance. After all the years of waiting, she was experiencing an odd reluctance to return to Stretton Wakefield anyway, and there was nothing there that needed her urgent attention, A few weeks, or even months, delay would do no harm.

She picked up the jug of hot water from the washstand and poured some in the basin. She would have to make sure she did not sign anything. She could arrange for the trustees to handle any documents and, if driven to it, she could sprain her wrist; but what about the receipt for the second-best jewellery and the animals... Fanny's legacy? If she asked Fanny to sign a receipt, it would give the game away instantly. She shrugged her shoulders, she would think of something, but it would have to be soon.

At precisely ten o'clock, Mrs. Daly, wearing a plain white cap for morning wear, presented herself at the door. Martha was warmly dressed in a grey morning gown of Marcia's, trimmed with black braid, and with a becoming froth of white lace at her throat.

She looks much better, thought Mrs. Daly, such a pretty lady, far prettier than her portrait downstairs. She must have been one of those plain children that grow into beauties.

'Good morning, Miss Marcia, are you ready to begin the tour?'

Two hours later, Martha, with a gleam in her eye sat snugly in the housekeeper's room with Mrs. Daly. While they both sipped what the latter euphemistically called a 'restorative', an extremely powerful elderberry wine, they reviewed what Martha, an inveterate note taker, had written on the little ivory tablets she liked to carry with her.

Every room had been inspected, from the attics to the cellars. All was spotless and, although the furniture was old-fashioned and most of the rooms shabby, beautifully kept.

The bedrooms not in recent use were closed, the furniture under Holland covers, but Martha was able to blink at the splendid example of Mrs. Corby's taste. Mrs. Daly stood back to let Martha drink in the profusion of crimson velvet swathing the tall windows against the daylight. Crimson velvet also hung in complicated folds from the hands of two gilt cherubs attached to the ceiling, nearly smothering the heavily gilded sleigh bed beneath. The walls were covered in a blinding paper of wide crimson and white stripes, dotted all over with a pattern of gold fleur-de-lys. The coverlet was crimson silk, heavily embroidered with gold thread repeating the fleur-de-lys pattern found on the walls. The expanse of crimson carpet was broken by white fur rugs placed on either side of the bed, and before the hearth. The fragile furniture was so overlaid with gilt it was impossible to discern the wood. The chairs were upholstered in yet more crimson. There was a profusion of gilded candelabra and ornaments and the whole room was repeated many times in the gilt-framed mirrors on the walls. Martha drew in her breath, a cloying

41

scent still hung faintly in the air. She wrinkled her nose. 'Is Mrs. Corby a tiny brunette?'

'Yes, Miss, how did you know?'

'No self-respecting blonde would be caught dead in this, this... I don't mind telling you, Mrs. Daly, but I'm sure a house of ill-fame would look like this. 'Tis designed to set-off the charms of someone dark, and as for small, look at the furniture,' she said witheringly, 'I would be afraid to sit on any of the chairs.' Upon hearing these strictures, Mrs. Daly's eyes met hers in a look of unspoken agreement. Nothing further needed to be said, so they continued on their way.

Martha admired the hall with its graceful oak staircase, looked with interest at the portraits, especially at the one supposedly of her and her putative brother. The artist had emphasized for posterity the slight cast in Martha's eye which made her look malign. This was unfortunate, for Martha knew the squint only denoted fatigue or boredom. She liked the one of Miss Charlotte and looked for a long time at the face of the adult Gerald beside it. It was easy to see where Fanny got her looks.

The withdrawing room was vast, handsome and cold. The library, lined with shelves of books, was delightful. Its tall windows looking towards the south, showing a prospect of parkland and rolling fields. There was a small sitting room beside it, which led to an enormous dining room dominated by a huge mahogany table and sideboard. To the front of the room, a door led to what Mrs. Daly called the Little Saloon, which was large and uninviting. Another door led from the dining room to the gunroom. The lingering smell of gun oil transported Martha back to her childhood when she used to love watching her father carefully clean his guns after a day's sport. As she sniffed the air she remarked without thinking, 'Oh, how I remember my father...' she stopped quickly, pleased to see that her companion noticed nothing as she opened another door.

'I expect you remember this room as well. The Master's study, although latterly Mr. Buchan used it as the estate office.'

The kitchens were a surprise, modern, spacious and bright, equipped with the latest in ranges. 'Miss Charlotte saw to that,' explained Mrs. Daly with pride.

When the denizens of the kitchen and servant's hall were presented to her, Martha began to think that there were far too many people to look after the comfort of one young girl... a French chef, his undercooks, footmen, chambermaids, kitchen maids, and other persons respectfully crowded around her.

Mrs. Daly formally presented her husband. Martha had to withstand a pair of unwinking brown eyes fastened upon her critically. She wondered why the butler should stare so and then remembered with a shiver, he had been footman when Marcia lived a Cobbleigh. Bravely, she smiled at him and put out her hand. 'Your wife tells me we have met before,' she said.

'Yes. Miss,' he bowed stiffly and barely touched her hand.

Of all the top lofty creatures, she thought. 'Well,' she confided as if she had noticed nothing, 'I hope you will not take this amiss, but I cannot say I remember you at all for it was so many years ago.' She smiled at him disarmingly and was answered by the beginnings of a smile.

She could not know he was apprehensive of finding signs of the mischief-making child who made his life a misery by teasing him when she knew he was not in a position to retaliate.

Both were relieved to end the encounter. She, because she had brushed through an awkward moment tolerably well, and he because he suddenly and unaccountably warmed to the lady and was ashamed of his misgivings. His Molly was right, the lady could be trusted.

Sipping her restorative cautiously, Martha asked, 'Why do we have two footmen and an underfootman?'

She felt a little self-conscious in using the possessive for the first time.

'That was Mrs. Corby's doing. Said it added to the Master's consequence. That is also why we got Mounseer. It upset Mrs. Martin no end, but she is a sensible body and she has learned plenty of foreign kickshaws by being his undercook.'

Mounseer, or Monsieur Leblanc, she remembered perfectly, he had bowed over her hand gallantly upon being presented. Must cost 'us' a pretty penny too, thought Martha. Mrs. Martin, yes, she was the plump little woman covered in a spotless white apron. Indeed she did look a sensible body.

'I expect Miss Fanny is awaiting you for luncheon,' said Mrs. Daly.

'Good gracious, look at the time,' exclaimed Martha as she glanced at the mantel clock, how the morning has flown.'

Fanny had, as usual, spent her morning in the stables and was so happy telling Martha of her doings, she did not notice her aunt's abstraction. She chattered on, while Daly benignly served the food, happy Miss Fanny had found a friendly ear. He saw that Miss Marcia, apart from an occasional encouraging sound, was not really paying much attention until she suddenly interrupted the flow.

'What was that you said, Fanny? How many head of stock you say we had?'

'About fifty,' replied Fanny 'why?'

'Fifty!' And that is breeding stock only?' Or does that include the hunters and driving horses?'

'Breeding stock. Some of it is more than ready to be sold. As I was explaining to you, we have not sold anything for three years.'

Amazed, Martha asked, 'Why not?'

Fanny began to pleat her dress as she hesitated. Then frowning, she said in a small voice, 'You see, dear Papa always looked after the sales and the last two or three years he never seemed to have time. Whenever anyone asked him what to do, he would say he'd think about it and then forget. I asked him many, many times about selling some of the youngsters and he would say, 'Oh, yes, I'll think on it.' In the end I gave up asking him and the foals kept arriving and the young stuff grew up.' Tears came into her eyes and she groped for a handkerchief, could not find one, and gratefully took the one Martha handed her. Fanny pulled herself together, blew her nose forcefully, wiped her eyes and continued, 'It was all right until Mr. Buchan died, but Papa did not replace... he'd lost interest... in everything.'

'Yes, Mrs, Daly has told me how it was,' Martha was gentle for she saw Fanny was still near tears. 'Tell me Fanny, who are your trustees? Mrs. Daly mentioned a Mr. Ackland.'

'Papa's attorney.'

'And the vicar, she did not mention his name.'

'The Reverend Theophilus Gore. Oh, Aunt Marcia, I am so frightened we will have to sell up.'

'Why?' Martha leaned forward, 'I always understood your Papa had many resources.'

'So did I,' admitted Fanny, 'But it seems Papa left more debts than money.'

'I do not promise anything,' said Martha, 'But you can be sure we will not sell everything out from underneath you... unless we really have to. Did they suggest you would be penniless?'

'Oh, no, but they said they would invest what was left in the Funds and then I would be able to live respectably in Bath. I do not want to live respectably in Bath. I want to live here.'

'That I can readily understand, Fanny. Besides any young lady out in the world with Cobbleigh Manor at her back, would be more likely to make an excellent marriage than if she was plain Miss Gilbert, lately of Cobbleigh. So we must see what is to be done. When am I to meet your trustees?'

'You will meet Mr. Gore at Church on Sunday. And both are coming to luncheon next week, when they will do nothing but gobble their food and wag their heads sadly,' said Fanny rather unfairly.

'That does not give us much time,' said Martha. She sat thinking for a few minutes then she smiled at the girl, 'But a lot can be done quickly when one sets one's mind to it. So do not despair. Now, what about that ride in the gig you promised me?'

'Whenever you are ready,' replied Fanny, 'And you must see the stables. It will be feeding time when we return and all the horses will be in.'

They set off in Fanny's smart gig. Highness, who had insisted on joining the party, wedged her plump body between them.

As they jolted down the front drive, Martha remarked that something must be done about the surface.

'What's the use?' Said Fanny gloomily, 'If, in spite of everything, we still have to sell.'

Clinging to the side of the gig as it gave another lurch, Martha said, 'Really, Fanny, I cannot have this pessimism, please try to see what I am suggesting. If, and it is a big if, we have to sell up, you will get a far better price if the place looks spick and span. A smooth drive, a lick of paint here and there, these gates hung properly for instance, and someone living in the lodge. What has happened to it? The roof is caved in at the back.'

'There was a fire, and the lodge keeper moved into Cobbleigh to live with her sister.'

'So, no one has mended the roof, and I suppose the elements have done their worst to the interior.'

'I did ask father,' began Fanny defensively, 'But you know how it was...'

Anxious not to upset the girl any further, Martha decided to keep such remarks to herself in future. Fanny was obviously still suffering from the unhappy life she had been leading. The way her spirits swung from elation to dejection meant Martha would have to be very patient with her moods. She devoutly hoped she had not made Fanny vain promises, and could succeed in bettering the poor girl's situation.

They turned into the lane where the gig was able to travel a deal more smoothly. Martha watched Fanny's capable handling of the reins and then looked over the satin-filled hindquarters of the stout cob, appropriately called Pork Pie. Beyond his intelligently pricked ears she could see a magnificent row of oak trees crowing a slight rise on their left.

'They must mark the Water Meadow boundary', she said. Not for nothing had she spent some minutes in front of the estate map this morning. 'They look as magnificent as ever.'

'Yes.' Agreed Fanny. 'A funny thing happened last year. Father received an offer for the Water Meadow from a new neighbour, a Mr. Patterson, a tea merchant I believe. Naturally Father refused, but asked him why he thought he would sell such a valuable part of his property. Mr. Patterson told him his wife desired him to buy it because she wanted to be able to look out of her upstairs windows in all directions and know they owned every foot of ground within her view. Father suggested Mrs. Patterson confine her viewing to the downstairs windows.'

Martha laughed, 'Whatever was Mr. Patterson thinking? Such a sale would have taken a huge bite out of your south boundary, and with all your riparian rights in the Cobb river and some of the best grazing.'

Although a little surprised at the extent of her aunt's knowledge, Fanny continued, 'Father said he thought Mr. Patterson hen-pecked and was nagged into making the offer. He also said Mr. Patterson was very apologetic. I have never met them, but I hear she is a tartar.'

'I expect we will meet them when we start entertaining,' said Martha lightly.

There was silence as Fanny negotiated the turn over the Cobb bridge, then she said quietly, 'Are we going to entertain? I thought because we are in mourning...'

'Oh, not right away, of course, but later on. I am sure there are many of your friends you would like to see. You could always ask one or two at a time to begin with.'

'I do not have any friends to ask, no one has called on me in a year. Neither have I had the heart to visit them since my dear Bramble left me.'

Oh, my God, thought Martha in horror, I do have to watch everything I say. Of course, no one would permit their children to call if their estimate of the Corbys coincided with mine.

'Well, my dear, now that things are different, you will find that your friends will begin to ask you to visit them again, as soon as you are out of deep mourning. You must have received many letters of condolence,'

'Oh, yes, from everybody.'

'I do trust you have replied to them all.'

'Of course.' Changing the subject she said, 'I am driving around the boundary today, we will not try for the Combes or Uplands,'

Martha thought it safe to ask, 'Who are at the Combes now?'

'Oh, the same people as always. Our tenants have not changed, you know, they are all on long leases. They are not very happy though. Old Mr. Mason at High Combe is quite nasty about it, but the Peters at Low Combe and the Cummings at Little Combe have not actually complained... yet.'

'What is it? Rents too high?'

'No, it is just that they expect us to do repairs, and we have not. Our carpenter needs help and he cannot get around to everybody immediately.' She caught sight of a middle-aged man working at a gap in the dry stone wall running along the side of the road, his black dog lying beside him. She stopped Pork Pie and said, 'Good afternoon, Bodger, have the heifers broken out again?'

The man who had straightened up on hearing them approach, touched his forehead in salute, 'Good day, Miss Fanny, yerse it do be them heifers. I'm shoring up the gap so they do not try again.' He tried not to stare at Martha, and Fanny divining his interest said, 'Aunt Marcia, I must introduce Bodger who has been our hedger and ditcher at Cobbleigh for many years.'

'An' me faither before,' he gave her a gap-toothed grin, 'Good day Miss Marcia, it is a good long time since I seen you an' faither would be right pleased to see you if you go that way, Miss, ninety if he's a day, all his wits about 'im, 'cepting he's blind now.'

'I am sorry to hear that,' said Martha. 'The name Bodger is familiar to me,' she speciously claimed, 'I suppose it would have been your father.'

'Yerse.'

'So you carry on the family tradition?'

'Yerse, not but that times 'avna changed, I used to 'ave five men under me, now I only 'ave young Ned an' 'e's at Huplands this week.'

'Good gracious,' exclaimed Martha, 'there are only two of you to do all the work?'

'Old Machin died an' the young 'uns went for to Stroud to take work in them cloth manufactories there an' I never could get the Maister..' he stopped and corrected himself hurriedly, 'an' I never could find others.'

As they drove up Cobbleigh Rise, Martha was very thoughtful. If what Fanny had told her about the carpenter and Bodger's disguised complaint were typical, she could readily understand why the estate was failing.

At the top of the Rise, Fanny pointed out the view of Cobbleigh with the Manor and the farm buildings beyond. Until now Martha had not quite grasped the extent of Fanny's inheritance and she made her wait until she had correlated what she had seen on the map with that which was spread before her. The Rise led into the village street with cottages and gardens built haphazardly on either side. At the end the street forked either side of the Green, with its scummy duckpond. Beyond it stood a solidly built Wool church. The left fork passed the Manor's back gates and continued round the boundary, the right fork led to the main Gloucester-Stroud road. Martha was interested to see that even this small village was able to support two inns, the Gilbert Arms, which gave the appearance of a superior establishment, and the Chevron. Also, there were a general shop, a cobbler and saddler, a wheelwright as well as a smithy. Although smoke was rising in the still air from most of the cottage chimneys, the clang-clickety-clang-clang of hammer on anvil ringing out merrily from the smith, was the only sign anybody was about. Two young men in smocks were watching the smith shoe a carthorse but, upon hearing the clop of Pork Pie's hooves, they turned to look at the gig. When she saw them, Fanny asked nervously, 'Shall I whip up and gallop through the village, or can you bear to stop and greet everyone?'

Martha laughed, 'There do not seem to be many people about today, I think they will probably prefer to curtain twitch. I shall have to meet them all on Sunday anyway, so we may as well begin with those men over there.'

At her words, Fanny looked uncomfortable, but not knowing the cause, Martha decided to await developments.

The taller of the two men took off his hat and spoke to Fanny.

'Good afternoon, Miss.'

'Good afternoon, Powell. I am sorry but there has been no change since I last spoke to you. Until I know what is to become of Cobbleigh – there is no work for any of you.'

'Then we'd best be off to Stroud, like young Tam,' muttered the shorter man.

'Aye,' agreed Powell, shaking his head, 'I don't want ter work away from the land, but I 'ave a family ter think on.'

'Wait a minute. Fanny, may I speak to you a moment?' The sound of Martha's voice brought their heads up.

'Of course, aunt.' Fanny turned to the men, 'Miss Gilbert and I will have our talk, will you wait over there for us?' As the men moved off, she asked 'What is it?'

'Fanny, did you want to rush through the village because you were afraid of being approached for work like this?'

'Yes, is it not dreadful, they need work so badly and I have had to say "no". Last time they said they would leave for the cloth mills, that is why I was not expecting to see them today.'

'Have many people left the village?'

'Quite a few of the younger ones. I do not understand how this came about, everyone used to have work, and now the Vicar tells me there are more people on the Parish than ever before. I know we have not been hiring, but there are other landowners in the district...' her voice trailed away.

'But, Fanny, this will not do. If this keeps up you will soon be unable to work the estate.'

'I had not thought of that, but what can we do?'

'Well, I have an idea, not a permanent solution mind, but something that will do for the moment, anyway, until I can talk to your trustees.'

'What is it?'

'Wait and see. Call the men back now, please.'

They returned with hopeful looks in their eyes. Martha asked them, 'If we can give you work, are you willing to do anything?' Upon receiving their eager assurances, she said, 'Good. The front drive needs repairing and put to rights, and I have no doubt the back drive is in a like case. For the time being, we will pay you by the day and hope we can arrange something more permanent later. Report on Monday morning to – whom Fanny?'

'Bodger,' said Fanny, looking very pleased.

After the men had thanked them and respectfully moved back to the smithy, Fanny asked, 'And how are we going to pay them?'

'No doubt the trustees can manage it. If not, I'll pay them myself – it would be worth it not to endure another shaking such as we had this afternoon.'

Pork Pie set off down the street at a spanking trot. No one else appeared, so Martha was able to look around undisturbed. Nearly every cottage needed work of some kind. Here a coat of paint, there roof tile replaced and more than one chimney needed repointing. The smart exterior of the Gilbert Arms made the general dinginess of the rest very obvious.

'Do we not own the Gilbert Arms, Fanny?'

'Yes, we do, but the landlord does his own upkeep. He attracts a lot of trade from gentlemen wishing to fish the Cobb. It does make the rest look shabby, does it not?'

They had passed the church and vicarage now and were approaching a pretty property called the Wool House, Martha remembered.

'That is where the Buchans live,' Fanny pointed with her whip. 'It belongs to us, but because we have no bailiff to replace Mr. Buchan, Mrs. Buchan and her daughter Margaret, continue to live there. There is a son, Hugh, but he went into the army. He was in the Peninsula and is a Waterloo Man, and is now part of the Army of Occupation in France. There's talk of him selling out.'

They passed through the Manor back gates – wide open. Hinges probably rusted through, thought Martha cynically, although she had to admit this lodge was occupied and very neatly kept. Which made a nice change.

Further on they encountered three very handsome red-headed boys, obviously brothers, ranging in age from about nine to eleven. They stopped and looked a little conscious when Fanny greeted them cheerfully with 'Had any sport?' The eldest said, 'Some, Miss Fanny,' his face going as red as his remarkable hair, the second brother hastened to say, 'We only took a rabbit with Copper's new ferret.'

'A new ferret, Copper. Do show me?'

The youngest boy brought out of an inner pocket a sinuous yellow creature with evil-looking pink eyes.

Martha quite forgot herself, 'I used to have one just like that,' she exclaimed. When everyone stared at her in amazement, she recollected herself and amended, 'That is to say, a friend of mine kept it, but he always said it was mine. How long have you had this one?'

'Me Da' got it for me, 'e's new an' 'e's fast,'

'I am sure he is,' agreed Martha with the air of a connoisseur.

'Micah an' Isaac pegged the nets an' I set ferret.'

'Only one rabbit,' said Fanny, 'What happened?'

Copper grinned, 'Ol' Stoney came along an' we ran.'

'Well,' laughed Fanny, 'I'll not tell tales.'

Pork Pie started up again and Fanny said to Martha, 'The Lees are poachers. They only take enough for themselves, so father tolerated them, and they keep away more predatory persons. They live in the cottage we are coming to. They own the freehold, but like us, they have no money for repairs. The neatest thing about them is their garden, they grow the most magnificent flowers and vegetables. To look at the cottage you wonder where ten people can be crammed into so tiny a space.'

A handsome woman bringing in the washing from the line responded to Fanny's wave of her whip with a flashing smile.

'They are part Romany,' Fanny continued, 'That is probably why they are so good with animals. We often use her husband at the stables, especially at foaling time.'

They turned up the deplorable front drive, but instead of stopping at the front door, Fanny took the gig around the side of the house through an archway and into the stableyard.

'This is where the hunters and driving horses are kept,' Fanny explained, 'the breeding stables are beyond. Look they are all waiting for their supper.'

Eyes shining, Martha looked at the alert heads watching over the half-doors. The yard had loose boxes on two sides, the first and third sides split by archways. The arch opposite the one by which they entered the yard led to the paddocks, and divided the grooms' quarters and tack and feed rooms from the coach house.

Going to the first box, Fanny gave a low whistle and a very pretty chestnut nickered back. 'This is my Badoura,' said Fanny proudly, 'she's the best mare I have ever had and I trained her myself, with the O'Brien's help, of course. We bred her ourselves, and I love her.' Martha caressed the velvety nose and assessed the mare's points, 'From what I can see,' she said, 'she looks wonderful.'

Fanny was puzzled, 'Aunt Marcia, Papa always said you hated horses. In fact, I should have remembered that before I started boring you with them.'

Martha's heart gave a lurch, but her hand never stopped gently stroking Badoura's muzzle while she replied, 'My dear, your father only knew me until I was ten. Yes, I was frightened of horses, but a kind old man took me in hand and taught me how to ride properly and taught me besides how to understand and conquer my fear. In fact, I now enjoy riding very much indeed, and I hope soon we can go out together. I suppose you have a mount for me?'

Fanny looked abashed, 'I beg your pardon. I am so glad you ride, it is sometimes lonely on one's own. You can have Juno over there,' indicating a brown head. Martha thanked her and they returned to the inspection.

The late Mr. Gilbert's hunters were good solid Anglo-Irish stock, most of which were of his own breeding. Whatever Martha might privately think of Mr. Gilbert's character, she had to admit he knew horseflesh. The other riding horses were of the same calibre and there was one bay mare Martha really liked.

'That one there,' said Martha pointing, 'will she accept a side saddle?'

'Tadpole? She was bought for Mrs. Corby, but she could not hold her so she was given Juno instead.' Martha grimaced in amusement at the implication. 'She's really called Belladonna,' continued Fanny, 'but that blaze looks like a tadpole.' She giggled, 'you should have seen Mrs. Corby. Tadpole ran away with her and then put her into a ditch, a muddy ditch, with stinging nettles. It was Mrs. Corby's fault she has no hands and no nerve.'

No nerve for riding, perhaps, thought Martha, but plenty of the other kind.

They looked into the coach house. Martha's first impression was of hundreds of equipages, and when she itemised them she was still amazed at the quantity. There were two curricles. Fanny's gig, and one other. A sleigh, a brand-new post-chaise, a huge old-fashioned coach on blocks, a closed carriage, a barouche, a Tilbury and a high-perch phaeton.

She was then shown all the driving horses. The late Mr. Gilbert's pair of match bays really took her eye, but the pair bought for Mr. Corby were merely showy without much bone. Fanny thought so too. 'He chose them himself,' she said with a sniff, 'Mick calls them a flash pair.' Martha looked at the post-horses, 'How many times did your father use the post-chaise?'

'Only twice,' admitted Fanny.

With a thoughtful face, Martha followed the girl under the archway, past the paddocks and in to a newer larger stableyard. They were met by Pat O'Brien, a slight, twinkly-eyed man, who greeted them pleasantly and was only too delighted to show Miss Fanny's aunt around.

As soon as he realised the older lady knew exactly what she was looking at, he was disposed to bring out and discuss every mare, every foal, colt and filly. Tired, Martha was only too glad to hear that more than half the stock was still in the far paddocks. As she was interrupting feeding time, she suggested she come back to see the rest another day. He agreed, but insisted upon showing her Lucifer, and called his son to bring out the stallion. Martha walked around him in admiration. He stood about sixteen hands, a dark bay with beautiful mottles over his barrel. He had magnificent shoulders, clean legs and powerful hind-quarters; a fine, proudly held head and an intelligent eye. 'We bred him,' said Pat, 'Miss Fanny called him Lucifer from some book she was reading.'

'"Paradise Lost".' said Fanny, 'Quite the most interesting part of it. I thought he look looked like a fallen angel.'

Mick turned the stallion around and walked him back and forth, then trotted him out to show he covered the ground with an even well spaced stride.

'An' he's a grand lepper,' said Pat, 'will clear a five-barred gate with ease. He's sired most of our foals for the past four years, he's only nine now. Mr. Cairnton over Bridgecombe way wanted to buy him last year for over 400 guineas, but the Master would not sell. He's sure a grand horse.'

'He's magnificent,' breathed Martha, 'And I am most impressed with all your stock. How much help do you have?'

Pat and Mike looked at each other, then the son said 'Just father an' me, and two grooms, and Timothy when he can spare the time from the other yard. His son, Tim, helps too but he is supposed to be the gardener's boy. Then there's James.'

'James?' echoed Martha, 'Who is that?'

'One o' the footmen, Miss.'

'Oh,' said Martha faintly.

'An' don't forget young Micah. He's only eleven, but he's as good as his da' with the foals and, of course, Miss Fanny helps us with the training an' exercising.'

They said goodbye to the men and left the yard. Martha was tired and she wanted to make notes while impressions were fresh in her mind. Fanny was concerned, thinking she had made her aunt do too much, she insisted on having some tea brought to Martha's room. Then she made her lie down and firmly told her to rest until dinner.

As soon as the door closed behind Fanny, Martha flew out of bed to get her tablets. She returned to bed and propped herself upon the pillows to begin her lists. She wrote a heading, 'Things to be Done' and underlined it twice. But after much cogitation, she had only added one sentence, 'Get complete authority to act from the trustees', before she fell asleep.

Fanny too had much to think over. It did not seem possible that her life could take such a completely new turn so swiftly. How could one person's presence in so short a time make such a difference? Fanny was now full of hope, for some reason she trusted her aunt to bring about the promised changes. But, she was so different from what she expected. Her father's jealous remarks had coloured her imaginings, she realised, but it did seem unusual that a lady who had lived in a town for nigh on thirty years should be so knowledgeable about the country. That ferret, for example, if her father was to be believed, her aunt Marcia should have been afraid of such an animal. There was another odd thing, it was plain she loved animals, and yet Highness was far too fat and under-exercised. Of course, her aunt had told her that latterly in Seacliffe, her time was fully occupied with nursing a sick friend. A selfless act her father would not have believed possible.

'And,' said Fanny to herself, 'she told us she had never fainted in her life before the other day, and yet father told me that as a child she could faint at any time she had a mind to it in order to escape unpleasantness. All very mystifying.' She sat thinking for a while, 'She's been very kind to me and seems really interested in helping me, so I suppose she must have changed a great deal, just as she said this afternoon. I do know,' thought Fanny practically, 'that she may do me a great deal of good, so I think I'll keep my thoughts to myself. Especially,' she smiled to herself, 'as she gives me lovely clothes like the white dress I am wearing this evening.'

Dressed for dinner and cosily sitting before the library fire, Highness and Tig stretched out on the hearth before her feet, Martha was startled out of her reverie when the door was flung open and a young lady ran into the room. She only recognized Fanny when she cried, 'Look, aunt, is it not pretty?' and spun around to show off the dress.

'Very pretty indeed,' said Martha wholeheartedly, 'Did Annie do your hair? 'Tis most becoming, but are you not cold, have you no shawl?'

'No, nothing to go with this dress,' Fanny looked disconsolate.

'Well,' said Martha briskly, 'Perhaps I have something suitable, though it will be a puzzle to find it.'

'Annie will know, what should she look for?'

'Violet silk, with a deep fringe. It will match the ribbons on your dress. Can't think why I did not think of it before... it should be in silver paper and lying flat somewhere, probably in a chest rather than the tallboy. I know the shade is a little old for you, but 'twill bring out the colour of your eyes.'

The shawl was found and the fashionable young lady became an ecstatic child who whirled about, stopping to curtsey to her new image in the looking-glass set in the over-mantle. Fanny's happiness was so apparent that Martha had no need of further recompense.

5 - 'Aunt Em' and Little White Lies

It should not be supposed that the advent of so interesting a personage as Miss Marcia Gilbert had escaped the attention of the neighbourhood. The recent scandalous activities at Cobbleigh Manor had kept villagers and gentry alike agog for many a month. The death of Gerald Gilbert had not caused a decline in their interest, for that event was closely followed by tidings of an extraordinary Will and rumours of insolvency to mull over. Not that her neighbours wished Fanny ill, they were merely following her problems as closely and as sympathetically as they would follow the plot of a play.

As it was, as soon as the travelling coach was dismissed, further tales filtered out from the Manor people to relatives and friends in the village.

Miss Gilbert was very ill, the doctor was summoned; Miss Gilbert was completely recovered. Miss Gilbert had come to remove her niece; no, Miss Gilbert has arrived to stay with all her pets and belongings; Miss Fanny was excited and relieved for it was reliably reported Miss Gilbert, with all her money, would save Cobbleigh; no, her aunt has no intention of undoing her purse-strings to aid her impoverished niece. So many stories were bandied about that interested parties resolved to see the lady for themselves, as if the sight of her would reveal the truth. And the soonest and most convenient occasion would surely be Morning Service at Cobbleigh Church. The lady had been seen driving through the village, so it was reasonable to suppose she would appear in the Manor pew on Sunday.

Wise in the ways of villages, Martha knew she was causing intense interest, nor could she blame people, the prosperity of the countryside was closely linked to the prosperity of the Manor. It was for this reason she suffered many qualms; could she maintain her role before so much scrutiny? She calmed herself when she realised that few would care to challenge her, and the possibility of anyone believing her to be an imposter was remote, but all the same she could not quiet the nervous fluttering of her heart. Owing to these hesitations, she and Fanny were late in setting off.

'Dear aunt,' begged Fanny, as she watched Martha distractedly hunt for her muff, search in her reticule for her handkerchief for the second time and drop her Prayer Book, 'pray do not twitter so, please do not be nervous, I promise you I will support you all the time.'

'I am not twittering... yes I am, oh dear, I shall never get through it, I shall forget everyone's name and worst of all, I shall forget whom is related to whom,' Realising she was doing exactly that which she had denied, she pulled herself up short and laughed. 'You're right, I am letting my nerves show. I'll have to do my best and treat everyone as if they are near and dear relatives of everybody else.'

Out they went into the pale March sunshine and set off at a brisk pace, for the day was chilly, and the walk did much to settle Martha's uneasiness. The bells, pealing out across the fields, ceased as they entered the church porch. Every head turned to watch them walk up the aisle to the Manor pew under the beady gaze of the carved oak eagle whose spread wings supported the Bible on the lectern. Upon entering the high-backed pew, Fanny nodded prettily to a family on the right and whispered to Martha, 'The Parks from Hampton Wick, they do not often come to church here, they usually go to their own, I wonder why... anyway I am glad to see them, Anna is a friend of mine.' During the service Martha took time from her devotions to study the Vicar, Mr. Gore, because she knew he would have to be convinced of her ability to help Cobbleigh. She listened intently to his sermon, and found from his gentle discourse a scholar of no mean attainment, but decided he was a most impractical gentleman. If she, who knew herself to be well grounded in general knowledge, could only follow his reasoning half-way, what, she wondered, did the villagers make of him? She subsequently learned he was their pride, for not only had he published several imposing tomes on abstruse spiritual theories, but he was highly regarded for his encyclopaedic knowledge of bees, no less than for his goodness and kindness. His unworldliness inspired in his parishioners a desire to shield him from life's buffets, and it was not until later that Martha was allowed to see that when called upon to act he could do so with common sense and despatch. However, for the moment she could not but wonder at Gerald Gilbert for so carelessly burdening this gentle man with half of the care of a great and impoverished estate.

He was waiting to greet his congregation at the church door and, because all hung back to allow Fanny time to introduce him to her aunt, once more Martha ran the gauntlet of curious eyes.

At Fanny's introduction, he took Martha's hand and smiled sweetly saying, 'Welcome back to Cobbleigh. You have no notion how amazed I was to learn that you had answered Fanny's letter by coming here. How did you manage to leave your house in Seacliffe, pack up your belongings and reach us so quickly? You must be a lady of swift decisions.'

His innocent words made Martha berate herself. With her sensibilities heightened by knowledge of her pretence, she could readily see that from another's viewpoint, her prompt reply to Fanny's appeal could appear unlikely in its swiftness. However, she managed to answer him calmly that she had been on the point of leaving Seacliffe, for she had planned on a much needed change of scene after so many weary months spent in attendance on her dying friend. 'So, Mr. Gore, it was the matter of a moment to inform the coachman of the change in my destination and here I am.' She added for good measure, 'it was a mercy

Fanny's letter reached me when it did, otherwise it would never have found me.'

'Most fortunate,' he agreed, quite unaware of the turmoil he had caused in Martha's mind. 'Ackland and I shall be visiting you on Tuesday morning, when I hope we can all put our heads together and help young Fanny.'

'I'm looking forward to it,' replied Martha, moving on to meet the press of people anxious for an introduction.

True to her word, Fanny stayed beside her and all went off well. Of the people presented to her, Martha 'recognized' old Bodger when guided to her by young Bodger. Except for his blindness, the old man was as spry as a sixty-five year-old and embarrassingly managed to recount at least two scrapes the young Marcia had fallen in to. As these were so uncharacteristic of the older Marcia, Martha was forced to conclude he had made up the stories out of whole cloth.

Mr. and Mrs. Park, flanked by their handsome family, expressed pleasure at meeting her and asked whether she was receiving callers, upon hearing the affirmative, they then introduced their eight children. The eldest girl was Fanny's age, the eldest boy a year older, and both were overjoyed to see her again. This was explained by Miss Anna Park saying they had prevailed upon their parents to attend Divine Service at Cobbleigh because they wanted to invite Fanny to join them in an expedition they were planning.

Mulling over this encouraging evidence that Fanny's isolation was ending, Martha was startled to be accosted by a farmer, dressed in a tight black broadcloth coat, and whose stock was threatening to choke him for his face was of an alarming purple.

'Name's Mason, from High Combe. You've heard of me?' Replying that she had, he continued, 'Well I'd like to know when I'll get me barn roof mended.'

'I have no idea,' replied Martha.

'Nonsense,' he said roughly, 'You're Miss Fanny's aunt, ain't you'

'Yes,' said Martha, 'but it is the trustees' responsibility, I have no authority to give such an order.'

'Poppycock,' he snorted, 'What do the Reverend an' that lawyer feller know about the workings of an estate?'

Martha said to him firmly, 'Mr. Mason, I really cannot answer you, I have only just met Mr. Gore, I have not yet met Mr. Ackland, and it is quite out of my power to assess their ability. I will pass on your request when I see them this week – Good day. Come Fanny.' As she left he laughed loudly, slapped his knee and cried after her, 'Lord, Miss Gilbert, don't take on so, I did not mean to anger you.' But Martha had sustained a trying morning, so she and Fanny made good their escape.

Sunday was a day of leisure for the Daly family, as they walked slowly back to the Manor they discussed Miss Marcia. Daly freely admitted he had been wrong, 'Molly, me old love, I think we can place our money on Miss Marcia, did you hear how she tackled Mr. Mason? Got him to apologise an' all. Did it well too. I am surprised, I don't mind telling yes, I never thought she'd turn out so nice, seeing as how she was such a horrible child. One would almost say she was not the same person.'

William, listening to his father as a good son should, broke in, 'Miss Fanny looks so much prettier and happier. Father, wouldn't you say everyone is happier.'

'That's because everyone expects great things from Miss Marcia,' said his mother, 'An' I for one intend to see she gets my full support.' Her menfolk nodded in agreement.

'I was talking to Timothy and the O'Briens,' said Daly, 'An' they say she knows horses, an' coming from them that's a compliment. Pat and Mick are convinced of her ability to bring Cobbleigh back to its former glory. None of us could quite say how she will accomplish this, but we're all sure she will. She does not miss much. Pat said he saw her eyes darting all over the yard and she knew well what she was looking at when she beheld our Lucifer.'

Even the Lees were interested and listened to Copper recount how Miss Marcia liked ferrets. But Micah thought their easy access to the Manor coverts might be stopped.

As for the rest of the village, they had all seen her looking so fashionable in church and were charmed by her handsome face, warm smile and pleasing manner. They gave her full credit for the improvement in Miss Fanny's looks and dress and were eagerly awaiting the other changes she was expected to bring to their lives. One or two people did express their surprise that she did not resemble her late brother, but they were silenced by their more knowledgeable friends who told them that brother and sister had never looked alike. One damsel, in piercing tones, voiced what several people were thinking, 'I don't believe she's forty years old, she looks far too young, much younger that there Mrs. Corby,' but she was hushed by her betters.

It was no longer possible for her to postpone her duty, so that afternoon Martha sat down at the imposing desk in the library to write a letter explaining her delay to Meg. When it was finished and addressed, she knew she now had to tackle the more difficult task of writing to the Thistlethwaites, and realised that a receipt for Fanny's inheritance, signed by Fanny, must be enclosed. She looked in the desk drawers to see if, providentially, Fanny had left anything with her signature upon it, but in vain.

She looked around the room for inspiration – Mrs. Daly was right, those curtains were a disgrace – her eyes stared unseeingly at the crammed bookshelves and immediately it came to her. The best-loved books were on a what-not near the fire. Martha took down a copy of Miss Burney's '*Evalina*', sure enough there was Fanny's signature on the flyleaf, somewhat immature, rather too high on the page and accompanied by the rider '*Her Book*'. Martha returned it and took out one of Mrs. Radcliffe's

Tales, Fanny had signed it, but again it was marred, this time by the date, last year's, of course. The third, entitled '*The Noble Art of Venerie or Hunting*', illustrated with charming woodcuts, had belonged to Gerald Gilbert, the fourth book she picked up had nothing written in it. The she found the perfect specimen in a well-thumbed translation of Xenophon's '*The Art of Horsemanship*', but alas, it was written upon the marbled end-paper. At last she found what she was looking for. A good signature, low on the page, and the paper bearing no other mark on either side. She looked at the spine, '*The Castle of Otranto*' by Horace Walpole – well, she thought – I hope Fanny does not want to reread this fantastical tale. She picked up some scissors and carefully cut out the page. That done, she returned the book, then settled down to write – forge – the receipt above Fanny's signature.

> *"Received in good order from the hands of Mrs. Thomas Grey the following items from my share of the estate of the late Miss Marcia Mary Gilbert, to wit:-*
>
> *Item – one jewel case containing such articles of jewellery as listed in the inventory, one copy of which is retained by the trustees and one copy of which is retained by the legatee.*
>
> *Item – one fawn-coloured female pug answering to the name of 'Highness' aged three years.*
>
> *Item – one male marmalade tiger-striped cat known as 'Tigris' aged four years.*
>
> *Item – one male African Grey parrot, called 'Voltaire' age unknown, believed to be about thirty to thirty-five years".*

It all fitted in nicely, and she fancied she had remembered the wording of the original quite well. She smiled and added the date under Fanny's signature, sanded it, folded it and set it aside. Then she started on the covering letter.

She began by thanking her dear friends for their hospitality and kindness, then went on to describe the journey, the circumstances of her arrival, her reception and the reaction of the animals to country living, making it as light and amusing as possible. She knew her friends would laugh at Voltaire's newfound loquacity:

> *"...Fanny and he have quite taken to one another and he croons to her whenever she is near. He is now settling down, not talking quite so much, and as it has been ascertained, amazingly enough, he does not swear as was originally feared, he is brought into circulation again. Fanny is his champion and what Fanny wants Fanny shall have. Why you may ask? Well, my dears, you can have no notion of what has been happening here, apart from mismanagement..."*

She continued by giving a concise and caustic description of the events leading up to Gerald Gilbert's demise, the neglect of Fanny and the estate and the depredations of the Corby pair. She then went on to explain her resolve to try and help Fanny:

> *"...So you see, my friends, I have to stay here for a while to render any assistance I may. My heart goes out to the poor girl, I am grown fond of her and I believe she is fond of me but most of all I see myself at that age, or nearly, having experienced a similar case*

all those years ago. I cannot in all conscience let Fanny struggle by herself. She does not seem to have any worthwhile relatives she can turn to, so I am determined that if at all possible Cobbleigh will be saved and Fanny shall have a decent patrimony. There is potential here, but it all hinges on the other trustee, whom I meet on Tuesday. Anyway Stretton Wakefield can wait, after ten years what are a few months more...?"

As she wrote these words, Martha wondered if she was not being over optimistic. Fanny was seventeen, nearly eighteen, nevertheless it would be four years before she was of legal age. Martha quickly stifled the chilling thought she was trapping herself in an impossible situation for four years. Naturally, she had written nothing of the identity she had adopted, understanding as her friends were, she could not lay the burden of that knowledge upon them. She concluded her letter by saying:

"...I must say that from what I have learned of Gerald Gilbert, he must have been VERY like his sister, but of the two I vastly prefer Marcia.

Here is the receipt for the delivery of Fanny's inheritance. I am afraid I mislaid yours, Henry, in the upheaval of my arrival. I hope the form is acceptable. If we find the other, I will send it on duly attested. Because I am writing about Marcia's estate, I have taken the liberty of using several sheets of paper, rather than crossing the lines, I am sure her estate can bear the expense.

Thank you again, my dear friends, for all

your kindnesses. I will keep you informed of further events, especially of my dealings with Fanny's trustees. As you can readily appreciate, all depends upon their approval of me, and whether they will allow a mere female to presume to attempt what they think they cannot."

She signed her name and made the letter into a fat packet. Sealed it securely with wax, using a seal she found in the drawer. She addressed it. Hoping Mr. Ackland would carry both letters to the Receiving Office in Gloucester for her.

She did not worry about replies causing undue comment, for she had a ready explanation. Any letter correctly addressed to Mrs. Thomas Grey care of Miss Gilbert would automatically come to her and she could declare them to be in connection with the estate of her late friend. Which was the truth, but not necessarily the absolute truth.

A steady light breeze was blowing, one of the best drying days they had experienced for a while, so Mrs. Daly, longing to get on with the Monday wash, was pleased to observe the Manor ladies come down to an early breakfast in their riding habits. The coppers were nearly boiling and the housekeeper paused in her chivvying of the maids stripping the beds and gathering the soiled linen, to watch from an upstairs window the tall, slender lady in bottle green velvet and the shorter, slighter girl in dark blue serge wait in front of the house for their mounts. What a handsome picture they made, she thought with pleasure.

'I will take Badoura, Timothy, please help Miss Marcia,' said Fanny.

He grinned and looked at Marcia, obviously wondering what was her skill. Martha, aware that both of them were covertly watching how she would do, put her hand on Juno's neck and said, 'Hello, girl, would you like a piece of carrot?' She held her flattened palm under the soft muzzle. Juno, displaying indifferent manners, slobbered the tidbit and crunched it happily. Meanwhile Martha walked around her looking at the mare's solid figure. She supposed she must be glad her first ride for some time would be safe, but as she pulled on her gloves she determined that she would soon be riding Tadpole. Timothy noted with approval that Miss Marcia was unobtrusively checking the tack, and was glad the lady appeared able. He reserved final judgment until he had seen her ride. He threw her lightly into the saddle and watched her settle herself with practised ease. Then he helped Fanny and waited to see them off.

'Where are we going today?' asked Martha as she urged sober Juno alongside the chestnut mare.

'I thought we should go over the Home Farm and then through to Uplands, it will give you a good idea of the rest, Or, we could go to the Combes, if you prefer?'

'What! Run the risk of another encounter with the fierce Mr. Mason, I think not,' she laughed, 'besides, the Combes are let, so we should see what is directly your responsibility first...'

'It's quite a long ride, are you sure you will not be tired?'

'Juno is so very comfortable, she has such a broad back 'tis like sitting in an armchair,' Martha replied sweetly.

Fanny, who had observed that her aunt's seat was excellent and her hands light, realised that Juno would definitely have to be replaced by Tadpole. A born horsewoman, Fanny knew her aunt was longing for a more forward going steed. She watched the mare being expertly brought onto the bit and thought she had never seen Juno walk out so well.

Although the purpose of their outing was a serious one, it was hard for either of them to be anything but happy and carefree on this pleasant spring day. The light breeze was touched by the sun, the birds were singing and the delicious scents of the awakening earth pushing forth primroses, violets and daffodils, assailed their nostrils as they took deep breaths of the sweet air.

They spent the entire morning traversing the Home Farm and Uplands. Everywhere Martha looked she saw land that had been neglected, but not irreparably. The heart had not gone from it entirely, but overgrazing in the pastures and the lack of proper crop rotation needed immediate correction. Hedges and ditches required trimming and cleaning out, and good drainage restored. Some work had been carried out, however, winter crops sown and some spring ploughing accomplished, so she felt that the Manor was lucky in the men who worked the estate. She was somewhat at a loss as to where to start. She knew she had been away from the land too long and resolved to study the treatise on farming she had noticed in the office in the hope that a thorough perusal would provide answers.

Before they turned for home, Martha impulsively suggested, 'Let us gallop, I just long for it,' and set a startled Juno into a hand gallop. Laughing Fanny held the faster Badoura in behind until they reached the end of the track, whereupon an imp of mischief prompted her to pass her aunt. She led her over a weak spot in an overgrown cut-and-laid fence, and was relieved to see the lady collect Juno and fly over in fine style. After they had circled round and jumped back again, Martha cried, 'That was fun, I have not done such a thing in an age.'

They slowed down to a quieter pace and turned homewards. Fanny chattering excitedly, 'It's so nice to have someone to show things to, and you do understand the country. No one ever did, except Papa and he changed.'

Martha cast a glance at her face as this thought brought sudden gloom. 'You must not blame your Papa too much,' she said gently. 'All that I have learned makes me sure that he was so unhappy at your mother's death that he became melancholy and in his melancholy he no longer cared what befell him. That does not mean he did not love you, I am sure he did, but he probably found you reminded him of your Mamma. It seems to me he would have recovered eventually, if he had not taken up with that precious pair of bloodsuckers.'

'But why?' cried Fanny in distress, 'Why did he let himself be taken in? Why? He was not a stupid man.'

'Hush, dear, no he was not a stupid man, but Fanny have you never been so unhappy that you have moped yourself into a melancholy and the more melancholy you became the worse you felt, and then you began to think the whole world against you, and you did not care what happened to you?'

She looked startled, 'Is that what happened to him? I never thought grown-up people felt like that. Are you sure?'

' Pretty sure, and I have no doubt he met the Corbys when he was on the point of making an effort to overcome it. Unfortunately, they encouraged him to go to the other extreme.'

The little face turned to Martha was unbearably sad, 'I did try to help him, I did.'

'I am sure you did, Fan, but sometimes one cannot always help the ones we love, we just have to watch them and try to understand.'

Martha brought Juno up close to Badoura and patted the girl's arm, 'No one can know the thoughts of others, not even the ones closest to us,' she told her sadly, 'But reflect, he did not leave the Corbys a solitary penny.'

'She was made my guardian,' burst out Fanny, 'so how can you possibly say that...'

'Fanny, Fanny, Martha laughed, 'Do you not see, he knew she would never accept, and he did it deliberately.'

Badoura stopped abruptly. Turning Juno, Martha was in time to watch the play of expressions pass across Fanny's face, then Fanny put back her head and laughed until her sides must have ached. Martha was so delighted with her cleverness, she began to laugh too.

Drying her eyes of her sleeve, for she had again forgotten her handkerchief, Fanny gurgled, 'Oh, Aunt, I wish you could have seen her face. She was furious and he was trying to hush her, If only I had realised then what Papa had done, I would never have been so unhappy. Thank you for pointing it out to me.'

Very well satisfied with her inspired handiwork, Martha smiled smugly to herself.

Timothy was awaiting them when they returned to the stable yard. 'How was your ride, Miss Marcia?' he enquired politely.

Martha fixed him with a stern eye, 'If ever,' she announced, 'you put me on Juno again, I shall ask Miss Fanny to dismiss you out of hand.' Her eyes twinkled, 'At the risk of hurting Juno's feelings, I must tell you she is the biggest slug in creation, that was the safest ride I ever had. Next time I want Tadpole.'

A wide grin on his face, Timothy meekly said, 'Yes, Miss, I did not think Juno would suit, but Miss Fanny said...'

'Miss Fanny!' She swung round, 'Fan, you little devil, you made me endure that rocking chair?' Fanny laughed with glee, 'But consider for a moment, we didn't know if you were another Mrs. Corby, or no. Now, of course, we know, do we not Timothy? You will never have to ride Juno again.'

Martha hugged her, 'You are a dear sweet child and I am so happy that you take care of your old aunt.'

As the ladies left the yard, Timothy heard Miss Fanny ask something, but strain his ears as he may, he could not hear the reply. Disappointed in his wish to add a tale to all the suppositions discussed at length with the O'Briens, he turned to supervise the rugging up of the mares.

Even if Timothy had heard Fanny's question, he would not have been much enlightened, except to confirm that relations between aunt and niece were cordial.

Fanny was merely asking, 'Aunt Em. Please may I call you Aunt Em? "Aunt Marcia" sounds so severe.'

'Of course you may. I agree "Marcia" is not a particularly felicitous name.' Truth to tell, she was more than pleased to grant Fanny's request. Although "Marcia" and "Martha" sounded alike, never having been an aunt and having answered to "Martha" for thirty-one years, she was constantly afraid she would not respond to "Marcia" in the proper manner.

'Thank you, Aunt Em. I am so glad you do not consider me forward, Now, what I was going to ask you was... do you not think I have been very forbearing in stifling my curiosity? Have I not let you go all over Cobbleigh and not asked a question? I do wish you would let me know your plans. Do you think all is lost at Cobbleigh? Or, can it be saved? Please, please tell me, I have been on tenterhooks, cannot you give me some idea of what you have been writing on those tablets...?'

'Very soon, Fan. Before I say anything I want to see all and there are two areas I have yet to see... the gardens and the farm buildings. Perhaps we could go round them now.'

'Immediately, Aunt Em. Come let us hurry, the sooner we see them the sooner I will know what you think. Quickly, let us go back to the house and put on pattens, the yards are muddy.' She seized Martha's hand and began to run with her.

'Patience, patience, Fan.' Protested Martha laughing, 'I promise we will have a serious talk before our meeting with your trustees. Fan, let us stop and walk soberly to the house, if Mrs. Daly saw us she would think there was a fire.'

Thus a happy afternoon was passed. They admired the extensive gardens flaunting their spring colours, and presided over by a crusty individual. They inspected the dairy closely; interviewed the egg-woman in charge of flocks of poultry; and, visited the granaries, haylofts, stackyards, cider press and even the dank cider cellar.

Their visit to the cowsheds at milking time was especially fruitful. Although the yards were muddy as predicted, the cowman kept his byres clean and his animals were gleaming with health. He met them with a request that he be allowed to sell off some of the older cows to make way for some very good heifers just coming into milk. He was disappointed to hear he had to await the trustees' approval for such a move, but was mollified by Martha's sincere compliments on his animals and their milk yield. To which he replied he was worried about grazing running short, they had far too many head. They left him with the hope he would soon be allowed to take his beasts to market.

They were not so happy with the pig man, his animals looked well and the styes tidy, but the sows in his charge did not appear to be as fertile as Martha had come to expect of Cobbleigh animals. She suspected, but could not prove of course, that Coggin had been quietly disposing of piglets ever since Mr. Gilbert had demonstrated his lack of interest. She intended to keep an extremely close eye upon him.

Tired, but with a feeling of accomplishment, the ladies parted, Fanny to make her usual visit to the stables, and Martha to return once more to her tablets. Nothing she had seen that day had made her change her previous opinion and she could barely suppress a feeling of immense excitement.

6 - The Trustees

'Good morning, Vicar, It is unusual to find you afoot, would you care for a lift?'

'Ah, good morning, Ackland, thank you... yes, my Trojan is lame, alas, and the youngster has a splint forming, I shall have to ask Miss Gilbert to lend me a mount.' He climbed nimbly into the smart black Tilbury drawn by the high-stepping hackney Fanny greatly admired.

'As trustees, it is up to us to decide whether we should lend you a horse, surely?' said Mr. Ackland driving down the village street.

'You jest, I believe, does not Miss Gilbert have any say in the matter?'

'Yes, I jest where the Manor stables are concerned, but in reality Miss Fanny is far too young to make any decisions without our advice.'

'Oh agreed, but I was speaking of the elder Miss Gilbert. Oh, I see... you did not know, I forgot that you are new come from Gloucester this morning. Yes, Miss Gilbert arrived last week and now all is changed.'

'Well, well, she actually came in person! It is fortunate we met when we did, now you can tell me what she is like. Will we have any difficulty with her?'

'What is she like? Well it is hard to say, I only met her briefly after Matins, but from all reports she has begun to make things hum. Already put some men to work improving the front drive – and none too soon – too bad she did not start with this one,' In spite of great care, the Tilbury from time to time jounced alarmingly from one rut to another. 'Said she would pay the men herself if we would not. Wanted to keep the men from leaving the district. Clever head on her shoulders, I think,' added Mr. Gore.

'Throws her weight around does she?'

'Good heavens no, man, she has been meticulous. Arrived here a week ago with all her bag and baggage, was indisposed for a few days, but soon recovered and was out inspecting the estate taking copious notes. Has not said anything much, just looked, which has had an extraordinary effect on the people. For some reason – perhaps because Miss Fanny likes her so – they all expect great things of her. Of course, she is wealthy in her own right, but I do not suppose for one moment she will frank her niece.'

Mr. Ackland was in a carping mood, 'She is of a frail constitution it would appear. Does she mean to stay as chaperone, or will she take Miss Fanny away with her? I do not suppose she will wish to stay at Cobbleigh for long.'

'She looks the picture of health. I understand she had a trying journey besides being fatigued by nursing a dying friend. I believe by her actions she means to stay, and she seems genuinely interested in Cobbleigh. She has already driven round the Manor boundary, ridden over the Home Farm and Uplands, visited every nook and cranny of the Manor House and farm buildings – nothing has escaped her attentions. My informants tell me, she is a very knowing lady. In fact, Mrs. Lloyd, a timid little thing, was quite hysterical with relief by the time Miss Gilbert had pronounced her butter delicious, admired the many cheeses and, in general, approved her management of the dairy.'

'I never cease to marvel, Vicar, at how very well informed you are, one would almost say you had been there.'

'It is easy to see you do not live in a village! You must remember my housekeeper is related either by blood or marriage to nearly everyone in the place, and she gives me a report every morning with my breakfast; how else would I know who needs a visit, or who is coming to see me... I call her my official remembrancer. If she did not keep me up to snuff, I would never have time for my writing or my bees. Talking of bees, do you know, I found...'

'Not now, Vicar, please, we must decide on how we shall deal with Miss Gilbert before we meet her. Do you think she will be difficult?'

'Like Gerald Gilbert, you mean?' Said the Vicar bluntly.

'Plainly, yes.'

'I think she will be reasonable, but I do not believe she will be put upon, she has her share of the Gilbert sense of worth. You should have heard her give old Mason a set down. He told me of it, not a whit upset, laughing all the while, which you must admit is an amazing feat considering the many valid complaints we have received from him.'

'So, she is formidable,' murmured Mr. Ackland.

At a loss to explain exactly what Miss Gilbert was, the Vicar could only say, 'You will have to meet her and decide for yourself.'

It was perhaps as well that they were unaware that the subject of this conversation had spent the previous evening preparing herself for the meeting. After the inspection tour, she had awaited Fanny before the library fire. Her purpose was to talk to Fanny and ascertain her true sentiments. Martha was sure she knew them, but before committing herself to the struggle to save Cobbleigh, she had to obtain Fanny's full approval for any action she might wish to take. If Gerald Gilbert's indebtedness was not as stupendous as Fanny had been led to believe, Martha was positive that with a deal of economy and reorganization, there was a good chance Fanny's birthright might be saved. Diminished perhaps, but still a Gilbert would live at Cobbleigh.

'Well, Tig,' she said ruefully to the purring cat on her knee, 'I never thought I would bless Papa for the fix he left me in, but it seems I learned much. Of course, dear Mr. Todd helped.' She did not often indulge in nostalgia because, inevitably, it led to painful recollections her losses that happened so quickly one after another. So she was glad to be interrupted by Fanny's tempestuous entrance.

'Cassandra has had her foal, a beautiful colt, the image of Lucifer. Pat and Mike are wild with delight.'

'I am glad,' said Martha, her dark thoughts instantly banished, 'I cannot wait to see him. How is the mare?'

'Both are well, thank you.'

'Good... Now, Fanny, sit down, the time come for us to have our discussion.'

The girl looked so apprehensive that Martha laughed, 'Do not look so worried, my love, Tell me, what are your exact feelings about leaving Cobbleigh?'

Alarm flared into Fanny's eyes, 'You know I do not... cannot leave, I would die,' she cried passionately, 'Aunt Em you promised...'

'Hush, Fanny, that is not precisely what I asked you, what I must know is... are you prepared to make sacrifices for Cobbleigh?'

'Of course, I would do anything. But I do not know what we can do, Mr. Ackland said...'

'I know Mr. Ackland thought you would have to sell up, and until I know the extent of your Papa's debts, I cannot say whether he is right or not. But Fanny, I have looked about the Manor and I have seen mismanagement everywhere.' At Fanny's gasped in protest she added, 'I am sorry, my dear, but your Papa was away too much during the last three years and was so uninterested when he was here, I have to call it mismanagement. There is a wanton lack of economy in the right places, drastic changes should be made and some money spent to put all to rights.'

'But there is no money,' wailed Fanny.

'Money!' exclaimed Martha, 'You have money everywhere. Did you not listen to your cowman, Thomas was it?' she glanced at her tablets, 'yes, Thomas, with all his complaints about not being allowed to cull the milch cows properly. We must sell off some of the beasts overgrazing your land. The land is not in good heart, but a little care and attention will soon bring it back. And your horses alone with bring in a tidy sum.'

She held up her hand as Fanny opened her mouth, 'No, my dear, there's no need to sell Lucifer, Badoura or Tadpole, but Juno will sell very well as quiet, and guaranteed not to upset the most nervous of females.' Her eyes twinkled as Fanny heaved a sigh of relief.

'And you have far too much young stuff eating their heads off and growing like weeds. None of us could possibly break and train all of them. Now, do you see what I mean?' Fanny nodded eagerly. 'Then there's your father's hunters, although to obtain the best possible price, they should be sold at the beginning of the hunting season rather than at the end. Now, I will not say any more, but I want you to think hard and, when you have thought, I want you to tell me that you will back me absolutely, no matter what I say or suggest to the trustees tomorrow. I need their approval to take over and I do not know how they will react to two women doing so-called "men's work". Your trustees are, I have no doubt good men, but I do not think either of them are countrymen – the Vicar I collect does not even farm his own glebe.' She paused to look at Fanny intently, 'If you do not have complete confidence in me, or you believe that the trustees know better, I would like you to tell me now. We should present an united front tomorrow.'

Pensively Fanny stared into the fire. She was thrilled that her aunt thought Cobbleigh could be saved. Now that matters had been brought to her attention, she agreed with her aunt's assessment. She was grieved her father had let things go, but with a new maturity she had begun to realize the depths of his despondency. She looked at the lady opposite her, sitting so quietly with Tig in her lap, who would imagine her to be so businesslike; so beautiful and elegant it was hard to believe she was interested in farming. Fanny spoke – she had made the decision that was no decision – 'Aunt Em, I am wholeheartedly behind you and if you can help save any portion of Cobbleigh, I shall forever be in your debt.'

Unaware she had been holding her breath, Martha let out a great sigh. Until now she had not quite grasped the extent of her own excitement at the prospect of what lay before hr. She could hardly wait until she could take the reins of government in her own hands. 'I am so glad. I do not promised miracles mind, but I do promise I will try my utmost to put matters to rights.'

Fanny flung her arms around Martha's neck.

'Wait, Fan, we have to convince your trustees, then we have to find a bailiff acceptable to them and who will work with two women, for my love, we will need help. I shall put it to the trustees in such a way that I am sure they will think the bailiff will manage everything for them and we'll be mere ciphers, but I do not propose that to be so, because I expect you to be able to manage Cobbleigh by the time you are twenty-one. That is, unless you get married.' Fanny blushed a little and said, 'I do not want to marry ever, it would mean I would have to leave Cobbleigh.'

'Not necessarily,' said Martha, 'Anyway, let us not dwell on matrimony now, but you never know Fan, you may change your mind.'

The four persons who held the fate of Cobbleigh in their hands arranged themselves comfortably around the library desk, while Fanny made the introductions. There was a little silence during which Mr. Ackland spread his papers. When he had completed the task to his satisfaction, he looked searchingly at the elder Miss Gilbert. He was amused to find he was being scrutinised just as intently by her. The Vicar, abstractedly taking snuff, thought of bees; while Fanny gazed anxiously from her aunt to her attorney, wondering what was going to happen.

Mr. Ackland was a surprise to Martha. A young man, not much older than herself, extremely precise in appearance, a thin careworn face out of which shone a pair of very keen grey eyes. He was no less taken aback to see a tall, elegant young woman with an air of common sense about her manner. Frankly, he had not known what to expect, all he had to go on was the petulant rantings of his late client. Of the two people, he felt he already liked the sister better than the brother, and she had obviously been kind to her niece. Both trustees were bachelors, but Mr. Ackland, unlike the Vicar who had vaguely noticed Fanny was looking uncommonly well, knew how much Fanny's improved appearance was due to a suitable, well cut dress. After all, Mr. Ackland was the sole prop and mainstay of a widowed mother and four unmarried sisters. Consequently, he was well informed in most particulars of feminine apparel. He gave the elder Miss Gilbert full marks for being sensitive to the needs of a lonely seventeen-year-old, but he wondered how she would be to deal with when the subject pertained to business. He did hope she would not try to wheedle him, he had enough of that at home and it was one of his sisters' pastimes he never could withstand. He looked at the intelligent face before him and became confident that he would not be disappointed. He had every hope their dealings would be as straight-forward as they would be pleasant.

Well, the only way to find out would be to put it to the test, so he said, 'Miss Gilbert, Mr. Gore has related how you were able to answer Miss Fanny's letter so promptly, now I ask you why you have returned to a place you left long ago and which must hold disagreeable memories? Would you tell me that?'

Martha's reply was careful, just enough selfishness to suggest Marcia, pure altruism would not fit what they thought they knew of her, but with enough sincerity to be believable, 'Fanny's letter arrived at a convenient moment. I needed a change of scene and an interest to occupy my mind. Apart from these considerations, there was this – the family dispute was between me and my brother, why should it be handed down to my niece? We are the last of the Gilberts and I deem myself honour bound to come to her aid – at least for a time.'

Not entirely convinced by these cool words, Mr. Ackland decided to wait upon events before he finally made up his mind about her. So he said, 'Forgive me if I appear cautious, but you – who have Miss Fanny's welfare at heart – as I do – understand my need to put you to the question?'

Composedly, although her heart was beating swiftly, Martha replied, 'Of course, Mr. Ackland, you do your duty and I would have been disappointed in you if you had not.'

Smiling inwardly at this riposte, he said, 'Well, to business, erumph, I am sure I have no need to tell you, Miss Gilbert, that Miss Fanny's affairs are in a bad way, suffice it for me to give you the extent of your brother's debts to date.' He named a figure that made Fanny turn white and Martha tighten her lips.

'I have, however, reason to believe that if further obligations incurred by him come to light, they will be of a comparative bagatelle. As to your late brother's account we have, of course, Miss Fanny's Trust which comes from her late mother. The principal is mercifully untouched, she will have the benefit of that when she comes of age, but the interest, amounting to about five hundred pounds per annum, was for her father's use and latterly he spent every penny.'

Fanny was stunned. All that money, where could her father have spent that amount? Mr. Ackland went on to answer her unspoken question.

'Mr. Gilbert lost a large part at play, the rest went in extravagant spending. One good thing I have discovered is that he had not mortgaged the Manor at all, although I am afraid he was negotiating to raise money on the parcels of land known as the Combes when he died. We may have to consider doing just that ourselves, if we do not have to sell outright. Two more items have turned up which makes me feel a little better.'

'Tell us, dear chap,' said the Vicar, who had left his bees as soon as they started business. Fanny sat silent while Martha was busy with her endless notes.

The attorney continued, 'Miss Fanny, did you know your father had bought a house in Bath, in Laura Place?'

Startled, Fanny said 'No! I did not. I wonder why he did that, my grandmother lives very retired in Bath and he always avoided her as much as possible...' a little frown wrinkled her forehead, 'Oh! I know why. Of course! Corbys!'

Her auditors understood immediately.

Mr. Ackland cleared his throat, 'Yes, well, erumph, the good thing about this occurrence is that the house was bought fully furnished and your father paid for everything, not one penny is owing. However, it is not being used. The other asset I have discovered is that your grandfather, Miss Fanny, bought some property in Gloucester, well placed by the Docks. Two warehouses, three houses and a large building where several merchants have offices. Your father was not interested in the property, although it brought him revenue. It was my partner's father, who administers several such holdings, who drew my attention to it. Everything is fully rented and brings in a fair sum.'

He shuffled his papers, 'The most distressing matter is the drop in the Manor revenues to half what it should be, each year brings diminishing returns. From what I can see, there is the necessity of spending a large amount of money to restore the place. That was why, Miss Fanny, I upset you so much last time by suggesting we sell. Glancing at Fanny's set face, he went on hurriedly, 'Now, don't you worry, we can now sell the Bath and Gloucester properties and perhaps the Combes or Uplands...'

'No!' cried Fanny positively, 'No, I do not want the Manor lands sold or changed, please Mr. Ackland cannot we use my Trust?' She turned to Martha 'Aunt Em please say something.'

Martha looked for permission at Mr. Ackland, who nodded. He sat back interested to hear what she had to say.

She clasped her hands in her lap to steady them. 'First of all,' she said, 'I am happy to hear there are a few more assets than you originally thought, and best of all that they are unencumbered.' She paused and drew in a deep breath, 'Mr. Ackland, Mr. Gore, Fanny and I have ridden over most of the estate, and I have taken careful notes of what is needed. The Manor is slowly running down like an unwound watch. The people on the farm, in the stables, and in the house, have been working the place by themselves without any guidance for the past three years. They have continued to do what they have always done very well, but they have not been allowed to make decisions, is it any wonder the revenues have fallen off? Oh, I know that since the end of the war there have been hard times, but that should not have affected the revenues by cutting them by as much as one half. Gentlemen, what the Manor needs is reorganization, some time and a little money spent on hiring more of the right people and the dismissal of the ones we have no further use for. This should be done in the house as well as outside. A programme for repairs to the buildings and the reclamation of the land should be instituted.' She paused for breath.

Sitting bolt upright in his chair, the Vicar asked, 'Where will we get the money and who will do it? It will have to be someone who knows what he is doing?'

'Mr. Gore,' said Martha, 'If you and Mr. Ackland agree, I will do it. With your help, of course, and also the help of a bailiff. Ever since the last bailiff died the land has needed another such as he.'

Mr. Ackland, who had been listening attentively his eyes never leaving her face, now spoke, 'What do you propose to use for money? We still have to pay off debts.' He was testing her, and her answer came without hesitation.

'Rent and take out a mortgage on the Bath property, people are always looking for desirable residences in Bath, and I presume it is a desirable residence?' He nodded with a slight smile. 'Mortgage all or part of the Gloucester property; that should settle some of the most pressing debts. Or, better still, compound with the creditors and pay the interest on the balance. That should also give us some cash to use until the Manor starts paying again. We would need to have the wages bill met and help with the housekeeping for three, perhaps six months.'

'Bless me,' exclaimed the Vicar 'you think you can make this place pay as soon as that?' Why, you will need every penny for extra help and supplies and where is the money going to come from, tell us that?'

Martha smiled, 'The animals have not been culled for three years; Mr. Gilbert's hunters should be sold and we have far too many young horses, not to mention useless items such as Mr. Corby's curricle and pair – how glad I am you would not let him take them – a post-chaise, used but twice, and so on... you follow my thinking?'

Both men nodded, while Fanny smiled with excitement. 'As for the house,' Martha continued, 'We mean to cut down on our expenses. Close the rooms we do not use and dismiss some of the servants. For example, Mrs. Corby's dresser whose surly presence upsets the servants' hall and who, I understand, was paid by my brother and not by Mrs. Corby, Shall I go on?'

'No, no,' said Mr. Gore in admiration, 'that is the most capital thing I have ever heard, what do you think Ackland?'

Mr. Ackland, drawing fantastic beasts on the paper in front of him, deliberately dipped his quill into the standish and finished a curlicue on a furry caterpillar, before looking up, 'How would you set about selling the surplus stock?'

'A few at a time,' replied Martha promptly, 'It 's no good flooding the market, it drives the prices down.' He nodded in agreement, 'And,' she continued 'to get the best price for the hunters they should not be sold until the season begins. However, once it is known that Mr. Gilbert of Cobbleigh's hunters are to be sold, I would imagine eager buyers will beat a path to our door, they are of very high calibre you know. Now, my niece is, of course, in charge of the stables, and she and I will train two or three of the youngsters so that when we sell them as suitable ladies' mounts, they will fetch a better price. All this will take time, that is why we need monetary assistance for the first quarter at least. Also, we cannot handle all this alone, we do need a bailiff. Can you recommend one?'

'Ah!' said Mr. Ackland, pleased, 'I'm glad you recognize you need help.' He frowned, 'We'll have to place an advertisement in the "*Gloucester Journal*" and further afield, I would suppose.'

'That will take time we can ill afford, I do wish there was a more immediate solution,' said Martha. The Vicar took snuff as he pursued a thought of his own, He sneezed, used his handkerchief, and then said, 'Young Buchan returned last night. A major now, he has sold out. Such a pity he would not do, his mother is in poor health you know, and it would be a hardship for her to remove from a house where she has spent all her married life.'

'Why would he not do?' demanded Fanny, remembering from happier days the pleasant young man who had not been too lofty to be kind to a small girl, 'He used to help his father before he went into the army.'

'That is so,' agreed the Vicar, 'Why not, Ackland? At least for the time being it would answer admirably.'

Mr. Ackland was dubious, 'Does he know enough about farming? He has been in the army all his adult life, I would imagine it might be too tame for him after the Peninsula.'

'Well,' replied Mr. Gore, 'All I know is what Janey told her mother – my housekeeper's youngest works for the Buchans – Janey said that he told his mother he had come to settle down to country life, because he was tired of racketing about.'

'Two things in his favour,' said Martha, 'he is used to handling men, and he will not be so knowledgeable that he will browbeat Fanny and myself. That is, of course,' she added hastily, 'if you agree we try to bring the Manor back to its former state.'

'And if all your hard work does not suffice and we still have to sell, what then?' asked Mr. Ackland.

'We will at least know we have done our best to save it and we will obtain a far better price if the place is seen to be neat and on the way to being prosperous. Besides,' she added with humour, 'we will have sold off the surplus animals to the ultimate benefit of lessening our indebtedness.'

The two men looked at each other for a few moments, then Martha rose and said, 'Fanny, let us find Daly and ask him to bring in refreshments.'

As they left the room, Fanny could hardly wait for the door to shut behind them before she burst forth, 'You were magnificent. How do you know so much about markets and prices and things? I declare I was positively awestricken.'

'You looked it,' said Martha kindly, 'your eyes were as round as an owl's.'

'You do tease,' giggled Fanny, 'but I was not the only one. The Vicar was amazed too. Mr. Ackland did not show how he felt though.'

'No,' agreed Martha, 'and he is the one we have to impress. The dear Vicar will follow his lead. We will know in a few minutes what they have decided. Now let us really find Daly.'

In the library, the Vicar was holding forth, 'An excellent lady, if we can manage what she suggests, perhaps Cobbleigh will be saved. What do you think?'

Mr. Ackland was not paying attention. While busily making computations in his head, he dimly realized there had been a question. His murmured, 'Quite so' was met with a baffled silence. When he reached a satisfactory total he looked up with a smile, 'Do you know, Vicar, I think Miss Gilbert is right, it can be done her way. I did not think of it before because we lacked someone to devote their time to Cobbleigh, both indoors and out, and in her we have found the very person. A capable young lady it seems.'

'Young – nothing – she is forty-one years old, I looked it up in the Parish Records.'

'Forty-one? I find that extraordinary. She does not look a day over twenty-eight. Another thing I find extraordinary is that she has a reputation for being mean-tempered and spoiled, and here she is a perfectly delightful person.'

'Yes, I heard that too. But children's characters do change when they become adults. At least,' amended Mr. Gore vaguely, 'I believe they do. Anyway, are we agreed we give this plan of hers a try?'

'Assuredly, but we must insist on regular accounting and a trial period of, say, six months?'

'Agreed. I am so glad that there is a chance Cobbleigh can be saved. During the past three years I've been most distressed at the late Mr. Gilbert's behaviour. Of course, he never recovered from his wife's death and then he fell into the hands of that pair of adventurers...' he stopped abruptly for the door had opened disclosing Daly bearing a tray with decanters and glasses. Behind him came an outwardly calm Martha and a very nervous Fanny. After they reseated themselves, the butler served ratafia to the ladies and maderia to the gentlemen; made up the fire, and withdrew, disappointed he had heard nothing of note to tell his anxious wife.

Mr. Ackland turned to Martha, 'Miss Gilbert,' he said impressively, 'Mr. Gore and I have decided that your ideas are perfectly sound, therefore, we entrust you with the task of reclaiming the Manor, with Miss Fanny's help, and we in turn will look after the rest.'

'Thank you,' said Martha striving to hide her intense pleasure, while Fanny clapped her hands in delight, 'but we must have a bailiff, do you sanction it?'

'We do,' he replied, 'And I see no reason why you should not give Major Buchan a try. What would you expect to pay him, have you thought of that?'

'Oh, yes,' said Martha, 'I feel we must offer him what his father was receiving.'

'But,' objected the Vicar, 'his father was a proper bailiff, and young Buchan is not trained.'

'I know, Mr. Gore,' replied Martha, 'but do not forget he is an experienced army man and the cost of everything has risen since his father's day.'

'Yes,' said Mr. Ackland, 'you are right, Don't you agree, Vicar?'

'Well, I suppose 'tis false economy to try and save too much on the wage bill.'

'Good,' said Mr. Ackland, 'then it is agreed that we will carry the wage bill and housekeeping for three months, and we shall give this scheme a six month trial.'

'Six months is not a fair trial period, gentlemen,' objected Martha, 'could you not make it a year? We could always have meetings in the meantime, so we can report to you and review the accounts, say once every two weeks to begin with and later, perhaps, once a month.'

The trustees communed with each other silently and then nodded simultaneously, 'Agreed,' said Mr. Ackland, 'I propose we hold our next meeting two weeks from today, and if you have the Major by then, he should attend as well.'

'Thank you,' breathed Martha. 'Now, there is one other favour I would ask of you.'

'What is that?'

'We have to dismiss a few people, how many I am not sure, I must first seek the advice of the Dalys. And, because I was not a member of the household, I feel I cannot give them proper references, but you can – as trustee. Also, they will have to be paid in lieu of notice. Do you think, Mr. Ackland, you could return Thursday and handle the dismissals. I shall have completed the list by then.'

'Do you really need me? Can it not be done by the housekeeper?'

'No, one should be fair to the people, after all it is not their fault we are overstaffed.'

'Very well,' he sighed, it was not his favourite way of spending a morning, 'I shall be here at ten o'clock.'

'And you will stay and partake of luncheon? How about you Vicar, will you join us?'

'Alas, Miss Gilbert, I cannot, I have to see my Bishop.'

Polite murmurs of regret were lost when Daly entered to announce luncheon was served.

Martha leading the way with the Vicar asked him, 'You pass the Wool House as you go home do you not?'

'Yes I do.'

'Would you kindly request Major Buchan to wait upon us as soon as possible, and, Mr. Gore, please do not tell him why, I do not want him making up his mind before we lay out our entire plans before him.'

'As you wish. I shall merely tell him you would like to see him.'

7 - Charles's Quest

The Mayor and Corporation of the town of Seacliffe in the county of Sussex liked to refer to Brighton, the fashionable seaside resort further along the coast, as their rival. Needless to say, secure in the patronage of His Royal Highness the Prince Regent, the Mayor and Corporation of Brighton found no need to refer to Seacliffe at all.

A generation or so ago, Seacliffe was a small fishing village nestling securely under the chalk cliffs on the east side of Cliffe Bay, well protected from chill winds. When the fashionable world, followed by the less fashionable but wealthy middle class, took to sea-bathing, Seacliffe split into two. Old Seacliffe retained its air of an overgrown village, narrow cobbled streets, houses crowded together, but New Seacliffe spread eastwards and upwards, Neat villas with little terraced gardens appeared to line the steep and winding Cliffe Road to Cliffe Head.

When the wind blew a gale from off the sea, waves broke high over the Parade and salt spray, carried by the wind, marked windows even in the topmost houses of New Seacliffe. The inhabitants of the villas assured each other repeatedly, any discomfort in living in the teeth of the wind was truly compensated for by the magnificent panorama before them. But on such a day, if they were wise, they remained indoors. Only the most hardy souls were abroad and then, only if they had important business.

Thus it was, one day in March, when a gale was blowing; Charles Grey hardly met a soul on his way to the address furnished by Mr. Todd. As one used to far worse, Charles paid no mind to the weather. Exhilarated, he wrapped his boat cloak around him and leaning against the wind, walked briskly up Cliffe Road.

At the corner of Mecklenburg Terrace, he paused for breath and looked without much hope across the Bay. No ships to be seen today, all would be lying snug in harbour or hugging the lee shore off the coast of France. Before Bonaparte was exiled, Charles had made countless voyages up and down this strip of sea, passing a mile or so from the very spot where Martha lived. Come to that, he had probably seen the lights of her window, if only he could have distinguished them from the many others twinkling across the Bay.

He turned away and walked along to 24 Charlotte Terrace. At first, he thought he had drawn a blank, for the house appeared closed, the blinds in the front windows down, a 'For Sale' sign in the window. Disappointed, he had counted on meeting Martha that day. Wondering what to do next, he was turning way when the front door flew open and a stout woman with snapping black eyes stood on the doorstep.

'You'll be the gentleman to view,' she announced and, not waiting for his reply, she continued, 'you are earlier than Mr. Thistlethwaite expected. Come away in, sir, so those nosey-parkers next door canna see you.'

Amused, Charles allowed himself to be urged up the steps. He caught a glimpse of a shadowy figure in the bow window of Number 26, as he passed over the threshold.

'They be that curious,' said the stout woman crossly, 'an' I won't accommodate 'em so there.'

As soon as they were standing in the hall, Charles produced his card, 'I have not come to view the house, I'm afraid.'

She took his card, '*Captain Lord Biscay*', she spelled out. As the glory of his name and the realisation of what the pussies next door were missing ran through her mind, she curtsied to Charles, introducing herself as 'Mrs. Bunnett, the housekeeper, her that was cook to the late Miss Gilbert.'

'I am delighted to meet you. Now, perhaps you can help me, I am looking for my cousin Mrs. Thomas Grey.'

'You're Mrs. Grey's cousin? She never told me she had a lord for a cousin. Oh, dear,' she was agitated, 'to think she used to polish the furniture, an' beat the carpets, when we were busy... an' all the time she was related to a lord.'

'Only by marriage,' said Charles, 'I daresay that does not count.'

Mrs. Bunnett was not placated, 'There! I knew she had fallen on evil days.'

Charles frowned.

'Such a nice lady and never a word of complaint, and Miss Marcia was that difficult. Why when I think...'

'She is not here, I collect, so where is Mrs. Grey now, do you know?'

'Why, sir, she should be at her home in Herefordshire. Stretton Wakefield, she told me. Do you know it? She'll be there by now, you'll find her there,'

Not wishing to upset Mrs. Bunnett, he asked quietly, 'When did she leave Seacliffe?'

'She went to stay a few nights with the Thistlethwaites, afore Mr. Thistlethwaite sent her off in a travelling coach with the animals.'

'Animals! What animals?'

'The ones Miss Gilbert left to her niece, Tig, Highness and Voltaire.'

This did not make matters much clearer to Charles, so he fastened on the one name that might help him. 'Who are the Thistlethwaites you mention?'

'He is trustee for Miss Gilbert's estate.'

'Where can I find him?'

'His office is on India Street, off the Parade, nearly opposite the Anchor Inn.'

'Thank you, Mrs. Bunnett, you have been most helpful,' he handed her a gold coin.

'Oh, my lord!' she cried in delight. 'Thank you ever so. And when you see Mrs. Grey, please give her my respects and tell her I do miss her, and Tig.'

'I will and good day to you.' He lingered on the doorstep to shake hands with her. As he passed Number 26, a spirit of mischief seized him. He bowed politely to the shadow in the window, and smiled at its hasty recoil.

Mrs. Bunnett shut the door behind him thoughtfully, Captain Lord Biscay – such a nice gentleman – was very anxious to find Mrs. Grey. His cousin, he said, but only by marriage. Just wait till I tell them pussies!

The firm of Blundell, Blundell, Watson & Thistlethwaite, Attorneys-at-Law, occupied a converted residence. Charles climbed the snow-white steps and pulled the shining brass bell. A boy opened the door and bowed Charles in. While Charles waited for his card to be taken up to Mr. Thistlethwaite, he looked about the busy office. It showed nothing of the traditional dinginess law firms were supposed to thrive in, and contrasted favourably to that of his London attorney's premises. He was struck by the quiet industry in the office glimpsed beyond the waiting room. None of the clerks were over forty-five years of age, and gave the impression that any new client could have great confidence that their affairs were in able, go-ahead hands.

'Please to come this way, my lord, Mr. Thistlethwaite awaits you.' Charles followed the boy up the stairs and into a spacious front room. Mr. Thistlethwaite came forward, his hand outstretched, and greeted Charles pleasantly. The boy closed the door behind him and Charles was led to a chair. When Mr. Thistlethwaite had seated himself behind his desk, he asked politely, 'How may I help you, my lord?'

'I believe,' said Charles, 'you can tell me where I can find Mrs. Thomas Grey.'

Mr. Thistlethwaite's response was to fasten his eyes on him intently. As both men sat in silence for a few seconds, appraising each other, Charles could not help wondering why the man had to stare so. Also, Martha appeared truly hedged about with solicitous solicitors. He smiled inwardly at his whimsical phrase.

Mr. Thistlethwaite in his turn, was wondering in what relation this man stood to Martha. He glanced again at Charles's card, rereading the name, rank, and title, but it did not help him. 'Forgive me, my lord, but would you tell me why you are looking for Mrs. Grey?'

'I am her cousin by marriage. She married my cousin Tom. Perhaps you know that her husband was an only child. When his father, Sir John Grey, died I inherited the estate as the son of his younger brother.'

'Yes, Mrs. Grey did mention something of the sort. But I do not recognise your name.'

Charles laughed, 'Until recently I was Captain Sir Charles Grey, K.C.B., and before that I was plain Captain Charles Grey.'

'Ah! I see. My felicitations, my lord, upon your ennoblement,' Charles bowed his head in acknowledgement.

Mr. Thistlethwaite bit his lip, staring at the bit of paste-board on the desk before him. 'Unfortunately, my lord, I do not know if Mrs. Grey would appreciate my giving you her address. Would you please tell me why you want to find her.'

Leaning forward Charles asked, 'How much of her story do you know?'

'All of it, I believe. My wife and I were honoured by her confidence a few days before she left Seacliffe.'

'So she has left,' commented Charles, 'I met a Mrs. Bunnett earlier who said she planned to leave for Stretton Wakefield. When did she leave?'

'A good three week ago. I saw her off myself.'

'Three weeks ago, great heavens, she has been missing since then!'

'Missing!' Exclaimed Mr. Thistlethwaite, 'no, no, dear sir, she's not missing.'

'You relieve my mind considerably, but, where is she? Her old nurse and her attorney are both worried for they expected her at least a fortnight ago. When they heard I was going to London, they asked me to visit Seacliffe and find out what I could. As I think I mentioned to you earlier, I, too, am most anxious to find her... I suppose you do know where she is?'

'Oh, yes. I received a letter from her recently.' He leaned forward and said earnestly, 'Before I tell you more, my lord. I must satisfy myself you are only interested in her welfare. She has not had much reason to like your family, I'm afraid.'

'Don't I know it,' said Charles, leaning back in his chair and crossing his legs. 'And it is in order to make her some reparation that I must find her. Believe me, Mr. Thistlethwaite, I have only recently learned just how cruelly my late uncle treated her...' and he went on to describe his recent findings.

Henry Thistlethwaite was horrified, 'Poor, poor Martha,' he muttered, 'I did not know the half of it. This is dreadful, dreadful...'

'It is indeed dreadful,' agreed Charles, 'that is why I must see her. You can tell me if she is well. How was she when you last saw her?'

'She had a hard time recently, and was tired to the bone, but still as beautiful as ever.'

'Beautiful,' said Charles and then he thought more carefully, 'I have not seen her since she was fourteen,' he said judiciously, 'Yes, I suppose she would grow into a beauty. Her parents were very handsome.'

'Her beauty is not in the ordinary sense. She has quiet good looks, very lovely sparkling eyes and a great deal of spirit. She is... er, would be, hard to forget.'

Tactfully ignoring Mr. Thistlethwaite's slip, Charles asked, 'Why was she tired? Meg, her nurse mentioned

Martha's employer dying. Was Mrs. Grey looking after her?'

'She bore the brunt of all the nursing. Fortunately the doctor insisted she continue riding twice a week otherwise she only took the dog for a quick run every day. Miss Gilbert hovered near death for a month. She'd been critically ill for six months before that and she was not an easy patient. Would have no one but Mrs. Grey around her. In fact, Marcia Gilbert was not an easy employer – and I should know, for she had me on the run over her Will, forever changing this and that – and Mrs. Grey told me as far back as a year ago she only put up with Miss Gilbert's megrims because she needed the money. Later she expanded upon it and said the money was to help pay off the mortgages on what was left of her father's estate in Stretton Wakefield. She had made a vow, she said, not to return to her village until all was paid. However, now she was free to return there, my wife and I had the impression she was hesitating, after all. She was badly treated by the neighbours as well as her in-laws. I gather.'

'Yes, you're right. Only heard about it myself recently. But, my dear sir, she must come home now. I am sure people have realised how wrong they were to listen to jealous gossip. Now, have I told you enough for you to trust me?'

Instead of replying, Mr. Thistlethwaite took his half-hunter out of his pocket, 'It's nearly noon, my lord, would you care to join us at luncheon? I always go home and I know Mrs. Thistlethwaite would be delighted and honoured to meet you. Mrs. Grey's letter is there too and you may read it.'

'Thank you, I would be happy to join you and your wife.'

'Well, shall we go? On the way I will tell you more.'

Jessica Thistlethwaite was indeed overjoyed to receive a visit from an old friend of Martha's. But she courteously hid her elation at meeting such an eligible gentleman who quite put Martha's erstwhile suitor, Mr. Greening, in the shade. During the meal she listened to the men talking while she studied Charles closely. By the time ratafia cakes and cream jelly were put on the table, she determined to promote immediate compliance by her husband to any request Charles made. She need not have worried, her husband never had any notion of not telling Charles of Martha's whereabouts. He fetched her letter, and proceeded to explain why he sent her to Cobbleigh.

'I was not surprised,' said Jessica, 'When Martha wrote she had decided to stay at Cobbleigh for the present to help the young Miss Gilbert. Though, I could wish that she had stayed here with us in Seacliffe if she decided against returning to Stretton Wakefield. I begged her to stay, my lord. I even hoped she would accept Mr. Greening's proposal of marriage, but she would have none of him.'

'Tcha! Greening,' exclaimed her spouse, 'Not the man for such as Martha, and well you know it, my love.'

'True,' conceded Jessica, 'but he is rich, and has built a big house...'

'All in the worst possible taste, and a widower with four young children... all he wanted was a housekeeper and someone to mind his children... Martha would be wasted on him. 'Sides he made his money speculating with army contracts. Not a pleasant fact a widow of a Lieutenant in the Royal Navy would want to live with... You were moongazing, my love, if you thought him suitable.'

'Only too true, and Martha said as much to me. But I do miss her presence. My lord, when you see her, please tell her I forgive her for turning down Mr. Greening, but I do not forgive her for settling in Gloucestershire instead of staying here with us.'

Charles left the hospitable pair with their good wishes and kind messages for Martha ringing in his ears. He was glad she had such delightful friends. Now that he knew she was temporarily residing in Gloucestershire, he rested easier.

Upon entering the inn where he was putting up, he immediately wrote letters to both Meg and Mr. Todd. He described what he had learned, and gave them Martha's present address, happy that he could put their anxious minds at ease. He also explained he would be in London for some time, but on his return he would at the earliest opportunity, seek out Martha if she still lingered at Cobbleigh.

Charles's business took longer than he had estimated. It was a good six weeks later when he returned to Stretton Wakefield. As his chaise bowled along the village street, one of the first people he saw was Meg. She waved to him, her white apron flying in the breeze. This time he stopped the chaise and got out.

'Well, Meg, did you get my letter?'

'Oh, my lord, I am so sorry you had the journey to Seacliffe for nothing.'

'For nothing?' His face lit up, 'She's here, Martha's come.'

'No, no, nothing like that, I'm afraid, 'tis just that I received a letter from her the very morning you left. I ran out of the cottage and tried to stop you – tell you... but you did not stop, I'm that sorry, my lord.'

'Don't be sorry, Meg. 'Twas my fault, I saw you... Thought you were wishing me luck. My journey to Seacliffe wasn't wasted. I learned much of Martha's life there. I'll send the chaise on and tell you all about it, if you'll regale me with your cowslip wine.'

8 - Plans Are Discussed

The sounds of vigorous brushing made Martha stop and look in the door. A young housemaid rose from her knees to bob and smile at her shyly. Martha motioned for her to continue with her occupation and took another look at the overpowering surroundings. There had to be some way to tone down Mrs. Corby's extravaganza, she thought, and half-closed her eyes to aid her imagination.

Presently, Patty was scurrying downstairs for a step-ladder. When she returned it was with James, who set up the steps under Martha's direction. He waited for further instructions but was told to hold the step-ladder steady while Miss Gilbert herself climbed up them.

'Whatever are you doing, Miss? Please be careful, you will fall,' cried Mrs. Daly who had come up to supervise Patty in her work. She was scandalized to find Miss Gilbert near the ceiling plucking the crimson velvet from the cherubs' greedy gilt clutches.

The heavy material fell with a thump and a puff of dust. 'There' said Martha gaily, 'I've found you your curtains for the library.'

'Now, why did I never think of that. Now come down, do, Miss, before you lose your balance.'

'Not I, certainly not while the steps are being held by James,' but with the help of the footman's arm she sedately returned to the floor.

'Now, I think we'll take down the valances. With that gilt fringe they are far too deep and heavy for the windows.'

'Let me do that, Miss,' said James, and set to work with a will.

Fingering the velvet, Mrs. Daly remarked, 'Beautiful material this, and it'll cheer up the library no end, but I don't think there is enough to cover all the windows, and there was not a scrap left over after Annie had finished sewing these.'

'I am of the opinion that at least two widths each side can be removed from the window curtains. The curtains should hang straight from the rod and those polished wooden rings and pole are too handsome to hide. You can have all the ties for the library and the valances should yield enough stuff to refurbish some of the cushions. Thank you James... Patty... that will be all.'

As soon as they were alone, the housekeeper turned an eager face to Martha, 'Now, Miss, can you tell me what the trustees said?'

'Of course. Well, they have given me complete authority to do what I think fit for the reclamation of Cobbleigh. I came in here on an impulse, but this is as good a place to start as any.' She laughed, 'I do not feel we have to make ourselves uncomfortable while we are economising.' She looked around her. 'There are one or two other changes I would like to make. I want Miss Fanny to be able to use this room for her friends when they come to stay. For instance, it shall no longer be known as 'Mrs. Corby's Room' or boudoir or whatever she called it. We shall name it something quite different. What about the 'Folly Room? No – not suitable, I suppose.'

'What about the 'Cherry Room', Miss?'

'The very thing, Mrs. Daly, you have hit it exactly right.'

Mrs. Daly picked up a pretty gilt music box, 'This would look ever so nice on the pie-crust table in the withdrawing room.'

'And three white fur rugs are excessive,' decreed Martha. 'One can be put in the sitting room, I do not think the hearth rug in there can withstand one more patch or darn, do you? And those cherubs are ridiculous flying around up there with nothing to occupy their hands. Mrs. Daly, do you have any more of the muslin you use as undercurtaining?'

'I always have a bolt on hand, you never know when fresh curtains are needed. I am sure I have enough to tent the bed.'

'Good – and they can be tied back with the original velvet ties, but I think the fringe should be removed, it would look handsomer in the library. Good heavens! This fringe is real bullion – not pinchbeck as I had supposed, feel the weight of it.'

'No expense was spared.'

'I should say not. 'Now... if the bed is tented in white and with a white rug on either side of it the contrast will not be so overpowering. We should remove some of the other bibelots too. I could do with another candelabrum in my room, I like to read in bed, you know. And if you would kindly see that pier glass and table are put in my room as well, then the cheval glass that is already there can be removed to Miss Fanny's room, where there is a dire need – I dare swear she has no more than a hand mirror. There, with those changes made, the 'Cherry' room will do very well. We will not shut it up, I believe all that crimson needs time and usage to dim it a little.'

'Are you thinking of shutting up some rooms, Miss?'

'That is what I would like to talk to you about. I need your opinion of my plans. I was on my way to ask you and your husband's advice when I stepped in here. But there is no reason why we may not have a preliminary discussion, you and I.'

'I am that eager to hear your plans, Miss Gilbert.'

'Let us sit down, on the bed I think, I do not trust those chairs. Now, Mrs. Daly, it seems to me a terrible waste of time and effort for this whole house to be kept open for just Miss Fanny and myself, so I propose we shut up the rooms we do not require, at least until we are out of mourning. For instance, I would like to close all the bedrooms on this floor except for mine, Miss Fanny's and this one. I do hope soon, some of Miss Fanny's friends will come and stay and if we can fill this room with her friends, she will then forget the original occupant. What do you think?'

'Oh, yes, Miss, of course, and the changes will help too. It will be quite a handsome room when we have finished with it, although nothing can be done about that dratted wallpaper,' she said regretfully.

'It could be whitewashed over, but 'tis expensive paper and would probably spoil. Now, I also think we should close some of the downstairs rooms. We seem to live in the library, quite the most comfortable room in the house in my opinion. So could we not close the withdrawing room and the dining room, in fact all the rooms on that side of the house, with the exception of the estate office?'

'Quite easily, Miss, but what will you use for a dining room?'

'The sitting room is large enough to put in a table that will seat six or eight people, why not do that?'

'Excellent, but after we have closed all the rooms, I shall have some idle hands and I do not like having to make work.'

'Oh, no you will not. I have already thought of that. Now, this is something we should discuss with Daly as well, I propose we let go several the extra people that have been hired recently, such as...'

'Mrs. Corby's dresser, I hope, and who else had you in mind?'

'The surly Miss Foote, naturally, and Monsieur Leblanc. He is an excellent chef, there is no denying it, but we do not need elaborate meals and his talents are completely wasted. Do you think Mrs. Martin would like to be reinstated as cook?'

'I am sure she would. I do hope, Miss, that neither Daly nor myself are asked to dismiss Mounseer, a proper French temper he has and when he runs on in French, it sounds so rude, and no one can understand him, which is perhaps a good thing.'

'Do not worry, Mr. Ackland has agreed to come and do that. Now, would you please find Daly and both of you join Miss Fanny and myself in the sitting room. We must all put our heads together.'

On entering the sitting room, Martha found Fanny coaxing Voltaire back into his cage. 'There you are Aunt Em, I wondered where you were. I've been talking to Voltaire and we were trying to decide where we should begin to save Cobbleigh. "Belay that" and "Avast the Port bow" is not much help, so I hope you have some ideas. What do we do first?'

'Start economising.'

'Scuppered' said Voltaire, flapping his wings, 'Pieces of eight'. They laughed as the bird bobbed his head. Fanny covered his cage with a cloth. 'There Voltaire, go to sleep. You're not helping.' She turned to Martha, 'But where can we economise? We do not lead an extravagant life now? Do you mean I shall have to make do with the dresses you gave me? You mentioned dismissing the servants, will we have to turn them all off? I would not like that at all, some of them are my very good friends.'

'No, my love, nothing quite as drastic as that. First, we must have a conference with the Daly's, they must be the first to know of any changes. If you have any objections to my plans, we should discuss them in private so as not to argue in front of the trustees..'

'Of course, I understand. But you did not have to say that, Aunt Em. I trust you implicitly... without reservation.'

Poor Martha, another load was added to her tender conscience, but she had, perforce, to say with gratification, 'Thank you, my dear.'

At this juncture, the Dalys arrived and at Martha's invitation joined them at the table.

Feeling sure Mrs. Daly had prepared her husband for the contemplated changes, Martha began by quickly running over her plans for Fanny's benefit. Then she asked Daly, 'Do you really need two footmen as well as William?'

'I never needed more than the boy,' said Daly scornfully, 'A great waste of time they are. James now, he is a good one, but his heart is in the stables as Miss Fanny knows, but as for Frank, I shall be glad to get rid of him, lazy he is.'

'This is the time to make your changes in the household. Are there any others you would like to dismiss?'

'Well, as I said before, there will be some idle hands,' said Mrs. Daly darkly, 'once we've closed the rooms.'

'No, there will not,' countered Martha gently, 'for I have further plans I'm working on. Now, I do not wish you to lack adequate help, if at any time either of you need extra people from the village, please tell me.'

'We can manage with the staff we have now, they can close the rooms before they leave,' said Daly.

'I must inform you that the trustees have assented to carrying our household expenses for at least one quarter, so we must bear that in mind when we make our changes.'

For another hour, Fanny listened with respect while the running of the entire house was reviewed. She had never imagined housekeeping to be such a complex task. Until now, her only interest was in stable management, in its way she saw a household was run on the same principles and a spark of interest was lit in her mind. After all, this was her home, her Manor, and she realized she ought to know everything she possibly could about her possessions and responsibilities, her aunt would not always be there to help.

The conference broke up at last with all members fired with enthusiasm at the challenge before them.

'Whew,' said Martha inelegantly, as the door closed behind the Dalys, 'What do you think, Fan? Were they completely convinced all these changes are necessary?'

'Oh, yes,' cried Fanny, 'they need to return the house to where it was in Mama's time ...before P-p-papa... poor dears, they hated the Corbys and were perfectly sweet to me. They never said a word, but they helped me in so many ways. Daly always covered for me when I was in the stables – through sheer pettiness Mrs. Corby tried to stop me from spending my time there – and Mrs. Daly went out of her way to shield me from h-his att-attentions.'

'What a despicable pair those Corby's are,' exclaimed Martha, realising that poor Fanny had not remained in youthful ignorance of their machinations. It made her burn with indignation to think whatever construction was put on her father's inaction, the poor girl had not only to carry the weight of her father's unhappiness, but also the realization he was either too blind, or too indifferent to the situation to intervene. Thank God, thought Martha, she had the servants for friends, but it was a shocking state of affairs when a gentleman's daughter could not rely on her own kindred.

The serious expression on Martha's face made Fanny wonder what was bothering her. Schooled by her recent bad experiences to be seen and not heard, she waited until Martha came back from her thoughts and said briskly, 'Let us go and visit Cassandra and her colt.'

The ladies made their way to the stables where Pat showed them the beautiful creature with great pride. The colt was handsome, alert with an enquiring eye and he would grow into a replica of his sire, save for the star he bore on his forehead.

'What shall we call him, aunt Em? I would like you to name him for me,' said Fanny.

Aware of the compliment Fanny was paying her, Martha said, 'With that star, "Orion", would suit him, for I am sure he will grow up to be a mighty hunter.'

'Excuse me, Miss, please, I don't think it's a good idea at all,' said Pat, 'it sounds too much like O'Brien.'

'No, 'tis a good name,' insisted Fanny, 'I think it is perfectly proper, after all Pat, 'tis you who are running the stables and what is more fitting.'

Amused that her careless words had provoked such a reaction, Martha was pleased to listen while Fanny dealt with the situation. Taken away from her recent troubles, she became a remarkably poised young lady.

Blushing with pleasure, Pat allowed himself to be persuaded, 'But,' he said to Mick later, 'we're going to have a devil of a time of it at the Chevron explaining that one.'

His son laughed, 'Well, Miss Fanny thinks it a compliment, bless her heart, so, Dad, we are stuck with it – we'll just have to live it down.' His father filled his clay pipe with care, 'That's not all Miss Fanny told me,' he said between puffs of smoke. 'She said Miss Marcia had talked the trustees round and she is to try and put Cobbleigh to rights.'

'No!' Exclaimed Mick, 'However, did she manage that?'

'Miss Fanny did not tell me because Miss Marcia stopped her, but I daresay she'll tell us later. Anyway, Miss Marcia said that she knew she could rely on us, and that she wanted our help in selling some of the youngsters, And, do you know, son, she and Miss Fanny plan to work with us and train some o' the three-year-olds to be ladies' mounts.' His son was astounded, 'Go on,' he said derisively, 'Miss Marcia is never going to work with us, Miss Fanny will, but Miss Marcia...'

'None o' that,' said his father sharply, 'Miss Marcia has all the right ideas. She wants to sell some of the youngsters, but not all at once. She explained that she wanted to get the best prices possible after, she said, all our hard work. She wants us to prepare some for the sale ring and she said the better broke they are the more they will fetch. Then she said she was going to get us some help, she could see we were understaffed. Now, m'lad, get a pencil and paper and we will start on a list.'

On the way back to the house the ladies stopped to pet the mares.

'Tomorrow,' vowed Martha to Tadpole, 'we are going for a ride, you and I, and no one is going to stop us.'

At the sound of footsteps, she turned and said, 'Good evening, Timothy, Miss Fanny has told you the news?'

'Oh, indeed, Miss,' he grinned from ear to ear, 'we are ever so happy, we are.'

Smiling at his pleasure, Martha asked, 'Did she tell you we mean to sell quite a bit, Mr. Gilbert's hunters, for instance?'

'Yes, she did Miss, and quite right too.'

'Please tell me, the postillions – we mean to sell the postchaise – do you need those boys? And what about Mr. Corby's groom? If they do not suit, we will find you other help.'

He scratched his head, 'Well, Miss, that Haynes is a good worker, quiet with the stock, but those postillions would never settle to be grooms – eat their heads off, they do and will not lift a finger unless I watch 'em the whole day. I would like them sacked.'

'Thank you, then we'll keep Haynes and dismiss the boys. Mr. Ackland is coming on Thursday for that very purpose. Now, you will need to hire some more help, have you anyone in mind?'

'Indeed, I do, Miss,' replied Timothy instantly. 'Mr. Gilbert's groom will come back, he is pining to.'

'Good gracious, what happened to him?' Asked Martha. Fanny, who had come up quietly and heard the last part of the conversation, realized Timothy was too embarrassed to answer, said 'Jack took exception to Mr. Corby's highhanded ways and Mr. Corby complained about him to Papa. Papa was inclined to laugh the whole thing off until Mrs. Corby took a hand in the discussion, twisted it, and made it appear as if Jack had insulted father and not just answered Mr. Corby back. Anyway, father dismissed Jack forthwith.'

'Oh, the poor man,' exclaimed Martha 'But perhaps he has another situation and will not want to return.'

'Not he,' said Timothy, 'It all happened the day the Master took so ill, and Jack thinks Mr. Gilbert was not rightly aware of what he had done, they had been together since they were boys. He has been living with his auntie in the village, hoping he will be asked to return.'

Martha turned to Fanny, 'We can ride that way tomorrow, Fan, and you may ask him to return, if you wish.'

'Of course I want him back, he taught me to drive a curricle.'

'Thank you, Miss,' said Timothy, 'Jack is just the man to get those hunters ready for sale and he's a right good 'un with the young stuff, the O'Briens will be that pleased.'

'We have made quite a start today,' observed Martha as they entered the sitting room.

'Yes, I suppose this is the reorganization you were talking of. Getting rid of bad servants and hiring new ones.'

'Only hiring new ones where they are necessary... Yes, what is it Daly?' The butler was hovering in the doorway.

'Major Buchan is here, Miss Gilbert, he said you had asked for him to call. I have put him in the library, the withdrawing room is already under Holland covers.'

'Thank you. Please tell him we'll be with him directly.'

9 - Hugh

To pass the time while he awaited Miss Gilbert, Hugh Buchan limped around the library inspecting the books. He was disappointed to find the handsome bindings on the shelves hid little more than fusty sermons and dusty memoirs, so he moved to a chair by the fire and sat staring into the flames. He was anxious to know why Miss Gilbert had sent for him so soon after his return to Cobbleigh. He feared it was to inform him the estate needed the Wool House and his family would have to move. His mother and sister, both faithful correspondents, had kept him informed of local events and, when he had first contemplated selling out, he had counted on Mr. Gilbert allowing him to take over his late father's position. Now, of course, Mr. Gilbert's unexpected demise had entirely changed matters.

Hugh had enjoyed army life, indeed he found he had an aptitude for it. In the camaraderie of his fellow officers he found a home, and the perils of being one of Wellington's soldiers during the advances and retreats of the tortuous campaign years in the Peninsula exciting. He was fortunate in that even though he had been badly wounded by a sabre cut on his thigh, he had survived it and the more debilitating night of exposure in the rain on a Spanish hillside. He was left with a pronounced limp, which discommoded him surprisingly little on the ground and not at all on horseback.

After Waterloo, where he had only sustained a bullet through the fleshy part of his arm, and a horse shot dead under him; he and his Regiment made part of the Army of Occupation in France. He found, to his regret, peace time soldiering was not for him. He had soon discovered that the funds at his disposal, sufficient for a soldier on campaign where it was more often or not a question of supply, and where the acquisition of a scrawny chicken or a bottle of inferior wine was an occasion for general rejoicing in the mess, were now totally inadequate. In war everyone was in a like case but in peace the rich men set the pace and, if a man of lesser means tried to keep up, he very soon ended in Queer Street. So, he sold out, and told his mother truthfully he was glad to be home for good. He was shocked at how frail she was and he now worried that, if they had to remove from the Wool House, he must find another residence for her quickly and, more importantly, a suitable position for himself in order to support her properly.

He frowned at the glowing embers in the grate, their reflection striking his strongly modelled face. He was not strictly handsome, his features were too rugged, but it was an agreeable face, his fine brown eyes showing humour and intelligence. He heard a movement in the hall, and he stood up revealing a not very big but strong shouldered wiry figure, carried with straight-backed military precision.

The door opened and a pug dog bustled in, her wide collar decorated with little silver bells chiming faintly. On seeing a stranger, the velvet ears pricked and the wrinkles deepened on her little black-muzzled face. Her tail in a tight double curl, she strutted to greet him. He was immediately charmed by her jaunty, high-stepping action, and bent down to caress her. He looked up to find a tall, smiling woman in black, watching him. She advanced with her hand held out, 'Major Buchan? How do you do, I am Fanny's aunt. It is good of you to come and see us so promptly.'

Murmuring a conventional phrase he looked beyond her to see Fanny, no longer the little girl he remembered.

'How glad I am to see you again, Major,' said Fanny in greeting. He smiled down at her, 'How delightful you look, Fanny. I remember a little girl, her hair in a tangle, who climbed trees, rode her pony bareback and who always called me "Hugh".'

111

'You were not a Major then, you see,' she smiled at him mischievously, 'I'll call you "Hugh" again if you agree to one condition.'

'And that is?'

'That you never remind me of my tom-boy days.'

'What, have they gone forever?' He asked in mock sadness.

'Of course they have,' she replied with dignity. Martha winked at her, 'Well... nearly.'

'Let us sit by the fire, Daly will bring us some tea in a minute,' Martha suggested.

Hugh, anxious to find out the purpose of this interview said, 'I've brought with me some of my father's farm diaries and account books, they are on the hall table. The Vicar gave me to understand you are to bring Cobbleigh back to what it was, and I thought the diaries might help you.' He held up his hand, 'Please do not distress yourselves, my mother and sister have kept me informed of the state of things and it occurred to me my father's papers could be of some use.' Before either lady could reply to this thoughtful offer, he continued, 'Also, I find we have not paid a penny in rent since my father's death, and I would like to know how much we owe you.'

Martha and Fanny looked at one another, each waiting for the other to speak, then Fanny said, 'Aunt Em please will you explain.'

'Perhaps I should, Fan.' Agreed Martha, 'Major Buchan, do you have any plans for the next few months?'

'No,' he replied, 'I am allowing myself some leave whilst I look around for a position,'

'In that case,' said Martha, 'would you like to act as out bailiff?'

He was surprised and very pleased. Just what he was wishing for had fallen into his lap. Then honesty made him say, 'I know little about running an estate...'

'That is exactly what we require,' replied Martha. He raised his eyebrows. She continued, 'Neither Fanny nor I want a know-it-all who will pooh-pooh our ideas. We also know little about estate management, but I have common sense and Fanny has horsemastership, and you know how to command men, how to organize and carry out plans. Between the three of us we should be able to do very well. Especially now, when you so kindly brought us your father's books to consult. The work on the estate has continued exceptionally well considering the lack of guidance and support the people have received over the past three years. All we really need to do is supply direction. Now, please do not think we will interfere with your running of the estate, we shall remain in the background, but for Fanny's sake, and because she will have to learn to cope sometime, we must have close liaison between us. Now, as to terms, we propose you keep the Wool House, and you be paid what your father was receiving latterly.'

Hugh was too astonished to speak, it was far more than he had possibly hoped for. Again, he felt honour bound to voice some objections. 'Miss Gilbert, Fanny, thank you for your offer, but I know I cannot step into my father's shoes.'

'We do not expect you to,' Fanny looked at him earnestly, 'Aunt Em explained why we need your help. Please Hugh, say you will.'

'I am not worth what you paid my father,' he protested.

'Let us be the judge of that,' said Martha firmly. 'After all, you have great experience, in another field granted, but you will soon learn. As we all will. Do you not see, we are starting at the same level. As for your salary, I asked Mr. Ackland what m-my b-brother paid your father and I find he was not over generous and, I may add, you may have not noticed it yet, but ask your mother or sister, the cost of everything is far higher than three years ago, so the amount we offer now is not so great, but it is all we can afford at present. So please say you will accept.'

'If you put it that way,' replied Hugh, 'There is only one thing I can do. And that is...' he smiled '...accept with pleasure.'

'Oh, I am so happy,' cried Fanny, 'just you wait until you hear what Aunt Em and I have planned.'

He looked at them questioningly and moved his chair nearer. Martha commenced outlining her findings, starting with help for Bodger to clear the ditches and trim the hedges, down to her suspicions of Coggin. Hugh listened with great attention, taking notes all the while, occasionally asking a pertinent question. Martha began to feel that in him they had found a person in whom they could repose complete trust.

'From what you've told me,' said Hugh, 'the most pressing matter is the sale of the overstocked beasts, before we have a murrain decimating the herds. I'd better visit the markets around here and ascertain current prices.'

'That reminds me,' said Martha, 'I must tell you about my market plans, perhaps you would spy out the land for me at the same time.'

Her audience looked at her in surprise. 'You did not tell me about any market plans before,' said Fanny, 'please explain, it sounds exciting.'

'From the first, it has been in my mind we are not sending enough produce to market. Our larders and still room are so stocked, I asked Mrs. Daly if she was expecting a siege, and she replied she could not abide waste, so every year she has made jars of jellies and jams and put up countless crocks of preserves. She agreed with me we would never be able to eat our way through it all, but as she said, what was she to do with them? Mrs. Lloyd in the dairy makes magnificent cheeses, but as far as I can see the surplus milk and butter milk, if it does not go to the pigs, is thrown away, after the needs of the estate have been supplied. When I enquired about her market days, it appears she does not like going to market and therefore only goes once a week to Stroud.'

'That is because she is very shy,' explained Fanny, 'we did not like to force her.'

Martha sighed, so typical of what was wrong at Cobbleigh, 'Well,' she said, what about the egg woman? It appears she only goes once a week too, and she certainly is not shy.'

'No,' giggled Fanny, 'but she only goes to support Mrs. Lloyd, she says. But I really suspect it is to collect the latest gossip.'

'I take it then, neither woman would mind if we relieved them of the responsibility of marketing and let them concentrate upon the preparation of their produce for sale?' Fanny nodded. 'Also,' said Martha, 'I am looking for a man who can read and write and who would like to go to market no less than three times a week. Not only to Stroud but to Gloucester and Cheltenham. I imagine the markets are held on different days.'

'I know!' Said Fanny, 'William – he likes meeting people, he told me, and he did well at school.'

'Does he know how to bargain and sell?' asked Hugh.

'I don't know that,' replied Fanny, 'I suppose that is very necessary.'

'How old is he?'

'Nineteen,'

'A little young for all the responsibility,' commented Martha.

'Not really,' said Hugh, 'but I think I've a better idea. I'll lend you Firkin, my batman, he would enjoy going to market and he could teach young William at the same time. Firkin was the best bargainer, scrounger, scavenger, I've ever encountered – in any language. He always managed to feed me and my horses well. If we put him in charge we'll have nothing further to worry about.'

'Will you not require his services yourself?' asked Martha.

'No, for I do not have enough for him to do. I think he'll jump at the chance to employ his astounding business acumen.'

'We must pay him. How much would you suggest?'

'Very little if you give him a percentage on what he sells. The more I think of it the more I believe we should take advantage of his talents.'

'Fanny, why do you not sound out William, and you Major, would you please ask Firkin if he would undertake our marketing for us. And, Fanny, we must consult the gardener because we shall most certainly want to send flowers and vegetables to...'

'I doubt it,' said Fanny drily, 'he does not like anyone touching his garden. He even begrudges the vegetables we eat, and as for trying to get cut flowers for the house...' she pulled a face.

'We will talk him round, bribe him or some such thing. I will not let a little matter like that stand in our way,' said Martha with a determined air. 'Now, Major, that is enough for today. Fanny and I plan to ride to the village and beyond, tomorrow morning, also we plan to start training some youngsters for the sale ring, so our day will be taken up. Perhaps we could meet here for dinner and discuss matters further. I doubt we'll have to tell many that you are now our bailiff, but we'll inform everybody we meet and let the newsmongers do the rest.'

'And I'll make a start by riding around the estate reacquainting myself with the land and the men,' said Hugh enthusiastically.

In the meantime,' said Martha, 'Fanny and I will read your father's diaries and see what he was doing at this time of year. We'll divide the labour. I'll take the account books and try to understand the revenues and expenditures. You Fanny can take the others.'

'And I?' asked Hugh.

'You have quite enough with all those notes you took.' Martha smiled, 'we will make a précis of our findings for you.'

Fanny groaned.

'What about money for incidental expenses?' said Hugh,

'The trustees have agreed to carry the wage bill for at least a quarter,' said Martha, 'But, of course, we shall need some ready cash for...'

'I know, there may be some in the strong box,' Fanny interrupted..

Martha was surprised 'What strong box is that, Fan?

'The one in the office.'

'Do you think your father, or the trustees for that matter, will have left any money in it?' said Martha with asperity.

'Yes, for they forgot to ask me about it, they were so busy ejecting the Corby's and Mr. Ackland seemed to have found quite enough papers in papa's desk as it was.'

'Let's go and look this instant,' said Martha rising from her chair.

The others followed her into the office. This room boasted a substantial desk, several bookshelves filled with works of reference and farmer's almanacs, two comfortable chairs and a large, highly-coloured map of the estate on one wall. On the opposite wall hung a steel engraving of the most obese bull Martha had ever seen, the copperplate inscription stated it was Mr. Newman's prize shorthorn bull 'Tiny'.

The strong box they were seeking was in the corner behind the desk, cleverly disguised as a small cupboard. Fanny opened the door of the cupboard, put her hand inside along the top edge and brought out a key which she inserted in an inconspicuous keyhole at the back. The false front opened to reveal a leather covered jewel case, several bundles of papers and a cash box. Fanny shook the box hopefully and was rewarded by a musical sound. Eagerly she opened it and tipped out the contents and counted them. Disappointed, she announced crossly, 'One pound, five shillings, six-pence and three farthings and two brass buttons.'

Preserving a straight face with difficulty, Martha said, 'that's a start, but not quite sufficient. I can see I'll have to lend Cobbleigh some money for the present. I did not bring much with me Fan, but I can add about fifty guineas and still have enough for emergencies. I'll go and get it now. Perhaps you would kindly prepare a receipt, Major, and both of you can sign it. I'll be back in a minute'

'That's a lot of money for her to be carrying about with her,' exclaimed Fanny.

'Not really, if she came all the way from Seacliffe,' observed Hugh. 'What do you suppose these papers are?'

'I've no idea, we had better look.'

Shuffling through the scraps of paper. Fanny laughed, 'These are the pedigrees of every horse we've bred on the place... 'til about three years ago. The O'Briens will be interested. What have your there?'

'Several bills,' he grimly replied, 'amounting to about sixty guineas.'

'Oh, no!' Fanny was shaken, 'Mr. Ackland was so sure he knew of them all. And what's this?' She picked up a paper that had fallen to the floor and read aloud, '"*Item – To one gold pendant, containing, viz., two diamonds...*" Oh!' she exclaimed bitterly, throwing the paper away from her, 'So that is what the necklace cost, the one he gave that woman last Christmas, I would like to strangle her with it.'

Martha returned to find Hugh trying to calm an outraged Fanny, her face white with anger. Suddenly she burst into tears and fled from the room. Martha let her go. A hearty bout of tears might make the poor girl feel better.

Seeing Hugh's distress, she said, 'We will let her go, Major, she will feel better directly. The poor dear has had much to contend with. I avoided discussing the Corbys in her presence earlier, but I think I should tell you about them now.'

'My mother mentioned Fanny was very unhappy about them, but no more. I collect that, apart from being a pair of vultures, they were also malicious.'

'Yes, well, she was certainly. In all fairness to Mrs. Corby, which goes against the grain, I might add, she was jealous of Fanny's youth and beauty, I believe. When I arrived, Fanny was abominably dressed in clothes more suited to a ten-year-old. He, of course, scared her dreadfully. I collect he cornered her one day and gave her a very nasty fright.'

The look on Hugh's face was positively murderous.

'Fortunately,' Martha continued, 'Mrs. Daly came along and saw him off with the rough edge of her tongue. In fact, Fanny's only support has been the servants. Thank God, Mrs. Corby refused the guardianship.'

'What?' roared Hugh, 'Mr. Gilbert left Fanny in the charge of that...' he bit off the words he was going to use when he realised they were extremely colourful and very impolite. Martha's eyes twinkled, 'My sentiments exactly, Major. But it was a very good joke you know.'

'Joke!' Thundered Hugh 'I do not see...'

'Certainly,' she replied calmly, 'And so I have pointed out to Fanny. The Corbys knew she was mentioned in the Will, my brother told them so. What he did not tell them that Mrs. Corby was mentioned as guardian to a beautiful young girl who would make her look her age or more, and that there was no monetary advantage to be had. She knew Cobbleigh's affairs were in a parlous state and she flatly refused the guardianship so the trustees immediately turned them out neck and crop.'

'Now I can quite understand why Fanny was so upset. Poor little Fanny.'

'I think that outburst is the culmination of many trials, she will feel better now.'

'But was Mr. Gilbert mad to take up with such a pair?'

'Not mad,' Martha said, considering, 'Very, very lonely. He missed his wife dreadfully, you know, and I think she had the stronger personality of the two. When he lost her support he drifted. That is another problem I have with Fanny. She is upset because he did not turn to her. I do not know how to explain to her that Mrs. Corby must have that same streak of iron in her make-up to attract him, that the late... er my... late sister-in-law must have had. In Mrs. Corby, of course, it manifested itself purely as self-interest, whereas in Charlotte it was in support of her husband.'

'I do not think you can explain that to Fanny – ever,' he frowned, 'if we carry on normally, surely she will forget... in time.'

'One does not forget injuries such as that very easily,' responded Martha, 'our only hope is to divert her mind. I could wish there were some young people around for her to meet. At her age she should be enjoying herself and not worrying her head over debts and the like.'

'There is no one nearer than the Parks, unless a new family moves into the neighbourhood. The youngest people around here are my age.'

'And there is a wide gap between the ages of seventeen and twenty-eight. Later, of course, the gap becomes smaller,' she replied absently as she put the cash box back into the safe, turned the key and handed it to Hugh. 'There, you had better have charge of that. I must go and see Fanny now.' She picked up the jewel case, the pedigrees and the bills. 'Goodnight Major, and thank you for coming to our aid. Will you be able to get home all right? 'Tis very dark, there's no moon.'

He laughed, '"El Soldado" is very sure-footed and he can see in the dark'

'"El Soldado"? Oh, he must be one of your chargers. I should have told you to ask Timothy for a horse whenever you need one.'

'I shall not need one, thank you. I brought my three remaining horses back with me. They served me well and deserve a quiet life, for they'll find Cobbleigh easy going, compared to Spain.'

'Three?'

'I have only three now. Firkin rode one and we used the other as a baggage horse. So they had to be Jacks of all trades.'

Daly was awaiting them with Hugh's greatcoat in the hall.

'I am happy to tell you, Daly,' said Martha, 'that Major Buchan has agreed to take his father's old position. He will, of course, be using the office to transact business. Please tell everyone how pleased we are.' She held out her hand, 'Goodnight, Major, we will see you tomorrow.'

She went upstairs and found Fanny in her room. Woebegone, but much calmer.

'Aunt Em, I am so sorry, I behaved very badly, I do not know what came over me. I hope Hugh was not disgusted – gentlemen dislike scenes.'

'The Major was very worried and when I told him more of the Corbys, well... he was so angry that if Mr. Corby had been in the room, he would have knocked him down.'

Fanny brightened, 'Really?'

'Yes, really. Anyway he quite understood why you were upset. So I should not mention it again. We will all forget about it.'

Fanny nodded her head in relief. She saw the box in Martha's hands, 'Why have you brought up father's jewel box?'

'Is it his? I thought it was yours?'

'No, mine is in the chest over there.'

'What is in your father's box? It's as well to know.'

'His fobs, pocket watches and snuff boxes, I expect. I already have his stickpins and signet ring.'

She was right. Mr. Gilbert had obviously liked fob watches, there were four. 'A watch and its fob is missing,' said Fanny, 'and one of his snuff boxes.'

'I wonder if they were left in his clothes, were they sorted out?'

'No,' said Fanny quietly, 'when Mr. Corby left he took his valet.'

'Did your father not have a valet?'

'Not after Simpson retired last year. Father shared Mr. Corby's'

'Mrs. Daly can go through your father's clothes tomorrow, it should be done before the rooms are closed.'

After her aunt had left, Fanny sat on the day bed reflecting on all that had happened that day. She really did feel much better. Her aunt was always so matter of fact and managed to have the right answer to her problems. She did hope Hugh would forget how ugly she must have looked with eyes red with weeping. She liked Hugh. Indeed, it was comforting to have two such kind people watching over one, she thought dreamily. For the first time in many months, all the tightness that had constricted Fanny's loving heart relaxed, and a wave of contentment flowed through her.

10 - Interesting Gossip

Before Mr. Ackland was allowed to commence the disagreeable business of the dismissals, he was handed the bills Fanny had found in the strong box. For her sake, he made no comment beyond a non-committal grunt as he leafed through them and Martha gave him full marks for not even raising an eyebrow when he saw the staggering cost of the diamond pendant.

'Is that all you have to tell me?' he asked without expression, 'Good, let us then get on with the business I came for. Here are the references in blank, Miss Fanny, perhaps you would be so kind as to write in the names. First, in the order of precedence I suppose, would be Monsieur Leblanc. If he talks French I shall have trouble, can either of you speak it?'

Fanny shook her head, 'Only with an atrocious accent, Miss Bramble was always in despair, and Monsieur Leblanc winces when he hears me.'

'I can,' admitted Martha. At their amazed stares she said defensively, 'there were many émigrés in Seacliffe,' which was no lie, there were. However, she had been taught the language by the vivacious lady who had married her Uncle Edward, a Naval Captain. Upon his death at the Battle of the Nile, Tante Elise had lived with them at Stretton Wakefield until the Peace of Amiens, when she had taken the opportunity to return to France. She had since remarried and Martha still corresponded with her. One of these days Martha intended to pay a visit to her at her chateau in Provence.

'I would be grateful if you would come to my rescue,' said Mr. Ackland, 'Daly please ask Monsieur Leblanc to come in.'

To everyone's surprise, Monsieur Leblanc, renowned for his vile temper, took his congé in good part. It was, he informed Martha, a pleasure to speak with her in his own beautiful tongue and it was a great pity he had not known he could so converse with her before, when he would have told her how he quite understood the necessity for retrenchment. Mademoiselle need have no fear that Madame Martin could not replace him. After all he had taught her, she was a good one that, not quite a light enough hand with the patisserie perhaps, but adequate. Mademoiselle was not to worry about him. A chef of his attainments would never be without an excellent position. In fact, be became confidential, Mademoiselle must understand he had plans of his own. He was on the point of quitting the Manor anyway. Of late, the simple meals required had not truly afforded him worthy scope for his talents. There was one request he had of Mademoiselle, were there any objections to him joining the landlord of the Gilbert Arms and turning this good inn into a truly magnificent one?

Martha, immediately seeing the benefits accruing to Cobbleigh, graciously gave Fanny's permission and the interview ended with great cordiality and many expressions of esteem by Monsieur Leblanc as he bowed over Martha's hand. He bowed to Fanny and backed out of the room as if he was leaving a Royal presence.

'Good God,' gasped Mr. Ackland, 'whatever did you say to him to make him so ecstatic?'

Martha quickly gave them the gist of the conversation and concluded gleefully, 'Not only will the neighbourhood benefit by having such an excellent chef at the Arms, but he will insist upon the freshest of produce and we will gain a steady customer right here on our doorstep.'

Fanny, still not used to this frankly mercenary talk of her aunt's market plans, scowled a little.

Mr. Ackland said, 'I hope the others are as easy to deal with.'

He was to be disappointed. Miss Foote, whose presence had been felt but rarely seen in the household, proved to be very different. She tried in various ways to claim more money. Then she said Mr. Ackland had no right to dismiss her because she was Mrs. Corby's employee. That was a mistake.

He said coldly, 'On the contrary, I have complete authority. You were never paid by Mrs. Corby, you were paid by the late Mr. Gilbert. You are lucky to receive an extra month's wages for, I understand, you have done little or no work. If you had made yourself useful and agreeable, you might have been kept on. Instead, Mrs. Daly tells me, you have been a thoroughly disruptive influence and I am completely within my rights in dismissing you.'

Angry at having to leave a comfortable place, for she was an insensitive soul and never heeded the dislike of others, she did not pause to think, but blurted out shrewishly, 'All right, sir, sack me, an' I'll have a pretty story to tell about Miss's father an' how he an' my mistress...'

'That will do!' Fanny jumped at the sound of Martha's voice, so unlike her usual soft tones. 'None of your insinuations are of interest to us, and,' said Martha firmly, 'if you continue to talk about that which you know nothing, Mr. Ackland will take steps to sue you for slander.'

The attorney regarded the angry woman before him with distaste. Looking down his nose, he gave such a masterly disquisition of the laws of defamation of character that, more by the splendour of his legal vocabulary than by the actual meaning, she was cowed. Whereupon Mrs. Daly took the opportunity to thrust her 'character' into her limp hand and escort the demoralised woman from the room.

'Horrid female,' breathed Martha. 'Mr. Ackland you were quite brilliant in your handling of her.'

Pleased at her praise, he smiled. 'Who is next?'

'Aunt Em,' Fanny said in a tiny voice,' what did she mean about Papa?'

'Do not worry about that Fan, she was so angry she was talking wildly. Mr. Ackland has ensured she now knows it is more than her place is worth to make up stories about her previous employers, so we will hear no further from her,' soothed Martha. 'She wanted to extract more money from us and thought she could try blackmail. Excessively silly woman, don't you think?'

Martha was relieved to see that Fanny after consideration, appeared to accept this explanation.

Dismissing the two footman was, to Mr. Ackland's relief, easily accomplished. Frank was only too happy to leave this dull place run by such a martinet as Daly. James, on the other hand, accepted his dismissal with dismay and ventured to ask if he could speak to Miss Marcia.

'Of course,' encouraged Martha, 'what is it, James?'

'It's like this, Miss,' James looked at her earnestly, 'we all know you are changing things around at the Manor, an' I know you need men to work in the stables. So, Miss, I was wondering, Miss, if you could see your way as to take me on as a groom, to help Mr. O'Brien like?'

Remembering Pat had said James was good with horses, Martha said, 'The person to ask is O'Brien. But are you sure this is what you want to do? Being a groom is a very different life from being a footman?'

'Oh, yes, Miss. 'Twas me father who sent me for to be a footman, not me.'

'Will your father agree to the change?'

'He could not say anything to it,' James replied triumphantly, 'for he's dead these two years come Michaelmas,'

'And your mother?'

'Her too. 'Sides I gave it a good try, Miss, but me heart is not in it.'

'Then you had better ask O'Brien if he will take you on. Come back here after you have spoken to him.' Said Martha.

'Thank you, Miss,' he left the room in a rush.

'I hope you think I have done right?'

'Yes,' said Mr. Ackland, 'you know more about these matters than I do.'

'He is good with horses,' confirmed Fanny, 'I am sure the O'Briens will be pleased. I know he wants to marry Annie, so he would not want to go far from here.'

'Nor do we wish to lose Annie,' said Martha. Then bearing in mind the tumbledown lodge at the front gates that displeased her tidy mind, she said, 'We must ask the Major to have the Front Lodge repaired. They could live there when they are married.'

'Mm., agreed Fanny.

'So the Major accepted. Did he?' said Mr. Ackland.

'My goodness, we forgot to tell you our most important news,' exclaimed Fanny.

'Well, tell me now,' smiled the trustee 'I must admit so much has happened, I am surprised more has not been forgotten. It seems Miss Marcia you are a Deus, no, a Dea ex machina, you descend upon us and all is set to rights.'

'I'm no goddess in a machine,' protested Martha laughing at Mr. Ackland's unexpected flight of fancy.

'Yes, you are,' cried Fanny, 'Of course your machine was a clumsy coach full of animals and you fainted as you descended.'

'Will I never live that down! Mind, that's the only time I've ever fainted in my life, so you must not keep reminding me of my momentary weakness. I am quite sure it was the shock of being at Cobbleigh,' joked Martha. She turned to Mr. Ackland and asked seriously, 'Sir, I do hope you do not feel I've exceeded my mandate?'

'Not at all. I am only too happy Miss Fanny has such a capable person to look after her. Now, Miss Fanny, he said to the silent girl who was sitting in a quandary, 'Tell me about the Major.'

She started, they were both looking at her, 'Oh, I'm sorry, I was miles away,' Indeed she was, for she again distinctly heard her father's voice saying, 'that sister of

127

mine could pull off a genuine faint whenever she wanted to escape unpleasantness.' Hastily, Fanny put the memory to the back of her mind to be examined later, and told Mr. Ackland all about the Major.

An excited James returned with Daly.

'Has O'Brien agreed to take you on?' asked Mr. Ackland kindly.

'Yes, sir, he has that, sir, he says I can start this afternoon, if Mr. Daly agrees. 'He looked anxiously at the butler. Daly smiled, 'Of course, lad, we are glad you are staying here.'

'Annie will be too,' added Fanny mischievously. James blushed and shuffled his feet. 'Miss Martha and I are going to ask the Major if the Front Lodge can be repaired for you both.' The young man was overwhelmed, 'Oh, Miss, thank you, Miss, that means we can be married soon? Please, Miss?'

Amazed to realise he was asking her permission, which made her feel she was grown up at last, she replied, 'As soon as the lodge is ready you can have the Banns read.'

'Do you not think you had better discuss all this with Annie?' Asked Martha.

'Yes, Miss Marcia, right away, Miss, thank you Miss.'

'Go on then, lad,' said Daly, pushing the incoherent young man out of the room.

They all smiled at each other to see such happiness. Suddenly, Mr. Ackland asked, 'Someone is, I hope supervising the people who are leaving? I presume your wife is watching Miss Foote pack, Daly?'

Daly was reassuring, 'Mrs. Daly is not letting her out of her sight, sir. But I must tell you, sir, when she was led away, Miss Foote was saying something about joining Mrs. Corby, and my wife remembered Patty, one of the upstairs maids, sir, and the only person Miss Foote ever passed the time o' day with, remarking some time ago that them Corbys had not gone to Bristol as was supposed, but

128

to Bath. Miss Foote had received a letter from Mrs. Corby and had shown it to Patty. Mrs. Daly and I put our heads together and we surmise, sir, Miss Foote has made it her practice to follow Mrs. Corby from one home to another contriving employment at the householders' expense and it was not by chance we hired her here. Perhaps that's why she was so angry at her dismissal, sir, she had not been sent for,'

His audience sat in stunned silence for a minute absorbing the implications of Daly's remarks. 'Bath' murmured Martha, 'Do you suppose...? she ventured. 'I wonder...' mused Mr. Ackland. Fanny was incredulous, 'They would not dare...!'

'No doubt at all,' confirmed Mr. Ackland. 'Always have their eyes on the main chance those two.' He thought deeply for a moment and the said, 'Ladies,' he paused significantly, 'Instead of asking my Bath correspondent to look after the business of the Laura Place house, I now find my presence is necessary, and I shall leave for Bath forthwith. The postboys can be dismissed on my way to collect my Tilbury, so I must bid you both a very good day.' He rose and gathered his papers.

Martha laid a restraining hand on his arm. 'Mr. Ackland, Mr. Ackland, please sit down, nothing is to be done until you have joined us in a glass of wine and then we will have luncheon, the Major is joining us, and then you may leave, if you must. If, as we surmise, the Corbys have the effrontery to use the house, they have had it – rent free – for over a month. I do not think half a day will make much difference, do you?'

***

'That right sleeve could be lifted a trifle, Annie, I think,' Martha smoothed the black velvet critically.

'Yes, Miss Gilbert,' was the muffled reply as Annie spoke through the pins held in her mouth, 'Miss Fan, drat it, be still or I shall stick you.'

Fanny craned her neck to look at herself in the cheval glass and was pleased.

'There now, Miss dear, please to turn around slowly so that Miss Gilbert can see you.'

Obediently, Fanny rotated before them, and was mightily relieved to hear the fitting was concluded. Much as she liked her new clothes, she did get tired of the endless standing before a looking-glass, and was longing to be out of doors.

There came a tap on the door.

'Come in,' called Martha, and Mrs. Daly entered the room. 'Miss Fan you do look ever so nice,' she exclaimed with a smile, 'I declare you look more like your sainted mamma every day.'

'Do I? But she was dark.'

'It is your eyes and the way you move,' Mrs. Daly told her. 'Now, you have visitors, Mr. and Mrs. Cairnton, they are below and asking whether you and Miss Gilbert are receiving.'

'Cairnton?' Martha's brow wrinkled in an effort to remember where she had heard the name before.

'They are from Bridgecombe, he was a great friend of Papa's, though of late they only met on the hunting field. She has not called for an age. I wonder what brought her.'

'Me, probably,' responded Martha. 'Very well, Mrs. Daly, we will be down directly. Fan, let Annie help you out of that dress – carefully, mind the pins. Put on your morning dress and sit down, love, and let Annie tidy your hair.'

Mr. Cairnton, a tall, burly, grey-haired man of about fifty, came towards them as they entered the room. With bluff heartiness he seized Martha's outstretched hand in both of his and greeted her jovially, 'Well, well, Marcia Gilbert, let me look at you. My word, you have grown into a fine handsome woman, who would have thought it from the little whiny slip of a thing who used to run after Gerald and me all the time. Such a nuisance you were. Do you remember, hey?'

'No, sir, I do not,' she said frankly, 'but a ten year-old's memory can be very patchy, I think.' She gently disengaged her hand and turned towards his plump little wife who regarded her critically. 'How do you do, Ma'am?'

'Well, thank you. Margaret Park told me you were receiving. Just as she told me you have new clothes, Frances, and were looking as fine as fivepence.' Fanny, used to her abrupt manner, smiled.

Martha's attention was claimed once more by Mr. Cairnton who said, 'I hear you have taken on young Buchan, sensible that. Mind you tell him if he needs advice he can come to me, happy to be of service.'

'Thank you, sir, I will tell him. He is not at all ashamed of his ignorance, and neither are we, you are most kind.'

'Nonsense, it is the least I can do for Gerald's daughter. Of course, I am only currying favour because I want Lucifer.' He laughed loudly at his joke.

'Of course,' cried Martha, 'Now I know, you are the one the O'Briens were telling me about, you wanted to buy him last year. Sir, I agree with you, he is worth quite what you offered for him and more, but Fanny would never sell him, you know that.'

'Yes, I do. But I have heard matters here are not as well as they might be, so that offer still stands and I'll add a hundred guineas to it. What do you say to that?'

'Most generous, but I am sure he'll be one of the last to go if we have to sell up.' Martha smiled at him slyly, 'Perhaps, sir, we could interest you in some other horse... as no doubt you know, we have some good ones.'

'Yes, that is one of the reasons we came to see you today, is that grey hunter of Gerald's available?'

'You must talk to Fanny, she is in charge of the stables.'

During the conversation with Mr Cairnton, Martha was aware that Fanny was undergoing a catechism from his formidable wife, and was looking acutely uncomfortable. To rescue her, Martha said, 'Excuse me for interrupting you, Mrs. Cairnton, but your husband is looking for a horse. Fan, I think he would like you to take him to the stables.'

Fanny leaped to her feet with an alacrity that was scarcely polite, bade Mrs. Cairnton farewell, and quickly made her escape.

Martha sat down beside her guest, conscious once again she was being scrutinised with a daunting openness bordering on the impolite. Before she could say anything civil to the lady, Mrs. Cairnton pronounced, 'You have caused a great change in Frances, she used to be such a nice, quiet child.'

Taken aback at the unexpected complaint, Martha retorted, 'Too quiet.'

Without a check, Mrs. Cairnton returned to the attack, 'So you have lived in Seacliffe all these years?'

'Yes,'

'You are forty if you are a day I know, but you do not look a day over thirty.'

'Thank you,' Martha was astonished at this woman's impertinence.

'And you speak French like a native, I hear?'

Good heavens, thought Martha, can nothing be kept secret. 'Yes.'

'How strange,' Mrs. Cairnton managed to deprecate the accomplishment and at the same time render the whole sinister in the extreme. 'I am told you are an expert horsewoman.'

'Thank you,' Martha knew she could stem the flow of questions and remarks that seemed to be the lady's only method of making conversation, but she was too amused. What an extraordinary woman, it is as if she were being interviewed for the position of governess for Fanny.

'You are not married.' This was a statement rather than a question.

'No,'

'You must have had your chances with all that money.'

Martha was nonplussed, to say "yes" would invite further questions in an area she would not care to explore further, so she said 'No'.

'O-o-oh?' This simple sound strung out on an upward note held a wealth of hidden meaning.

This time Martha thought the game had gone far enough so she asked, 'Do you have any children Mrs. Cairnton?'

'No.'

'O-o-oh?' She imitated Mrs. Cairnton's tone so exactly, the lady audibly drew in her breath, stared at Martha with very bright eyes and then burst out laughing. She laughed until she cried, then wiping her eyes with a large man's linen handkerchief, she said, 'Oh, my dear, I was waiting for you to put me in my place and you did it beautifully. I was worried you see, about poor little Frances, so I was determined to see if you were right for her. Otherwise, I would have spoken severely to her grandmother.'

'You know Mrs. Powys?'

'My dear, yes, such a stupid lazy woman. Of course, she was more a contemporary of my elder sister, we lived near them when I was a girl. I shall see her when I next pass through Bath. I much prefer Mrs. Powys's step-mother, Mrs. Birch, who is eighty or more and is as bright and sparkling as you or I, but the poor creature suffers so from an infirmity of the legs and spends most winters in a warm climate. One of her husbands was an Italian Prince, so she has estates south of Rome. If you had not been suitable, I would have written to her and she would have stirred up her step-daughter to take some sort of action.

'I never realised Fanny had more than three living relatives, her grandmother, her aunt Augusta and... er myself.'

'Oh, dear me, yes, she has many half- and step-aunts, uncles and cousins. They are, of course, remote. Mrs. Birch was married three – no – four times and had children by three of her husbands I believe, and at least two of them already had children by their previous marriages. Mrs. Birch happily took them all under her wing regardless of blood ties or not and is looked upon as the head of the family. She has no fixed abode, she travels from one branch of her family to another and they all adore her. During the war, through I do not know what connections with Government, she continued to travel to and from Italy with extra-ordinary ease. A remarkable old lady.'

With a gleam in her eye she edged her chair a little closer and said confidentially, 'Now, my dear, I know I am a nosy old woman, but the goings on in this house were so disgraceful these last few years, and although I say it to you – a Gilbert – I have no doubt you'll agree, a lack of decorum, an unseemliness...

'Say no more, Ma'am, I agree wholeheartedly, I only wish something had been done for Fanny before this.'

'I know. No sooner had I heard you had come to Frances's side, than I determined to visit you.'

The two heads, one grey and the other a glossy chestnut, were close together while Mrs. Cairnton happily regaled Martha with the stories current in the neighbourhood. Martha had only to preserve a discreet silence and let her guest rattle on.

The purchase of the grey was swiftly and amicably concluded when Fanny and Mr. Cairnton returned to the library to find the two ladies chatting quietly.

'Well, Mr. Cairnton,' said his spouse, 'have you found what you came for?'

'Yes, indeed, I've had my eye on that grey ever since Gerald bought him. Well up to my weight and lovely gaits, such...'

His wife, used to his passion for horseflesh, stopped him without ceremony by making her move to leave.

'You never warned me about her,' accused Martha as soon as Daly had ushered the callers out.

Fanny laughed, 'I am truly sorry, I did not expect her to ask questions like that, she probed very deeply, all about you.'

'I have nourished a viper in my bosom,' Martha wailed dramatically, 'I saved you, and you let me walk right into the pit without one solitary word.'

Fanny giggled, 'She really is very kind, and so is he and I'm glad our first sale was made to him.'

'Yes, but she is a tattle-tale. I learned many things about people I do not know and am not likely to meet, but she means very well by you. She tested me severely and in the most alarming manner in order to ascertain if I was a fiend in disguise. I imagine your father had something to do with that.'

Ashamed for her father and his obsession, Fanny took Martha's hand and squeezed it. 'Papa did not have the good fortune to know you.'

Which was precisely the conclusion Mrs. Cairnton had arrived at and was saying so to her husband.

'William, Gerald Gilbert must have exaggerated when he talked of his sister, I find her an admirable woman, and I have never seen Frances as happy as she is now, at least not since her mother died.'

'You know how it was,' said her husband comfortably, 'Gerald was jealous of his sister. It beats me,' he added gloomily, 'how he could have neglected this fine estate the way he did.' He shook his head in disgust as the curricle passed the Front Lodge. On their way to Cobbleigh, his love for the land had been affronted by the glimpse afforded them of tumbled stone walls, and ditches so full of debris from the recent rains the water was across the road in places. 'At least Marcia Gilbert is taking immediate steps to repair the ravages caused by his lack of interest. I had a long talk with Major Buchan, a good young man that, and heard what is afoot.'

'Yes, Marcia told me something of their plans. She is a force to be reckoned with, Frances need have no fear now, and so I shall have the infinite pleasure of writing and telling that odiously selfish Caroline Powys.'

11 - A Managing Woman

There were two letters beside Fanny's plate at breakfast next morning.

She and Martha had been up betimes to look over the horses the O'Briens deemed suitable for training. Pat had shown them seven and they spent an agreeable hour watching Mick ride each of them sidesaddle. On the ground he made a comical figure with his legs draped in sacking to simulate a lady's habit. He found his improvised skirts a great handicap and, upon hearing Fanny's clear laugh ring out, he executed several mincing steps, tripped over the tail of his 'habit' and fell flat on his face. Once in the saddle, however, Martha saw he knew exactly what he was about, as he assessed which animal would prove most amenable. One, a showy chestnut, was eliminated immediately for bucking. It did so determinedly until Mick was dislodged from his unaccustomed perch.

'I'll make him accept the saddle,' Mick insisted from the ground, unwinding the sacking tangling his legs.

'It would take too long,' said Martha, 'we'd be better off concentrating on the ones that accept the change of saddle at once.'

In the end they were left with five to choose from. Martha picked a handsome bright bay mare, with black points, for as she explained to Pat, 'She's a horse to appeal to a lady, distinctive colouring combined with good temperament, and I think this one will sell very well. Which one will you take, Fanny?'

Fanny wanted to take three, and asked Martha if she would look after the other one as well as the bay, but Martha persuaded her that there would be occasions when they would probably not be able to devote as much time to them as they would like, if other matters at Cobbleigh needed their attention. In the end a compromise was reached, Fanny chose an iron grey gelding with a silver mane and tail, and both of them agreed to take turns in working a third, a dainty strawberry roan mare.

Pat said, 'Miss Fanny and I were discussing Major Buchan.'

'If he's as half a good a man as his father, we'll do,' said Mick with satisfaction, 'I reckon you are wise, Miss Marcia, we were worried you was going to try to look after everything yourselves.'

'Oh, no,' said Martha, 'The trustees and I agreed we need a bailiff to keep an eye on things for us, and we are so glad the Major said he would take the position. He will be around to see you today. I know you will help him as much as you can. He is going to help you in selling your stock.'

'Aunt Em,' called Fanny 'I'm starving, I expect breakfast is ready are you coming?'

'Right away,' replied Martha, 'Goodbye Pat, Mick, we shall be back tomorrow at the same time.' She left the yard with Highness strutting beside her.

Eagerly, Fanny discussed the merits of the three horses, She was sure the grey would fetch more than the other two, but Martha maintained the bay's temperament was better and the roan prettier, more amused at Fanny's arguments than through any real conviction. 'If you're so sure, why not place a wager with me?' she suggested. Fanny's eyes widened in shock, 'Bet? With money?' she gasped, then giggled, 'Why not, who's to know?'

'Who indeed,' murmured Martha, 'What about a guinea?'

'A whole guinea, can you afford it?' said Fanny with an impudent grin.

'What do you mean, can I afford it? Your grey will lose.' said Martha haughtily, trying hard not to laugh at Fanny's volte face.

'We'll see, we'll see... so the bet is on?'

'Done,' agreed Martha as they ceremoniously shook hands.

But now Fanny, her breakfast forgotten, was grimacing horribly. She had recognised the handwriting on the top letter. It was from her grandmother, although aunt Augusta had penned it.

Martha, who had seen her pretty mouth turn down at the corners asked, 'What is it, Fan?'

'A letter from grandmamma,' she replied glumly, 'I wonder what she wants now, I suppose it is to insist on my going to Bath.'

'You will not find out its contents by staring at the superscription, open it.'

Fanny slid a knife under the seal, spread the sheet and looked closely at the crossed lines. After considerable trouble she managed to decipher what was written.

'It is as I feared... they are shocked that I am living here without a proper chaperone... they demand I leave for Bath immediately. What shall I do?'

'Write and thank them kindly for their very generous...'

'Generous! Aunt Augusta only wants me so that I am at her beck and call...'

'Generous,' repeated Martha imperturbably, 'invitation but, unfortunately, you are unable to avail yourself of it at present as you are entertaining your father's sister Marcia, who has consented to live at Cobbleigh as your chaperone. As a sop, you may tell them that perhaps you will visit them later on in the year, when Cobbleigh affairs permit. In the meantime, you are their loving and dutiful granddaughter and niece, etc. etc.'

'Do you imagine that will stop them?'

'Do you think your grandmamma really wants you to stay with her? I am sure she has a certain routine which your presence will upset?'

'N-no, I suppose not, but aunt Augusta...'

'Does not your grandmamma rule in her own house?'

'Oh, I see.' Fanny's compassion was aroused, 'poor aunt Augusta, I do not think she has much of a life.'

'No, I would not think so, but at the risk of seeming harsh, my dear, why should you be condemned to the same life, when you have many people here who depend upon you. Cobbleigh, in its way, is just such a hard taskmaster as your aunt and grandmamma.'

'But I love Cobbleigh.'

'Precisely.'

Fanny was stunned at what was to her original thinking and, after mulling it over for a few minutes, while Martha continued with her breakfast, she said, 'Do you mean I do not love my relations as I ought?'

'Have your relations shown themselves as loving you?'

'No, I suppose I am a duty, a cross for them to bear.'

'The why should you feel badly in not allowing them the gratification of doing their duty? Now, Cobbleigh is a duty if you will, but you do not find it so because you love it. However, if you ever stopped loving the place, then it would become a burden. Do not feel slighted by the way your relations think of you, after all relations are thrust upon us but friends we can choose.'

'But you are a relation and I do not feel that way about you.'

'Thank you, my dear, but let us say that we are fortunate that in one another we combine advantages of near relationship with the pleasures of friendship.' After this sententious comment, Martha thought it as well to change the subject. 'Not wishing to pry, Fan, but I do hope the other letter is more to your liking.'

Fanny put down her toast, 'I had forgotten it. She opened it and gave a cry of delight. 'It's from Anna Park, she and her mother will attend Matins at Cobbleigh again next Sunday and hope to take me back with them to Hampton Wick. They leave for Cirencester on Monday to stay with Mrs. Park's sister. That is the expedition they were telling me about. They say that Mrs. Orchard, Mrs. Park's sister, is acquainted with the Duke of Beaufort's steward and she has an invitation to take a party over Badminton while the family is away, and also see the stables and kennels. They knew I would be interested, especially as the Orchards also have a fine stable. And here is a note from Mrs. Park for you.'

Martha read out to Fanny a very civil invitation for her to join the party. Martha immediately decided to decline, she did not want to expose herself too frequently to local society, thinking it better to confine her activities to the valley of the Cobb where she was less likely to meet persons who might recognise her from her other life. Besides, Fanny should be allowed to make a journey away from Cobbleigh on her own, if only for a few days. She had not had much opportunity to mix with people of her own age and it would do her good. So Martha said, 'Do you know, Fan, I do not think I will join you.'

'Why ever not? It'll be most agreeable and everybody will want to meet you.'

'I know, my love but it is scarcely a week since I rose from my bed after that dreadful journey. I would like to stay here quietly and get on with my market plans. I will write my excuses to Mrs. Park and invite her and Anna to partake of luncheon with us before they carry you off to Hampton Wick. Do you not think it a good idea?'

'Are you sure? I would have loved taking you with me. But if you wish to stay at home, then of course you must.'

'Thank you,' Martha was flattered by Fanny's sincere disappointment. 'Oh, by the way, if you would like to invite Anna to stay, you must do so, the Cherry room will be ready by then.'

'Annie has told me all about the changes she is working on. That was a very good notion of yours.'

Fanny's quiet acceptance of the room's transformation hid a wealth of admiration for her aunt's tact and foresight.

'Then Annie must stop and alter that black silk dress of mine with the pearl grey underskirt for you.'

'For me?' squeaked Fanny, 'that is quite your favourite dress.'

'No it is not, I've had it this age. Besides, you will need something suitable for evenings.'

'But what about my white?'

'Your white is lovely, but only when you are en famille. Now, the black will look very nice on you and I'll tell Annie to cut the neckline a little deeper, no need for you to be dowdy. Do you have a pearl necklace?'

'Mother's... and earring to match.'

'Good, Now for the rest of your stay. You will take a riding habit, I imagine, and to travel in I shall lend you a dashing bonnet to dress up your pelisse. We really must find time on your return to shop in Cheltenham, I understand there are some excellent modistes.' She smiled at Fanny, 'I am sure I do not have to remind you that if there is dancing in the evening, which I doubt there will be, for everyone will know of your recent bereavement, but if there should be, I am afraid you must refrain,' Fanny nodded her head seriously.

'And, my dear,' continued Martha, 'if you should have an opportunity, please take care to mention you are selling off your Papa's horses.'

To Martha's surprise, Fanny objected, 'Must I? I do not feel comfortable being a... a horse coper.'

'Horse coper?' I should say not!' exclaimed Martha. 'All I ask is that if you find an occasion to remark to your hostess, "Alas, I have decided to sell Papa's hunters," or, "this year we have so many youngsters coming up we are seriously over-stocked and we have to sell a few", it will be sufficient. Even if the Orchards are not interested, they may tell someone who is. How do you expect us to sell the animals if no one knows they are for sale? Naturally, you would not have anything to do with the actual transaction, you would refer anyone expressing an interest to the Major, after all that is why we have him.'

'I see. Yes, of course you are right. But aunt Em, may I say something else? You told me to tell you if there was anything I particularly disliked.'

Wondering what she was in for now, Martha was wary. 'Of course, Fan.'

'It's this. All your talk of going to market and how you want to organise it on a business-like basis, all this talk smacks of trade and Papa always looked down on tradesmen. He never invited Mr. Patterson to the house because he called him a... a counterjumper...' her voice trailed off.

Mentally consigning the late Mr. Gilbert to the devil, in whose presence he was no doubt already occupying a prominent position, Martha said, 'I am not proposing that you and I open shop, because there is no need. But,' she added vehemently, 'if I had to, I would. And I am sure I would make the best of shopkeepers too.' Seeing Fanny's eyes widen in surprise at her reaction, Martha smiled and continued in a milder tone, 'There is nothing wrong, Fan, in making an honest living. Some people do it by trade; some own land; and, some by working for others. But let me tell you this, it is all the same in the end. There are people with enough money who do not have to soil their hands, and there are people who have to labour for it. Any man who has made his living by honest toil, whether it be manually or mentally is more to be admired than a man who has inherited it from a forebear who may, and I say "may" advisedly, have gained his wealth honestly. Look at some of the great houses today, Fan. Some scions fritter away their fortunes in a frivolous manner, others have gone into public service because they have the substance to do so, and some have not rested upon their fortunes and have continued to amass riches. Bridgewater, for instance, with his love of canals, managed to make a tidy sum while enabling the fast, easy passage of goods and coal to and from cities. Many colliery owners are people who happened to find coal on the land and they are exploiting it to the full, employing many so they – in their turn – may earn a living. I could go on for ever.'

'I-I see,' said Fanny doubtfully, stunned at the discourse unwittingly brought upon herself. 'B-but what about your intention of removing their perquisites from Mrs. Lloyd and the eggwoman, after all, their right to sell the extra produce augments their incomes...?'

'I never planned to leave them with less than they earn now. Mrs. Lloyd, for instance, how much does she earn by selling butter at the dairy door? Not much I'll wager.'

'Well, no, she's far too timid and, because she knows everyone and has a soft heart, she can never bring herself to charge the full price, practically gives it away.'

'And people take advantage of her,' said Martha, 'and the eggwoman, how much does she make?'

'Not as much as she would like. She has a loose tongue and her gossiping frightens away most people. The ones who brave her tongue very often do not want to pay the high prices she charges, she is not very clever I'm afraid, although she knows her poultry.'

'I should have explained myself more carefully. I mean to pay each woman more annually for not selling their extra produce at the door, than they would make by selling the excess themselves. We will sell it all instead through the village shop. That way we will have more control to the benefit of all. I was never going to take away their rights and privileges without giving them something in return.'

Fanny was contrite, 'I'm sorry, aunt Em. I did not understand.'

'I'm glad you told me you were not happy with my plans and we have cleared up this misunderstanding.' She rose from the table, 'Is it not time we set off to speak with your father's groom? I am longing for my first ride on Tadpole, and do you suppose we can manage to go as far as the Combes?'

Their errand was easily accomplished. Fanny had no difficulty in convincing Jack he was needed to help Timothy. Overjoyed, he set out immediately, eager to discover for himself how his beloved charges had fared in his absence.

The ladies continued in their intent to view the Combes, their passage through the village considerably hampered by having to talk to everyone they met. By the time they had escaped the last importunate well-wisher, Martha knew without question Tadpole was the mount for which she had been searching all her life. Well mannered and tractable, with the added spark that required a tactful and sympathetic rider. As they flew at a fast gallop along the track leading to the Combes, skirting the lower slopes of Cobb Beacon, she determined that when the time came for her to leave Cobbleigh, she would buy the mare and take her to Stretton Wakefield. That is, of course, if Fanny would be magnanimous enough to forgive her for the deception she was perpetrating. Pushing that sombre thought to the back of her mind, she gave herself up to pure enjoyment.

As they pulled up, Martha laughed out loud from sheer happiness, she had not felt so alive for years. Fanny, finding such joie de vivre infectious, chimed in merrily. The mares stopped of their own accord puzzled at the strange behaviour of their riders.

It was late in the afternoon when they again reached the back drive.

'I meant to ask you the other day,' said Martha, pointing to an old stone house screened by a grove of beech trees on their left. 'Who lives in the Dower House... er... now?'

'No one since your aunt, my great-aunt, Elizabeth died. Excepting for the Hills... they looked after her and now they act as caretakers.'

'I would like to go over it... er... see it again after all these years.'

Obediently turning Badoura, Fanny remarked, 'I like the Dower House. Perhaps 'tis because 'twas the original house we Gilberts built, in – I think – the fourteenth century.'

'Thirteenth,' corrected Martha with a quirk of her lips. Not for nothing had she endured many a lecture from her late employer on the length of the Gilbert line.

Upon close inspection Martha found the Dower House enchanting. Privately she thought its haphazard lines and unusual angles made it a far friendlier dwelling than the more pretentious Manor. To a person brought up in a sprawling half-timbered house, the Manor's strictly balanced shape, fashionable at the turn of the previous century was austere, almost forbidding. The Dower House was constructed in mellow, honey-coloured Cotswold stone and, like her own home, had started as a Great Hall with later additions built on in all directions. It abounded in nooks and crannies, uneven steps and rooms leading from one into another. No plan had ever been made, this house had grown with the needs and tastes of succeeding generations of Gilberts, and Martha found the effect quite charming.

The Hills, an elderly couple, were cast into a flutter. Put out because they had not been given proper warning and it took all Fanny's persuasion to calm them down. Here Martha had a scare. Mrs. Hill remembered the young Marcia and Martha had to listen to her voluble wonderment at the changes time had wrought. Fortunately, Mrs. Hill's memories, garnered from afar as became the village blacksmith's daughter, were necessarily vague.

To Martha's surprise the house was in good repair, but like so much of Cobbleigh, it needed painting. The garden was a delight, its untamed growth, more attractive to her than the formal flowerbeds and paths laid out in a regular pattern around the Manor.

After they said goodbye to the Hills, Martha, who had been thinking hard, said suddenly, 'Fan, I have an idea. Now, if you do not like it, please tell me and we'll say no more, but I've just thought of a way to make some money if, after our conversation this morning, you will deign to listen,' she teased gently.

'That is wonderful, but until you tell me what it is, I cannot know whether I'll like it or not. Is it very horrid?'

'Depends upon how you look at it.'

'Then tell me. Don't keep me in suspense, I beg you. It must be detestable with all this preliminary.'

'I was thinking that the Dower House is so lovely that it deserved to be occupied. Every house should be lived in, but this one especially needs to be loved. I was wondering Fanny if you would consent to renting it to a nice family, there are at least six bedrooms.'

'Seven, counting the small pink room at the back,' replied Fanny abstractedly. There was a pause while she thought. 'Aunt Em, could it be rented to a family with children my age?'

'I do not see why not,' agreed Martha, delighted with Fanny's immediate acceptance of her idea.

'Then let us ask Mr. Ackland, when next he comes, to look for tenants right away. A family with at least two girls. The house does not need much refurbishing, the furniture is shabby but comfortable, so perhaps they will not mind.'

'We can ask the Major to put some men to painting,' said Martha, amused at this burst of enthusiasm, 'Not much else is needed because the kind of family who would like the Dower House would probably like the old-fashioned comfort.'

'The stables must be cleared and cleaned out, they have been used for storing all manner of objects,' said

Fanny, never far away from the true subject of her heart. 'I'll oversee that myself.'

12 - An Unscrupulous Pair

As was their custom, Giles and Angelina Corby were discussing their activities of the previous evening at the breakfast table, when suddenly they were in the middle of a furious quarrel. They had always fought, but recently Giles realised their quarrelling was becoming more virulent and far more frequent. Ever since leaving Cobbleigh, he feared Angelina was moving further and further out from under his controlling hand.

In this instance Giles admitted, but only to himself, he should not have boasted of his cunning in winning so large a sum from Quincy Fairchild. Although he had noticed signs of Angelina's unusual partiality for a man whom Giles classed as a dull dog, he was truly amazed when Angelina announced that, as she had hopes of snaring Quincy into marriage, he was to stay clear of her prospect. He laughed and said, 'Fairchild is not that foolish.'

She flared up immediately. Seizing a plate from the table, she launched it at his head. It missed him and smashed against the wall, followed by her cup and saucer.

'Careful!' he said keeping a wary eye on her, 'you nearly smashed the looking-glass. I don't want the cost of replacing it.'

The act of violence had calmed her. 'Why should you worry? It's not yours.'

'True. But there'll be a day of reckoning I've no doubt. As soon as the Gilbert trustees find out we are living in Gilbert property. Broken crockery may be overlooked, but a cracked glass for all to see – never.'

'How could the trustees possibly know of this house. 'Twas a secret and Gerald only completed the purchase for me in November. And 'tis mine – he bought it for me, you heard him say it.'

'To live in, perhaps, but he never gave you the deeds, now did he? There was a canny streak in old Gerald. Hard to overcome even when he was in his cups.'

'I would have managed it, if he hadn't died too soon. He hid them somewhere, I never could find where... but I did find the key, two days before he died. Oh, how I laughed up my sleeve at that dragon of a housekeeper in her ridiculous cap, her very stays creaking with disapproval, she never even suspected... all she worried about was me taking my sheets. My own silk sheets, bought for me... But that's beside the point, Giles. Please promise me you will not win any more money from Mr. Fairchild. I truly have a mind to marry him and I do not want him wasting any more of his substance.'

'You're serious?'

'I am serious. I am going to marry him. 'Tis time I arranged myself, as the French say.'

Giles said reluctantly, 'Alright, if you are in earnest, I suppose I will have to stay my hand. Though 'tis a waste, if ever there was a man with no card sense... Are you sure he has enough money for you, he's been running through his inheritance as fast as bedamned? An' I should know, a deal of it is in my pocket this very minute.'

'He has enough. Only let him be married to me, I'll ensure he no longer wastes it. And, dear Giles,' he looked at her suspiciously, when she called him "Dear Giles", she always wanted something from him, 'Dear Giles, could you please come the heavy brother and exact a settlement for me?'

He laughed, 'I'll do more than that, I'll see you safely married, then I'll clear out and leave you two love-birds together.' They understood each other perfectly once more.

'And,' she went on sweetly, 'we must divide the spoils equally. After all, I earned it just as much as you did. I've beguiled your pigeons for you while you've had the pleasure of plucking 'em.'

'Don't tell me you never enjoyed exercising your wiles, for I've seen you. Right from the day we first met, when you were happily setting your uncle's family at each others' throats... all to relieve your boredom.'

She rose to the bait, the memory of her humiliation still raw after all these years, 'I hated them!' she spat, 'they were so virtuous, so kind to a poor relation, the penniless daughter of a man who had killed himself,' she ground her teeth, 'they were too goody-goody, namby-pamby, niminy-pimini...'

'Well, I took you away from all that.'

Instantly her mood changed, she was all smiles as she threw herself against him and flung her arms around his neck, 'Yes, yes you did, dear Giles and I never cease to be grateful but, Giles dear, I must settle down,' she looked deep into his eyes and bravely made an admission he never believed he would ever hear from her, 'I am not getting any younger, you know, and must attach a man before I begin to lose my looks.'

He patted her soft cheek, and said kindly, 'Lose your looks. Never!'

She smiled at him beguilingly, 'Thank you, Giles,' kissing him sweetly.

Although they had not been lovers since the first heady days after she left their uncle's house to go adventuring with him, she never lost her appeal. He kissed her back heartily and grinned at her. 'If you can bring Fairchild up to scratch, you will have earned your half of the money. Wait.' He crossed the room and opened the desk in the corner, pulled out a piece of paper, looked at it, scrupulously added last night's winnings and said, 'As of today, here is the total, half of which is yours.'

She was agreeably surprised by the amount, although she merely said, 'And Giles, I keep the jewellery. For outward show, of course,' she explained hastily.

'It shall be my wedding present to you.' He could afford to be generous for he had carefully forgotten to include in the total, sundry IOU's safely reposing in his wallet.

Once more in perfect agreement, they returned to the breakfast table. Giles picked up the newspaper and appeared immersed. In reality he was congratulating himself on brushing through the morning's events with a whole skin. For some time he had thought Angelina a liability, and now she had revealed her plans for herself and they excluded him, he was free to make his own future without her. Only let her catch Fairchild, he prayed. And he determined to aid her in any manner possible.

These thoughts were interrupted by his valet, Turner, entering to announce, 'Biddy has come and asks to speak with Miss Angelina.'

'Biddy!' Exclaimed Angelina, 'I did not send for her! I wonder why...? Oh, send her in.'

Miss Foote rushed into the room, not entirely sure of her welcome, 'Miss Angelina, I know you did not send for me, but I've been turned orf,' she cried, 'so I came to you straight away.'

'Oh, Biddy, I'm not ready for you yet,' Angelina was quite put out, 'What happened?'

Giles folded his paper, while Angelina petulantly poured Biddy a cup of tea. Biddy took a sip or two of the tepid liquid, set it aside, and began her tale.

'You'd never recognize Cobbleigh. 'Tis all at sixes and sevens.'

'Good heavens, why? Are they selling so soon?'

'I'll tell you,' said Biddy enjoying herself, 'After you left, Miss Fanny's trustees said there was no money. Mr. Gerald was near to bankrupt and Miss Fanny would have to sell and come and live here in Bath with her grandma. I was about to write and warn you when Mr. Gerald's sister arrived...'

'What, Gerald's despised sister?' Both Corby's were amazed.

'That's her. Well, she arrived with her bag and baggage and her smelly animals, looking as if she were to stay. She was in her bed for a week, then when she got up at last, she went all over the Manor and estate making notes. She an' the trustees came to some agreement. She's running the estate now, at least so she thinks, but them trustees are keeping an eye on her an' there was some talk afore I left they're employing some young man as bailiff to 'elp 'er.' She took a gulp of cold tea, made a face, and continued, 'Then yesterday morning that Mr. Ackland, you know the one that read out the will...' she cast a malicious little glance at Angelina, but was rewarded with a blank stare.

Giles hid a smile at Biddy's look, and Angelina' lack of response. Angelina had the happy faculty of dismissing nasty reminders of her faults and failings instantly from her mind. He was sure that by now she had carefully forgotten how her untimely hysterics had ruined all possibility of negotiating a settlement of some sort out of Gerald's estate. 'Go on, Biddy,' he said, 'what happened next?

'Well, he was there at Miss Marcia Gilbert's behest to turn orf ever so many on the estate. Mounseer, the footmen, an' me. Without so much as by your leave,' Biddy conveniently overlooked the wages paid to her, 'I 'ad to pack me traps an' was taken to Gloucester.'

'Oh, Biddy, I was hoping you could stay there until I was ready for you,' said Angelina sighing. 'Never mind, you're here now. And who knows, if all goes right, we may be settled permanently in a nice house in Twickenham soon.'

'Oh, Miss, you 'ave prospects?'

'Indeed, yes. However, 'tis early days yet.'

'You'd better 'urry, 'tis my belief that Ackland is a sharp 'un. 'e'll find out about this 'ouse any day now.'

Giles had a great respect for Biddy Foote's animal cunning and her ability to ferret out interesting secrets. It was one of the reasons why they left her behind at Cobbleigh, that and a disinclination to pay wages when someone else was available to do it for them, 'What makes you think that, Biddy' asked Giles on the alert.

'Nothing reely, 'cept them trustees and Miss Marcia are turning every which way to discover where Mr. Gerald spent all his money. Any day now, they'll come acrorse them deeds for this 'ouse, I shouldn't wonder.'

'Hm,' said Giles, 'perhaps we should think about leaving.'

'Oh, no!' cried Angelina, 'not until Mr. Fairchild...'

'Not leaving Bath,' said Giles, 'finding somewhere else to live.'

'No, Giles, I won't! What reason would we give for removing? We'd never find such suitable, genteel lodgings. And we must never give Mr. Fairchild reason to think we're down on our luck. He'd smell a rat. And I do not wish to give him the slightest reason to question...?'

'Oh! We can say the roof is leaking, wood worm in the floorboards, or some such...'

But Angelina would not be convinced there was any danger of being caught out by the Gilbert trustees. She became extremely upset and threatened a further bout of hysterics. So against his better judgment, Giles relented. Although he did, however, suggest they start packing, in case a sudden removal from the premises became necessary, and privately he determined to look about him for other lodgings.

Mr. Ackland did not know it, but he was only a few hours behind Miss Foote when he arrived in Bath. After leaving his valise at the King's Arms on Broad Street, he called on his colleague with whom he frequently did business and put some enquiries in motion.

Early the next morning, armed with a magistrate's order, and with a stout constable at his elbow, he was banging on the door of the Laura Place house, trusting the occupants of the house never rose early.

Turner, like his master, was not at his best at this time of day. Yawning, he opened the door. As soon as his blear-eyes saw who was on the doorstep, he instantly tried to close the door in their faces. The constable stepped forward and placed a large booted foot on the threshold and leaned his weight against the door, Turner was forced to give way.

Once in the hall, Mr. Ackland demanded Mr. Corby. Turner did his best to usher them out of the hall and into the withdrawing room, but Mr. Ackland declined to budge. He much preferred to keep the front stairs within his sight, sending the constable to stand by the back stairs, while he prepared to wait upon events.

More than twenty minutes elapsed before Giles Corby, attired in a splendid dressing gown, made his leisurely way down the front stairs.

'Mr. Ackland,' he said, holding out his hand, 'Pray forgive me for being unshaven, 'Tis an unconscionably early hour for me...'

Mr. Ackland ignored this overture and said curtly, 'Corby, you have no right to be in this house. I presume your ...er... wife is abovestairs?'

Mr. Corby smiled, 'You of all people very well know, Mr. Ackland, Miss Angelina Corby is not my ...er... wife. She is my cousin. Yes, she is abovestairs.'

'Be pleased to send for her, now.'

'No need to bother her. Can we not settle this amicably between us?'

'No we cannot. You have both broken the law.' He waved the paper he held in his hand. 'I have a court order...'

'Come, come now, Mr. Ackland, do you think your client, Miss Fanny Gilbert or Gerald's sister for that matter, would care to have Gerald's dirty linen aired in public? Just think of the stir, the gossip, the innuendos... As you yourself can testify, my cousin Angelina has no discretion when she is crossed. The scene at Cobbleigh will be nothing to the sensation she'll cause if you take us to court.

Can you imagine the revelations... the juicy tidbits... she'll let fall... and we will call a parade of witnesses, my valet Turner, for instance... he was privy to much... acted as poor Gerald's valet too, latterly...'

Mr. Ackland looked grim.

'There are also,' continued Giles smoothly, 'the other occupants of Cobbleigh... we could, for another example, call Miss Fanny to the stand...'

Mr. Ackland's mind boggled at the very thought.

Knowing he had said enough, Giles merely added, 'All this and more will happen if you charge us. And I should warn you, moreover, Angelina truly believes Gerald bought this house for her, and she is very convincing when she knows herself to be in the right. The key to the house is in her possession...'

'But not the deeds!'

Biddy Foote was woken by Turner. Hastily he explained what had happened. Both of them, long in the service of the Corbys, were well used to such alarms, so she dressed hurriedly and ran down the back stairs to find out more. There she found the constable on guard. He told her to return to her room and wait to be called for. She did not argue, retreated up the stairs and went to waken Angelina.

Unwillingly Angelina opened her eyes. 'What's that you say?' She yawned and stretched.

'There's trouble, I say. A constable is guarding the back stairs an' Mr. Giles is talking to that Mr. Ackland in the hall.'

'Who?'

Mr. Ackland, I told you he was a clever one.'

'I'd better get up. Hand me my gown. No, not the old grey one, the pink with the ruffles.' Angelina went to the wash stand and threw water on her face, and brushed her teeth. Sitting down at her dressing table, she said, 'Come quickly, help me dress my hair... make me look as ingenuous as possible.' Biddy brushed the shiny tresses into a curly mass, while Angelina touched her wrists, neck and arms with lavender water, and wafted a light dusting of powder over her face and shoulders. 'There,' she studied herself critically, 'that'll have to do.'

Silently the two women went to the head of the stairs and listened to the voices rising up from the hall.

'It's as I said, 'tis that there Ackland.' Whispered Biddy.

Angelina motioned her to silence. She took a deep breath to steady herself and, clutching her pink dressing gown to her as if she had just left her bed, she tripped lightly down the stairs.

'Giles,' she said, 'what is happening? Who are you talking to?'

'Mr. Ackland, my dear.'

'Mr. Ackland?' She reached the bottom step and looked sleepily into Mr. Ackland's face with a guileless smile, 'How do you do, sir? Pray why are you standing in the hall? Please enter the withdrawing room, and I will send for some refreshment.'

Although Mr. Ackland was fully conscious of the art she displayed in her charming undress, he was not about to be cozened by it. 'We will stay here, Madam, until you have packed up your belongings and you and Mr. Corby, and your servants, have left the premises.'

'Oh, sir, you would not be so unkind as to throw me out into the street so early in the morning. Why I have this very moment woken up.' She shivered, allowing him a delightful glimpse of her white bosom, 'And I confess I am feeling cold. Please, come, let us go into the other room and discuss this out of the draught.'

'Madam you have only to put on more suitable clothes.'

'Oh! Mr. Ackland how can you be so cruel,' she moaned, great tears welled into her eyes and spilled over. Crying she threw herself into his unwilling arms. 'I am so afraid,' she sobbed against his chest, 'I've nowhere to go, only you can save me. Please help me. Only you can help me. I beg you... don't be so heartless... I'll end in debtor's prison and I'll die...' Angelina had matters well in hand.

All but forgotten, Giles cheerfully stood at one side. He had seen his cousin employ this, one of her most effective manoeuvres, often enough and was eagerly waiting for Mr. Ackland to succumb to these blandishments. Meanwhile an audacious plan was forming in his agile mind.

But Mr. Ackland was not the brother of four sisters for nothing. He calmly unwound her clinging hands from about his neck, and firmly put her from him. 'Madam,' he said sternly, 'Compose yourself.'

'Oh, how can I?' she wailed, 'If you throw me into the street, I've nowhere to go.'

'Madam, I have no doubt a roof will be over your head this very night, even if you have to undo your purse strings and pay for it yourself,' he said dryly. 'Now go, pack up your bags. Take nothing from the house that is not yours, mind.' He waved a paper in her face, 'There was an inventory along with the deeds, and the constable will check it off before you will be allowed to leave.'

Unwilling to acknowledge he was proof against her charms, she was about to try again, when Giles stepped in. He put his hand meaningfully on her arm, 'Go, my dear, please do as Mr. Ackland requests.' They might quarrel, but they were attuned to each other, and she knew immediately he had an alternate plan. She pouted pettishly, and with a great show of show reluctance, retired upstairs.

Bearing in mind Angelina's conviction she would soon marry Mr. Fairchild, and his own wish to continue adventuring alone, preferably on the Continent, Giles determined to act on his brilliant idea. First, he must convince Ackland. 'Mr. Ackland,' he said, 'is there nothing I can say to prevent you from carrying out your plans to prosecute us?'

'I do not see how you can possibly expect any leniency.' Replied Mr. Ackland austerely.

'Well, I have a suggestion. You do not prosecute us, and Gerald's behaviour does not become food for scandalmongers...' he trailed off suggestively.

'Go on, there is more I am sure.'

'Yes, there is. My cousin and I expect to leave Bath shortly. But there is one matter to be resolved before we do. If we undertake to leave this house in, say, three...' he paused, his mind calculating rapidly, 'no let us say...four, yes four, months at the outside. Would you..?'

'No! Out of the question. You must be mad to believe I would leave this house in your hands for four more months...'

'Hear me out. Please. What I propose is this. We pay you a reasonable rent for the full four months, and we undertake to quit the house, probably even before then, leaving all as we found it.'

'Hm...' Mr. Ackland rubbed his chin, reluctantly admiring Giles Corby's effrontery. His proposition even had merit. It had to be faced, here was an opportunity to recoup some of the money the Corby's had bled from Cobbleigh and, what was more important, without a breath of scandal. On the other hand, even if the Corbys were prosecuted as they so richly deserved, it was doubtful any money would be forthcoming, and whatever the outcome, the Corbys would ensure a great deal of noise was made. He grimaced at his thoughts, not only would Miss Marcia dislike her brother's peccadillos made known to the wider world, he knew Miss Fanny would suffer greatly. Could he trust Giles Corby? Well he would tie him up legally as tightly as possible and he would set someone to watch over the house. After more deliberation, Mr. Ackland said unwillingly, 'Well... your idea has some merit, I suppose... However, before I agree to anything, you must pay rent for the two months you have already spent in this house, up to the end of this month.'

Giles, in his calculations had expected no less, shrugged his shoulders. He hid his elation for he had not finished with Cobbleigh and its inhabitants, but he had to wait until the time was ripe, and why not wait in comfort in Bath?

'There must be a signed lease for the full term, and the balance of the rent must be paid in advance,' stipulated Mr. Ackland.

'Done,' said Giles, 'as long as the sum you name is reasonable.'

'And... a sum equal to one month's rent, repayable at the end of the lease, but only if there are no breakages, or losses, and only normal wear and tear on the contents and fabric of the house.'

'I am agreeable, again only if the sum you name is reasonable.'

Mr. Ackland mentioned the amount he had in mind. 'Half of that,' Giles countered instinctively. 'Three-quarters,' offered Mr. Ackland. 'Done,' said Giles, who hoped Angelina, pacified at not having to move, would not scream at him for this sudden extra expense. If, however, she did not snare Quincy Fairchild, they would probably have to pawn her jewels again. So, he thought grimly, she had better manage it for he did not relish having to wrest Gerald's pendant from her grasp.

Mr. Ackland had not finished, 'And I, or my representatives, be allowed to inspect the premises whenever we choose.'

'Within reason. Daylight hours, and not more than once a month.'

'Daylight hours, and twice a month,' said Mr. Ackland firmly.

13 - Shocks for Martha

The sweet scent of gillyflowers pervaded the air and enveloped Martha as she rounded the side of the Dower House on her return from the stables. She was feeling content. Earlier the gelding she was now training had, at long last, overcome his aversion to cows and had passed the herd without balking once. The morning was laden with the heavy hum of bees visiting flowers, flying busily to and from the skeps placed, upon the advice of the Vicar, at the bottom of the garden. The birds sang drowsily as the heat of the sun climbing the sky warmed the day. Tig appeared meowing a welcome, and joined her when she sat down on the stone bench in the shade of an old lime tree. These last few days had not been as occupied as formerly and she no longer felt guilty if she spent a few minutes in quiet contemplation.

She looked with pleasure at the Dower House, her first impressions were borne out, they were very comfortable there. So much had happened during the last few months, and the estate was beginning to look as it should. She was happy in the knowledge that not one roof needed repair, every ditch was cleared, nearly all the hedges trimmed, tumbled walls rebuilt, whitewash and new paint gleamed everywhere. The Major was a strong believer in smartness and in the maintenance of outward appearance, but he had not allowed any sacrifice in the quality of workmanship. Nowadays, when she rode down the village street, she was pleased to see that the Gilbert Arms was no longer conspicuous, every building looked well kept and, although a few chimneys still required attention and a gate needed rehanging here and there, the work would soon be completed. The estate was employing all who required work, for there remained a great deal to be done. A few of the younger men were still drawn to the mills in Stroud, but now some of the disillusioned were returning when they heard of the changes at Cobbleigh.

The biggest change of all was the removal of Fanny and her household from the Manor to the Dower House. This had been caused by Mr. Ackland. He had received Fanny's proposal to let the Dower House with enthusiasm; listened kindly to her wishes with regard to the choice of a young family and promised to advertise immediately. Then, when casting about for suitable tenants he heard of the Wentworths. There were eight children, three boys older than Fanny, two girls about Fanny's age, and three youngsters still in the schoolroom. Mr. Wentworth's uncle owned a large estate in the next Parish. He was elderly, crippled and convinced he would soon die, so he insisted his heir be near him. However, afraid that a large and energetic family would disrupt his comfortable bachelor ways, his nephew sensibly sought a residence within easy riding distance of his uncle. The Dower House being too small to accommodate the Wentworths, Mr. Ackland had the happy notion of offering them the Manor House instead. Fearful that Fanny would categorically refuse to move even for such an advantageous tenancy, Mr. Ackland approached her with extreme caution, Martha wisely staying in the background. Fanny was reluctant at first until she learned of the young people, then she insisted they move in immediately. Mr. Wentworth had already assigned the small property he owned in Kent to his eldest son and was able to transfer the rest of his family to Cobbleigh forthwith. He brought his own upper servants, so the Dalys, Annie and Mrs. Martin moved to the Dower House and the Hills were pensioned off. All this activity provoked intense interest in the village and, when it became clear there would by a hiring of more people, there was rejoicing at these signs of renewed prosperity.

Martha and Fanny had awaited the Wentworths with anticipation. Although Martha was still wary of going too much into local society, she had become so used to her role as Marcia she relaxed her taut nerves and thought no more about meeting these strangers.

The day the Wentworth family arrived Martha and Fanny waited to welcome them in the withdrawing room. The furniture, released from its Holland covers was dusted and polished until it gleamed. Although still shabby, Martha thought the room was looking at its best with bowls of Mrs. Daly's potpourri perfuming the air and vases of flowers strategically placed by Fanny on various surfaces.

When the family entered, Fanny, overcome with a fit of shyness, was quite overwhelmed by what looked to be an invasion. This soon resolved itself into an orderly receiving line. At their head were Mr. and Mrs. Wentworth who were affable and pleasant. He, a good-looking man in his late forties, with a spare frame, was grey haired and energetic in his speech and movements. She, more rounded than her spouse, had been a beauty and was the more placid of the two. It was easy to see where the family got its looks.

After polite enquiries as to their journey, their comfort and health. Mrs. Wentworth called her family to be presented. 'Our eldest son, James, is not with us. He is newly married and he and my daughter-in-law remain in Kent to look after the property. They will visit us later in the year.'

'When they will bring the hunters' said Mr. Wentworth with satisfaction. Fanny, immediately interested, was on the point of asking about them when Mrs. Wentworth presented the two older boys. George, as befitting a young man preparing to go up to Oxford, bowed elegantly and Frederick, equally handsome, smiled charmingly showing an engaging gap between his front teeth. With obvious pride, Mrs. Wentworth then brought forward her eldest daughter, Arabella, who was quite lovely. Dark haired and dark eyed with a cleft chin giving her exquisite face great character. Her sister, Louise, bid fair to be equally lovely, but had not quite yet reached the perfection of her sister. Hers was a softer, more rounded, face and looked remarkably like her mother. The younger two daughters were twins, Amelia and Caroline, both very alike and yet could still be told apart. Now at the coltish stage and still in the schoolroom, they showed promise of future beauty. Their governess, Miss Plum, stood between them firmly holding the hand of the youngest child, a boy of about five, obviously a handful. In spite of her efforts, he would not stand still, he wriggled and at last managed to squirm free. He ran up to Martha and Fanny and made an impressive bow. 'Hello, Ma'am, Miss,' he piped, 'I'm Henry Edmund Robert Wentworth, you may call me Harry.'

Fanny laughed and held out her hand, 'Hello, Henry Edmund Robert Wentworth you may call me Harry. I am Frances Charlotte Geraldine Gilbert and you may call me Fanny.' He chuckled and took her hand, whereupon Highness, who was no doubt pleased to find someone her size, left Martha's side, bounced up to Harry and licked his face. He squealed and said, 'Silly dog, you've a funny face.' The little dog wagged her curly tail, barked joyfully and bounced around him. Everyone laughed and the ice was broken.

'Do you have other funny dogs?' demanded Harry. 'Really Harry.' Hissed Miss Plum despairingly.' Do try for a little more comportment.'

Fanny laughed, 'No, but I do have a parrot.' This excited the company and she was bombarded with questions. 'A parrot, Oh, what kind?' Where is he?' Can we see him?' What's is name?' The young Wentworths clustered about her, while Highness leaped around them barking.

Martha put her hands to her ears, 'Fanny why don't you take everyone to see Voltaire. Stop it Highness. No. Sit.' The little pug sat and sadly watched them leave. Harry's voice floated back 'Why can't the funny dog come to see Voltaire... that's a silly name, this is a funny...' 'Harry' admonished Miss Plum and as Harry subsided.

Fanny said kindly, 'I did not name him, Harry. I call him Volly for short.'

'I can't let Highness go with them. The parrot has learned to imitate her bark, which annoys us and confuses her so, that she barks back in a frenzy. You can imagine the pandemonium. So we keep them apart whenever possible.'

Smiling, Mr. Wentworth said, 'Well, Miss Fanny has found her way into my children's hearts with her parrot. They'll be wanting one of their own, I've no doubt.' A thought struck him, 'you don't by any chance have a monkey as well, do you?' Martha laughed, 'No, that parrot is quite enough.' 'Thank goodness.' Mr. Wentworth heaved a huge sigh of relief.

Smiling at his comical expression, Martha became conscious Mrs. Wentworth was gazing at her fixedly. Martha returned her look with slightly raised brows. The lady went a little pink and said, 'Forgive me, Miss Gilbert, but have we met before? I am sure I know you from somewhere.' Martha's heart plummeted and then began to beat rapidly. Steadying herself, she said as calmly as she could, 'No, Mrs. Wentworth I am sure I would have remembered you if we had met.'

'Have you ever visited our County, Kent?'

'No, never.'

Mrs. Wentworth frowned, 'I know I know you from somewhere. It'll come to me, I expect, probably when I am doing something else. Have you always lived at Cobbleigh?'

'Oh, no. Until about six months ago I lived at Seacliffe in Sussex.'

'Seacliffe, of course! Mr. Wentworth and I visited Seacliffe to stay with friends, two or three years ago it is now. That must be where... it'll come to me... let me think.'

Martha berated herself for her carelessness in allowing herself to be lulled into complacency and she steeled herself for the whole sorry story to come out.

'I've got it!' Mrs. Wentworth exclaimed triumphantly. Martha drew in her breath sharply and waited for the axe to fall. Mrs. Wentworth continued, 'You are quite right. We've never actually met, but I remember seeing you nearly every day the se'ennight we were at Seacliffe.'

Martha allowed herself to breathe but was now very confused, 'Seeing me? Nearly every day?'

'Yes, because you drove an extremely smart Phaeton, dark blue with red accents, drawn by two beautiful match greys, your groom in dark blue and red livery, riding behind on a black cob. You had your companion with you, and always drove along the Parade at a spanking trot. You handled those greys so well my husband was all admiration, weren't you Mr. Wentworth?'

'Eh! What's that my dear?'

'Seacliffe, Mr. Wentworth, the phaeton with those greys, you coveted them... remember.'

Obediently her husband withdrew from admiring the view and bent his mind towards Seacliffe. Mrs. Wentworth continued with her recollections, 'We told our friends that we had seen a very smart turnout and they said it was one of the sights of Seacliffe and it belonged to Miss Gilbert, so that's where I've seen you.'

Martha was heartily relieved, she thanked her lucky stars the Wentworth's friends had obviously given them the wrong impression. Yes she had driven the greys because, although Marcia liked to be up to the mark with a smart equipage, her dislike of horses made her an unsympathetic and indifferent driver. When the horses bolted with her one day, Marcia screamed and dropped her hands, thus allowing the pair to pick up speed. Martha, instead of awaiting their rescue by the groom, seized the reins and in short order brought the pair to a quivering standstill, she then walked them calmly while Marcia recovered from her fright. From then on Martha was allowed to drive. This was not an unalloyed pleasure, for

Marcia was not above criticising Martha's form, and always complained she drove too fast. In reality Marcia enjoyed looking for her friends and having her hands free to acknowledge their salutes and bows as she viewed them from her elegant turnout tooling smartly along Seacliffe Parade. They drove nearly every day during clement weather, until Marcia's illness made even the gentlest of expeditions too much for her.

'Ah, yes, I remember those greys well, lovely movers, do you still have them?'

'Alas no. When my ...er... companion became ill and driving out was too much for her, they were sold. I do regret them, but they needed to work and it would have been a crime to have kept them doing nothing.'

'Quite right too,' approved Mr. Wentworth, 'I wish I'd known they were for sale,' he said wistfully.

'Well, we have plenty of horses at Cobbleigh for you to look at. Fanny loves showing them off. She is in charge of the stables here.' And, to Martha's relief, the conversation turned elsewhere.

The advent of Wentworth family was held to be a great asset to the neighbourhood. Fanny introduced them to the Park family and Anna and her brother were soon joining them all in their many pursuits. Martha was pleased to see Fanny growing in confidence and was happy to let her join in the social events now forthcoming. After her narrow escape from being recognized she was even more relieved to leave the chaperonage of Fanny to either Mrs. Wentworth or Miss Plum. Happily Mrs. Wentworth proved to be a sensible woman and was on the way of becoming a good friend and Martha felt free to confide in her some of her worries about Fanny. That experienced matron was in complete agreement that a girl as beautiful as Fanny should be given the chance of a London season and she offered to present her at the same time as she presented Arabella.

'After all,' she told her husband, 'It will be as easy to present two girls as it is one. I had hoped it would be Louise, but she is not quite ready for the fashionable world, as you will agree. Miss Gilbert is frank in her inability to sponsor her niece, but she said all Fanny's expenses would easily be met. She feels, as I do, that a pretty thing like Fanny should have every opportunity. Mind you, Edmund, I would not have suggested it if Fanny cast our Arabella in the shade, but I am convinced they will both take very well. A dark one and a fair one, a lovely contrast...'

'You are kind and generous, as always... that is why I esteem you so highly,' he responded and with that happy turn in the conversation, no more was said about Fanny that night.

Martha turned her head, though a gap in the trees she could see the Home Field, where she had ridden the gelding amongst the cows. How well they all looked, and so pretty; their glossy hides patches of red, blue, white and black, against the lush green grass. Nearly all the surplus beasts were now sold profitably, the land was beginning to reward the recent work put into it and now there was ample grazing. Although the spring had been wet, crops were progressing and if today's weather held, the hay would be ready for scything soon.

But Martha had received her set backs. The first one was, surprisingly, with William Daly. He had not taken to the intricacies of marketing. Firkin, who had carefully planned his every move to break into the business, had tried his best with William, but both he and William had soon arrived at the conclusion the young man would be happier following in his father's footsteps. To replace him, Firkin took on Isaac Lee who was, as Firkin said repeatedly, 'So sharp he'll cut himself one 'o these days.' From their first meeting, Martha had liked and respected Firkin. A cheerful man, who immediately grasped her intent and, she found, even improved upon her plans. Within a day, he had talked the waggoner into giving him one of his light wagons and, instead of accepting a pair of farm horses, he prevailed upon Timothy to let him use a fine pair of hackneys, but not until he had demonstrated to a critical audience his ability to handle them. Timothy, waxing enthusiastic, found a very handsome set of harness, gleaming with brass. Firkin washed the wagon and painted it a dark green with wheels picked out in yellow. Along both sides of the wagon he inscribed in the same yellow paint and in beautiful flowing copperplate the legend "Fine Fresh Produce from Cobbleigh Manor". When his handiwork was greatly admired by Martha and Fanny, he casually let fall he was once apprenticed to a sign painter, found it a dull life, and had run off to join the army. During the weeks prior to his first journey to market, Firkin and the Major visited all the likely towns within reach of Cobbleigh and, by using their eyes and ears, were able to plot their entry into local commerce accordingly.

When the day came for the first wagonload destined for Gloucester market, everybody on the estate assembled to watch Firkin and Isaac pass in spite of the early hour. Smartly turned out in identical jackets and breeches, with highly-polished boots, everyone commented on how well they looked. Both of them had leather driving aprons wrapped around their waists which they would change for spotless white cloth when they reached the market. Martha, who had found the money for this outward show, quite agreed with Firkin in the necessity of being conspicuous and clean in order to inspire confidence in prospective customers. 'Besides, Miss Gilbert,' explained Firkin earnestly, 'I want the cottagers to see me coming on my return from market, so they can run out and buy what's left unsold for a fraction of the price. That way we should clear everything.'

Upon their return the first day, Firkin reported a small profit, but what was more important, he had a list of orders for the following week. By now, Firkin had built up a regular route and was becoming renowned for the excellence of his cheeses, his preserves, and for his clutches of eggs that hatched out only a reasonable number of cockerels.

Thus Martha was able to agree with the Major that Firkin was a gem. He had even, in his unobtrusive way, found time to keep an eye on Coggin, and the fertility of the Manor pigs improved sharply.

As for the Major himself, she and Fanny found him so sensible and capable that they enjoyed a pleasant friendship as well as reposing complete trust in his judgment. In fact, Martha knew she was more than a little fond of him, but her awkward position of being, as all Cobbleigh believed, twelve years older than he was, made her even more aware of the impossibility of her situation. With eyes sharpened by susceptibility, she saw that he had the same effect on Fanny. Fanny was, apparently, young enough not to be aware of her feelings. Also, George Wentworth was there to divert her attention. With the advent of the Wentworths and the summer, there were many more activities for the young people than Fanny had ever enjoyed before and, although she was still in mourning, she entered a social round that left her quite breathless. Nevertheless, she found time to continue training the ladies' mounts for sale. The wager between Fanny and Martha was happily settled when Fanny's grey was sold for a guinea more than the roan and three guineas more than Martha's choice. Immediately Fanny took on another candidate for training and was also shouldering her share in the running of Cobbleigh. In fact Martha was happy to see Fanny's new-found friends, who had easily absorbed Anna Park and her family into their circle, did not take up all of her time, and she was certainly a much happier girl. Her merry laugh and her voice raised in song were now heard frequently. However, her efforts to whistle through her teeth in the manner of Frederick whose convenient gap between his front teeth made him so proficient, met with such extreme disapproval from Daly that Martha, hiding her amusement, asked her to desist. But nothing could please the household more than the excellent spirits and cheerful noise prevailing amongst the young people. As Mrs Daly remarked, 'I never thought I should see the day when I would be glad to live in a bear garden.'

The other disappointment for Martha was when she was forcibly made aware that her penchant for putting people into places she knew would suit them best was not always what they themselves would choose. She had hoped her idea of apprenticing Copper Lee to Stonewall the gamekeeper, using the precept "Set a thief to catch a thief" might curb the Lee's poaching. But neither was Stonewall happy with the boy's incorrigible belief that all was his for the taking, nor was the boy happy with the gamekeeper's heavy hand. So Martha had to resign herself to the fact that the Lees would continue to poach and evade the gamekeeper.

'It is shocking we should allow them to take whatever they fancy,' complained Martha to the Major,

'There's nothing you can do about it,' replied Hugh, 'The Lees have always poached.'

'I do not see why they should. Did m-my brother not mind? I'm surprised he did not hale them before a magistrate.'

'Did you not know they have the right?' he grinned.

'The right? I do not believe it.'

'Oh, yes, for the Lees are your cousins, several times removed, of course.'

'What?'

'Surely, my dear Miss Marcia, you did not think such red hair was natural in Romanys? Did you not know your great-grandfather, Marcus Gilbert, fell in love with a gypsy and set her up in the house the Lees still own? He had several children by her and these are the descendants.'

'Now I understand why the Lees are so indulged.' She thought of the portrait of the heavy-eyed roué, with the sardonic curl to his lips, adorning the hall in the Manor. 'I never knew he had red hair, the painting shows him in a wig. What a thing. Did his wife not mind them being right on her doorstep?'

'No. For the story goes that after she had given him heirs, she found an interest elsewhere.'

Why be surprised, she thought, her own family – the Wakefields – had their open secrets too. 'Thank you for telling me, Major. Does Fanny know of her disreputable ancestors?'

'I don't think so, but one cannot tell with her, she learned to keep her own counsel at an early age. Of course, she knows there is a tradition that the Lees are allowed more latitude than is customary.'

'I've just realised, Major,' said Martha in a humble tone, 'I've a dreadful tendency to push and pull people into places and situations where I think they would do best, regardless of how they feel in the matter. I am glad you told me of the Lees, now perhaps you would tell me there is any other...?'

'Absolutely not, Miss Marcia. I find you are a kind and very capable woman and can only feel sorry your brother did not know you. I do not want you to judge him solely by his actions during the last few years. He was always good to me. He allowed me the run of his stables and, when I joined the army, he sent me off with one of his choicest hunters. After I was wounded and he learned I had lost one of my horses, he sent out another as a remount. My father told me he had personally tried out several of the horses with a view to finding which had the easiest paces so that my bad leg would not be jarred too much.'

'Major, I only fault him in his handling of Fanny. For myself, I do not care, it is all finished and done with a long time ago.'

The trustees were agreeably surprised when the Major repaid some of the sums of money outlayed to cover the wage bill. Martha herself had long since been reimbursed the fifty guineas she had lent the Manor, and Fanny at last had some new clothes and was no longer beholden to Martha for her cast-offs.

'Not that I did not appreciate wearing your clothes, they're so elegant,' she prettily thanked her aunt, 'but you can have no idea how splendid it is to have something of your very own and absolutely new.' Martha, who had a very good idea, smiling wryly to herself merely said, 'I can imagine,'

Mr. Ackland's hurried journey to Bath which confirmed their suspicions the Corby's were living in the Laura Place house like cuckoos in another's nest, and his practical solution to the problem, was met with both Fanny's and Martha's disapproval. However, when he delicately explained the nature of Giles Corby's veiled threat, Martha was proud of Fanny's response. Fanny had listened to Mr. Ackland's reasoning calmly, and quietly congratulated him on his excellent handling of a very difficult matter.

He then described with feeling Angelina's attempts to bend him to her will. He displayed a hitherto unsuspected talent for acting, and his audience laughed when, with appropriate expressions he demonstrated how, when Angelina cast her sobbing weight upon his bosom he received her in his reluctant arms. Fanny said he mimicked Angelina's voice uncannily when she cried she was destitute and had nowhere to go.

When they were serious again, Mr. Ackland told them of hiring a sharp boy to keep watch on the Corbys and report daily to his Bath colleague. 'Because,' Mr. Ackland said, 'even though my fellow solicitor will visit the house every two weeks on my behalf, I do not trust that precious pair. I took the precaution of enquiring about them before I approached them. In Bath they are known as brother and sister. At present, they're busily setting a trap for a middle-aged gentleman of middling intellect, but considerable newly-inherited wealth. The Corbys are, it appears, helping him spend his gold in riotous living, and she is hoping to marry him. And I have no doubt she'll nab him. She has a sinuous charm, you know, that could be fascinating to someone who cannot see through her to the calculating mind behind those melting eyes.' Mr. Ackland stared into the distance for an instant, then recollecting himself, shook his head and continued, 'When I left, a betrothal was expected any day.'

Martha was curious, 'Do you think they really are brother and sister?'

'I do not know, but they were never husband and wife. In fact, Corby himself told me they were first cousins.'

'Well, I for one, am full of admiration for you, you had a very difficult time with them.'

As he was still shuddering at the recollection of his ordeal, and if truth be known, his narrow escape, all the balm of their sympathy and admiration was needed before he could even begin to smile at the episode.

Reviewing these events while sitting on the stone bench, Tig purring beside her, Martha allowed herself a small measure of pride of accomplishment. But with the added time at her disposal, she now had the leisure to examine the basic dishonesty of her imposture. Her longing to set matters to rights and her certainty in her ability to run Cobbleigh on sound economical lines had led her impulsively to take on her late employer's identity, but now that she was not essential to the smooth running of the estate, her position was hateful. What worried her more than anything was the shock to Fanny when she discovered that the one person she trusted unreservedly had been living a lie.

Martha knew she was cowardly in putting off her confession, but she justified her pusillanimity by the knowledge that she was doing Fanny good. Something will turn up, she hoped optimistically, besides, she rationalised the delay, she could not break the news to Fanny and leave, without someone else being available to take her place. Behind her pleasure in Fanny's happiness lay an uneasiness which she could firmly suppress only when estate affairs occupied her mind. But in the still of the night, she was wakeful, her thoughts chasing one another around and around and, when she did fall asleep, she suffered appalling nightmares. The vivid memory of awfulness often remained with her during the day, although the actual events of the dream dissipated upon waking. Indeed, she was afraid Fanny had noticed all was not well, recently she had looked enquiringly at her on joining her for breakfast. She fervently hoped Fanny's natural reticence and tact would prevent her from commenting.

Once more making a stern resolve to break the news to Fanny just as soon as she could screw up enough courage, Martha rose from the bench, disturbing Tig from his slumber. She walked down the flagstoned path towards the front of the house. On turning the corner, she beheld a smart curricle and pair being driven to the stables by a groom. Visitors, she thought, idly wondering who they were.

Daly met her at the front door displaying an ill-suppressed air of excitement, 'I was about to send William to find you, Miss Marcia, you have a visitor.'

'Who is it?'

He drew himself up to his full height and announced portentously, 'Captain Lord Biscay.'

14 - Reunion

'That feckless Hill woman,' grumbled Mrs. Daly to Annie who, instead of paying attention, was holding her needle and thread in the air. From her position in the Minstrels' Gallery overhanging the Great Hall, she was watching the butler greet a strange gentleman at the front door and ceremoniously usher him into the withdrawing room.

'I wonder who he is,' whispered Annie, 'he's never been to Cobbleigh before, I swear.'

'Have you not basted that linen case yet?' Mrs. Daly stripped the cover from the cushion she was holding. 'Whatever are you gawping at, we've not got all day. What with the move an' all we're all behind like a cow's tail as it is. All these winter covers must come off. Tcha! That woman has let the velvet matt and fray... Annie?'

'Oooh! Mrs. Daly, didn't you see him?'

'See who?'

'Why the lovely gentleman Mr. Daly put into the withdrawing room... ever so tall an' handsome he is.'

Mrs. Daly dropped the cushion. They moved as one accord to lean over the carved balustrade. Daly was crossing the hall in answer to his wife's beckoning finger, when he was diverted by Miss Gilbert entering the front door. The women were too far away to hear what was said and had to contain their impatience until Miss Gilbert vanished upstairs.

'Now, Molly, what is it?' he said innocently, knowing full well what his wife and Annie were after.

'Who is he, Mr. Daly?' asked his wife.

'Captain Lord Biscay.'

'Biscay?' echoed Annie, 'What an odd name.'

Always pleased to demonstrate his superior knowledge, Daly said, 'It is the name of a bay off the coast of France and Spain, which you might know if you read more worthy periodicals than those fashion books and foolish romances you are ruining your eyes with.'

'They're not foolish. Miss Fanny and Miss Marcia read 'em and enjoy 'em too... so there.'

'Anyway,' said his wife, 'How can you expect Annie to read the newspapers when you always take so long...' this was an old complaint so Annie cut in impatiently, 'An' who is Lord Biscay, Mr. Daly, is he a foreigner?'

'I am wondering that meself,' he admitted. 'No, is he as English as you or I, but 'tis very strange, he asked especially for Miss Gilbert, but she does not know who he is either. Ah, well, 'tis probably a new creation, there have been many ennoblements since Napoleon was defeated.'

'Well, whoever he is I think he's a handsome young gentleman, so tall and fair...'

'Not fair, Annie,' corrected Daly, 'Iron grey with a white streak on one side. I can tell you one thing, he's military or morelike a naval gentleman, his face is that weather beaten an' so are his hands.' He considered a moment then added judiciously, 'Nor would I call him handsome, nor young, but if you ladies like grey hair, a brown complexion, a scar down one cheek, a broken nose set out of true, and...'

'Oh. Give over do,' said his wife not believing him, 'You make him a monster.'

'Not at all,' returned her spouse with an injured air, 'It's the truth, although he is a pleasant gentleman.'

Charles was not given to thinking about his appearance. It sufficed him to be neatly and correctly dressed. He stood in the bay window contemplating the pleasant prospect before him. His hands firmly clasped behind his back, a habit his junior officers knew well, their Captain was thinking deeply and should not be disturbed. Again, he was a disappointed man. No one knew Martha at Cobbleigh. The thrill of the chase was palling on him. Where the devil was she?

Irritated, he drew in his breath. The scent from the charming profusion of flowers and shrubs reached him through the open window. He looked at the likely looking horses standing nose to tail, lazily whisking at flies in the shade of tall trees beyond the sunken fence.

Eagerly he swung round as the door behind him opened, only to disclose the butler.

'Miss Gilbert has but this minute returned from her ride, my lord, and she begs you will grant her twenty minutes in which to change her habit.'

'Of course, er... what is your name?'

'Daly, my lord.'

'Thank you Daly, I will be pleased to await her.'

'Would you care to partake of some refreshment, my lord? May I pour you a glass of...?'

'No, I thank you Daly. That will be all.' He turned back to the window and his thoughts.

Sorry he was so summarily dismissed without assuaging his curiosity, Daly quietly withdrew. He would very much like to know who this fine-looking man might be.

The horses beyond the ha-ha broke into a melee, fleeing from a gadfly. The sudden movement served to jerk Charles from his reverie and he looked about him more attentively. This was an extremely fine property. He did so wish he had found Martha residing here in comfort. He wondered, not for the first time since finding those infamous letters, how much further this chase would take him. His call at the Manor House had brought him the intelligence she was not known there. The lady of the house suggesting perhaps Miss Gilbert would be able to help him. Now he was awaiting an unknown young lady who, he hoped, would be able to give him some more positive news.

A quiet voice behind him said, 'Captain Lord Biscay? How do you do, I am Miss Gilbert, you wished to see me? I am sorry to have kept you waiting.'

In turning he presented his right profile to the room. There was a strangled sound, and the same voice gasped, 'It cannot be...T-Tom? Oh, my God!'

Surprised at the horror in the tone, he moved quickly across the floor to the side of a woman who, a stricken look on her white face and eyes tightly closed, stood trembling with her hands clasped to her breast. His strong hands caught her as her knees buckled. Gently supporting her, he guided her to a nearby chair, sat her down and inexorably held her head down over her knees.

Martha had received a severe shock. Her mind roiled with a mass of conflicting thoughts. Part of her brain was amused by the ruthless manner in which the gentleman cured an attack of the vapours. An hysterical giggle rose up inside her, while another part of her mind was examining her mixed emotions. She was startled to discover that, in believing the stranger to be her long dead husband, her own feeling was one of acute dismay. Forcing herself to recover her equanimity, she struggled to sit up. His hand still firmly on the nape of her neck, the gentleman said, 'Rest quietly until you are sure you will not faint on me.'

'Oh, no, I'm quite recovered now, please let me up.'

He released her to anxiously study her face. It was regaining its normal colour. 'Why,' he said in surprise, 'you're Martha. My God, woman, you've led me a merry dance.'

Martha was equally astonished, 'I know who you are, you're ...'

'Charles. Though why you should think I was Tom...'

She brushed her hand across her brow, 'You were in silhouette against the light you – you're both of the same build, and with your hair... Oh, God, you gave me a turn,'

'My dear girl, I am so sorry. I had no idea you would mistake my grey hair for Tom's blond thatch. God, no wonder you were shocked. You thought you'd seen a ghost.' He smiled with amusement, 'That's quite the most startling reaction I've ever provoked.' He frowned in puzzlement. 'I asked for a Miss Gilbert and, come to think of it, that is who you said you were. Martha... What is going on here?'

Not wanting to answer that question at present, Martha countered with, 'Well, you announced yourself to Daly as Captain Lord Biscay, so I had no inkling as to your identity. When did you become Lord Biscay? I never read of it in the papers, was it recently?'

He threw back his head and laughed, 'Just the same Martha. When you wanted to avoid answering a question you always posed questions. But I shall have to know the truth sooner or later, there is something havey-cavey going on.' He said it kindly and Martha, who remembered how he used to shield her from the consequences of her own youthful indiscretions, felt relieved. She would be able to confess her deception to him. He would believe her and understand how it all came about.

'Yes, Charles, I will tell you, all in good time, for I'm in a terrible pickle. But first, I must know how you found me, and why... the why is important, I think.'

He looked at her gravely, 'Where to begin?'

Irrepressibly Martha suggested, 'How and when you became Lord Biscay, of course, I'm dying of curiosity.'

'Oh that,' he said carelessly as he sat in a chair opposite her, 'That is easily told.'

'Well?'

'You knew that my uncle died, of course ? Yes, Meg said she had written of it to you.'

'Dear Meg, she writes rarely. Yes, I knew of it. So, you've seen Meg, how is she? And how did you manage to cozen my direction out of her, as if I did not know? You were always her favourite, why I recollect...'

'Quiet.' Naturally and easily they had fallen into their childhood patterns of conversation. 'You wanted to hear my story, did you not? Meg is well, and my natural charm and address served me with her, of course.' His clear grey eyes twinkled as they grinned companionably at one another.

'To continue, I was at sea when I became Captain Sir Charles Grey, Sixth Baronet.'

'K.C.B.,' added Martha, 'I read you were knighted, although I must have missed your elevation to the Peerage.'

'Yes, yes, but the knighthood was before. Now, where was I... my ship returned to Plymouth for a re-fit just as Napoleon was exiled to Elba. My Lords of the Admiralty saw no point in continuing with the re-fit and I found myself on the beach. There was nothing needing my attention at Stretton Court, so I indulged myself in a journey I'd always wanted to take. A Grand Tour of Europe. I now had the time and the means to gratify my wish, visiting those places hitherto only names on a map to me. I had a most interesting and delightful time.'

'I can imagine,' said Martha enviously, 'and then?'

'The belated news of Napoleon's escape from Elba found me in a small town somewhere in Hungary so, dispensing with my coach, my man Barlow and I rode to Belgium, where a confrontation was likely.

'On Waterloo day, as we later found out, we were somewhere between Brussels and the battlefield. Suddenly we came upon several soldiers – deserters – stealing the horses of a young man and his two servants. They were putting up a strong fight, but were outnumbered. I didn't even have to speak to Barlow, he drew his cutlass, and I drew my pistols. Then hemming the unwilling baggage horse between our mounts, we rode down on the skirmish at full gallop – yelling as if we were the hounds of hell. This attack from their rear discouraged the deserters. They fell back and were quickly routed. The young man and his men were but slightly wounded. He was profuse in his thanks and it was with amazement I learned we had rescued a German Princeling, a cousin of King George's no less. After binding up their wounds, we all rode into Brussels where I took my leave and thought no more of the matter. Brussels was in chaos. We'd missed the battle, but were of some assistance to the authorities who were trying to alleviate the problems arising from the masses of wounded and refugees suffering in the aftermath of battle.'

'I read about it in "The Times"'. Said Martha sadly, 'And the Major, Fanny's bailiff, was there and has given us a brief account of the battle,'

'Then you have a good idea of what it was like,' he said. 'Upon my return to England a month later, I called at the Admiralty to see if they had need of my services and learned "my" Princeling was enquiring for me and Barlow. We immediately waited upon him at his hotel. He presented Barlow with a fat purse, and bestowed upon me the ribbon and insignia of his principality's Order of the Great Bear – First Class, no less. I'll show it to you some day. He also insisted upon my accompanying him to the Regent's next levee. With some misgiving, because I did not feel court life was for me, I went with him. Imagine my surprise when, not only was I embarrassingly introduced to the Prince Regent as Prince Ludwig's "saviour", the Regent informed me he was graciously pleased to grant me a Barony, at Prince Ludwig's insistence. With a tact and sensitivity that few people, I fear, credit him, the Regent told me this creation was not only for the singular service I'd rendered his cousin, but also in recognition of my services to the country. He explained his brother, the Duke of Clarence, whom I had espied nodding and smiling at me behind Prinny, had reminded him that I was, and I quote his exact words, "one of our gallant Captains who kept Wellington's supply ships safe." He also said that, for my deeds in the Bay of Biscay I should take the title of Baron Biscay of Stretton Wakefield.' Charles stopped his tale, and asked her anxiously, 'I hope you do not mind that title?'

'Why ever should I? I think it a very appropriate one,' she replied warmly.

'Well, Stretton Wakefield has been the Wakefield demesne for centuries...'

'It is no longer,' relied Martha briefly, 'And there's no one I would like better to have it than you. Tell me more,' she begged, 'Is the Regent as fat as they say? Had you met Clarence before?'

'Later. I've told you how I became Biscay, now I want to know how you became Miss Gilbert, and no more procrastination, Martha.'

'Don't call me that,' she cried in alarm, 'my name is Marcia.' He knit his strongly marked brows in a heavy frown. She knew she could no longer put off confessing the whole.

Even though she needed to tell someone of her imposture, and even though she remembered Charles's kindness and solid good sense from their childhood days, her story did not come easily. She brought the tale up to the present and included her worries about confessing her deception to Fanny.

She fell silent. With a sinking heart she recognized Charles's grave look. But never, even after her worst childhood escapade had he ever looked so serious.

'Martha, my dear, you must tell the girl and quickly. You know it as well as I do. I know you started out with the very best of intentions, but just think for a moment what a terrible blow to young Miss Fanny's faith in you if she found out from another source you are not her aunt.' He shook his head, 'This is your worst scrape yet, how could you have been so feather-brained?' The seeing her strained look, he took her hand and added kindly, 'Do not worry that I will give you away, I will not. I promise. It's not right, but I do promise. But for everybody's sake you must own up as soon as possible.'

'I know it, but I'm so afraid Fanny will hate me, and I've grown so fond of her.'

'She would be an ungrateful brat if she hated you, but she may very well be disappointed in you. I think she is a lucky young lady to have had you at her side.'

With tears in her eyes, she said, 'Thank you Charles, you can have no notion of how pleasant it is to see you again and to hear you scold me. 'Tis quite like old times. I will do as you say, I will.'

He now thought the discovery of the unpleasant bundle of letters was a happy circumstance after all. Despite this unfortunate imbroglio of Martha's making, he was charmed by the easy renewal of their old friendship.

'You still have not told me what prompted you to search for me. You said I had led you a merry dance, but if you spoke to Meg, she must have told where I was.'

'Ah, but at the time, you see, Meg did not know you were here.'

'But I wrote to her months ago informing her I had decided to act as chaperone and companion to Fanny.'

'Yes, but I set out in search of you the day your letter arrived and Meg could not stop me in time, so off I went to Seacliffe.'

'Seacliffe! Now I see. I am truly sorry you had that long journey for nothing.'

'Not for nothing. I enjoyed Seacliffe. I met Mrs. Bunnett who, by the way, asked tenderly after you and Tig, or was it Tig and you?'

Martha laughed, 'The latter to be sure.'

'And I met your friends the Thistlethwaites, whom I liked very much. She, I might add, asked me to convey her displeasure. She takes it ill you decided to settle in Gloucestershire instead of staying in Seacliffe, if you decided against returning to Stretton.'

'Jessica never wrote of your visit, I wonder why?'

'Because I asked her not to. She is a most understanding lady. I wanted to find you myself, Martha, because we Greys have treated you abominably and you have cause to dislike us heartily...'

'Not all of the Greys, Charles, I married Tom remember, and there was always you and your mother. How is she? She must be very proud of you.'

'She died, alas, before my uncle. But in her later years, what with my Captain's pay and prize money, I was able to make her comfortable, and she no longer had to depend on my uncle's bounty... do you know Martha, that hurts still.'

'I well remember how you hated being beholden to him. You used to tell me there would come a day when you would throw it all back in his face.'

'I did,' he replied with satisfaction, 'the very day I received my first substantial sum of prize money, I wrote him an impertinent letter. I never received an acknowledgement, but Mother's allowance ceased immediately. Mother used to try and make me laugh at his foibles, telling me he was quite satisfied if, during her visits, she thanked him no less than twice a day for his goodness. But I did not find gratitude marched well with my pride.

'Do you remember that last summer we were all together? You were fourteen, or thereabouts, a streak of lightning... never quiet for an instant.' His eyes took on a faraway look for a moment, then he put his head to one side and bent a critical gaze upon her. 'You have changed. You now have a restful capacity for stillness, and you've become a very handsome woman.'

'Dear Charles, for this encomium, much thanks. You have not changed much. Except for your nose and that scar... which I must tell you are most becoming. How did you acquire them?'

'The scar from a splinter of wood, always a hazard in a fighting ship and the nose, well,' he ran a lean brown finger over the bumpy bridge, 'I was trying to quell a brawl. I plunged into the fray instead of putting a belaying pin to good use.' He laughed reminiscently, 'The ship's surgeon, a man with a sense of humour, wanted to put a splint on my nose, but I was not going to allow my shipmates more reason for mockery than they had already, so the result is as you see.' He grinned at the recollection.

'Yes, well, as I was saying before you diverted me with more questions, that last summer before the Peace of Amiens was broken, when I was nineteen and Tom must have been sixteen or seventeen, I realized Sir John was afraid of my influence, even then Tom was restive, straining to leave that unhappy household. Later my uncle blamed me for encouraging Tom to go to sea. It must have soured him more than ever when Tom was the one to be killed and I, as the son of his younger brother, became his heir... I am sorry Martha, that was clumsy of me.'

'No, no, please, 'tis of no consequence. It was a long time ago and belongs to another life.'

He blurted out, 'Why did you marry Tom, Martha? Surely you knew Sir John would be vindictive?'

'We never gave it a thought. I was young. In love for the first time. Father approved. Poor father, he thought it would protect me from Sir John.'

They sat in undemanding silence with their own thoughts until Martha said, 'What prompted you to seek me out?'

'Eh? Oh, a bundle of letters I found. I'll give then to you, you'll want to read them when you are alone. Some of them are addressed to you although they've all been opened.'

'But surely a bundle of letters would not send you on a journey across England?'

'Well, the first one I came across gave me a very nasty turn, I can tell you. You see,' he told her gently, 'when I read it, it appeared I had no right at all to Sir John's estate.'

'What can have made you believe that?'

'It was your letter to Lady Grey announcing you were increasing. A funny stilted note, not at all your usual form of expression.'

Dawning comprehension widened Martha's eyes. 'But I lost...'

With compassion, he said, 'I know, my dear, that was in the next letter. Then there are other letters which you should have. But my main reason for seeking you out is because you have been cheated of your rights. I should have come to you sooner, I already knew Sir John had made no provision for you in his Will, and when I realised you could have been the mother of the sixth baronet, my disgust with him was boundless. Meg told me of all you had to bear; the gossip and innuendos when your hasty marriage became known, spread no doubt because of my uncle's refusal to acknowledge you as his daughter-in-law, and the fight you had to retain what little of your father's property that was left. Thank God, you had Mr. Todd at your side. Meg sent him to see me. I needed his approval before they would let me have your Seacliffe direction. I took to him immediately, and I shall employ him myself. Although I like your Henry Thistlethwaite even better. Anyway, I determined to find you and offer you a proper allowance and the choice of...'

'No, really Charles, you do not have to do that, I have managed very well on my own.'

'That you have,' he replied, 'but I must insist, it is your right. Especially since my inheritance was greatly enlarged at the expense of yours.'

'No, no. You keep it for your heirs, I have all I need.'

'Martha Wakefield, you're stubborn, stiff-necked, and, and...'

'And pig headed,' she laughed, 'you always used to call me pig headed, Charles.'

'Do not divert me, I want you to have the allowance, and do not cite my heirs, I do not have any, bar a remote cousin or two.'

'Not even a wife?'

'Not even a wife.'

'But you are not...?'

His lips twitched, 'No, Martha, I am not. And before you ask me more indiscreet questions and quite put me to the blush, let me tell you, I have been presented to numerous eligible young ladies and I've been wined and dined by prospective parents-in-law until I am ashamed to accept their hospitality under false pretences. How could I tell them that in not one of their daughters, charming and accomplished though they were, did I find the one person with whom I desired to spend the rest of my life. That is why I travel.'

'Poor Charles,' said Martha mournfully, with a wicked twinkle in her eye. 'Never to have loved...'

'I did not say that.'

Seeing his sudden frown of pain, she desisted from teasing, immediately regretting she had allowed her lively tongue so much freedom. Her lack of proper respect for his feelings came from her pleasure in meeting his again. She was treating him the way they used to treat one another those many years ago. Biting her tongue, she waited apprehensively for him to give her a sharp set down.

Instead he attacked, 'You, Martha, why have you not married again?'

'For the same reason as you, Charles, I've become over nice in my requirements for a husband, I fear.'

'Yes, Mrs. Thistlethwaite thought so too.'

'You never discussed me with Jessica? Really, Charles...'

'Oh, in the kindest possible way. I learned of Mr. Greening, for instance.' He grinned at her annoyance, 'Come let us call a truce on that subject.'

She agreed with relief. But she was mightily intrigued, she would dearly like to know what manner of woman had caused him that sudden grimace of pain. But she merely said, 'How long can you stay with us, Charles?'

'I called in here on my way to Somerset. I am standing godfather to my First Officer's new son. We decided, that is Meg, Mr. Todd and I, you should be allowed to return

188

to Stretton in your own good time, but I did wish to make sure you were aware that you are eagerly awaited.'

'Must you leave so soon,' she cried, 'surely you can at least stay for luncheon?'

'I would be delighted, I am looking forward to meeting Fanny. This afternoon, however, I have to be on my way,'

'Perhaps you could visit us for a longer period on your way back?'

'I was hoping you would invite me, I shall be returning the following Saturday, and I can stay for a few days – I saw a likely inn in the village. When I leave, then perhaps, you will be ready to come with me. I should be happy to escort you to Stretton.'

'Thank you, but no, Charles. Even if Fanny wants to throw me out neck and crop, I still would not be ready, I could not leave her without a suitable chaperone, and I doubt a suitable one could be found quickly. But I do promise I will eventually return to Stretton when all this is over.'

'And you will accept a proper allowance?'

'I'll think about it. Thank you again, Charles, you are very kind.'

'Nonsense, it is your due.'

Fanny's voice was heard in the hall, speaking with the Major.

'There's Fanny and the Major now, luncheon must be ready. Quick Charles, remember, I am Miss Gilbert, Marcia, or aunt Em, as she calls me, and you and I met, oh, where? I know, when you were visiting friends in Seacliffe.'

'Miss Gilbert, I am yours to command,' bowed Charles, 'and I do believe 'twas your Mr. Greening who introduced me.'

15 - An Unreliable Bird

Presiding at the head of the table, Fanny's lively curiosity knew no bounds. She would like to know what this pleasant gentleman, so suddenly introduced into their midst, meant to her aunt. It was obvious they were good friends, although it appeared they had not seen each other for a long time. And he was doing aunt Em a deal of good for she had recovered some of her sparkle after looking tired and wan recently.

Charles enquired of Hugh, 'Major, you have sold out, I collect. What was your Regiment?'

'The Twenty-eighth, my lord.'

The North Gloucestershires?'

'Yes – you know them, my lord?'

'I saw the Sphinx Badge at Corunna – we evacuated some of your regiment. A shocking business, we were late to rendezvous – contrary winds off Vigo. I'll never forget the terrible sights on that beach. Were you there?'

'I was. After two hundred and fifty miles on foot over desolate mountains and through inhospitable country.' He shuddered at the recollection and smiled grimly, 'I was one of the lucky ones – I had boots. D'ye know, my lord, we lost more men due to bad weather, exposure and the like, and lack of supplies than we did to Soult? Even though the ships were late, my lord, there was never a more welcome sight.'

'And Moore was still able to pull off a miracle before he died – saved an army to fight another day. You were in the Peninsula as well, I would suppose?'

Hugh nodded, 'Talavera, Salamanca, Vittoria,' the sonorous names of a few of his Regiment's Battle Honours rolled off his tongue, 'then – Waterloo.'

Fanny's eyes were shining, she and Martha exchanged speaking looks. Hugh had never spoken to them of his army career except to tell amusing tales of campaign life.

'And you, my lord, what was your ship?'

'Dragonfly,' replied Charles.

Hugh was excited, 'Sir, I mean, my lord, are you er – were you the Captain Grey, who captured La Belle Héloïse?'

Charles admitted he was.

'I was never more pleased to meet you in my life,' exclaimed Hugh. He turned to Fanny, 'I must tell you how we gloried in the stories of the Dragonfly's exploits. The very knowledge she was cruising off the coast, harrying the enemy so our transports could get through, made us feel our backs that much safer. Whenever we could lay our hands upon a newspaper we used to read all the published reports from beginning to end. The news, my lord, of your storming that French battery, I forget its name, cheered us no end.'

'Yes, well,' said Charles with a slight smile, 'that shore battery was placed so the enemy could run their ships under its guns to safety, and 'twas a plaguey nuisance. Something had to be done, so we looked to the example of Cochrane and the Imperieuse who were so successful in the Gulf of Lions. Let me tell you, Major...'

Martha listened with a pride she freely acknowledged to be proprietary, as an earnest discussion sprang between the two men. She was distracted when Voltaire, from his cage in the window, suddenly rattled his feathers, he then opened his beak and, to her horror, said, 'Martha, Martha' in a perfect imitation of Marcia's voice. Martha, who in that very moment was raising her wineglass had only, by a supreme effort of self-control, managed to put it down without a quiver. Talk was halted, as she calmly turned to the hovering Daly and said, 'Cover his cage, please, we cannot have him join in the conversation, or worse still start barking, he is so raucous.' Everyone laughed, and the men became conscious they had monopolised the conversation long enough, and turned back to the ladies.

While Hugh and Fanny discussed a colt suffering from colic, Charles said to Martha in an undertone, 'I admire your audacity, but it worries me. I like your 'niece', and she is very fond of her 'aunt Em'. I am confident she will not be too hard upon you.'

They exchanged a conspiratorial look and Fanny, happening to glance towards them, caught it speculating upon its meaning. Her intuition had already told her this gentleman was more than a mere acquaintance of her aunt. An aura of quiet pleasure in each other's company hovered around them and Fanny knew a pang of envy. She tactfully withdrew her gaze and returned to her conversation with Hugh.

After luncheon, as they prepared to go their separate ways, Fanny, as she bade Charles farewell, said hospitably, 'We looked forward to your return, my lord, when I hope you will stay long enough to see around Cobbleigh.'

Martha said, 'If you must be on your way so soon, Charles, I'll walk with you to the stables.'

He stood looking down at her. Now that he had had the opportunity of observing her with that delightful girl, he realised what an astounding woman she was. All was serene although he knew there must be turmoil in her heart. She had given Fanny more than a chance to save her heritage. With her quiet affection and strong common sense, she had procured for Fanny the stability she so desperately needed.

He repeated, 'I like your 'niece', my dear, but you must confess your secret. I told you someone else may tell her before you, although I did not expect it would be a confounded parrot. 'Twas fortunate we were deep in talk when he called out your name.'

'Yes and copying so exactly Marcia's voice that it gave me a terrible fright, but' seeking his reassurance, 'he was not very clear, was he? And it's the first time he'd said that, perhaps he'll forget, and not do it again.' she added hopefully. 'Perhaps,' he said doubtfully, the scar stretched one corner of his mouth upwards, emphasising his humorous look, 'How you kept your secret this long beats me. Anyway, I suggest a fatal accident should overtake that damned bird quickly, before he has time to do real damage.'

'That is too much to hope for, I would not, could not, condone it. Fanny adores him.'

'How will you explain matters to Fanny, my resourceful one, if you have still not told her the truth, when that indiscreet bird really lets the cat out of the bag, so to speak, as it very probably will? I urge you to tell her today.'

'I-I'll try. I'll definitely try. I will.' Not convinced, he took her hand and led her out of the room begging her not to rely on thinking she could get away with it indefinitely.

They reached the stables and Martha was able to approve, in perfect sincerity, Charles's curricle and matched bay geldings. He looked down at her in amusement, 'I'd forgotten what a keen judge of horseflesh you are, I am honoured you like them.' He took her hand in farewell, 'Upon my return you must do as Fanny says and take me around Cobbleigh, I want to see everything you have described.'

'With pleasure. I am never tired of showing the place, and there's an ideal hunter for you, up to your weight and with manners to burn - are you looking for a horse?' she asked with an impish grin and they laughed together as happily as in the old days. Barlow, at the bays' heads, sharply observed this elegant lady in black to whom his Captain was reluctantly bidding farewell. It was many months since he had seen the Captain look that carefree and he silently blessed whoever she was.

Martha stepped back as Charles climbed into the curricle and gathered the reins. At his order Barlow released the bays and quickly hopped up beside him. With a smile for Martha and a flourish of his whip, Charles drove the equipage out of the stableyard.

'Barlow,' said Charles, as they drove through the newly painted and properly hung front gates. 'What have you been telling them at the Manor?'

'Nothing, my lord.'

'Do you expect me to believe that, man. What did you talk about with that stableman, for instance?'

'I only told him about our seafaring days, my lord.'

'Nothing about why we were here?'

'No, my lord, seeing as how I truly don't know why we're here, my lord.'

'Yes, you do. When you 'my lord' me that many times. I know you're hiding something. Out with it.'

'Well, my lord,' he grimaced and began again, 'Well, Captain, I know as how you're looking for Mrs. Thomas Grey, an' I would say, from seeing the lady you were talking to, you've found her. But Captain, they at the house and in the stables never mentioned a Mrs. Grey, all they can talk of is a Miss Gilbert an' a Miss Fanny, so I kept quiet, Captain.'

'Good man, I knew I could rely on you. As far as you are concerned, 'tis Miss Gilbert we came to see, and it is Miss Gilbert we visit again upon our return. Now, what else did the people talk about?'

'About hows they'd fallen on evil days until Miss Gilbert came and rescued them,' and he went on to report all he had learned. Charles, not particularly surprised, was gratified to hear Martha had wrought more finely than perhaps even she imagined.

Later that afternoon, Fanny was cleaning out Voltaire's cage. As was her habit she was talking to him as he perched on her shoulder supervising the operation. Suddenly, in the manner if his kind, he cocked his head on one side, cast a knowing look at her and favoured her with his new party piece. She was not really listening at first, and had not understood what she was hearing but, as soon as the meaning became clear, she listened intently for a few minutes. There was an odd sensation in the pit of her stomach. With infinite care she returned the bird to his cage, took off her apron, folded it deliberately and went in search of her aunt.

Meanwhile Martha, seeking to reflect on her pleasure at Charles's sudden appearance and also wishing to delay reading of the letters he brought, had repaired to her favourite bench under the lime. She sat thinking while her hands were busy with whipping a fringe she had knotted onto a white shawl for Fanny. Panting extravagantly, Highness lay spread-eagled at her feet. From a low branch overhead Tig watched them. When Fanny joined them, Martha exhibited her work and said, 'I think I'll embroider a pattern in violet where the fringe joins the silk, 'twill match the trim on your new dress admirably. What do you think?'

Without preliminary, Fanny said, 'Who is Martha?'

Totally unprepared, Martha, in suppressing her start of surprise, jabbed her needle into her finger. With considerable poise, she put down her sewing, licked away the drop of blood and carefully wrapped the injury in her handkerchief, while thinking furiously she was not prepared, not ready to tell all, in spite of Charles's strictures.

'We lived together in Seacliffe, as companions, why?' Her outward calm successfully hiding her inward turmoil.

'No reason. Except Volly has been talking in your voice and a strange lady's voice, and the strange lady said "Martha" all the time, and your voice said "Marcia".'

'How extraordinary! Well, to answer your question,' Martha temporised, 'I suppose it was because,' she began slowly then in a rush as inspiration came to her aid, ' because we used to amuse ourselves by trying to encourage him to speak and we thought the similarity of the names would double the intensity of his training. Not that it did any good.' Why now? When I am not ready to reveal the truth, did that ridiculous bird have to remember, she thought despairingly. 'Has he said anything entertaining?'

'No, except to call "Highness" in your voice, and complain in the other voice that Tig had again been on the sofa and left hairs.'

Fanny, for reasons she would not allow herself to question, had not rendered the true version of Voltaire's remarks. What he actually said astounded Fanny, for the whiny voice he used had been of the Martha person and yet he had said 'Martha, that odious cat has left hair on the sofa again' and even more peevishly, 'Martha, fetch my drops.'

Her aunt's carefully hidden agitation did not escape Fanny's eagle eye, but, although she sensed a growing mystery which should be cleared up, she hesitated from taking an irrevocable step. She loved and respected this woman and rather than make a decision on the spot and perhaps bring grief to all, she determined to let matters rest for the nonce. She tucked the episode away with the other little discrepancies she had noticed about her aunt, and managed a gay little laugh saying, 'I wonder when he will shock Daly by imitating him?'

Heaving a sigh of relief at this reprieve, Martha returned some inconsequential reply.

The letters lay spread out on her bed. Martha stood for a long time looking down at them, reluctant to start what she knew would pain her almost beyond bearing. To postpone the raking up of old memories, she picked up the communication from Mr. Todd that Charles had also brought to her.

A personal note rather than one of his official documents, Mr. Todd had allowed himself to show his true friendship.

He wrote in his clear hand,

> *"I would be remiss, if I did not urge you to*
> *accept the generous allowance Lord Biscay*

proposes, and also the Malt House as your residence in Stretton Wakefield, if you should not wish to end the tenancy of your Manor. You need have no compunction in accepting these things from his hands because, as he was eager to point out, they are your due. Both Meg and I find him an honourable man we hope he can persuade you to return, if not with him but soon, to your rightful place..."

The letter continued with reference to a minor piece of business awaiting a decision from her.

She must think deeply before putting herself under an obligation to Charles. She was sure she need never fear him, but she was wary of being in anyone's power after being independent for so long.

Fortified by Mr. Todd's concern, she turned to the other letters. She was not going to like this.

In date order, the first was her own letter written to her mother-in-law. Charles was right, it was stilted. She remembered her dislike at being forced by Tom to write in a letter what she had wanted to keep to herself as a cherished secret.

"Dear Lady Grey," the spikiness of her writing showed her irritation,

> *"I am requested by my husband, your son, to inform you that I am increasing and we expect our child to be born in about five months' time. I will let you know as soon as I am safely brought to bed.*
>
> *Meanwhile I remain your dutiful daughter-in-law.*
>
> *Martha Grey."*

Young prig, thought the older Martha. No wonder Lady Grey did not answer it. This must have been the letter that stunned Charles.

She picked up the next one, again addressed to Lady Grey. She recognized Helena Blake's hand. Vaguely she recollected asking her kind friend to write to Lady Grey, but she had never seen the letter before.

"Dear Lady Grey," it ran.

"It is with deep sorrow I tender you my condolences upon the loss of your son, and it is with a heavy heart that I have to lay a further sorrow upon you. Martha has asked me to write this for her and give you the sad news that, worn out with the recent loss of her father and the shock of the death of her husband, she lost the child she was carrying. At present, too weak to hold a pen, she has asked me to tell you her anguish at not being able to present you with a grandchild, and begs your forgiveness."

There had been no reply to Helena's letter, and Martha had never written to the Greys again. Ten years later, Martha could feel compassion for Lady Grey, a much tried woman. Now, she could excuse her silence, but it had hurt at the time. So completely under Sir John's thumb and he so unforgiving of the despised daughter-in-law who had failed him.

The next letter puzzled her. How could one of her letters to Tom be in this bundle? Then her horror rose when she realised what had happened. She had never received his effects. His Captain had called upon her when he was next in harbour and had personally expressed his condolences. At the time, she remembered, he had shown surprise at finding her still in Plymouth, he had expected her to be with the Greys at Stretton Court, where he had despatched Tom's sea chest.

In her mind's eye, she could see what she had written in that letter. It was the one where she had told him of the circumstances of her father's death and of her condition. She did not need to reread it, she could well remember her mixture of emotions when she told him the news. In his reply, he had been perfunctorily sorry for her loss, but far more interested, not so much in the prospect of becoming a father, but in the benefits accruing therefrom.

She picked up the next paper and gasped in pain. It was an unfinished letter of Tom's addressed to her. In this letter he reprimanded her for not obeying his previous instructions, and peremptorily commanded her to return to Stretton, because, as he callously pointed out, "*If the old man is ever going to forgive you,*" wryly Martha noted the pronoun, "*now is the time for him to do so.*" Here the letter stopped as if he had been interrupted. She looked at the date and a wave of nausea washed over her, he must have been writing it when the enemy was sighted. She crushed the letter in her hands; just as well she had never received it. Perhaps he would have softened the tone if there had been time for him to finish it properly, but as it was fate had been kind in misdirecting it to Stretton Court.

The next letter was from Charles, again addressed to her at Stretton Court. It had also been opened. She spread it out. It was his letter of condolence after Tom's death. A kindly and compassionate expression of concern, it ended with his sincere request that if ever she needed his assistance, she had only to ask him. Well, she had never received it. She supposed when he did not receive the courtesy of a reply, he no longer thought of her.

There were two letters from Tom's Captain, one addressed to her at the Court and the other to the Greys. Both with broken seals. Numbly, she read the kind but stock phrases of condolence. When she had finished the last sentence, she let the papers drop and sat huddled miserably in her chair, staring into space.

Suddenly tears welled into her eyes and she began to sob wrenchingly. She cried for the young Tom and the young Martha. She cried for the lost child, for her father and even for the unhappy Greys. She cried until it seemed she could not stop. At last no more tears came. She sat up, pulled herself together with an effort and went to the wash stand to bathe her face. That done, she picked up the scattered letters, folded them carefully along their accustomed creases and locked them securely into her writing box. Exhausted by her bout of weeping and drained by the day's unusual events, she took off her dress and lay down on her bed. Instantly she fell into a deep sleep.

16 - The Debt of Honour

Save for the squeak of quill on paper and the occasional drumming of Fanny's fingers on the table as she counted, silence reigned in the Morning Room. The ladies of Cobbleigh were observing their Saturday morning ritual. Fanny was bringing the Stables Book up to date, and Martha was studying Firkin's market accounts and weaving further plans in her head. She looked up at Fanny's sigh of despair, 'What is it?'

'I can never remember how many pints to a quart and how many quarts to a peck. I wrote it all on a piece of paper for quick reference and now I can't find it.'

'It's on the floor by your foot, I collect.' Fanny retrieved it, 'Thank you. Ah, it's eight quarts to a peck,' She was about to return to her work when Martha said, 'Fanny, may I give you some advice?'

'Of course you may.'

'If ever Firkin comes to you and asks you to lend him money to go into business for himself, I beg you Fan, much as you dislike trade, I beg you not only to advance him all the money he needs, but also make very certain you become his partner. Silent partner, if you wish, but definitely you should become his partner.'

'If you recommend it, aunt Em then of course I will, but why are you giving me this advice now?' There was a look of fear in her eyes, 'You're not leaving me are you, not right away?'

Martha, who had been trying for such an opening ever since Charles had left said, 'Fan, I've been meaning to speak to you, but I've been putting it off.' She tried to gather her wits after this unpromising beginning. 'It is true I shall not be with you forever. When you know the story, I do hope you'll forgive me.'

'I would forgive you anything, aunt Em. But when you marry Lord Biscay, you'll go so far away...'

Her mind on her confession, Martha's usual quickness deserted her. Startled she said feebly, 'What? Oh, I have no intention of marrying, Fan, that's not what I have to tell you.' As she said this they were distracted by the sound of a carriage drawing up at the front door. They looked at each other interrogatively.

'It is far too early for Charles, I wonder who it can be?' Reprieve, thought Martha, she found confession far harder than she had ever anticipated. All week she had tried for an opening, but Fanny proved elusive, almost as if her social engagements had taken over her life. Martha even suspected Fanny, for some reason, was avoiding a tete-a-tete with her.

In the hall voices were raised in annoyance.

'That's strange,' commented Fanny, 'Daly is having an argument... Oh, the Devil' she turned a stunned face to Martha, 'It can't be...'

'My love, you really should not use such an exp... what is it?'

'Giles Corby,' said Fanny, only half believing what she said.

'Are you sure?'

'Yes, I've heard his voice too often to mistake.'

The door opened and a flustered Daly marched into the room. Very upset and breathing hard, he almost shouted, 'Miss Gilbert, Mr. Corby has arrived with this.' Outraged, he thrust the sheet of paper into her hand. 'He demanded to speak with Miss Fanny, but I told him that if a member of the family wished to communicate with him they would do so through Mr. Ackland. But he insisted. The matter was too urgent, he said, there was no time to be lost. So I've left him in the hall with William to watch him, and I took the liberty of telling him that you, Miss Gilbert, would receive him at your convenience.'

Martha read the paper. As she did so, she drew in her breath, it was worse than she could possibly have imagined. Fanny hovered at her elbow, 'What is it pray, what does it say?'

Martha included the butler in her reply, 'Bad news, I am very much afraid. Mr. Corby wants quite a large sum of money from us.'

At Fanny's shocked exclamation, she added with more assurance than she felt, 'Do not be upset, my love, we will come about. I'm sure something can be arranged satisfactorily.' She looked at Daly, 'Have you read this?'

'I took the liberty, Miss Gilbert. This is a copy, he would not let the original out of his hands.'

Fanny looked askance, so Martha explained, 'This purports to be a copy of an IOU from your father in which he engaged himself to repay a loan of five hundred guineas with fifty guineas interest exactly six months from the date of signature.' She read the paper again, 'Good heavens, that is today. If your father or his heirs and assigns... that's you, Fan... are in default, Mr. Corby could and would take immediate possession of the collateral which, in this instance is, and I quote *"that parcel of land known as the Water Meadow"*.' As the enormity of it dawned on her, Fanny gasped in horror. To lose the Water Meadow would mean the loss of the very heart of her Manor property.'

Daly said sadly, 'Come to think of it, Miss, I mind when the Master signed that paper. Yes, 'twas during that extraordinarily hard frost before Christmas last. You remember, Miss Fanny, the Master and his guests were unable to hunt an' they passed the time by playing games of chance.'

Fanny's lips trembled as she nodded.

Daly sighed, 'Mr. Corby chose well.'

'Yes,' said Martha briskly, they could not afford to repine, 'And we now have to pay him off. If the original is genuine.'

'No doubt of it, Miss, I am more than sorry to say. I only saw it for an instant, but it was the Master's hand right enough.'

'We do not have much time, the note is due today.' Martha stared in front of her for so long Daly and Fanny started to fidget, wondering if she had forgotten them.

She came out of her trance at last to say bracingly, 'Well, the first thing we must do is confirm the IOU is genuine. If Mr. Corby insists upon the letter of the IOU we must then find five hundred and fifty guineas before midnight tonight. I do not suppose he will take another note from us, so it will have to be actual money. What I cannot understand is, why he did not go to Mr. Ackland.' Brightening, she repeated, 'Mr. Ackland, someone must ride to Gloucester and fetch him immediately. I'll write a letter of explanation.' She picked up her quill, but put it down when Fanny wailed, 'Oh, no, do you not remember, this is his week to visit Bristol? But perhaps his partner?'

Martha replied in exasperation, 'Things have been wretchedly planned – the Partner is in London for a month, Mr. Ackland informed me of it the last time he was here.'

Seeing Fanny's face fall, she said quickly, 'There is nothing we can do about that, so we shall have to start gathering money ourselves. We must have no compunction in borrowing all we can and pay of the horrible man. What do you suppose Mr. Corby wants with the Water Meadow?' A dreadful thought struck her, 'Oh, my God, but of course, he is in a perfect position!'

'Perfect position for what?' asked Fanny.

'Either hold us up for ransom,' seeing Fanny's puzzled little face, she explained, 'force us to buy back the Water Meadow at far more than five hundred and fifty guineas, or...', 'Or?' Prompted Fanny. 'Or, sell it to Mr. Whatever-his-name is... the tea merchant. You told me, did you not, Fan, his wife desired it?'

'Yes.' Agreed Fanny gloomily, 'and he'd pay handsomely.'

'An' no questions asked, Miss,' corroborated Daly.

Their downcast expressions spurred Martha to speak in a rallying tone, 'We are not finished yet, not without doing everything we can to raise the money. First of all, Daly, show in this Mr. Corby, if you please, then stay with us, I want you to confirm my brother's fist.'

Left to cool his heels in the Great Hall under the disapproving eyes of the young footman, Giles Corby nonchalantly seated himself on the uncomfortable oak settle. He helped himself to a pinch of snuff from a beautifully chased gold box. Returning the box to his pocket, he crossed one exquisitely booted leg over the other and looked about him. His face was bland, but the thoughts tumbling about in his mind were full of annoyance.

A badly botched mess they had made of the whole Gilbert adventure. This was a lovely old house, and from what he had seen coming up the front drive, the place appeared to be thriving. He had never seen it so prosperous. He and Angelina should have either sat it out, or cut their losses and left at least a year ago, when it became evident she was unable to cozen Gerald Gilbert into entering a formal liaison. It was almost as if they had lost their touch. From the very day they met Gerald, matters had gone awry. To begin with, as Angelina continuously pointed out, it was unfortunate they were introduced to Gerald as husband and wife but, as he repeatedly explained to Angelina, it was as husband and wife they lived in Cheltenham with the Carrington-Smiths and, if he had taught her nothing else in the years they had been together, surely consistency in their stories was the one precept he had managed to drum into her.

Of course, at the time he had not fully taken into account her growing recklessness. In a momentary fit of boredom, she could quite suddenly do something stupid and jeopardise their positions without thinking. By and large, however, their years together were pleasant and even profitable. It was not until they fastened their hooks into

Gerald he noticed Angelina was changing, and for the worse. Usually he could control her, but she eluded his dominance when he noted with dismay her jealously of Fanny. He should have cut the connection then and there, as he admitted to himself, he was also tiring of that particular game and perhaps some of Gerald's inertia was gripping him because he let matters slide until it was too late. He even, and he shuddered at his crass stupidity, let himself get so bosky one day, he cornered Fanny meaning, he assured himself, only to drop an avuncular kiss upon her averted cheek. Her dragon of a housekeeper saw him and swept down upon him. Made a terrible fuss and the household resented them more than ever. He was thoroughly ashamed he had allowed himself to lower his guard and it was right then and there he resolved to leave Cobbleigh, with or without Angelina. By that time, unfortunately, Gerald was already suffering from the chill which killed him. Then came the mortification of watching while Angelina, his careful coaching gone for naught, completely lost her head. Instead of being bought off handsomely, they were lucky to escape as they did.

Restlessly, he rose from the settle. He was tired of kicking his heels awaiting Miss Gilbert's pleasure. He took a turn about the hall.

Well, Angelina had married her swain, and he gave her away with a brotherly flourish. He wished them joy in each other. Giles smiled grimly to himself, Quincy Fairchild was less foolish than he appeared and, although he was generous in his settlement on Angelina, it was only after he was assured Giles was off abroad for a prolonged visit.

Without rancour, and with a fairly plump pocket, punctiliously he had taken leave of the happy pair. Even with the Gilbert debacle, the last years had turned a modest profit and he declared that perhaps Italy would prove a pleasant place in which to establish himself. Even with the money he had accumulated for such a venture, it seemed foolish not to avail himself of the sum due him from the Gilbert estate. He liked the odds, he could not get less than five hundred and fifty guineas, and he might secure a great deal more. Not at all dismayed at the reception accorded him by Daly and William, he was complacently sure that, as he had managed Gerald, he could as easily manage Gerald's despised sister.

Daly returned to the hall and said austerely, 'The Misses Gilbert will receive you now,' and held the door barely wide enough for him to pass through.

Martha was agreeably surprised by her first sight of Mr. Corby. He looked every inch the gentleman from his carefully dressed hair, well-tied cravat, excellently tailored coat to impeccable breeches and boots. He wore a gold signet ring on the little finger of his left hand and a handsome fob hung from his watch pocket. His good-looking face lit with a charming smile which would have quite taken her in if she had not already heard all about him.

'Giles Corby at your service,' he bowed smoothly. 'Miss Gilbert, I understand you are dear Gerald's sister.' Martha moved her head a fraction in haughty acknowledgement. Undeterred by her frosty glance, he smiled sweetly and turned to Fanny who was endeavouring to retire behind Martha, 'My dear Miss Fanny, how pretty you look, I do hope I find you well.' Fanny, in imitation of Martha's manner, nervously jerked her head. Undisturbed by the prolonged silence, he turned back to Martha and, with commendable poise, said, 'I take it you wish to verify the original IOU. Here it is.'

While Martha perused it, Giles Corby regarded the two ladies with pleasure. Angelina was quite right to be jealous, he thought, properly dressed – even in that dreary black – Fanny had turned into quite a beauty. The elder lady was a surprise, he had not expected to find Gerald's sister a tall, handsome, imperious woman whose speculative glance seemed to strip away his carefully maintained mask of assurance and leave him bare of all pretence.

Martha had seen enough examples of Gerald's schoolboyish scrawl to be reasonably sure the paper was genuine. She showed it to Fanny who whispered, 'Yes, it is Papa's hand,' and to Daly who also agreed with a sigh, 'Yes, it is the Master's right enough!' She studied the signatures of the witnesses whilst she thought out her approach to Mr. Corby. He appeared reasonable. She looked at him searchingly, this time noticing the imperceptible indications of strain. Constantly living by one's wits, nerves at a stretch, waiting for the axe to fall was wearing, as she had good cause to know. Only too well.

She spoke at last, 'Mr. Corby, I see that my late brother's estate does indeed owe you this money, but alas, you have chosen to come on a day when the trustee who can authorise the bank to pay out such a sum to you is away from Gloucester.'

This was no news to Mr. Corby. The previous day he had called at Mr. Ackland's chambers and was informed he was away until next Tuesday or Wednesday, by which time he planned to be well on his way to the Continent. It was only when he received this set back he realised that, perhaps, he could squeeze more money from Fanny than he could ever hope to obtain from Ackland.

'Mr. Corby, could you not possibly wait until next week for your money? Asked Martha persuasively.

'Dear lady,' a form of address Martha did not care for, 'I'm afraid I cannot. I really must insist upon the letter of the IOU. Payment by this date, or I take possession of the Water Meadow.'

'Will you not accept a note?' Martha knew this was a useless offer.

'Dear Lady, I regret I cannot. I need the monies for a venture which is awaiting me. I must not delay.'

In other words, thought Martha viciously, he is as desperate as we are.

Nothing showed on her face. 'Very well, Mr. Corby, I suggest you wait at the Gilbert Arms and return here at ten o'clock this evening.'

He was disappointed and protested, 'I had thought to conclude my business with you immediately.'

'It is you who insists upon the letter of the bond, so we have the option of waiting until the stroke of midnight if we so wish... ten o'clock, Mr. Corby.' She repeated in minatory tones.

Seeing her beautiful eyes flash and harden with resolution, he gave in gracefully, bowed and left the room, not at all sure he had won the encounter. From what he remembered of Gerald's description of his sister, he had not been prepared for this forthright creature and he would be lucky to get away from her unscathed. It was certain she lacked Gerald's careless, easy going manner.

Fanny and Martha stood looking at each other in consternation, while they waited to hear the front door close behind their unwelcome visitor. They only relaxed when Daly returned to the room and asked, 'What are your orders, Miss?'

Immediately, Martha sat at the desk, pulled out a sheet of paper, picked up her quill, dipped it deliberately into the standish and began to write a note to Mr. Ackland. She stopped what she was doing and asked, 'Fanny, do you have any money?'

'Not much, aunt Em. I should never have bought those new riding boots, nor my amethyst habit and that lovely length of white silk...' Martha was sorry to see she was restlessly pleating the material of her skirt, a nervous mannerism she thought the girl had overcome. 'What are we going to do? We can't afford to lose the Water Meadow...'

'Hush, my love, we are not going to.' Martha touched wood and showed Fanny her crossed fingers. 'Bring me what money you have left, please. Also, bring down from my room the walnut box and my reticule. And Daly, please ask William to be ready to ride to Gloucester with a note, and also ask Mrs. Daly for what she has in the housekeeping purse.'

Fanny flew out of the room and up the stairs, while Daly followed at a stately trot. Martha continued her cry for help to Mr. Ackland on the off-chance he had cut short his visit to Bristol.

Fanny returned with a very long face. 'I've only four pounds, fourteen shillings and nine pence. Here is your box and reticule, how much do you have?'

By the time Martha had searched her reticule – one pound, three shillings and sixpence, and looked in her walnut box – one hundred and thirty-six pounds, fifteen shillings, a drastic remedy had occurred to her. 'Fanny, I need your consent to a very difficult decision. If we borrow all we can from everybody we can think of... such a pity today, of all days, the entire Wentworth family has gone to pay their respects to that uncle... I doubt we will be able to raise the necessary amount without we shall have to sell something someone has been wanting for a very long time. I mean, and I am sorry to have to suggest this, Fan, Mr. Cairnton has coveted Lucifer for years.' She waited for Fanny to protest, but the girl surprised her. She gravely gave the matter a moment of consideration and then nodded her head.

'You are quite right, the Water Meadow is an asset we cannot afford to lose and we do have Lucifer's progeny. We are in a desperate case, so I agree.'

'I shall take him over,' said Martha, 'and rest assured I shall endeavour to get a good price for him. Who knows, if we collect enough, perhaps I shall only have to sell half of him, or perhaps I can negotiate a loan using him for collateral. I shall appeal to Mr. Cairnton's kind nature and I'm sure he will help us in any way he can.'

Determined that Fanny should have no time to brood, Martha asked her to find the Major. 'There must be some money in the estate cash box. And Fanny, would you explain what has occurred to the Vicar, after all he is a trustee, perhaps he can lend us a button or two from the Collection Plate.' That sally made Fanny grin wanly, but she did say, 'I think I shall go over to the Parks, Mrs. Park will gladly lend us whatever she can.'

'Excellent notion, my love, and be sure you write a receipt for anything received, and make a note of it for us. We'll pay everybody back, with interest, as soon as Mr. Ackland gets here.' There, thought Martha, as Fanny went to change into her habit, that should keep her occupied for most of the day.

Having rapidly changed into her favourite habit of smoke grey cloth, with darker grey velvet facings, Martha ran down the stairs to find Daly awaiting her at the foot. 'Miss, Miss,' he cried, 'Mrs. Daly has only six pun' in the 'ousekeeping, but we 'ave fifty-three pun' of our own we would like to give to Miss Fanny. Mrs. Martin, Miss, 'as given me seven pun'.' His excitement was measured by his accent slipping back into the idiom of his youth.

'Bless you all,' Martha was touched. She took him into the morning room and asked him to write down what had been collected so far.

'Miss Fanny and I are riding out, so I would like you to be in charge of what we collect. Please make sure that every contributor's name and the amount is listed, and they have a receipt.' She smiled as he inscribed in careful copperplate *'List of Contributors and their Contributions to the Fund for Saving the Water Meadow'*. At the top of a large sheet of paper.

Swiftly Martha made her way to the stables, as she passed Timothy she told him to saddle Tadpole and then she squared her shoulders and went to talk to the O'Briens. She had a difficult interview ahead.

After she had explained what had happened, Mick so far forgot himself in his wrath as to swear in front of her. Pat, horrified at his son's social lapse, nudged him in the ribs. But Martha, who was in very much the same frame of mind, ignored the byplay and commiserated with him, 'I know, I know, but perhaps we can work out a reasonable settlement with Mr. Cairnton.'

'I doubt it,' said Pat gloomily, 'I hear tell he keeps large sums of money by him, that's why he keeps them big dogs about the place. He'll want to buy Lucifer outright, just you mark my words.'

The journey to Bridgecombe was accomplished as quickly as possible. Pat, mounted on his useful cob, leading a fresh Lucifer, set a spanking pace across country, as if he wanted to get the distasteful transaction over and done with. If Martha had not been so worried she would have enjoyed the ride. It was not until O'Brien slowed down at the last mile in order to cool out the horses that he spoke of his feelings.

'I am that put about, Miss Gilbert, yon villain needs hanging, upsetting you an' Miss Fanny this way. To think we have to lose Lucifer a 'cause o' the likes of him. Miss, they has been nothing but trouble from the start. I never liked them Corbys, as you know. Mick and I was only saying just now as how's we'd like to knock him about a bit like an' scare him off, but you says he has the right of it, an' that you believe the best way to rid oursel's of him for good is to pay him and get that paper?' Martha nodded and said, 'And I shall make him sign a form of quit claim so we shall never be bothered again. If Mr. Ackland does not get here in time, I shall ask the Major to help me.'

'Ah, I'm that glad, Miss, you an' Miss Fanny will not see him alone. Anyroad, me an Mick will be outside iffen you needs us.' He said pugnaciously, spoiling for a fight.

Martha laughed, 'Thank you, but really I do not feel that will be necessary what with the Major and, I hope, the Vicar. Mr. Corby will see we are well supported.'

They turned into the gates leading to Cairnton House, Martha rehearsing her speech to Mr. Cairnton.

As it so often happens when elaborate preparations are made, Martha's speech was not needed. When they drew up at the front steps, Mr. Cairnton himself came out to see who was visiting him. His two bull mastiffs barked their defiance throatily until he admonished them to be quiet and sit. After the dogs had obeyed him, he exclaimed, 'Miss Gilbert, what a delightful surprise, but why have you brought Lucifer? Good morning, O'Brien, good to see you, man, he looks very fit. Does that mean you are going to sell him to me after all?' His jovial laugh ceased abruptly when he saw Martha's face.

'Miss Gilbert, whatever is amiss? But please, dismount and tell me, here let me help you. Come into the house. O'Brien take the horses to the stables and refresh yourself. Come in, my dear, let us find Mrs. Cairnton.'

'No, no,' protested Martha, 'Please, sir, I would like to speak with you on a matter of business. Let us sit here while O'Brien goes to the stables. I would like to see Mrs. Cairnton later, perhaps.'

She sat down on the stone mounting block opposite Mr. Cairnton who perched on the low balustrade running around the terrace in front of the house. Taking a deep breath, Martha began, 'Sir, do you truly want to buy Lucifer?'

'Indeed I do.'

'Then, sir, you may have him for three hundred and seventy guineas, if you can pay me cash immediately.'

'Cash! Good God.'

'Please, sir, we need the cash desperately.'

'Well now, the price is not high enough, even so I do not have that amount of cash in the house.'

'But, sir, rumour has it you always keep a lot of cash on hand...'

'Rumour, as is usual, exaggerates. Tell me this, what's all the hurry?' Why are you in such desperate straits? Will not Monday do? I could have it all then, and I quite expect to pay more for a stud of Lucifer's calibre. He fixed her with a stern eye. 'There is more to this. Now let's have it – all.' So Martha embarked upon a complete explanation. He listened grimly but did not interrupt once. At the conclusion of her recital, Martha said, 'Now you understand why we are desperate.'

'I do indeed,' he moved away from the balustrade and walked up and down for a few moments thinking hard. 'Well, one thing is absolutely clear, I will not buy Lucifer under such circumstances.'

'Please,' begged Martha.

'Wait. Hear me out. What I will do is this – lend you what money we have in the house, it will not be enough to cover the full amount, but it will help, then perhaps you can persuade Corby to forgo the rest or some such. Now, let's find Mrs. Cairnton.'

'Dear Mr. Cairnton, thank you so much, but we cannot allow you to make such a sacrifice... turning away a chance to obtain Lucifer,' She thought rapidly, 'All those who are lending us money will earn interest upon it. I have a suggestion, as well as the interest, let us say you may send two mares to Lucifer free of charge. Would that make up for your loss?'

Mr. Cairnton smiled, he dearly loved to haggle, 'Six and no interest.'

But he did not know Martha, 'Four and no interest.'

'Done,' he agreed, holding out his hand, she shook it as they solemnly sealed the bargain. If he has a goodly sum by him Martha thought, she had come out of it rather well.

Mrs. Cairnton, who was discreetly observing them from her sitting room window, met them as they entered the house. Upon being told the whole story, she threw herself into rounding up her contribution. He was able to produce one hundred and seventy pounds and she, by dint of cleaning out her reticule and her housekeeping purse, added thirty-two pounds to it. Martha was overjoyed, 'You are the best and kindest of friends. Fanny and I thank you both. Now, we only have to find about a hundred and seventy odd pounds, and I have not yet seen the Major. You will see me again as soon as Mr. Ackland reaches us. Now I must get back. I am so grateful.' She was incoherent with relief, 'And O'Brien will be overjoyed when he learns he is not to lose Lucifer.'

The Cairntons watched the small cavalcade trot down the drive and experienced that immense gratification which comes from knowing they had rendered a great service without any real exertion on their part.

The return journey was one of pure delight. Pat softly sang Irish ballads in a slightly off-key tenor, Martha relaxed and enjoyed the beautiful day, while the horses stepped out keenly for their heads were pointed towards their stables and home.

17 - Friends to the Rescue

As soon as she left her aunt's reassuring presence, Fanny was fretting again. No longer shocked by the vast sums of money her father had squandered, but the advantageous position held by Mr. Corby, whereby he could squeeze even more money out of the estate, threw her into a panic. Her old fears of losing her beloved home returned to haunt her, and it was a very disturbed young lady who set out to look for Hugh.

She found him in the estate office. He was sitting at the desk, his back to the window, immersed in his farm journal. Like his father before him, he continued the excellent practice of keeping detailed records. It made him proud to find that he was keeping the work in hand almost as up to date as his father had. Intent on verifying a point in one of the diaries, it was a few seconds before he noticed Fanny in the doorway. His frown of concentration changing into a welcoming smile he greeted her, 'Good morning, Fanny, that is a new habit, is it not? Very fetching,' and was disconcerted to find his compliment thrust to one side with a 'N-never mind that, Hugh, the most dreadful t-thing has h-happened.'

Seeing her terrible agitation, he leaped to his feet with an exclamation. Swiftly limping around the desk, he put his hands on her shoulders to steady her and said quietly, 'Tell me.'

It took him some minutes to unravel Fanny's story, and with understanding of the full import of her tale, his brow grew blacker and blacker.

'Do not be so unhappy, my dear Fanny, we will deal with that blackguard, never fear.' He said fiercely. She raised her eyes and tried to smile. The gallant little grimace quite wrung his heart and without pausing to consider, he wrapped his arms around her and cradled her against his chest telling her not to worry, he would look after her. Marvellously comforted by his warm embrace, Fanny slowly moved her head back to look up at him and said softly, 'Hugh?'

He regarded her searchingly for a moment and then gently kissed her lips. If that first kiss was a question, the second kiss gave the answer. Neither of them was aware of moving, but they found themselves once more together, oblivious of all but their discovery of one another.

Hugh was the first to recover his senses. He raised his head and gently put her away from him until she was at arm's length, saying, 'Fanny, I apologise. I seem to have picked quite the worst time to lose my head. I never meant to put you in an embarrassing position. I...'

Fanny was confused, 'Hugh? Did you n-not mean...?'

Horrified to think she doubted his sincerity, he hastened to gather her to him once more and said gently, 'I mean, this is no time to make a declaration of my love for you, but I will. I do not want you to misconstrue my actions, thus.' He kissed her again and then, holding her hands in his he made a little bow and said formally, 'Miss Gilbert, will you do me the honour, the very great honour of becoming my wife?' He smiled lovingly at her. Laughing joyfully, she drew close to him and put her arms shyly around his neck, saying, 'Silly, of course I will.'

She was so happy, all her problems had quite disappeared until Hugh brought her back to earth by saying, 'I could stay with my arms around you like this for ever, my love, but first we must finish with Mr. Corby. Let us set about collecting the money.' He put her gently from him and continued, 'Besides I should never have done this, first I should have asked leave of your aunt to pay you my addresses.' He looked worried, 'Fanny, I do not want to act in a hole in the corner and improper fashion, so I think we should keep this our secret until such time as I have spoken to Miss Gilbert.'

Fanny, partly because she wished to savour this magical moment, and partly because she did not want to delve into the mysteries still under the surface of her relationship with her aunt said, 'I agree, Hugh, I do not think now is the time to approach her.'

Something in her voice made Hugh ask anxiously, 'Why, Fan, do you think your aunt will not approve? I know I am older than you by ten years. Do you think 'tis too much? From something she once said to me...'

'No, of course you are not, you have always been ten years older than me, that is a fact that cannot be altered, just as I have always loved you, I think,' she added meditatively.

'And I you, my darling, but I did not think I had a chance. Recently, every time I saw you, you were either with young Park, or George or Frederick or all of them. You were enjoying their company so much I was convinced you never thought of me, except as an old friend and someone with whom to discuss Cobbleigh.'

'Hugh, d-dear, I am sorry... I did not realise how it appeared to you. 'Tis because I never had brothers or sisters, and I've so enjoyed being part of their family. Oh, Hugh, it has always been you I loved, from the time when I was just a little girl and you used to give me rides on the swing, and took me bird's nesting and frog spawning. I like George and the others, they are wonderful friends and we always laugh so much, but 'tis you I love. So, for the present, let us enjoy our love for each other quietly without outside interference, the two of us, something of our very own.'

Fanny had unformulated thoughts in her mind, nebulous feelings hard to put into words. Long used to keeping her own counsel it now stood her in good stead. Ever since those episodes with Voltaire, she tried to forget her unworthy suspicions of her aunt. All week Fanny had done her unobtrusive best never to be alone with her for any length of time because she was not ready for a confrontation. Now, some instinct made her keep her plans to marry Hugh secret. She was still of the opinion that time would bring answers, but before she took Hugh into her confidence, she wished once more to give her aunt every chance. After all, aunt Em had been instrumental in the miraculous changes in her life and deserved her every consideration.

'I am so glad you agree,' said Hugh, 'and it will not be for long. I'll speak to Miss Gilbert as soon as we finish off Corby once and for all.' He gave her a hug and a kiss on the top of her head. 'Now, we must go to work. First let's look in the cash box'.

Eagerly they counted the contents, but it was not nearly as much as Fanny had banked on. 'I paid the quarterly bills recently,' explained Hugh. 'However, I can contribute something and I'll go home and ask mother for the housekeeping and Margaret for her pin money. I'll also call on the Vicar,' and with swift kiss they parted. Fanny, in a very different mood from that of half-an-hour before, gaily informed Jack he was to saddle up and ride with her to the Parks.

Hugh and Daly were awaiting them in the morning room when Martha and Fanny returned that afternoon. Fanny smiled shyly at Hugh, she was rewarded by a straight-faced, flickering glance and the suspicion of a wink, which sent a warm glow to her cheeks. Quite unaware of what was going on over her head, Martha was at Daly's side and bending over the table anxiously watching him painstakingly add their contributions to a list that was surprisingly lengthy. She commented upon this and Daly told her word had spread out all over Cobbleigh and people had come to the door to offer whatever they could spare.

Fanny had tears in her eyes, 'I know,' she said, 'Bodger and Powell stopped me on my way back from the Parks and gave me some shillings. And Mrs. Park gave me whatever she had too. She was so angry, Anna had to dissuade her from coming over this evening to give Giles Corby a piece of her mind. People have been so good.'

Hugh said Coggin, of all people, had handed him some coins tied up in a neckerchief. He put the little bundle on the table and when it was untied they counted out eighteen shillings. 'Well, he might have given us more,' remarked Martha crossly, 'after all he made free enough with your piglets, Fanny.'

'Hush, aunt Em, I think it is very kind of him to contribute.'

Martha was pleased rather than affronted by this dignified little rebuke. She studied Fanny's face and wondered what had happened to the worried young lady she had left that morning. Now, she was perfectly calm, even happy, which was all to the good because they had a very trying evening ahead of them.

When he had completed the entries, Daly showed them what he had written. They exclaimed anew at everyone's kindness.

'Who is Mrs. Peachey?' Asked Martha.

'The eggwoman,' replied Fanny, 'but no one ever calls her by her real name. Oh, look James and Annie have given us a pound, bless them.'

'And the Lees, and all at the stables,' Martha read aloud, 'Thomas cowman, oh, people have been so generous.'

But strive as he might, even with Hugh's assistance, Daly could not make the total add up to more than five hundred and twenty-eight pounds, eight shillings and nine pence, which left them over fifty pounds short.

'It is too bad Firkin does not return until late,' lamented Martha, 'he usually brings in about fifteen pounds. However, I think we can safely say that today it will be no less than ten pounds and probably more. In the meantime, we must think... Is there no one else we can approach?'

At that point another carriage was heard arriving. 'Charles!' exclaimed Martha unguardedly, expressing such joy that Hugh was dazzled, 'Why did I not think of him before this,' and without further ado she ran after Daly into the hall crying, 'Charles, Charles, I'm so glad you've come, you must help us, we are in such a fix.'

'What again?' Charles was grinning, relinquishing his hat and driving gloves to Daly so that he could take her hand properly. He raised it to his lips. 'It appears some things never change. How may I serve? At least,' he added, surveying his anxious audience, 'it would appear you are not alone in your scrape this time.' It was fortunate his familiarity was lost upon the others. He is going to give the game away if he is not careful, thought Martha, but thank goodness he has arrived.

'Charles, we need all the money you have with you.'

'I've about twenty-five pounds, will that suffice?'

'No,' said Martha baldly, 'but 'twill help, thank you.'

Thoroughly amused at his unorthodox reception Charles looked forward to the explanation of it. He remembered, from childhood on, life was never commonplace when Martha was involved in one of her escapades. By this time they were in the morning room and he saw the list, 'What is this?' Everyone explained at once.

As soon as Charles sorted it out and was in possession of the facts, he opened his pocket book, 'Well, here's my twenty-five pounds, I wish it was more but I'm near the end of my journey.' He watched while Daly inscribed his name and the amount, 'How much more do we need?'

'Just under twenty-five pounds, my lord.'

'I strongly believe we can make Corby accept whatever we choose to give him.' Said Hugh with the light of battle in his eye.

'I've no doubt we could coerce him into accepting even less,' said Martha, 'but I would rest easier if we had the whole sum. That reminds me, we must make him sign a quit claim so he can never bother us again.'

'I was thinking the same thing,' agreed Hugh. 'My lord, are you versed in the drawing up of legal documents.'

'Not in the least,' said Charles cheerfully, 'but I'm positive you and I can come up with something that will fairly tie him in a knot. Let us work on it immediately.'

'Here are quills, paper and ink, my lord.' Daly was only too thankful Lord Biscay and the Major were taking all responsibility into their hands. 'May I offer you some refreshment?'

'Please, what about you, Major? Do you think a glass of wine will help us concentrate?'

'Indubitably, my lord,' Hugh grinned as he watched Daly pour them both a glass.

Charles looked at the ladies and said with the candour of an old friend, 'Marcia, you and Fanny look quite done up. Why do you not have some tea and take a rest. You've both been through a lot and the day is not near ended.'

Laughing good humouredly at this summary dismissal, Fanny and Martha were graciously pleased to act upon his high-handed advice and retired gracefully to the sitting room next door. Freed of their presence the men were left to wrestle with the document in peace.

Tea was exactly what she needed, thought Martha, gratefully sipping the hot liquid. She pondered the day's events. Fanny, not yet of an age to fully appreciate the beneficial properties of the beverage, drank enough to quench her thirst, and replaced her cup in its saucer. Quietly revelling in the knowledge of Hugh's love and support, she had lost most of her nervousness, but she still worried about the lack of twenty-three pounds. 'What are we to do? If Mr. Corby does not receive all the money? Knowing him, he'll insist upon every last penny, if he doesn't get it, can he not legally take the Water Meadow from me anyway?'

'Do not agitate yourself so, Fan. Firkin will bring in enough, of that I am sure, he took a particularly large load with him today, remember?'

But Fanny was not satisfied, 'Oh, why did Mr. Ackland have to be away this week? And why did the Wentworths have to visit their old uncle 'til Monday? Not that I'd have liked to approach them, but as a last resort...' she sighed heavily, 'It's too bad...'

Martha shut her ears, let Fanny talk herself out, it would ease her. If the truth were known, Martha too would have been much happier if they had managed to raise the full sum, and she cast about in her mind to find an acceptable substitute. Jewellery was the answer, of course. In Marcia Gilbert's bequest to Fanny there were several pieces that would certainly be suitable. A ring or a brooch, worth more than the necessary sum, should appeal strongly to a man of Mr. Corby's ilk. Martha's conscience, more tender each day she postponed her confession, was exercised in an internal debate as to whether she had the right to give away any of the pieces without consulting Fanny. Perhaps she could say that the jewellery was due to be Fanny's inheritance and ask her to choose what she liked least from the case.

Sparing herself nothing, Martha secretly wondered if her care in making this fine distinction was not mere hair splitting when her basic dishonesty, in pretending to be someone she was not, quite over shadowed such niceties in her behaviour. After all, why should she boggle at using jewellery belonging to Fanny in order to save Fanny's land. Not entirely happy she had found an answer to quieten her uneasy conscience, she was running over Marcia's jewels in her mind when Fanny's question impinged upon her thoughts. 'What was that you said?'

'I only asked what you thought of Mr. Corby?'

'Oh, a very fine looking fellow indeed, fine as five pence.'

'He was always extremely nice in his dress. Was he what you expected?'

'Frankly, no. You had led me to believe him the complete rogue... a villain with cloak and dagger... you know how one's imagination always outstrips reality. Instead, I found him an agreeable surprise. I was very disappointed, he should at least have had the common courtesy to be vulgar in the extreme, flashy in manners and dress. Someone it would be a positive pleasure to dislike. But, the person of my imaginings would never have attracted your father, and I should have taken that into account. A successful adventurer would always have the appearance of a gentleman, part of his stock in trade.'

'Yes, 'tis easy for him to maintain the look of a gentleman,' said Fanny with asperity, 'when he makes it a habit of acquiring appurtenances belonging to his friends.'

'Now, why do you say that with such conviction?'

'Because he was wearing Papa's watch fob, I saw it hanging from his pocket. Do you not remember, the very one we discovered was missing when we were looking for the watch? I recognized it at once. 'Twas Papa's favourite.'

Martha suddenly sat upright in her chair, 'Are you absolutely sure?'

'Yes, I am.'

Martha clapped her hands, 'Oh, we have him now,' she exclaimed with glee, 'Oh, yes, we have him. How careless of Mr. Corby. How stupid,' she crowed. 'Can you recall, Fan, if he was wearing your father's watch as well?'

'I'm sure he was because it matches the fob, although I did not actually see it... he did not consult it while he was with us. Aunt Em, do you think he has Papa's snuff box too?'

'Obviously he approves of your Papa's taste, so I have no doubt of it. We must find out, of course. Anyway, Fan, we no longer have to worry about paying off Mr. Corby. We can have him taken as a thief, the fob alone is proof enough, but 'twould be better for our case if he was also wearing the other things. Rather than create a scandal, I am certain he would accept half the money we owe him, or even none at all, if he thought the story would be bruited about. And we can assure him it will. He would be terrified of losing his plausibility, if anything truly detrimental was known about him.'

'Do you really think so?' Fanny came alive, 'this is wonderful news. If it is truly so, we have no more worries.' She relaxed, sinking back in her chair, sighing, 'Oh, what a relief!.'

Martha closed her eyes in brief respite – now there was no further need to raid Marcia's jewel case.

'Let's ask Daly if he saw father's things, he would recognize them too, Papa wore them nearly every day. But I do not understand how Mr. Corby could have been so silly as to wear them here.'

'Even the cleverest people make foolish mistakes.'

Unaware of the hidden meaning in Martha's words, Fanny declared, 'Well, if it was me, I would not have dared wear them at all, I would have sold them at once.'

'Probably thought they were too handsome and they enhanced his turn out... or, he may have conveniently forgotten how he came by them,' said Martha.

A shout of laughter was heard through the connecting door to the morning room and Martha gave Fanny a mischievous smile, 'It would be a shame to disturb them when they are getting along so well. Come, let's go up and change for dinner. We can keep our news until later when we can all take a hand in planning tonight's strategy.'

18 - The Debt is Cleared

'It would appear we've had similar ideas,' Martha said to Fanny while they were standing admiring themselves before the pier glass in Martha's bedroom. 'There's nothing like knowing one is looking one's best to give one confidence.' They smiled at each other's reflection.

'You do look lovely, aunt Em. I've always seen you in black, so didn't realise cream became you so well.'

'Thank you, my love. I'm so tired of mourning and on such an important occasion as this evening, I did not think it would matter it is not quite six months since your Papa died. After all, 'tis only my underdress that's cream, I think the overdress of black lace a nice touch.

She had spent many minutes wistfully admiring a glorious pale yellow silk dress and one of a daring cut in rose muslin. Regretfully, she had turned away to pick up the old black silk Annie had laid out for her, when something inside her rebelled. She returned it to the cupboard in favour of the one she was now wearing. Soon she could wear bright colours again, but for tonight this would do very well. In keeping with her mood, she replaced her modest string of pearls in its case and had recklessly taken from her own jewel box the fine diamond pendant and diamond earrings inherited from her mother. To complete her ensemble she found one of Marcia's fans of black lace mounted on mother of pearl sticks.

'Now, Fan, turn around and let me look at you.' She nodded, the girl looked lovely 'yes, Annie has made you a beautiful dress, the fit is excellent.' Fanny's cheeks glowed warmly with excitement and her pretty eyes matched the violet motif embroidered around the square neckline of the white silk bodice and on the bands marking the three tiers of flounces at the hem. The colour was again picked up by the violet taffeta ribbons tied high under her bosom. Draped across her elbows was the shawl of Martha's working.

Anxious her putatative niece should look her very best, Martha had a daring idea. 'Your pearls look very nice, but I think you may now wear coloured stones. In this box are some amethysts. Just the thing to round off your toilette.' She opened Marcia's case took out a star shaped pendant the stones set in gold, and fastened it around Fanny's neck. 'There, now for the earrings,' she handed her a pair of matching miniature pendant stars. Fanny put them on and admired herself in the looking-glass. 'Oh! They're beautiful, thank you, aunt Em. Thank you.'

'Do not thank me, they were your grandmamma's and are... would have come to you anyway so why not have them and wear them now.' Fanny's rapturous delight was cut short by a knock at the door. Mrs. Daly entered at Martha's bidding.

'Oh! Miss Marcia, Miss Fanny, if I may say so, you both do look ever so lovely.'

'Thank you Mrs. Daly, just look at what my aunt has given me, they were grandmamma's.' After admiring the jewels, Mrs. Daly told them. 'Daly sent me to say the gentlemen have arrived, and that we would all like to wish you the very best of luck this evening. Mrs. Martin sends her compliments and hopes you will enjoy the dinner she prepared specially, and Daly has been across to the Manor cellar and chosen some of the choicest wines. We are all hoping that this evening will go off very well.'

'Thank you all,' said Martha, touched by their practical display of sympathy. 'Miss Fanny and I will do our best not to let you all down'.

'No fear of that,' said Mrs. Daly her staunch support emphasised by the agitation of the ruffles on her cap.

'No, indeed,' said Fanny. 'I do not scruple to tell you Mrs. Daly, I was afraid – very afraid – this morning, but I've now no fear at all since I found out what splendid friends I have. Please tell everybody so from me. I will thank them all properly later.'

Daly thought the old dining room had never seen a finer sight. From his vantage point behind Miss Fanny's chair he proudly surveyed the scene. The sun, beginning to set on this warm evening, glowed through the open casement upon the polished mahogany table, making it shine richly. The silver gleamed, prismatic lights danced on the cut glass, spotless white napery dazzled the eye and ruby red wine smouldered in the glasses. All this offset the sombre splendour of the table's occupants. He had never seen the ladies in such looks and, he was interested to note, the Major was unable to take his eyes off Miss Fanny. While Lord Biscay was more circumspect, he was regarding Miss Marcia in a mighty possessive manner. The Vicar, silver haired and dignified in black, with the white bands of his calling, lent an air of propriety to the gathering, while the two handsome and vigorous younger gentlemen in their dark evening coats and high white cravats, represented a force to be reckoned with. Mr. Corby had no notion of what he had got himself into, decided the butler as he directed William in his duties, and it would serve that parasite right.

While they ate Mrs. Martin's delicious dinner, they discussed the ways and means of catching Mr. Corby out. Firkin had returned around seven o'clock and had come to the Dower House with twenty-one pounds and some change. He had heard of their difficulties from the Lees and had thought to bring his personal contribution to the fund as well. He was warmly thanked, but Charles and Hugh had privily decided this money should be held in reserve. They resolved to make Mr. Corby suffer some measure of what he had made others suffer. They would make him accept the watch, fob and, if he had it, the snuff-box, in lieu of full payment. On hearing this Fanny became stubborn, 'I want them. They were Papa's,' she said flatly. In spite of all representations she was adamant.

'Of course we'll get them back, if you wish it,' soothed Hugh, 'First of all, we must verify that the things are your father's. My lord, do you have any suggestions how we can make him show us not only the watch, but the snuff-box as well. Do you take snuff? I do not.'

'No, I don't,' said Charles, 'Filthy habit.'

'Well, I do,' said the Vicar mildly, 'I'm sure you are quite right, my lord, 'tis a filthy habit, but I cannot stop myself, even during the Lenten Season, I give up honey instead...'

'I beg our pardon, sir,' said Charles hastily.

'No, my lord, I'm not offended, I know you are right. What I meant was, perhaps I can induce Mr. Corby to offer me his sort.' He paused for a moment's thought, 'If I left my box in this room, somewhere Daly could not find it, and then asked him to fetch it, surely Mr. Corby...?'

'Excellent,' said Hugh, 'I'm sure he'll offer his box because he'll wish to be conciliatory, especially if we do not give in easily to his demands.'

At that point Martha and Fanny left the table to the gentlemen and their Port. Too keyed up with the evening's drama still ahead of them, the gentlemen were not long in joining the ladies in the withdrawing room. By now it was twilight. The last rays of the summer sun painted the evening sky as Daly lit the candles, no end pleased he had a part to play in the downfall of Mr. Giles Corby.

'We have a good hour before he comes,' said Martha, 'I think we should enjoy the evening as if we were not expecting to be interrupted. Perhaps some music, or cards? Fan, my love, do you think you could entertain us at the pianoforte, while the four of us play a hand or two of whist?' Fanny, who played the piano very well, but did not enjoy cards, was only too glad to have something to do. The others settled down at the card table and, to their amazement, managed several exciting games.

The clock on the mantel struck the quarter-to and Fanny stopped playing in mid-phrase. The card players dropped their unplayed cards face down on the table.

'Mr. Corby should be here soon,' said Martha, 'When he does arrive, Fan, why not come and sit beside me. I shall make the introductions and we'll not have to talk further, unless you wish to. In the meantime, continue playing as if his coming is of no moment, and let us finish the hand and start another, if you are agreeable.'

Before they resumed play, Hugh went over to Fanny, 'Nod to me as soon as you confirm the watch and snuff-box belonged to your father. I'll be watching you. Daly, please do not leave the room after you have shown him in, you can be busy snuffing the candles, or some such.'

Charles put the money on the side table. Neatly laid out beside it were a fresh quill, ink-well, sander and the quit claim. Earlier in the evening the Vicar had read and approved the document. He complimented the authors, saying he doubted Ackland could do better.

They then returned to their cards while Fanny played a lively tune. The bell pealed, the clock showing three minutes to ten. 'Your Papa's watch keeps good time,' Martha said to Fanny as she finished the piece, closed the lid of the instrument, and moved to sit by her. Obviously music had relaxed her, she was smiling, 'Nothing but the best for Papa.'

Some instinct bestowed upon those who live by their wits, made Giles Corby ignore Martha's suggestion he wait at the Gilbert Arms. While he did not anticipate trouble, he was unsure how the inhabitants of Cobbleigh would behave towards him if they recognized him. He had, therefore, prudently retired to Gloucester and spent a day kicking his heels at the New Inn.

Although he had experienced many awkward moments in his life, nothing quite prepared him for what awaited him at the Dower House. Instead of meeting two defenceless women and, perhaps, their butler, he was confronted by what at first sight appeared to be a room full of strangers. He stopped dead in the doorway. He took a deep breath, as if readying himself for a plunge into deep waters, then let it out slowly. The formidable array of people staring at him in disapproving silence, resolved itself. The butler was there right enough, and so were the two women. But they were no longer defenceless, they were supported by three other men. He had no difficulty in placing the Vicar, but it was the other two who alarmed him. The taller looked at him with a dispassion that made him cringe inwardly, and the slighter glared at him belligerently. All this made him fear he would not leave the room with a whole skin.

It took all of Mr. Corby's resolution to bow to the assembled company and say 'Good evening,' imperturbably.

'Good evening' returned Martha politely, while the others watched him stonily. She turned to Charles, 'My lord, allow me to present Mr. Corby to you.'

My lord fractionally inclined his head.

Vicar, I believe you know Mr. Corby?'

'We have met,' the Vicar was courteous as always.

'Major Buchan, this is Mr. Corby.'

Martha was punctilious, 'Mr. Corby, Captain Lord Biscay is our advisor.' Mr. Corby bowed obsequiously, while Fanny, who had never seen Charles in other than an easygoing mood, was astounded to find how very unapproachable he was when he looked down his nose from his great height.

'Major Buchan is our bailiff and speaks for all of us.' Again Fanny's eyes widened as her kind Hugh became a cold stranger, who curtly nodded his head in response to Mr. Corby's brief bow.

The Major was the first to speak, 'Sit down Mr. Corby,' and indicated the straight-backed chair Daly had deliberately placed in the centre of the room. 'First of all, we wish to see the IOU.'

231

Mr. Corby handed over the paper in silence. While Hugh and Charles pretended to study it minutely, the Vicar was fumbling in his pockets. 'Where is it,' he muttered, 'Oh, dear, where could I have put it,' with enough commotion that everyone was made aware he was searching for something. 'Ah, here it is... no... 'tis my honey pastilles... Daly have you seen my snuff-box? I think I must have left somewhere in the dining room. Would you please look.'

Mr. Corby looked up as the Vicar sent Daly from the room, then immediately returned to keeping an eye on that precious piece of paper. It was borne upon all that Mr. Corby was not going to rise to the bait. The next few minutes were spent watching him, trying not to show they were holding their breath. Daly, throwing himself into the deception, allowed enough time to elapse for him to have conducted a thorough search and returned clearly empty-handed. 'I'm sorry Reverend, but your snuff-box is not where you say you left it.' He took in the situation at a glance, and improvised, 'Are you sure you brought it with you this evening, sir?'

'Yes, yes,' insisted the Vicar, 'I'm never without it, for I'm afraid it is a bad habit of mine I cannot break...' He heaved a sigh, 'Well, I shall have to do without, I must hold up the proceedings no longer. I shall manage...' this last was said plaintively, his voice breaking pathetically.

This by-play had not been lost upon Mr. Corby, but all his thoughts and anxieties were centred upon the other two men. Mr. Gore heaved a heavy sigh. Hummed a little tune. Tugged at his white bands. Let his fingers, like pink spiders, wander restlessly over the card table. The deprivation of snuff making him increasingly unhappy, his fingers commenced drumming on the baize cloth. The insistent sound so distracted Mr. Corby, he at last put his hand into his pocket.

'My dear Vicar, please allow me to offer you a pinch of my special sort,' and he pulled out a lovely gold box, flicked open the lid and proffered it to the reverend gentleman. Mr. Gore eagerly helped himself to a generous pinch murmuring, 'How kind, thank you.' He held the snuff to his nostrils, sniffed strongly, sneezed. Wiping himself with his handkerchief, he beamed sweetly upon his audience.

Fanny caught Hugh's eye and nodded excitedly. Hugh smiled fleetingly at her enthusiasm and turned to Mr. Corby, 'We have your money here, Corby, please count it.' Mr. Corby, trying to disguise his eagerness rose from his chair, Hugh barred his way, 'But before we let you take it, there are a few things we want from you.'

Mr. Corby looked alert.

'First,' continued Hugh, 'We want the IOU receipted.'

Within an ace of reaching his goal, Mr. Corby could afford to be conciliatory, 'That goes without saying, Major.'

'Second, we have prepared a document for your signature stating you have no further claim upon Miss Frances Gilbert or the Cobbleigh estate whatsoever.'

Reluctantly, Mr. Corby nodded, he was naturally averse to putting his signature to documents of that nature.

'And third, we want this back,' Hugh leaned over and dexterously pulled the watch by its pendant fob out of Mr. Corby's breeches pocket.

'Sir!,' gasped and outraged Mr. Corby stepping back, 'How dare you.'

'Major, that's my late master's watch and fob. I would know them anywhere. They disappeared at the time of his death,' cried Daly, enjoying the high drama.

Fanny too thought it was time she spoke up, 'I recognize them as well, and the snuff box. Mr. Corby, how could you?' She turned huge reproachful eyes upon him, 'You've stolen from me as well as tried to extract money from me, O-o-oh...! She wailed and sobbed loudly into her handkerchief which, for once, she was carrying with her. Martha, watching the spectacle, put her arm around Fanny and soothed, 'There, there, love, we'll not let him get away

233

with it. Charles, please do something for this poor girl.' When she turned back to Fanny, the little minx under cover of her handkerchief, whispered, 'Look at him, he is nonplussed. I did that so well I think I'll go on the stage.' Martha stifled her laughter.

Mr. Corby was living a nightmare, matters were slipping from his grasp. He was further alarmed when Lord Biscay said in the coldest of voices, 'Mr. Corby, we are taking you to the nearest magistrate and we'll let him deal with you.'

Mr. Corby paled, 'B-but,' he stammered desperately, 'G-Gerald gave them to me, on his death bed. I didn't steal them, I swear.'

'He did not,' asserted a very much recovered Fanny, 'For I was there, so were you Vicar.'

'This is most distressing,' said Mr. Gore, 'But Miss Fanny is quite correct, you did not receive anything from Mr. Gilbert's hands. You should be punished, you are a thief... However, perhaps Miss Fanny will be lenient. What do you say my dear child?'

She thought for a moment, then asked, 'That paper Mr. Corby is to sign, could we not add his confession of stealing to it?'

'The very thing,' agreed Hugh and wrote in several sentences at the bottom of the sheet. 'Here we are, Mr. Corby,' he said, his cheerfulness quite horrible to Mr. Corby's ears, 'Just sign here, and under the addition, and we shall witness your signatures. Now, give me the snuff-box.' Knowing he had no choice, Mr. Corby put the box on the table. With an effort he composed himself and managed to sign his name with a steady hand.

'Now receipt the IOU, if you please,' added Hugh as he sanded the signature.

Mr. Corby recovered enough poise to protest, albeit feebly, 'But I have not received my money.'

'You'll have it as soon as you've signed.'

'Oh,' said Mr. Corby visibly brightening, he had quite forgotten he was dealing with honourable people.

When all was completed, Charles indicated the money, 'It's all here, but you may count it. I would strongly suggest you use it to travel abroad – extensively. You may live quite cheaply in Europe, I collect. If ever I hear of you or see you in this country again, I shall be compelled to enquire very deeply into your affairs.'

'Yes, my lord, thank you, my lord,' Glad to be seeing the end of his ordeal, Mr. Corby was only too eager to leave this accursed place as quickly as possible. He crammed the money into the bag Daly had thoughtfully provided without bothering to count it. Although he was tempted to flee the room incontinently, he drew himself up, managed creditable bows all round, and was shown the door by a supercilious butler.

As soon as the door closed behind them, there was an immediate sigh of relief then an outburst of jubilation. 'Mr. Gore, you were absolutely superb,' said Fanny, 'I thought he was never going to offer you snuff, but he did. Your mournful cry was masterly, enough to break my heart. And thank you my lord, Hugh, aunt Em... everybody. You were all wonderful.'

'Fanny, 'twas your reproaches that finally undid him, I swear,' laughed Hugh, 'They really threw him off his stride. Addled his wits.'

'What's this?' asked Charles as Daly entered the room with a large bottle wrapped in a napkin.

'I anticipated a celebration, so I ordered champagne,' explained Martha. 'Daly, I hope you brought a glass for yourself, you deserve our thanks as much as anyone.'

'Oh, yes,' agreed Fanny, 'you've been a tower of strength throughout.'

After seeing everyone's glasses charged, the highly-gratified butler took a glass, poured in a small amount of champagne, raised it and said, 'If I may be so bold, my lord, ladies and gentlemen – on behalf of us all at

Cobbleigh, I would like to make a small toast... to Miss Fanny and Miss Marcia and to Cobbleigh!'. At the murmured 'Hear, hear,' he drained his glass, set it down on the tray and quietly left the room.

'Very good man, that,' said the Vicar, 'I truly believe if we had not been to hand, he could have dealt with Mr. Corby singlehanded.'

The enjoyable discussion of the day's events was brought to a close when the Vicar said regretfully, 'I have to go... Holy Communion at six tomorrow,' and the party reluctantly broke up.

After renewed thanks and protracted goodbyes, Martha and Fanny took their candles and wearily climbed the stairs. It had been a long day. Fanny, still buoyed by all the excitement and champagne, chatted happily, 'What a day this has been. I was quite ready to give up completely this morning,' she confessed, 'until you took charge, oh aunt, what would I do without you.'

'We all saved Cobbleigh,' maintained Martha. 'I only set matters moving. Something had to be done and done quickly. It was an unusual set of circumstances. If Mr. Corby had behaved like a normal person, Mr. Ackland would have dealt with him. I must say we were lucky in having both Charles and the Major with us, it quite took Mr. Corby all aback.'

'Yes, we are lucky to have them,' Fanny's cheeks flushed remembering how splendidly Hugh conducted the interview with Mr. Corby. She suppressed a yawn, 'Goodnight, aunt Em, and thank you.' She kissed Martha lovingly, 'I'm so glad we didn't lose Lucifer after all.'

19 - Enter a Formidable Lady

The next morning Fanny and Martha were nearly mobbed after Church. There were those interested in Fanny's welfare and there were those interested in getting a closer look at the tall stranger, a Lord no less, who rumour had it was courting Miss Gilbert.

While Charles chatted to Hugh and the Vicar, Fanny and Martha spent considerable time warmly thanking all those people who had so readily come to their assistance. Mrs. Park and Anna had purposely attended Matins at Cobbleigh in order to inveigh once more against the iniquities of Mr. Corby and demand a complete description of all that had befallen.

There was one person, however, who was inclined to take umbrage. Mr. Mason, as he had no hesitation in informing Martha, took it very ill she had not applied to him for aid. He told her, in a voice loud enough to be heard to the bounds of the Parish, he always kept a goodly sum of gold by him and Miss Fanny was welcome to it at any time. Martha tactfully smoothed him down by saying that if Lord Biscay had not come to their aid, the Combes were the very next place she would have visited. That he had only been bested by a Lord mollified him and he allowed himself to be led away, informing his embarrassed son who firmly held his arm, that he might get high tempered every now and again, but he hoped he could always be trusted to help anyone in need.

The next two days were pleasurably spent in showing off Cobbleigh to Charles. Mounted on one of the late Mr. Gilbert's remaining hunters, he enjoyed viewing the prosperous estate, admiring all he saw. Looking at the place as though through the eyes of a stranger, Martha was proud of how very much had been accomplished in so short a time. She felt it quite permissible for Fanny, Hugh and herself to preen themselves.

The four of them had reached the happy and informal ease of social intercourse that friendship brings. The two men liked and respected each other and, in no time at all, were addressing each other by their Christian names while contentedly discussing and arguing points on a wide range of subjects.

While they all awaited Mr. Ackland, it was without impatience. On Wednesday he made his appearance. He had returned from Bristol the night before extremely pleased with himself, for he had handled, in what he modestly thought a masterly fashion, a tricky piece of conveyancing. His self-satisfaction was abruptly terminated when he read Martha's hasty note. He realised she was a very competent woman, and reassured himself that if she could beg, borrow or steal enough money to pay off Corby, she would have done so. But he was extremely annoyed with himself for not foreseeing such a contingency and he belatedly resolved to make some arrangement whereby Cobbleigh would always have ready access to money. On his early morning journey to Cobbleigh, he tried to believe Miss Gilbert, if she did not succeed in paying him off, would detain Corby on some pretext or other. Sadly, he was not sanguine because he was sure the wily Corby was the kind to profit by the absence of a trustee.

He arrived at Cobbleigh just as the two gentlemen were joining the ladies in their mid-morning ride. They abandoned their plans without a backward glance at the glorious day, and immediately took the attorney to the Estate Office, where Fanny poured out the full story of Mr. Corby's perfidy and rout. The others looked on with wide grins of satisfaction. Martha was proud of Fanny... gone was the shy, gawky, schoolroom miss of her first acquaintance... now here was an elegant and poised young lady consulting her man of business. Martha happened to look at Hugh and noticed his eyes were on Fanny with so tender an expression, she was troubled. Now what do I do? She asked herself. Nothing, she decided, he is too great a gentleman to take advantage of the situation. She ceased her musing and caught Charles's eye. For the space of a minute, the room, Fanny's eager voice, Mr. Ackland and Hugh, all faded into the background until all she knew was dear Charles's battered face. Mentally she shook herself and once more the office and the other people in it came back into focus.

Mr. Ackland was saying '...congratulate you all, I am so glad I do not have to buy back the Water Meadow at a vastly inflated price – for that is what we would have to have done. Miss Fanny, I must apologise to you and Miss Gilbert, I am kicking myself, I should have foreseen... should never have trusted that even the closest monitoring of the Corby's actions was an adequate precaution against...'

Fanny stopped him gently, 'Oh, no, dear Mr. Ackland, no one could have foretold this would happen.'

'You are very good, but rest assured now, although I fear it is too late to be of use, I shall make arrangements so that this kind of occurrence can never happen again.' He shook his head and picked up the quit claim 'My lord, Major, I am particularly impressed by this document,' he re-read the paper and added, 'perhaps there are one or two very minor points I would have included, not the sort of thing a layman would think of. I think you gentlemen have done very well, one would almost say you have had the benefit of some legal training.' Charles and Hugh exchanged amused glances. 'An army or naval officer, Mr. Ackland,' said Charles, 'has to be prepared to turn his hand to anything. Paper work rules an officer's life. We do not live by action alone, you know, we are paper men, we live by lists and manifests.'

'And reports,' said Hugh, 'Reports for this, requisitions for that – mountains of 'em, we were buried under 'em.'

Mr. Ackland murmured, 'Quite so,' but did not feel much sympathy. In his opinion, a life ruled by orderly and accurate records was the only way to conduct a business or, for that matter, a war. So he turned to Martha and Fanny and once more exclaimed in admiration at the manner in which they had collected such a large sum of money in so little time. He drew the list of contributors towards him and remarked, 'Yes, well, perhaps we should plan on how to reimburse these good people as quickly as possible.'

The four of them passed the next few days riding about the countryside. It took a long time to repay even the smallest amount for everyone had to hear the story from Fanny's own lips, and Martha admired her patience. The girl had wisely elected to repay the smaller loans first, so it was several days later they were riding back from the Cairntons. Those kind people were pressing in their hospitality and nothing would satisfy them but they all stay and partake of luncheon. The afternoon was well advanced by the time they started on their way. The day was hot and the lavish entertainment they received disinclined them to strenuous exercise. Walking their horses on a loose rein, Fanny and Hugh drew a little ahead, so Martha and Charles, while they kept the couple in sight, fell naturally into talk about Stretton Wakefield and their youth.

The game of 'do you remember' began with Charles remarking on how much he liked Tadpole, and Martha replying she wished to buy her from Fanny when she left Cobbleigh. 'She reminds me of that nice mare you had, I forget her name, what happened to her?'

'Vashti? Sold with all the others,' she said unemotionally, 'she went to a very nice family, I am happy to say.'

'My dear, I am so sorry.'

'Don't be sorry. I admit it was a wrench at the time, I loved her dearly, but I never think of it now.'

'Well, recently I've been thinking a lot about those days. I suppose meeting you again has brought it all back. As a boy, when we stayed at the Court, I could never wait to visit the Manor. Your father, and Captain Edmund, Meg and your Tante Elise always made me so welcome.'

'Yes, I remember, it seemed as if you and Tom were always there. Meg used to be in despair, no sooner than she had me clean and properly dressed, than I would follow you boys into some scheme or other and come home dirty and with torn clothes. Did you two never propose an adventure that would leave us tidy?' She laughed, 'Remember the time you two made a raft and poled it towards the island in the lake? Tom never wanted me along on your jaunts, but you always used to say I was a good little thing and never any bother. I remember that day. As soon as I joined you on the raft, it tipped and into the water we all went. Ugh! I'll never forget the sensation of stinking mud oozing between my bare toes. Tom was so angry – blamed me for tipping the raft and ran off. 'Twas you who fished me out and took me home to Meg. It was always you who took me home when I had done something so rash that I scared myself out of my wits.'

'You did not wreck the raft, it was Tom abandoning ship... the sudden loss of his weight upset the balance. I do remember he tried to frighten you afterwards – said you would die because you swallowed frogs when your head went under water. But that you did not believe.'

'Oh, yes I did, I believed it – until I found I was not ill. Looking back I can understand why he did not want me tagging along. In those days I was always striving to do exactly as he did. When you were not there, we were very good friends you know, but your presence made him ashamed of me, because I was female and younger.'

'Young chub,' he commented, 'I think the first time I really noticed you was when you climbed that oak tree, after Tom of course. You could not get down. He managed to shinny down quite easily, and he stood under the tree making fun of you.'

'I remember', said Martha with feeling, 'It was you who helped me down. You who climbed up in your beautiful new coat, of which you were very proud, and guided my feet. It was not the height that bothered me, you understand, but I could not see where I was going.'

'You never let on how frightened you were, but you were shaking by the time I got you to the ground.'

'Yes, and that was the first time I took you to Meg to get your clothes repaired.'

He smiled ruefully, 'Dear Meg, she reminded me of that only the other day. Her beautiful repairs always saved my bacon, except that particular time. I lost a button, and she had to replace the whole set. Mother noticed and I got no end of a scold.'

'I'm sorry for that.'

'Oh, mother's scolds were nothing, she was always trying not to laugh, except the time you fell off the stable roof... remember?'

'Do I not.' Martha shook her head in wonder, 'What can have possessed me to have climbed on to the roof, I cannot imagine. I remember the thump when I hit the ground to this very day. Charles,' she turned her head to look at him, 'I was following Tom, so why were you taken to task?'

'He told you not to follow him, but that did not deter you. He knew he'd been too rash when you fell. He disappeared in a hurry.'

'Yes, it was you who picked me up and took me home. But I do not see why you were blamed, you did not climb onto the roof.'

'It was held by my uncle that as I was the eldest, I should not have allowed either of you to be so daring. And I did not climb up there because it did not seem worth it, or very formidable.' Martha's eyes widened. He smiled at her, 'Not to a very young Midshipman who learned to climb a swaying mast without flinching. You were very brave, you did not cry although your bruises must have hurt abominably.'

'Most probably I was stunned. 'Twas not until some well-meaning person remarked to Meg, in my hearing, how lucky it was there were no broken bones that I began to howl. It had not occurred to me before that bones... my bones... could be broken. What happened to Tom? Was he whipped? He never said. He would not talk to me for days after.'

'No, he was never whipped, you know that.'

'Yes,' she agreed, 'He was a past master at getting out of unpleasantness scot free. Do you remember the time he took your uncle's new team with his sporting curricle and lamed one of them?'

'Vividly!' He smiled wryly, 'I do believe 'twas the last time my estimable uncle ever spoke to me.'

'He was beside himself with rage. He would not listen to reason. All he could see was you holding the team's heads while Tom was feeling their legs and Sir John immediately believed it was you who had taken the team. Tom expostulated, of course. But in retrospect, I now realise he spoke so skilfully, it only confirmed your uncle's suspicion it was you who had done the deed and Tom was trying to shoulder the blame.' She fell silent, a frown disfiguring her forehead.

Wishing to smooth out her brow, he hastily said, 'Well, whatever we did was really comparatively tame, when I look back upon it. It would appear we were merely clumsy – no vice in us.'

Her laughter ran out, 'That's a good one. Especially when it comes from the gentleman who shot my great-aunt Sophia.'

'What! I never did.'

'Oh, yes, you did,' she replied with a wicked glint in her eye, 'She bears the mark for all to see to this day. Don't you remember, you were showing me how David slew Goliath with a sling. We were in the long gallery one rainy afternoon and you pierced her portrait.'

As he recollected the incident, he excused himself, 'It was not much of a shot, the target was immense.'

'Yes father always said she was proud of her ample charms. Although, as I recollect it, you said you were aiming for the suit of armour standing beside the picture. I suppose that expanse of pink flesh was a temptation.' She turned in her saddle to look back at him as he stopped his horse with a shout of laughter. 'What amazed me, my dear Charles, was that 'twas early three months before anyone else noticed the puncture. Meg wanted to blame me, but she knew I was no sort of shot, so she blamed Tom and was more than usually terse with him – she never truly liked him you know. Even though Tom was innocent for once, I never told anyone the truth.'

'I am glad the tables were turned on cousin Tom for a change.'

No more was said for the couple ahead had reined in to wait for them to catch up. Charles and Hugh then took their leave. They would change and rejoin them for dinner later.

The ladies rode on into the stableyard. While Fanny conferred with Jack over a youngster that had been kicked, Martha studied the very smart chaise being washed, she had never seen it before.

'Whose carriage is that?' she asked Timothy.

'Mrs. Birch has come.'

'Mrs. Birch?' said Martha. Who was Mrs. Birch? She tried to remember, she was sure she had heard that name somewhere, and recently.

'You know, Miss Marcia. Mrs. Birch, her as was married to Miss Fanny's great-grandfather.'

'Fanny,' Martha called, 'It would appear your step-great grandmamma is visiting you.'

'Grandmother Birch? How wonderful! I've not seen her since mother died, she has been in Italy this age. I wonder why she did not let us know she was coming to stay.'

Fanny ran excitedly towards the house. Martha followed more slowly. As far as she knew Mrs. Birch and Marcia Gilbert had never met, so she dismissed the old lady from her mind. She was more occupied in trying to arrange to see Fanny alone. The events of the past few days had put her confession out of her mind, but Charles had again spoken to her severely this morning and she had promised once more to tell Fanny all.

Martha took a short cut through the rose garden and found Mrs. Daly, a basket in the crook of her arm, cutting masses of pink and white roses. Hearing Martha's step she looked up and said with a pleased smile, 'I'm gathering roses for the dining table, Mrs. Birch always says she is starved for Cobbleigh roses. I expect they told you at the stables, Miss Marcia, Miss Fanny's step-great-grandmamma has come.'

'Yes, I'm hurrying to change so as to be down in time to greet her.' Martha made as if to pass. But Mrs. Daly detained her. The housekeeper was an admirer of Mrs. Birch from the day she, a timid little apprentice ladies' maid, who cared for Miss Charlotte Powys and her sister, was suddenly called upon to attire their dashing relative. No one, in her opinion, had ever surpassed the brilliance and charm of that youthful looking creature who had, at the time, been thrice married and twice widowed. Her third husband was a handsome Italian gentleman of large fortune and distinguished lineage and, Mrs. Daly always maintained, there never was, nor never would be, such a dazzling couple.

She was eager to impart her pleasure in serving the lady once again, so, with a creak of her stays, she set down her basket, and with a hand in the small of her back, straightened up. Determined to impress upon Martha the importance of the new arrival, she began by assuring Martha that, because Mrs. Birch was a great favourite with Miss Charlotte, she was regarded equally so by Miss Fanny, and more than customary care was to be taken in the accommodation of this still enchanting lady. She had therefore put Mrs. Birch in the spacious room leading off the Minstrel's Gallery, so she had one half flight of stairs to negotiate.

'Perhaps you were not aware, Miss Marcia,' she said, 'but Mrs. Birch, although somewhat infirm in the lower limbs, is a very active lady for her age. Eighty if she is a day and, in the summer when 'tis warm, she's able to move about unaided save for a cane. Very particular she is, in her choice of canes, none of those crooked ones, just a straight stick with a lovely gold knob on the top, or ivory, amber or... oh, she has a choice of dunnamany styles, for she is always so elegant.'

After expressing her approval of these arrangements, Martha was at last free to make her escape. She entered the house by a side door and went straight upstairs to Fanny's room. It was empty. Frustrated in her purpose, Martha went to her own room. She left the door slightly ajar, in case Fanny returned and could be intercepted.

Annie, putting her black and cream dress on the bed, explained her presence, 'Miss Fanny changed so quickly I scarce had time to brush her hair, that eager she was to see Mrs. Birch. So I've come to see if I can help you.'

'Thank you, Annie. At what time did Mrs. Birch arrive?'

'About two o'clock. Miss Ross – that's her maid – tells me that Madam, as she calls her, never travels far each day and likes to arrive early in the afternoon so she can take a-a see yesta, I think she said, before dinner. Madam lived for many years in Italy where they takes them things every afternoon. Lazy, I calls it, but 'tis a good idea for an old lady like Mrs. Birch. Very active she is, Miss Ross says, and loves travelling. Has relatives everywhere, she has, seeing as how she was married four times.'

Martha's silence encouraged Annie, fascinated by these details, to chatter on, 'Four husbands. Fancy that. Married and widowed four times, an', I dunno how many children. She married gentlemen who had children of their own too. That's what happened when she married Miss Fanny's great-grandfather, he was her second, I b'leeve, an' the one after him was a Princhippy, that I do now.' Seeing Martha's puzzlement, Annie added helpfully, 'Italian, he was.'

Martha smiled inwardly, she should have been able to work that one out for herself.

'Miss Ross was pressing Madam's dress. Miss Marcia, you wait 'til you see the lovely silk. Nothing but the best for her, says Miss Ross...chemises hand embroidered by nuns... lace so fine... I could not believe it. And her dress, Miss Ross let me study as to how it was made. It is beautiful.' She sighed at the recollection, 'New it was, a silver thread running through it... they had bought it in Italy, seeing as how they have just come back from visiting her family... her Italian family.'

Bemused by this wealth of information, Martha wondered how Mrs. Birch had managed to overcome the loss of four husbands, and her heart went out to her. Not that it did not appear the lady had managed to recover. All the same, Martha was looking forward to meeting this redoubtable woman.

By the time Annie had helped her into her dress and Martha cast a critical eye at her reflection in the looking-glass, the hour was well advanced. Quite easily she resigned herself once more to not having her talk with Fanny before she went down to the withdrawing room. She vowed she would speak to her before they retired to bed for the night.

Eager to see her most favourite, no – come to think of it – not quite her most favourite relative – aunt Em was that now, Fanny tapped on the solid oak door.

'Enter, Frances, enter. There Ross, you see I told you 'twould not be long before Miss Frances came to see me. Come and give me a kiss... dear child.'

Fanny flew across the room into the welcoming arms of the spritely lady who was sitting on the day bed propped up by numerous pillows. After a warm embrace, she put Fanny away from her and said, 'Now, let me look at you. See Ross, I was right, she has turned into a beauty.'

'Yes, Madam, that she has, not but I always thought she would,' said Ross, 'but still cannot hold a candle to her mamma, I reckon.'

'Nonsense,' said Mrs. Birch, 'Her mamma's beauty was of a different order. Come sit here, child,' she patted a chair beside her. 'Now, tell me, what's this I hear from your grandmamma... Cobbleigh bankrupt... It cannot be, for if ever I saw prosperity, I saw it when I reached your lands.'

Fanny looked into the shrewd unfaded blue eyes and said flatly, 'Grandmamma was right, but she is a little out of date.'

Mrs. Birch nodded her head and remarked scathingly, 'That's not all your grandmamma is, but I digress. Go on child. Apart from wishing to see you after all these years, I also wish to hear everything down to the last detail.' The mischievous smile accompanying these words transformed her face, instant evidence of how she had attracted four husbands and retained their devotion until their dying day; and how she was also a popular friend and confidante of her own sons and daughters, the children of her husbands and the descendants of both. The nefarious doings of Napoleon Bonaparte notwithstanding, she had managed, most years, to spend the winter months in Italy. The rest of the year found her a welcome guest amongst her English families and it was to pay her customary visit to her step-daughter, Fanny's grandmother, that she had gone to Bath.

Caroline Powys was one of the few members of Mrs. Birch's extended family for whom she never felt much affection. Consequently, her effort to be agreeable was always the greater. The woman annoyed her. To a person of Mrs. Birch's boundless energy and vivacity it was, perhaps, natural for Caroline's indolence to exasperate her. For her part, Caroline Powys dreaded the matriarchal descents which upset the quiet life she had succeeded in arranging for herself so admirably.

She frequently complained to her daughter, Augusta, 'She exhausts me so, always wanting to be up and doing, really at her age it is positively indecent they ways she runs about.'

'Hardly runs, mamma, hobbles,' corrected the long-suffering Augusta with a titter, for the brunt of entertaining Mrs. Birch always fell upon her.

'Well, 'tis most annoying for she manages to make even her hobble look graceful,' grumbled her mother. Mrs. Birch arrived in Bath to find her step-daughter lying on a sofa in her withdrawing room, wrapped in shawls, complaining of a summer cold.

After greeting each other with cool politeness, Mrs. Powys commanded Augusta to twine another shawl around her for there was a draught whistling about her shoulders. 'Nonsense,' said the hardy Mrs. Birch, 'It is a lovely day without a breath of breeze, you should be out enjoying the sunshine.'

'Mamma, you know my complexion cannot tolerate the sun,' wailed Caroline, resentful at being reduced to the schoolroom even at sixty years of age. Mrs. Birch restrained herself from throwing the curtains back and opening a window, and recollected herself in time to keep a vigorous answer between her teeth. She could never force Caroline to do anything against her will. So she sat herself gracefully on a chair opposite her and said, 'Very well, Caroline, what has been going on since I saw you last?'

'Nothing to speak of, you know how quiet we like to keep ourselves.'

Hearing this Augusta sighed. She would not have minded if they went to the play now and then, instead of everlasting playing cards with her mother's cronies and visiting the Pump Room every morning, if the weather was not inclement, of course; and it was an age since she had attended a concert or an assembly. Mrs. Birch heard the sigh and wondered, not for the first time, why Augusta did not make a push at living her own life. Her mother could well afford a companion. Putting aside the temptation to meddle, she said instead, 'When can I see Frances? Where is the dear child? I was excessively shocked to hear of Gerald's death and that Cobbleigh was to be sold.'

'She is still at Cobbleigh,' replied Caroline.

'What!' Cried Mrs. Birch thunderstruck, 'Have you done nothing for the child?'

'I did not have to do anything,' said Caroline defensively, 'I offered to give her a home here with us, but she would have none of it. Instead she wrote to that sister of Gerald's asking her for help, if you please.'

'And?'

'Oh, she went to Cobbleigh. And has done very well, from what I hear from Beatrice Cairnton. Although what reliance I can place upon Beatrice's judgment I do not know. She was the one who recommended Miss Porter, the governess I had to turn off for walking out with that lawyer person behind our backs.'

'Well, she married her lawyer, did she not? Besides, what's that to the purpose?' Mrs. Birch was irritated. 'D'you mean to tell me, Caroline, you have not communicated with Frances since you heard from Beatrice Cairnton?'

'Augusta was going to write to Frances next week, were you not Gussie?' Her daughter, still annoyed at not having Fanny at her beck and call, was slow to reply. However, to deny any knowledge of the intended letter would, as soon as they were alone, bring her mother's wrath down upon her head, so she said sulkily, 'Mother asked me to write only yesterday.'

Mrs. Birch had a pretty good idea that neither Fanny's grandmother nor Fanny's aunt were interested enough in the girl to bestir themselves, so she resolved then and there to rest for a day, then journey on to Cobbleigh and see for herself how matters stood. Quelling her disgust at the pair of them, she said, 'I am only here for a day, my dears, for I am on my way to Chester. I think I will call at Cobbleigh on the way. I shall, of course, send you a report of what I find. I do not place much reliance on the Gilbert side of the family being of any use to Frances.' Silently she added the rider, 'either' to that remark. She wondered, not for the first time, where she had made a mistake with Caroline, believing it her fault Caroline was so lazy and selfish. Like most people with boundless vitality, Mrs. Birch never realized how enervating she could be to anyone with Caroline's lack of stamina, and it was inevitable Caroline always showed the worst side of her nature in her step-mother's presence.

Except for telling Fanny that her grandmother and aunt Augusta sent their fondest love, Mrs. Birch did not explain the reason for her unheralded visit, beyond saying she had made up her mind so quickly she knew she would arrive before a letter.

'Now, Frances, what has been going on? Your grandmamma told me terrible tales. How Gerald left no money, only debts, and your trustees wished to sell Cobbleigh. And what's all this about Marcia Gilbert residing with you? I'm amazed. Is it true?'

'Yes, quite true, grandmother Birch. Papa left so many debts I was quite at a stand. I did not know where to turn. Then aunt Em came and, somehow, she has managed to change things so, I no longer have to sell

Cobbleigh. She is a marvel. Why, she and the Major between them...'

'The Major, who is he?'

Happy in the tale she had to tell, Fanny unconsciously avoided stressing the disagreeable part played by the Corbys and the deleterious effect they had on her father. She concentrated more upon the retrenchment and reclamation of Cobbleigh. The old lady was enthralled but puzzled. This did not sound at all like the Marcia Gilbert she knew of. However, in the enjoyment of the narrative, she let it pass. She approved the appointment of the Major, asked many searching questions regarding the present state of Fanny's finances and rejoiced in the girl's glowing looks.

'We discovered you had rented the Manor House on our arrival, I deem it a very sensible move. I have always liked this house and I see you are comfortable here. Now, Frances, we shall go down to the withdrawing room, for 'tis near six o'clock and your guests will arrive soon. I am looking forward to meeting the gentlemen and, of course, Miss Gilbert.'

20 - Truth Will Out

As Martha descended the stairs, Daly told her 'Everyone awaits you in the withdrawing room, Miss Marcia.' In reproach for her tardiness, he flung wide the double doors and loudly announced 'Miss Marcia'. Heads turned towards the door. Fanny sat on a stool beside the wing chair enthroning a handsome, straight-backed, old lady. They stopped talking to the men standing together before the empty fireplace, and everyone watched her unusually ceremonious entry. Recollecting her social obligations, Fanny jumped up and ran to her and took her hand to lead her forward, 'Grandmother Birch, may I make known to you my aunt Marcia. Aunt Marcia, this is my great-great grandmother, Mrs. Birch.'

Mrs. Birch, immediately approving the elegant figure moving gracefully towards her, took a second look at the smiling face.

'Good Gad!' she exclaimed. 'You are not Marcia Gilbert.'

Martha's blood froze. Unable to think clearly, her response was as involuntary as it was truthful. 'No, Ma'am, you are quite right, I am not Marcia Gilbert.' Stunned by her unexpected unmasking, she was barely aware of what she said. Fanny's warm little hand tightened its clasp on hers until it hurt. This support served to make her aware of Charles's encouraging nod, and Hugh's bewilderment.

'Then, who are you?'

'Grandmother, this is my...'

'Let her answer for herself, Frances.'

'B-but...' stammered Fanny.

'Hush, my love.' Martha's words were for Fanny alone, 'I'm so sorry you had to learn the truth in this way...

lord knows I've been trying to confess to you for days. Please don't be angry with me...'

Mrs. Birch, rapped her cane on the floor. 'Answer me, if you please. Who are you? Explain yourself.'

Charles stepped forward to stand on Martha's other side. He faced the old lady and said, 'I can tell you who she is...'

'Please. Charles, no. Let me,' Martha smiled up at him gratefully, 'Thank you, but I must explain my own actions. I must do what you've been urging me to do ever since you first came here.' She turned back to Fanny, 'My name is Martha Grey, she that was companion to the late Miss Marcia Gilbert.'

'Late?' said Mrs. Birch.

'Companion,' murmured Fanny, 'so that's how...'

'How and when did she die?' demanded Mrs. Birch.

'A few days after her brother. She was ill for many months. Fanny's letter arrived as I was closing the house and making it ready for sale. I was about to return to my home in Herefordshire when Marcia's attorney asked me to break my journey and carry the news to Fanny in person and, incidentally, convey Fanny's legacy to her.'

'And what legacy is that, pray? Marcia Gilbert was a wealthy woman.' Mrs. Birch's tone was accusatory. Some twelve years ago she had visited Seacliffe to recuperate from the death of Mr. Birch. At the time she had met and heartily disliked Marcia Gilbert. Realizing Marcia Gilbert could only have heard of her as the Principessa di Donato and had no means of connecting that aristocratic name with a mere Mrs. Birch, she had not enlightened her of their family connection. As soon as she had heard of Fanny's aunt Marcia setting about the salvation of Cobbleigh so energetically, she was somewhat puzzled and her lively curiosity was aroused. The marvellous tales Fanny told of her aunt, strengthened her wish to meet the miraculously changed woman who, in her estimation from her admittedly brief encounter, did not sound like the cold, selfish woman she had met. Now, of course, she understood. She looked at the young woman standing before her, head held high. She could not help but admire her, resolutely refusing all support from Lord Biscay – who was obviously in love with her – answering all questions calmly. Mrs. Birch could tell she was not calm underneath, a tiny vein throbbed in her temple. It would do this Mrs. Grey no harm to be catechised, and Mrs. Birch decided not to spare her until she discovered why this woman had assumed another's identity. The old lady did not show it, but she was vastly entertained. The unravelling of all the whys and wherefores of what had taken place at Cobbleigh was a powerful stimulant to one who thrived on excitement.

'Marcia Gilbert left all her property, real and personal, to the orphans of Seacliffe, with the exception of a few bequests to the servants, all her beautiful clothes to me; and, to Fanny the jewellery that was her mother's.' Fanny touched the amethyst pendant at her neck. 'Also, Voltaire, Tig and Highness. A parrot, a cat and a dog.'

Fanny chuckled, 'So that's why your coach resembled Noah's Ark.'

'This is no time for levity, Frances.' Reprimanded Mrs. Birch, hiding her secret amusement. Nevertheless, she asked sternly, 'When did you decide on this masquerade?'

'I did not.'

There was an incredulous stare from Mrs. Birch and a perplexed look from Hugh. He was sad to think his friend Marcia had lent herself to such a deception and, as he could not think ill of her, cast about in his mind for an acceptable reason.

Martha hastened to explain, 'I was exceedingly unwell when I arrived here. Stupidly, I fainted on the doorstep. When I came round you, Fanny, addressed me as 'aunt Marcia' and Mrs. Daly persisted in calling me 'Miss Gilbert'. When I tried to explain, more than once, either no one heard me or did not listen to what I was trying to say. Before I had gathered my wits and was feeling strong enough to correct the error, I'd heard enough of Fanny's plight to feel that perhaps I could be of some assistance.

'My home had not seen me for many years, so a few more weeks would not matter. Also, I fully understood what Fanny was undergoing because, years ago, I nearly lost my all, without I had not received timely help, so – rightly or wrongly – I kept quiet and searched for ways and means of assisting Cobbleigh back on its feet.' Depressingly, she saw no weakening in Mrs. Birch's countenance, so she said, 'N-now, I'll g-go and get your aunt Marcia's jewel case, Fanny,' and whisked herself out of the room before she broke down in front of them all. She left consternation behind her.

Daly was in the hall. Martha managed to say quite naturally, 'Please put back the dinner by one half hour,' and paid no attention to his expostulations at the dinner's ruination and his fears that Mrs. Martin, in her despair, would throw a tantrum to rival Mounseer's.

Her unmasking had been far worse than Martha could ever have imagined. She blamed herself for lacking the courage to speak to Fanny before this evening. 'Serves me right,' she muttered as she picked up the jewel case. She rested on the window seat in her bedroom, breathing deeply, until she had herself once more in hand. Bravely she returned downstairs, knowing her momentary calm was precarious. It would take very little to break her down. Her insides trembled.

Martha's audience was left in stunned silence, until Fanny burst out, 'She means more to me than any of my real relatives. I love her. She's kind and generous and...' tears welled up and ran down her cheeks. Hugh went quickly to her side and led her to a chair. He turned to Mrs. Birch and said 'In all our dealings I have found Miss Marcia... er... Miss... er... Grey, fair and upright. She has a keen businesslike brain and she alone brought the trustees, honourable gentlemen though they are, to see reason.'

Charles went to Fanny and placed a reassuring hand on her shoulder, said earnestly, 'Ma'am, I've known Martha Grey since we were children and I can vouch for her absolute integrity. She is the widow of my cousin. She had a very hard time when she lost her father, her home and her husband one after the other within the space of a few months and that is the reason – as she told you – why she knew she could sympathise and help Fanny in her predicament. Generous and warm-hearted, she has ever been impulsive, but always with the very best of intentions, and her probity is unquestionable.'

'You are a trifle partial, my lord,' was Mrs. Birch's dry comment. 'Nothing of what you say takes away from the fact that she has done wrong – she has imposed upon us, she is an imposter.' Charles moved to protest, but she held up a hand, 'And,' she continued, 'such an imposture must be severely punished.' Fanny's cry of disbelief at her great-grandmother's words was drowned by the noise of Martha opening the door.

The words 'imposter' and 'imposture must be severely punished' rang through her head. Numbly, she held out the jewel case, 'Here are your jewels, Fanny, the inventory is with them and you will find everything as it should be. P-please f-forgive m-m-me.' She could not continue. Tears welled into her eyes. Blindly she turned towards the long windows, open to catch the evening breeze, and ran into the garden.

'Grandmother, how could you be so cruel?' Fanny demanded in horror. She put down the box without so much as a glance at it, and started to follow Martha.

'No, Fanny, let me,' Charles moved past her.

'Mrs. Birch, I think 'tis time I took my leave,' said Hugh, 'I shall return in the morning with all the estate books so that you may...'

'Nonsense, Major! Stay here. Frances sit down.' They looked at her in surprise. 'Lud! Sit down, I say, both of you. I want to hear the whole tale from you and I will judge who is to be blamed and who is to be praised. It seems to me, Frances, your family is shockingly remiss in allowing a complete stranger to take over and...' she paused with a wicked twinkle in her eye 'do so much good.'

'Grandmamma!' Shrieked Fanny, joyfully casting her arms about Mrs. Birch's neck, 'I knew you were not so unfeeling as you appeared.'

'By George, Ma'am!' exclaimed Hugh 'You had me very worried.'

'Now, Frances, what you told me earlier was not the whole story, was it?' Fanny shook her head, 'Well, I want it now... all of it... so begin at the beginning, please. Where, for instance, was the excellent Miss Bramble at the time of your Papa's death...?'

The tensions and anxieties of the past week, culminating in this evening's disastrous scene, sent Martha into a hearty bout of tears. Charles came upon her in her favourite spot, beneath the lime tree. She was sitting on the bench, her arms wrapped about herself, sobbing her heart out. Wisely, Charles let her cry. It was not until she had sniffed and gulped herself to a standstill that he made his presence felt by silently handing her a large white handkerchief.

She wiped her eyes and firmly blew her nose. 'You warned me,' she said in a small voice, 'But please do not say "I told you so".'

'Did I – ever?'

'No. You were kind. Every time you extricated me from my d-difficulties you were always most s-sympathetic.'

He sat down beside her.

'It is now brought home to me just what I have done,' she continued, 'First, I have to make my peace with Fanny, then I shall gave to apologise to the whole of Cobbleigh, beg their pardons for impersonating Marcia... oh dear...' the prospect daunted her. 'It is a good thing no one connects you with the name Grey,' she said as lightly as she could.

'Martha, my lovely, idiot, do not be silly,' he took her hand, 'I have a very good solution to all your problems – listen to me – become my wife and everybody will be so busy exclaiming at Lady Biscay there will be no time for people to think of Martha Grey.'

Her misery was such that several seconds went by before she turned her tear-marked face towards him. His heart went out to her, she was not one of those lucky people who cried beautifully. Infinitely dear to him though she was, she looked as plain as he had ever seen her.

'Oh, Charles, how very kind you are.' She exclaimed with an artificial brightness that was quite dreadful for him to hear. 'Thank you. But no. I cannot, will not take advantage of your generosity. I have to take my punishment and I will not embroil you. Thank you from the bottom of my heart, but no. I will not marry you.'

Damnation! You hamfisted idiot, he railed at himself. He opened his mouth to rectify the false impression he had given her, but before he could utter a word, she agitatedly pulled her hand from his, rose from the bench and ran away. His Martha running away twice in one evening, he could hardly believe it. His Martha, he liked that. Although his proposal had been unplanned, it was heartfelt. To himself he had been calling her his ever since he began to search for her all those months ago, and the more he learned of the adult Martha, the more his interest in her had grown. It took him but a few minutes, when they met again, to know this was the woman he wanted for his wife, even though, or perhaps because, she was in one of her scrapes – he did not know which. But one thing he did know, he did not want to live without her. And now he had frightened her away.

Her slim figure disappeared down the flagstone walk. It showed him how upset she was, his Martha never used to run away, she was ever a valiant soul. Glumly, he returned to the withdrawing room where he found the three occupants looking, to his jaundiced eye, horridly happy.

Mrs. Birch saw his face and turned to Fanny saying, 'My child, take the Major in to dinner, Daly has been trying to catch our attention this age. Lord Biscay and I will follow presently. Sit down my lord, you will be pleased to hear we have absolved Mrs. Grey from any wrong doing. I was hard on her, I know, but I had to find out exactly what was going on. Those two youngsters have filled my ears with her many excellencies and I cannot tell you how shocked and ashamed I am to be allied to such a ramshackle family. I am more shocked at myself for not having the sensitivity, the nous, to realise years ago all was not well here. And as for Frances's grandmother, words fail me. There again, I feel responsible, after all I brought her up.' She sighed, 'I think your Mrs. Grey saved Frances from a complete mental decline and I must thank her. Where is she?'

'She ran away from me. I'm afraid she's very unhappy.' An unusually resourceful man, in this instance he was completely at a loss to know what to do. 'I've upset her even more than you did. Although it was the farthest thing from my mind,' he added miserably.

'Bless me!' Mrs. Birch smiled knowingly, 'You asked her to marry you and she will not have you?'

'How did you know?'

'I have eyes, my lord,' she replied mockingly. 'Well? Did you?'

'Yes. Made a hash of it... blundered... badly.'

'You must have,' she agreed. 'I suppose you told her all the good reasons why she should marry you except the important one.'

He looked at her questioningly.

'Did you tell her you love her?'

He grimaced, 'No, I didn't have a chance.'

'Fool.' Mrs. Birch's laugh was kind, 'Do not worry, you will next time.'

'She'll not have me because she says she alone must bear her punishment and she is glad I am Biscay and no longer known as Grey. I am not to share her disgrace.'

'So! You did not take her in your arms and kiss some sense into her? And she is so overcome with guilt and remorse she is wallowing in her misery... punishing herself by refusing you. Here's a pretty kettle of fish.'

'What shall I do?' He asked humbly, 'If you can help me change Martha's mind, I would be eternally grateful.'

'My advice will probably not be to your taste, but 'twill serve in the end.'

'What do you propose?'

'Go home for a week or two. Let her settle down and begin to miss you...'

'Do you think she will?'

'I'm a sharp-eyed old woman who, having had four husbands, can tell you a thing or two about the human heart.'

'But you have only just met us.'

'Ah, but I saw her look at you the first time she came through the door and I've also seen how you look at her.'

'I did not realise it showed.'

'As I said before, I'm a knowledgeable old lady, Now go away for a spell. Mrs. Grey will stay here. I'll see to that, and we'll let her recover her equilibrium. I imagine her false position has weighed her down.'

'It has. She has an active conscience and I've not helped her by urging a full confession to Fanny.'

'So, she must be given time. I'll write and let you know when to return and, when you do come back, do not waste time on reasons... act.' She closed her fan with a snap, picked up her silver-topped ebony cane and prepared to rise. 'Agreed?'

He smiled ruefully, 'Agreed, ma'am. But you will not let her run away, will you? I would follow her to the ends of the earth – I've already chased her the length and breadth of England – but I would be happier knowing she is safe here with you.' He put his hand out to assist her to her feet, 'I would hate to have to start looking for her again, and if she took flight it would be to anywhere but Stretton Wakefield now.'

'I will keep her by me' she reassured him. 'Now, we will dine and then you will take your leave. I do not imagine Mrs. Grey will be with us tonight. Do not return tomorrow.'

He protested 'I cannot leave her without so much as a word of farewell.'

'Write her a pretty note, if you must. Let Mrs. Grey start missing you immediately.'

Martha's mind was in a whirl as she lay back on her bed staring at the ceiling. Instinctively, she had run to her room to hide and brood. Inextricably woven in her disordered thoughts were fears Fanny would never forgive her, Mrs. Birch's disapproval, Charles's sudden proposal – so hastily turned down – the shock on Hugh's kind face and her dread of having to meet everybody on the morrow. Gradually she composed herself, trying to form a rational plan to solve her problems. First and foremost, she must see Fanny. With that thought she rose from her bed, washed her face and took up her hair brush. Running the brush through her long hair soothed her, allowing her to think more clearly. The feeling uppermost in her mind was regret she had refused Charles so abruptly. She heartily wished she was not in such a dreadful scrape and could have accepted his proposal with a clear conscience. Her hands paused while pinning her hair, what was she thinking of? Why, when he had made no mention of loving her and had, indeed, merely given her to understand he was offering her the protection of his name, did she think so longingly of giving in and laying all her problems on his shoulders? There was no mention of love between them. Perhaps that was why she refused him so swiftly, and yet he must have some feeling for her, otherwise why should she have the impression he would do anything for her? It was really very puzzling and she must think the matter over more deeply later. First, she must see Fanny, she would attempt to overcome her other difficulties and embarrassments one by one. And then what should she do? Where should she go? Not to Stretton Wakefield, the dear place would be no haven to her now. She had it. She would return to Seacliffe – Jessica would welcome her and later she could visit Tante Elise in Provence. On that last thought she opened a drawer in the tallboy and piled the contents on the bed ready for packing.

Fanny spoke from the doorway, 'Aunt Em... er... Mrs. G-Grey... you were not with us at dinner. You must be hungry, would you like a tray brought up?' Then she saw what Martha was doing, 'No, no,' she cried, 'you must not leave me.' She ran to Martha's side and took the lawn shifts from Martha's hands. 'You must not leave, Aunt Em, I need you...' She looked earnestly into Martha's face 'Oh, Aunt Em. You've been crying, indeed you must not, grandmother Birch is not angry with you anymore. Hugh, Charles and I explained how it was, in fact grandmother now she wishes to thank you.'

'It's you, Fan, who should be angry with me for deceiving you. I would not blame you if you threw me out of Cobbleigh neck and crop.'

'Throw you out of Cobbleigh! I should think not, indeed! How could I, when you have done so much for me and Cobbleigh. Without you there would be no Cobbleigh for me to throw you out of.'

'But I've deceived you grossly. I would not blame you if you never trusted me or indeed trusted anyone again.' Wearily she sat down on the edge of the bed, 'Believe me Fanny, I did try to tell you, many, many times. It was Charles who brought home to me the evils of my situation, but I promise you, I had tried to screw up my courage even before his arrival. But every time I was ready, something always happened to put me off. Mr. Corby coming, for instance, and even this evening. I was going to tell you while we dressed for dinner, but I was foiled by the arrival of Mrs. Birch.

'Aunt Em...'

Martha winced, 'Oh, please don't call me that. Could you not call me Martha?'

Fanny laughed and hugged Martha, 'I was not truly deceived you know. I had my suspicions.'

'Voltaire!'

'Yes, Volly, but other things. Long before he opened his beak. Little matters, when you fainted and told us you never fainted. Completely to the contrary of what Papa used to tell of you. And you were not quite in the character father had painted. Nothing in themselves, but they added up to I knew not what. Even taking into account Papa's love of exaggeration, I suspected you far too kind a person to be my aunt Marcia. Also, I was surprised at your ease and ability in matters pertaining to country pursuits. In fact, you were far too nice to have been a relative of mine.' Fanny's eyes filled with tears, and with one accord she and Martha put their arms around each other and cried on each other's shoulder Soon the sobs turned into giggles, and Fanny hiccoughing a little, said 'Look at the pair of us, a pair of ninnies,' and Martha smiled in watery agreement.

'Do you truly not hold it against me that I masqueraded as your aunt?' Fanny nodded emphatically, 'And Mrs. Birch has forgiven me too?'

Fanny smiled, 'And she says you and she will have a conference tomorrow and decide how the news best be broken to the neighbourhood. I have no doubt she is looking forward to it, as she dearly loves excitement, especially when it smacks of intrigue. We, that is, Hugh and I, were all for not telling anyone, after all I call you aunt Em and you could continue to be Miss Gilbert until such time as you should wish to leave, no one need know any differently. But grandmother and Charles both thought neither could it, nor should it, be kept a secret. If grandmother and I make nothing of the matter, then no one else can possibly do so either. So grandmother is undertaking to sponsor you in the neighbourhood, and she is delighted to sacrifice grandmamma Powys for your benefit. Her ill-health, you know, precludes her from taking as close an interest in me as she might do. And on her deathbed aunt Marcia, the real aunt Marcia of course, enjoined you to look after me as best you might. Do you not think it a famous plan?' Fanny's eyes sparkled, 'I must say I'll enjoy the telling of it, just as much as grandmother Birch. Charles did not think it would do for everybody, in fact he insisted the Dalys be told the truth, and the trustees, although it will be pointed out their wanting to sell up made us desperate enough to decide you should masquerade as aunt Em.

'Charles is right. And I must tell the O'Briens and Timothy. Oh dear.' Martha shuddered, 'Although I am loath to confess my duplicity to them all, I do owe them a true explanation.'

'Charles agrees. He made grandmother agree, too. She would love to continue hoodwinking everybody. Anyway, aunt... I mean Martha, you need not worry further. I very much hope you will stay with me and make your home here for as long as you wish, although I know you have a perfectly good home in Stretton Wakefield... for Charles told me so.'

Martha was touched and near tears again, 'Thank you my dear, dear Fanny. But now Mrs. Birch has matters in hand, I do not think you have any further need of my services. I will stay until we have cleared up the least misunderstanding over my not being Marcia, but then...'

'You may stay forever if you wish, but Charles, before he left, said he hoped very much you would return to your rightful place in Stretton Wakefield.'

'Yes, well... I must talk to Charles tomorrow,'

'You'll not be able to do that I'm afraid. He took leave of us tonight. Something about an urgent summons calling him home earlier than expected. He left his best wishes and deepest apologies at not being able to say goodbye to you himself, but he quite understood that you had shut yourself in your room.'

'Charles has gone?' She felt completely bereft,

'Yes, but he did say he hoped to return before long.'

With that vague promise Martha had to be content. She kissed Fanny goodnight and, worn out by the events of the evening, she hastily prepared for bed. Yawning widely she lay down, meaning to think about the tumultuous events of the evening, but was asleep as soon as her head touched the pillow.

Next morning, Annie brought a note from Charles with her hot water. Couched in formal terms it merely reiterated his message of the night before, which left Martha dismally convinced she had, by her brusque refusal of him, completely alienated her one and only true friend.

21 - Resolution

When the extraordinary tale whereby the elder Miss Gilbert was not Miss Gilbert at all, but a widow, a Mrs. Thomas Grey, filtered out from the Dower House, the sensation it caused was a nine days' wonder. Who was this Mrs. Grey? No one had heard of her. Matters were clearer when it was said that Mrs. Thomas Grey had taken Miss Gilbert's place, at the request of the true Miss Gilbert on her death bed, in order to render Miss Fanny any service within her power. Still the inhabitants of Cobbleigh were taken by storm and for a time nothing else was discussed. There were the usual well-informed few who insisted they had always suspected there was something dashed smokey about the lady. And the maiden who had said Miss Marcia looked far too young for her age, unwisely attempted to say, 'I told you so', to her mother and had her ears soundly boxed for her impertinence. In the main, however, it was held a very good thing Mrs. Grey had come to set Cobbleigh to rights. The unpredictable Mr. Mason maintained loudly that she was the best landlord Cobbleigh had ever had and hoped Miss Fanny would be half as good.

As it was generally believed Mrs. Grey's (one must remember to call her Mrs. Grey) arrival ushered in a new prosperity to manor and village, Martha found she was treated with even more respect, if it were possible, than when she was believed to be Miss Gilbert. These intense discussions occupied manor and cot alike until another fascinating occurrence took precedence. Farmer Fieldfare's heifer gave birth to a five-legged calf and, in no time, people were too busy assessing how much money he would make exhibiting the unfortunate creature at fairs and sideshows, and the strange tale of Mrs. Grey faded into the background.

Martha steeled herself to face the Dalys. Before she had done more than apologise for imposing upon their goodwill, Daly stopped her and said, 'Mrs. Grey, we, that is to say, Mrs. Daly, William and I, would like to say that no one, no one else could have done what you've done for Miss Fanny and we, that is to say...' he halted confused and Mrs. Daly took up the speech, 'What Daly would like to say for all of us, Ma'am, is Miss Fanny has told us the whole story and no one in our hearing will be allowed to say any other but what you did was right and proper, and so we shall tell everybody.'

Quite overcome Martha said, 'Thank you from the bottom of my heart. Bless you, you have no notion how relieved I am you've taken it this way.' She turned away unwilling to let them see the tears in her eyes, she cried so easily these days.

Her interview with Mrs. Birch was far easier than she anticipated, although Fanny had told her the old lady was on her side. They soon discovered they had a lot in common, and found not only did they agree on many diverse subjects, but they could discuss and argue amicably and thoroughly enjoy each other's company.

They were united in their disapproval of Gerald Gilbert's behaviour in his later years; stigmatized the Corbys as a rascally pair; minutely discussed Marcia Gilbert's foibles; and, sorrowfully dismissed Caroline Powys as a selfish lightweight. Mrs. Birch was more than grateful Fanny had come to no harm and was truly mortified her family had sat back leaving room for an outsider to step into the breach. She bound Martha to Cobbleigh by insisting she continue on as before. Whereupon Martha, still uncomfortable with her conscience, responded by assigning herself more and more tasks to keep herself busy and thus hold her growing unhappiness at bay. All the while Mrs Birch watched her knowingly, and did not protest at the lengths Martha went in tiring herself out.

When Martha, with Fanny and Mrs. Birch in support, made the rounds of their friends the Cairntons, the Parks and the Wentworths, Mrs. Birch's unqualified approval of her enabled them to accept her as Mrs. Grey, thinking it a marvellous tale and admiring her for her daring.

The trustees were a different matter. Mr. Ackland took a very grave view of the imposture, and shook his head so gloomily that Mrs. Birch told him acidly that if Mrs. Grey had not taken matters into her own hands, Cobbleigh would be sold up by now. Mr. Ackland forced to accept the accuracy of the statement said, 'Mrs. Grey I see we have much to thank you for, but I can only wish you had confided in us when you arrived. I do admit that if we had not supposed you to be a relation, we would never have given you the right to carry on as you did, so I must be thankful you did not tell us.'

'Mr. Ackland,' replied Martha warmly, 'you are more than generous.'

'Hmph!' was Mrs. Birch's comment.

The Reverend Mr. Gore, rebuked Martha gently, more in sorrow than in anger, which she found hard to bear. He too wished she had been open with him, but he too had to concede he would never have allowed her the latitude she had enjoyed if he had even suspected the truth. 'So all's well that ends well,' he said 'for Fanny's sake we'll say no more but thank you.' And Martha heaved a sigh of relief.

One day, when Martha and Mrs. Birch were alone in the morning room, the old lady broached a subject that had been exercising Martha's mind for some time.

'I like Mrs. Wentworth, and her girls are very pretty and well brought up.'

'Yes, Mrs. Wentworth's a thoroughly nice woman. Arabella and Fanny get along so well, Mrs. Wentworth has offered to give Fanny a season when Arabella makes her debut. I have – had – rather been trying to contrive because, Ma'am, Fanny should have the chance to go out into the world a little, especially...' she looked at Mrs. Birch.

'Especially because she is very interested in Major Buchan... Yes, I've seen that too. He would make an excellent husband for her, of course, but she is too lovely, one cannot help but feel she might do a deal better for herself.'

'She is so very young to have formed a strong, lasting attachment,' Martha looked worried.

'No younger than I was, when I married my first husband – not that it was an altogether successful marriage,' she added in a reminiscent mood. 'He killed himself in a carriage accident, just after my second child was born. So I cannot tell... it might have turned out very well... but looking back I have my doubts. What about your marriage?'

'We were very young too,' said Martha evasively, she did not feel she could discuss Tom with an equal frankness.

'When one is so young, one's judgment is not always of the very best. Marriage is a gamble,' pronounced Mrs. Birch, 'and no marriage is perfect. If it was, how very dull life would be to be sure. Often difficulties can be overcome with patience, and I enjoyed the challenge.' Her eyes sparkled like a girl's.

In appreciation, Martha said, 'I'm sure you did. But to return to Fanny, she has not had a happy life in recent years. I thought a season would give her some gaiety, give her a chance to meet a different circle of people, get away from Cobbleigh... although she'd never consent to leave for long, I know that. Before Mrs. Wentworth's offer I did not know what to do.'

You're absolutely right, but before I take her to London... oh, yes, I shall give her a season with Mrs. Wentworth and Arabella... I shall take her, and Arabella if Mrs. Wentworth agrees, to Bath. Not the Bath Fanny complained of, and not to the assemblies and parties as she is still in mourning, but to concerts and plays and then, on to Italy to visit my Italian family. There are several grandchildren of her age, and in London and elsewhere, Fanny will not lack for company. Who knows, the two girls might make a hit. I was, you know. At their age I was a toast.' She nodded her proud head with its finely modelled bones, and Martha could well believe her. 'I shall enjoy it all hugely, I have not had anyone come out under my aegis for many years. And you shall come with us – you deserve a holiday – would you like to be frivolous with us?'

It was a temporary solution to Martha's problem, so she was pleased to reply with gratitude. 'I would enjoy it above all things, and I accept your kind invitation with pleasure.'

'Good, that's settled.' said Mrs. Birch, 'Now, that does not solve the problem of the Major.'

'He loves her, of that I am sure.'

'Enough to let her go?'

'Is that not asking too much of him?'

'I do not think it unreasonable,' said Mrs. Birch firmly.

'Well... I do think he is conscious of the ten year age difference.'

'And Fanny? Would she consent to go away, if we put it to her that before she settles down she should see something of the world beyond Cobbleigh. No, I think I would mention that any man who was a soldier might not settle down for ever with a know-nothing miss who'd never been further than the next county.'

'No names, general statement en passant. Simple,' said Martha. 'But, Ma'am, do you want Fanny to marry elsewhere or would you accept the Major for her? I must say they do seem well suited and I doubt she would ever settle happily away from her beloved Cobbleigh.'

'Oh, I agree, but we cannot have Fanny married to him and later, through lack of experience, elope with some pretty young man within a year or two. After all the Major is no Adonis.'

But Fanny was wiser than the two ladies so busy in planning a life for her. She looked to the Major as the rock upon which to build her house. She knew she loved him and would not change, but upon Mrs. Birch's representations she should acquire a little knowledge of the world – a little polish – more for her prospective husband's sake than for her own, she agreed wholeheartedly. She had also come to the conclusion her grandmother very much wanted to make it up to her, in some measure, for the neglect she had experienced and would enjoy having her having her as a protégée and travelling companion. Fanny also knew Martha was unsettled and unhappy and she had a greater obligation to her. Until Martha had, in some sort, worked out her destiny, Fanny did not feel free to pursue her own interests. She owed Martha far too much to ignore her prior claim.

Fanny and Hugh had not truly had a minute alone since that momentous day in the Estate Office. Now she sought him out and found him in the cider cellar, which smelled deliciously of fermented apples.

'What are you doing?'

'Checking the casks to see which ones need repairing for this year's pressing. We'll have a bumper crop.'

'I did not know you knew anything about cider.'

'I don't, except to drink it. But according to father's notes, now is the time to look over the barrels.' Her turned to her, 'Did you want to see me about something, Fanny?'

'Yes, I did. Let's talk here where we will not be disturbed.' She sat on a small keg and looked up at him leaning against a barrel. 'I would like your advice, Hugh,' she said earnestly, 'Granny Birch has asked me, Martha and Arabella, to go with her to Bath and then on to Italy.

That is, until the London season begins when we are to join Mrs. Wentworth in London.'

'I see.' He said noncommittally, 'And what are your feelings?'

'Oh! That I must go.'

He was silent, no clue to his thoughts showed.

She was worried. Why he did not say something? She took a deep breath and continued 'I believe some time away from Cobbleigh would be most interesting and instructive.' Still he did not respond to this stiff little speech, but continued to look at her expressionlessly. 'When I return...'

He stirred at last, 'When you return? So, you will come back you think?'

'Of course I shall come back to you.' There it was out. Then in a rush, 'I would like to become betrothed to you before I go – but they would not understand...'

He moved at last to catch her hands in his, 'But Fanny, if we are betrothed, what if you meet someone more to your liking?'

She was emphatic in her denial, 'I will not! Oh, Hugh, I know what I want and what I shall always want. Martha and Granny Birch do not understand me. Because their first marriages were not entirely happy they fear for mine. But I'm not like them, you are not the gay, careless, lovers they chose, you are solid dependable and loving. I love you, Hugh, and I do not really want to do the season, but I am under a great obligation to Martha. And Gran has invited her to go with us. I cannot leave Martha while she is so unsettled.' Her brow puckered with worry, 'Where is Charles. Hugh? He should be here with her.'

'I agree, but give them time. I am sure they'll be together soon.'

'If they do come together,' said Fanny, 'I shall have no hesitation in refusing Granny's plans for my season. I'm under no real obligation to her. Although I will accept her invitation to visit Bath and Italy, I would like to see something of the world before I settle down with you.' She smiled up him lovingly.

He took her in his arms, 'I'll speak to Mrs. Birch and ask her permission to pay my addresses to you. Though I suppose it should be Mrs. Powys...'

'Oh, no. Granny Birch is the one. She likes you and she can manage grandmamma Powys admirably.'

His mouth brushed hers, 'I love you Fanny.' He kissed her again with great tenderness, she opened her mouth to reply in kind and found it impossible to think of anything further than his deepening kiss.

After an interval if dizzying delight, Hugh came to his senses. He raised his head and looked into Fanny's adoring eyes. 'Stand over there, my love, I have to talk to you and I cannot do it rationally with you in my arms.'

Disappointed, Fanny reluctantly obeyed.

'Listen to me,' he ran a hand through his hair distractedly, 'Now, listen to me,' he repeated, 'I will not be betrothed to you. No, let me finish. We will, however, make an agreement and that is, if you, after your travels no longer feel the way you do now, you are to say so.'

'But Hugh I know I'll not change my mind. We Gilberts marry young and are happy...'

'You may change your mind, my lass, and I do not want an unwilling wife, bored with me and...'

'Hugh!'

'Think, Fanny, think - am I not right?'

She was quiet. 'Y-yes, I suppose you are. And I make the same agreement for you.' There were tears in her eyes as she said forlornly, 'I do hope we are not being too sensible...'

'No love, we are being cautious and 'tis only for six or seven months... less if Charles comes up to scratch. Now, come here, kiss me, and then go.'

She ran into his arms, was scooped up, resoundingly and thoroughly kissed and the propelled inexorably towards the door. As the door closed behind her Hugh sat down on the keg and bowed his head in thought. He hoped his gamble on her return to him would pay off. He looked at his clenched hands resting on his knees. He opened them slowly and saw they were shaking.

Mrs. Birch's letter reached Charles two weeks later. He had begun to fear she had forgotten her promise. Much relieved, he ordered his curricle and set off immediately.

He neared Cobbleigh by three the following afternoon. He swept around a bend in the lane leading to the Manor gates, and saw Fanny on Badoura. She was talking to Hugh who was leaning against a gate, an uncocked gun over his arm and a pair of spaniels at his feet.

Charles drew up beside them and Fanny greeted him with excitement, 'We are so very glad you have come. Do hurry to the Dower House, everyone will be so pleased you are here at last.'

'Fanny!' exclaimed Charles in consternation, 'Does all the world know my business?'

'Not all. 'Tis because Martha has been getting worse and worse.'

Thoroughly alarmed, Charles tightened his hands on the reins, making the horses throw up their heads and step backwards, 'My God! She's not ill?'

'Not ill.. precisely,' said Fanny.

'Do not tease him, Fan,' chided Hugh, hiding a smile.

'By worse and worse, I mean she never stops. She's not ill, unless you call turning the house upside down and inside out... being ill. She has cleaned out the attics, refurbished and repaired all she can lay her hands on and, any day now, I know she'll want to start on the Manor attics. The Dower House has nearly wilted under her ministrations. She is driving Mrs. Daly quite demented. Poor dear, I believe she's still trying to atone.'

'Or, rather, she's trying to keep so busy so as not to think,' said Hugh sympathetically.

'Whatever the reason, 'tis only because they like her so much the servants have not given in their notice. Charles, 'tis all your fault, you have stayed away far too long,' Fanny accused.

'But I was only obeying Mrs. Birch's instructions,' explained Charles.

'Granny Birch had a hand in this? I might have known. Charles hurry, at this very moment on this beautiful day, Martha is in the linen room, with my poor Annie, going through the linen. And 'twas all done not four months gone when we moved.'

Charles gathered the reins, 'Right. Where's the linen room?'

'Up the stairs, along the passage to the left, the second door on the right.'

'I'm infinitely obliged to you,' Charles gave the horses their heads.

'How I wish I could be a fly on the linen room wall,' said Fanny wistfully, watching the cloud of dust kicked up by the curricle's passage.

'Much better to pay attention to our own affairs, my love, now that Charles is dissolving your obligation to Martha,' said Hugh firmly.

Charles left his curricle in the stableyard, and walked over to the Dower House. He entered the front door, wide open to the summer air. Encountering nobody, he left his hat and gloves on the hall table and mounted the stairs two at a time. Following Fanny's directions he reached the linen room. The door was ajar. He could hear Martha saying '...and two makes one and a half dozen. These need re-bleaching, please add them to the pile.'

Silently, he pushed the door wider. The clean, sweet smell of the lavender used to scent the linen met his nostrils. Martha, her back to the door, was standing tip-toe on a three-legged stool putting something on the top shelf. Annie, standing below and behind her, caught sight of Charles. Her eyes grew round in surprise and was about to speak, when he stopped her from uttering by putting a finger to his lips. He jerked his head meaningfully towards the door. She nodded and quietly passed him, putting the linen she was holding into his hands. She went through the door and pulled it quietly to as she did so.

'Please pass me the rest.' Martha put her hand down without looking. Charles obeyed, remarking as he did so, 'You know, my love, I do think you would be much happier looking after your own linen in your own house.'

Martha swung around so suddenly the stool toppled. Her cry of 'Charles!' was a glad sound as she fell with considerable force against him. With great presence of mind he clasped her to his breast as their combined weight hit the wall with a thud. He did not let her go and cut off her exclamations by kissing her warmly and at great length, and was glorying in her enthusiastic response. When they at last broke apart, he found she was laughing, 'Oh, Charles, what a man you are to catch me like this...'

'Quiet,' he commanded, 'you, my love, are going to marry me immediately.'

'Immediately? But...'

'Immediately, no buts. I've obtained a Special Licence since I last saw you and I will not have any argument from you. I love you, my beautiful idiot, I think I've always loved you and I hope you will come to love me and that's all there is to it.' He pulled her back into his arms. This time the kiss was broken by Martha moving her head, 'Charles...'

'Quiet.'

'No, Charles, listen... I love you too.'

'You do? Since when?'

'You've always had a corner of my heart, but I felt love the day you came and flung yourself into helping us confound Mr. Corby. I was so proud of you.'

'Then why could not have accepted me when I proposed to you before?'

'Because you did not say you loved me. I-I thought you were only getting me out of yet another scrape.'

'So, Mrs. Birch was right,' he muttered.

'What has she to say to anything?'

'A great deal. She told me I should have grabbed you and kissed some sense into you. Like this.' He seized her once more and swung her around, kissing her passionately, 'We have a deal of lost time to make up for,' he said, as his shoulders leaned against the linen room door. Their weight pressed the door shut, enclosing them into their little world. Martha's hands went to his face, stroked it lovingly, and then her fingers moved to link themselves firmly around his neck, as if she would never let him go.

When Charles's weight snicked the door shut, Annie, avidly listening outside, was nearly trapped by her hair. She had remained there, crouching against the jamb all the while, with her ear pressed to the crack. Now, frustrated in her wish to know more, she abandoned her post and hurried away. For she had heard enough and was eager to be first in spreading the news. She burst into the kitchen and breathlessly blurted it all out. When her listeners understood the reason for her excitement, they rejoiced and hastened to send the tidings rippling out to relatives and friends. By the evening, the information of the approaching nuptials had reached every inhabitant of the Manor and village of Cobbleigh, and beyond.

--- THE END ---

Thank You

Both the author Sarah M Jefferson and Ex-L-Ence Publishing hope that you have enjoyed reading this book. Please tell your friends and write a review on your favourite social networking site.

Also by Sarah M Jefferson: 'The Ranee's Tears' and 'The Major Meets his Match'.

For further titles by other authors that may be of interest to you, please visit the publisher's website
www.ex-l-ence.com
where you can also, optionally, join an information list.

Lightning Source UK Ltd.
Milton Keynes UK
UKOW06f1920230816

281282UK00001BA/1/P